Best of British Science Fiction 2018

Best of British Science Fiction 2018

Edited by Donna Scott

NewCon Press
England

First edition, published in the UK August 2019 by NewCon Press

NCP 210 (hardback)
NCP 211 (softback)

10 9 8 7 6 5 4 3 2 1

Introduction copyright © 2019 by Donna Scott
Cover Art copyright © 2019 by Les Edwards
This compilation copyright © 2019 by Ian Whates

"Providence" copyright © 2018 by Alastair Reynolds, originally appeared in *2001: An Odyssey In Words* (NewCon Press)
"Talking to Ghosts at the Edge of the World" copyright © 2018 by Lavie Tidhar, originally appeared in *Infinity's End*
"The Miracle Lambs of Minane" copyright © 2018 by Finbarr O'Reilly, originally appeared in *Clarkesworld*
"Territory Blank" copyright © 2018 by Aliya Whiteley, originally appeared in *Interzone*
"Throw Caution" copyright © 2018 by Tim Major, originally appeared in *Interzone*
"Golgotha" copyright © 2018 by Dave Hutchinson, originally appeared in *2001: An Odyssey In Words* (NewCon Press)
"Salvation" copyright © 2018 by Dave Bradley, originally in *The Hotwells Horror & Other Stories* (Far Horizons)
"Waterbirds" copyright © 2018 G.V. Anderson, originally appeared in *Lightspeed*
"Buddy System" copyright © 2018 by Mike Morgan, originally appeared in *Mind Candy* (CreateSpace)
"Do No Harm" copyright © 2018 by Anna Ibbotson, originally appeared in *Shoreline of Infinity*
"A Change of Heart" copyright © 2018 by Hannah Tougher, originally appeared in *Idle Ink*
"Birnam Platoon" copyright © 2018 by Natalia Theodoridou, originally appeared in *Interzone*
"Good" copyright © 2018 by Sunyi Dean, originally appeared in *Flash Fiction Online*
"Hard Times in Nuovo Genova" © 2018 by Chris Barnham, originally appeared in *Intergalactic Medicine Show*
"The Escape Hatch" copyright © 2018 by Matthew de Abaitua, originally appeared in *2001: An Odyssey In Words* (NewCon Press)
"P.Q." copyright © 2018 by James Warner, originally appeared in *Interzone*
"The Purpose of the Dodo is to be Extinct" copyright © 2018 by Malcolm Devlin, originally appeared in *Interzone*
"Cat and Mouse" copyright © 2018 by David Tallerman, originally appeared in *Bubble Off Plumb* (Feral Cat)
"Before They Left" copyright © 2018 by Colin Greenland, originally appeared in *2001: An Odyssey In Words* (NewCon Press)
"Harry's Shiver" copyright © 2018 by Esme Carpenter, originally appeared in *Shoreline of Infinity*
"The Whisperer" copyright © 2018 by J.K. Fulton, originally appeared in *Leicester Writes Short Story Prize Anthology 2018* (Dahlia Publishing)
"Death of the Grapevine" copyright © 2018 by Teika Marija Smits, originally appeared in *Café Stories* (Comma Press)
"Rainsticks" copyright © 2018 by Matt Thompson, originally appeared in *Aliterate*
"The Veilonaut's Dream" copyright © 2018 by Henry Szabranski, originally appeared in *Clarkesworld*
"F Sharp 4" copyright © 2018 by Tim Pieraccini, originally appeared in *Triangulation: Harmony And Dissonance* (Createspace)

All rights reserved, including the right to produce this book, or portions thereof, in any form.

ISBN: 978-1-912950-35-5 (hardback)
978-1-912950-36-2 (softback)

Cover art by Les Edwards
Cover design by Ian Whates
Text layout by Storm Constantine

Contents

Introduction by Donna Scott	7
Providence – Alastair Reynolds	9
Talking to Ghosts at the Edge of the World – Lavie Tidhar	15
The Miracle Lambs of Minane – Finbarr O'Reilly	23
Territory Blank – Aliya Whiteley	43
Throw Caution – Tim Major	55
Golgotha – Dave Hutchinson	69
Salvation – Dave Bradley	75
Waterbirds – G.V. Anderson	81
Buddy System – Mike Morgan	99
Do No Harm – Anna Ibbotson	111
A Change of Heart – Hannah Tougher	119
Birnam Platoon – Natalia Theodoridou	121
Good – Sunyi Dean	133
Hard Times in Nuovo Genova – Chris Barnham	137
The Escape Hatch – Matthew de Abaitua	155
P.Q. – James Warner	161
The Purpose of the Dodo is to be Extinct – Malcolm Devlin	167
Cat and Mouse – David Tallerman	199
Before They Left – Colin Greenland	211
Harry's Shiver – Esme Carpenter	217
The Whisperer – J.K. Fulton	227
Death of the Grapevine – Teika Marija Smits	237
Rainsticks – Matt Thompson	245
The Veilonaut's Dream – Henry Szabranski	263
Doomed Youth – Fiona Moore	279
F Sharp 4 – Tim Pieraccini	291
About the Authors	305

Editor's Acknowledgement

A huge thank you to Ian Whates and Newcon Press for once more inviting me to edit a *Best of British Science Fiction* anthology. I can't describe the immense pleasure seeking out these stories brings me. Thanks to all the editors and publishers who have allowed me to reprint their stories; Pete Sutton and Neil Williamson who also gave me recommendations, and to Tom Jordan, my beta reader. Thank you all for your invaluable help.

2018: An Introduction

Donna Scott

I am writing this introduction shortly after a flurry of genre shortlists have been announced, and the writing community is abuzz with excitement and anticipation.

It makes a change from a couple of weeks ago when there was more of a sense of outrage and scorn, after a big-name literary author deigned to dip his toe in genre waters proclaiming that he was going to be writing "not in terms of travelling at 10 times the speed of light in anti-gravity boots, but in actually looking at the human dilemmas of being close to something that you know to be artificial but which thinks like you." The old 'silly spaceships' argument about the shallowness of genre is inferred once again. We see it again and again in many forms, like remakes of *War of the Worlds*, which is in itself fought over by those who would claim it to be a 'classic' or 'genre' work of fiction from time to time.

So, Ian McEwan sounds just like a real science fiction writer – like an Ursula Le Guin, or a Stephen Baxter, or a Gareth L. Powell! – but he is also *not* a real science fiction writer, because he's turned out to be superior in his thinking to all the actual science fiction writers, just like the Adams in his novel *Machines Like Me* are to men. So, is he saying he is in fact a robot? And always has been... Wow, that's meta.

There is an additional motivation to review his book (a lot of them are good) from the ton of extra hype such fuss generates, and for a while it has been practically the only book I've seen advertised on railway station posters. So how wonderful that all the great stuff that was written in 2018 is now coming along in a burst of news to eclipse it.

Not least, that one of the stories in this volume made it onto the

Donna Scott

shortlist for the BSFA Best Short Fiction Awards this year: Malcolm Devlin's "The Purpose of the Dodo is to Become Extinct". Another contributor, Aliya Whiteley, has found her novel *Loosening Skin* on the shortlist for the 33rd Arthur C. Clarke Award, and Alastair Reynolds' *Elysium Fire* and Lavie Tidhar's *Unholy Land* are on the Locus 2019 Finalist Science Fiction Novel shortlist. I extend my congratulations to all of them.

It almost goes without saying that science fiction writers do write about the human condition; about our present situation. And yet, we do need to be reminded of this it seems, because of the scrutiny invited by those big-name literary authors who come along to play in the sandbox every so often and cast a little shade in the process.

In choosing stories for this volume, I did feel inclined to avoid the sorts of stories that made big pronouncements in the narration about the *way things are*. Instead, there were plenty of great stories to choose from that evoke real human relationships, tangible characters facing soul-shattering dilemmas, imbued with emotional realism; stories which placed us in the heart of uncannily familiar worlds. This is the zeitgeist of 2018, turning to 2019 and looking beyond. We have stories that offer dreamlike glimpses of pristine worlds that will destroy us before we destroy them; we have stories of work-based friendships, mistrust and isolation; of alienation and othering; we have stories of slavery given an acceptable face through beautiful voice and the ever-present need to keep fighting injustice; we have stories of bodily choice being made a crime; we have stories of rebellions we thought we'd already had but need to have again; we have another end to childhood. And we have the murder of story itself… involving an AI.

Many of the writers selected for this anthology aren't big names backed up by huge marketing departments, but hopefully discovering them here will pique your interest. If story is a mirror, reflecting ourselves back to ourselves, welcome to the hall of mirrors. Be entranced by skilful storytelling and beautiful language; be immersed in fascinating landscapes; be inspired to seek out more work by these wonderful storytellers… In fact, I suggest you make that your mission for 2019. Do believe the hype.

Donna Scott
Northampton, May 2019

Providence

Alastair Reynolds

They threw petals into the capsule before sealing me in. Pastor Selestat hammered the door, the final signal for departure. I nodded, read his lips:

Goodbye, Goodwoman Marudi.

I braced. The ejection sequence shot me out of the hull, into interstellar space.

The capsule wheeled, trimming its orientation. I had my first good view of the *Dandelion* since being packed aboard with the other pilgrims, before they showed us to the dormitories.

Ten kilometres long, whale-bellied, speckled with ten thousand tiny windows. And at the far end, where there should have been the swelling of its Inflator Drive, a scorched and mangled stump.

"This doesn't have to be the end," I said, voice trembling as I took in the desperation of my fellow crewmembers. "We can still make something of the expedition."

"Maybe you haven't been paying attention," said Selestat, falling into the sarcasm that had served him well since the faultlines appeared. "We have no engine. Not since you and your technician friends decided to run a systems test without adequate ..."

"Don't blame Marudi," said Goodman Atrato, one of the propulsion clerics. "Whatever decisions were taken, she wasn't part of them. And she's right to look at ways in which we can salvage something. We have an obligation – a moral prerogative."

"Don't talk to us about morals ..." started Goodwoman Revda, open and closing her fist.

Before someone lashed out, I strode to a wall and brought up a schematic I'd pre-loaded. It had a drunken, sketchy look to it, my coordination still sluggish.

"Say we're here," I said, jabbing at a point two thirds of the way along the line that connected Earth and Providence. "Doesn't have to be exact." A smudge-like representation of the *Dandelion* appeared under my fingertip, skewered by that line. "Given the engine damage, there's no way for us to slow down now. Any sort of settlement of the target system is out of the question."

"Tell us something we don't know," Selestat said.

"But we can still redeem ourselves," I said, tapping at the wall again, making the ship zip along the line. "When we reach the target system we'll sail through it in only a few days. We can use that time to gather information."

"No use to us," Revda said.

"No," I agreed. "But one day Earth will send out another ship. We'll be able to give them the data we didn't have. Maps, surface conditions ...weather systems, atmospheric and oceanic chemistry, detailed biomarkers ... they'll be able to shape the expedition much more efficiently." I swallowed, knowing that the truth needed to be stated, however unpalatable. "We'll die. That's inevitable. But we can do this one good thing for the pilgrims to come."

"One chance," Atrato said, looking grim. "Better make sure we get it right."

I touched the wall again, making the ship spring back to its earlier position. "No. Two chances. We commit the *Dandelion* to one approach. Most of our eggs in that basket, yes. But if we launch a service capsule now, it can give us a second pair of eyes, an observational baseline."

A slanting line peeled away from the ship. As the ship moved, a dot diverged along the line. That was the capsule, putting more and more distance between itself and the mother vessel.

"Just one snag," Revda said. "The service capsules don't run themselves. Some fool would need to be inside that thing the whole time. Or did you forget that?"

I met her scorn with a smile. "I didn't, no."

I watched the *Dandelion* diminish, fading to a dim grey speck.

Ahead was a red star only a little brighter than any of the others. Still much too far for the naked eye to make out its accompaniment of planets, much less any useful details. But that would change by the time I emerged from hibernation.

As I readied the capsule for the long sleep, Selestat asked me how I was doing.

"I'll be fine," I said. "I've got a job to do, something useful. That's enough for me. Just make sure you get a good set of observations from your end of the baseline, and we'll give Earth something to really make them grateful."

"It's a good thing that you're doing, Goodwoman."

"Duty," I answered, moving my hand to close the communication link. "That's all."

I opened my eyes to silence and loneliness. And squinted them shut just as quickly.

A sun's brightness flooded the capsule. I raised my palm to the window glass, trying to catch some of that life-giving warmth. That was the light we had been promised, the light that should have been giving us sustenance as we made a home on Providence, establishing a human foothold around another star.

But this distant warmth, conveyed to my skin through glass, was the closest I would get to feeling that star's nourishment. Providence would never be ours. The best we could do now was turn our long-range instruments onto that planet, imagining the breezes we would never feel, the shorelines we would never touch. But we do so dutifully, pouring our souls into that work, making the best observations we could, and committing our findings back to Earth, so that a second expedition might begin their journey with a huge advantage compared to our own.

My own part in this endeavour was trivially small. I was under no illusions about that. At best, I'd be filling in a few unimportant gaps in our coverage.

What mattered was the symbolism of my journey. By proposing the idea of the capsule, and then volunteering to crew it, I had provided a unifying focus for the crew. Selestat, Atrato and the others had pulled back from the brink. My sacrifice was visible, unarguable. It had inspired cooperation and reconciliation across the divisions. The ship's destiny remained unchanged, but at least now we had found a purpose, a common dignity.

I felt a quiet contentment. I had done the right thing. *We* had done the right thing.

A comms squirt came in from the *Dandelion*.

"Thought you'd appreciate these images of Providence," Selestat said, after some awkward preliminaries. "We've been weeping over them for hours, so it's only fair to share some of our sorrow. It's more beautiful than we ever imagined, Goodwoman Marudi. Pristine, untamed – an Eden. It'll make a lovely world for some other pilgrim."

"But not us," I whispered.

He was right. The images were gorgeous, heart-breaking. Azure seas, gold-fringed coasts, green forests, windswept savannahs, diamond-bright mountain-ranges. A world we could have lived on, with little modification. A world that could have been ours.

I swallowed down my sadness. It was wrong to be envious of those who would come after us, those who would actually know the airs of their world, its fragrances and evening moods. Better to do something that would guide their passage, something that would help them. They would be grateful, I was sure. They would build monuments to our generosity.

Something caught my eye.

It was from the capsule's own sensor summary, nothing to do with the images Selestat had sent.

The capsule had picked up something on the unlit face of Providence. It was on an area of that world which would never be visible from the main ship, one of the blindspots I was supposed to fill-in for the sake of completeness.

A thermal signature.

I stared at it, waiting for some transient fault to clear itself. But the signature remained. If anything, it was growing brighter, more distinct against background darkness.

I told the capsule to concentrate its sensors on that area, while it was still in view.

The image sharpened.

The thermal smudge was on a coastal inlet, exactly where we might have chosen to place a settlement. It was a harbour city, with spidering lines radiating out to more distant communities. These too were warming, beginning to glow against darkness. Lava-lines of communication and travel and energy-distribution. Hot moving sparks of vehicles, returning to the sky.

I understood.

They had dimmed their lights, turned off their power, during the period when they would have been a risk of detection, even when they were out of direct sight of the main ship. But now they thought they were safe. They were bringing their city and its surroundings out of dormancy, restarting generators, resuming normal patterns of life.

I felt puzzlement at first.

Then suspicion.

Finally, a slow rising fury.

Earth had already got here. By some unguessable means they had come up with something faster than our Inflator Drive. While we were sleeping, they had reached Providence and settled it.

Our efforts were pointless, our noble intentions irrelevant. The people on Providence knew of our existence. They were aware of our survival, aware of our plight, and still they wished to hide their presence from us.

Not because we were a threat to them, or of any larger consequence.

I think we were an embarrassment.

We were like shabby old relatives stumbling out of the night, bringing unwanted gifts and favours. Our existence made them uncomfortable. They wanted us to go away. So they damped their fires, battened their doors, shuttered their windows and kept very, very still, pretending no one was at home.

All of which would have been theirs to know, their secret to hold, their shame to live with, except for one thing.

They had not known of me.

So, something of a dilemma.

My fury hasn't gone away. It boils in me like a hot tide, demanding release. I want to send this news back to the *Dandelion*, so that they can share in my righteous anger. That would be the proper, dutiful thing. My fellow pilgrims do not deserve to remain in ignorance about this callous, calculated act of deception.

They should learn, and know, and decide in their own time how to communicate the fact of that knowing back to Providence.

What a bitter astonishment it would be for those people on that world, to learn that their cleverness had not been sufficient. To learn that we had seen through their lie and exposed their shame and furtiveness for what it was.

It would change no part of my fate, and make no ultimate difference to the people on the main ship. But there would be some minor solace for me in the sharing of my discovery, unburdening myself of some fraction of the anger I now carried.

So, yes, I thought long and hard about that.

In a corner of the capsule I find a dried petal.

The people on the *Dandelion* still think that they've done a good and noble thing, and I won't rob them of that. Let them continue thinking that Providence is unsettled, that their observations will wing their way back to a grateful Earth, moved to tears by their selflessness. Let them have the contentment of knowing that their information will pave the way for another expedition, that their kindness will ring down the centuries.

Let them have that.

The only snag is, I don't trust myself.

I can't let this knowledge find its way back to them. And even if rescue isn't feasible – and it probably isn't – I can't trust myself not to crack. It would be too easy to send a signal back to the *Dandelion*. At the moment my resolve feels total, unwavering. I believe I can hold a secret until my last breath.

But what I believe now, and what I'll feel when the air is guttering out, are two different things.

I'm just human, and the one thing we're not very good at is taking secrets to the grave.

I flip down the emergency panel over the pressure vent release. I settle my hand on the heavy red lever, ignoring the increasingly strident tones of the automatic warning message. I allow myself one last thought: this is also a sort of kindness, albeit not quite the one I had in mind.

And pull.

Talking to Ghosts at the Edge of the World

Lavie Tidhar

The small plane flew high above the Kraken Sea. A crimson sky. Lakes of liquid methane down below. A storm was gathering on the horizon, flashes of lightning etched in dark glass.

Rania loved flying. The stubby little plane was an extension of her body. She sat in the single-occupant cockpit in her outdoors suit. It kept her warm and plugged into the small oxygen tank. Flying high above the landscape she could see the bays and coves of the Kraken Sea, perfect pirate hideouts. They said Nirrti the Black was stirring again, in her crusade against the Ummah.

The Disconnected, she called her army. People who were born without a node or, worse, tore them out of themselves, ripping the fragile aug out of their brain stem with crude surgery, left little more than zombies. It was appalling, but it was far away, she seldom stirred herself from her rumoured base on the Mayda Insula. Rania could see the island, far to the north.

She couldn't imagine what drove Nirrti, what fear or hatred of the Conversation, that all-encompassing flow of data everyone was part of.

Yet she could imagine some of it. She shut all but emergency channels from her consciousness, entering flight mode. She loved the peace of it, the isolation. No other mind beside her own. You could still be alone, on a world like Titan.

She flew her little plane, hugging the coast, veering west at last towards the flashing beacon of the small settlement of Al Quseir. She kept hoping for a rare glimpse of Saturn in the sky, but the clouds had covered the horizon.

She could see the small settlement as she began her descent.

Flying was easy on Titan, the thick atmosphere was like a soup and in the busy streets of Polyphemus Port where she lived it was not uncommon to look up and see flyers with wings strapped to their suits, freewheeling above the dome.

Al Quseir had started as a small mining community in the early days of settlement. Rania could already see the giant drilling rig that had been left over from that time, a huge platform that now stood forlorn in the winds. The early settlers had dug deep down for water, and for a time Al Quseir was famed across all of Titan for the quality of its exported oxygen. For a time, it was a prosperous town, but the water reserves had grown low and the remaining residents lived deep underground, where they maintained small farms. The plane landed gently, and Rania taxied to the shelter of an old hangar before she climbed down from the cockpit. She'd been here a few times before, and always for the same purpose.

Only two people waited for her inside the hangar. She nodded, then followed them through the airlock. She took off her helmet and warm, humid air engulfed her, and with it came the sweet smell of frangipani and protea.

"I am sorry for your loss."

Umm Nasr with a face tanned by years under hydroponic lights, lined with age, green eyes as rare and startling to find as Great Tinamou eggs. She nodded thanks.

Nasr, her son, with a mouth that looked ready to smile easy, a farmer's hands. "Thank you for coming," he said.

"Of course."

She followed them to the elevator. Everything here was old but well-maintained. No rust, the hoist ropes oiled and silent. They journeyed down, into Al Quseir. The upper levels passed by one by one, storage units, farms, air reservoirs.

The doors opened, and they stepped into the town.

In all the years of settlement this main cavern had been repeatedly dug, extended. Now the ceiling rose so high overhead it seemed like sky, and Rania could look as far as the horizon. Lanterns bobbed gently in the hazy air. A brook bubbled gently nearby, and butterflies flitted between the numerous flowers that grew everywhere. Rania could hear voices in the distance, snatches of song and laughter, and over the canopy of trees saw a group of small children kite-flying, looping and swooping in a race against each other. Cautiously opening her node to a wider broadband, Rania felt the flood of the Conversation from all sides, though it felt more muted here, somehow. She could see Saturn rising, and the gathering storm, and the black data-less patch that was Nirrti's island. She could see people talking to each other across Titan and across the Outer System, could see the firefly dance of spaceships against the fiery reds and orange of Jupiter, and across the narrow gulf to the Inner System where the massive data-clouds of Mars and Earth itself coalesced.

She brought it down to a murmur.

"This way, please," the man, Nasr, said, politely.

She followed mother and son along a quiet path lined by trees. It wasn't far to their home, hewn into the side of the rock. They stepped through the gate and into a courtyard where fig and olive trees grew. A fire burned in the centre.

The rest of the family was gathered there. They turned at their approach. Murmured greetings, a thank you. Rania, again: 'I am sorry for your loss.'

How many times had she spoken those words since she'd returned to civilian life? She'd lost count. She wasn't all that used to talking to the living. Mostly she just spoke to the ghosts.

The deceased was lying in wait on a thick woven carpet. He was old when he died. He looked at peace. She knelt beside him. Gathered herself together.

There'd be no ceremony involved. That came before, or later. But hers was just a job.

Gently, she reached out her hand, touched her fingers to the back of the man's head.

Closed her eyes and felt the ghost still there.

A decade back and over four astronomical units away, Rania had served a stint as a combat medic in the Galilean Republics of the Jupiter system. It was one of those skirmishes that barely even get designated wars or given a name of their own, though the dead were real all the same. They were always warring, the Great Houses of Ganymede and Callisto, among each other. And the pay was good.

She had been one of a large shipment of young, inexperienced recruits from Titan crossing that great space between Jupiter and Saturn. She had hoped to see the famed flower gardens of Baha'u'llah Prefecture, and the ice palaces of Valhalla, where the lords and ladies of Odin's Hall live and dance in splendid isolation.

Instead, war turned out to be somewhat different. All she knew was the taste of legumes and tofu and puréed goat meat; the stink of bodies and the motion sickness of abrupt gravitational change; the whisper of hollow-point bullets fired in the close confines of boarded ships and the screams of dying combatants. Most of this long and intermittent war between the Houses – of which this was merely a skirmish, one amongst dozens over the eons – was fought in near-space, a huge bubble of nearly seven light seconds in radius. That space was filled with the military debris of centuries of sporadic fighting: sentient mines and boobie-trapped dead ships, mimic tech and self-replicating Conversation-nulling hubs, robots of all sorts, some as large as destroyers, and tiny clouds of deadly nano-mites. All these had long ago forgotten which side of the war they were on, if those sides even existed any more, and now functioned semi-independently as abandoned hardware still determined to carry out its deadly goal at all costs.

Then there were renegades: robots who abandoned war in search of higher truths, new converts to Buddhism or the Way of Robot or Ogko. Sentient mines discussing obscure philosophies on high-encryption channels; missionary probes on their way to extending the Conversation in the outer reaches of the Up and Out, Von Neumann spiders crawling in search of any usable matter to convert into more mirrors and routers and hubs.

The battles skirted Europa. A no-flight zone enforced by a miniature Dyson Swarm of angry dust mites. The Galileans had Priests of Water – a strange religion worshipping chthonic deities under the subsurface ocean of that ice-encrusted moon. Rania had learned all this but never found out if it were true. She learned to shoot, and get around in free-fall. Her node was loaded with hostile takeover protocols and Others-level shielding. She learned to take care of the dead.

Every unit had one spirit talker. They'd come in firing – near-space crawled with hostiles' habitats, rings, converted asteroids and ships as large as moonlets. As the firefight moved on, she'd come upon the dying and the dead. After a while, she became proficient…

Kneeling down, her boots dyed with fresh blood, soldiers on the floor no older than herself. One girl, the first time… Callisto-white. Rania had never seen such skin. Dead eyes staring at a utilitarian ceiling where broken lights still flashed emergency frequencies. She reached down and touched the base of the skull. Fleeting code tried to attack her node – the feel of it like sparkles of live wire. She pushed, her fingers sinking into the skin and through, searching for and finding the *foramen magnum*, that oval hole into the brain through the skull. Inside her mind the ghost screamed, defences rising, but she nullified the attacks until all that remained was the digital part of the dead human, naked and open to her like a mouse pup.

She retched. But her fingers found purchase, closed around the physical infrastructure of the node itself. It felt like a small ball or marble.

The node had grown with the girl, from the womb or shortly after. As it grew it became a part of her, the biological and digital fusing together into one form. The node sent filaments into the brain, like roots through earth, fusing and infusing. Now the girl was dead and the brain no longer functioning, but the node remained, a ghost, one part of her. Rania *wrenched*, grey brain matter tore and for a moment the root system of the filaments flashed an electric blue. Then it went dead, and she bagged and tagged it, the remains, the ghost to be taken elsewhere for what they euphemistically called strategic debriefing.

Then, one day, the war was over, and they all got shipped back home again.

There was no ceremony now. Rania worked quickly, gently – she'd become an expert by this time. During the war it had been brutal, messy, hurried. But now she worked to excavate the ghost, decant it, preserve as much of it as there was left. She barely left a mark. In moments she was done.

She rose. Her knees hurt more, these days. She said, "You wish to speak to him?"

Umm Nasr held on to her son's arm. "It isn't him," she said. "Not really."

"No," Rania agreed, gently. "And the choice is yours."

"I have my memories. And my children."

She nodded. Nasr made to stop her, hesitated.

"No," his mother said. "It's for the best."

He nodded, slowly.

Some families kept their ghosts in ghost house shrines. Some made sure to erase this last remnant of the person that they'd known, to allow them the last true rest.

In other places, other times… There were hells, it was said, black market Cores, *verboten*, where the souls of the dead could be kept in eternal torment.

Or so they said.

"What were his final wishes?" Rania said. "Heaven, or the archives?"

The archives of Titan were famed across the solar system. A database of sleeping lives beyond count. The Cores they ran on were buried miles underground, were some of the safest in the entire solar system. They said they rivalled even those of Clan Ayodhya on Earth.

"Heaven," Umm Nasr said.

"Of course."

Rania gently took her leave. The job was done, and they would not thank her to linger. What was left behind was all anyone ever left behind, when it came to it. They'd bury Abu Nasr, and mourn his passing, and then return to their lives, for that was the nature and way of the world.

She made her own way back. She knew the road. Only once she was interrupted, as a young girl ran after her, catching her almost by the elevator.

"Yes?"

The girl, suddenly shy, kicked dirt. "Umm Nasr said to give this to you, please," she said.

Rania accepted the small offering. The smell of fresh, sweet strawberries was like a reminder of a time when she was young.

"Thank you," she said, touched.

"Can ghosts taste strawberries?" the little girl said.

"I suppose... I don't see why they can't," Rania said.

"Uncle Qasim always loved strawberries the most," the little girl said, and then she smiled. "If you talk to him, will you tell him that—"

"What?"

But the girl looked down. "Never mind!" she said, brightly, and with that she turned and ran back towards the house.

Holding the small pail of strawberries, Rania rose back to the surface. Closed back the suit, climbed into the cockpit. The strawberries and ghost shared berth in the cargo hold.

She sped along the tiny runway. In moments she was flying, into that glorious, thick nitrogen soup. The wind whispered against the tiny airplane, lifting it high like a toy.

Rania loved flying.

The ghost materialised beside her. It looked at the roiling red and purple skies, and for a moment they both saw Saturn and its rings as it rose in the heavens above.

"It's beautiful," the ghost of Abu Nasr said.

Rania looked at him sideways. The ghost flickered in and out of her field of vision. She turned her eyes back to the flight path. The storm had lashed down on the Kraken Sea, lightning flashing over the bays and alcoves of the shoreline, and for a moment she thought she saw a fleet of black ships illuminated on the waves, sailing away from the Mayda Insula.

Rania tilted the plane and swooped in a long curve south, away from the storm. She looked down on her world, the quiet and the splendour of that land of methane lakes and seas. It wasn't perfect. Nowhere was. But it was home.

"Yes," Rania said. "Yes, I suppose it is."

The Miracle Lambs of Minane

Finbarr O'Reilly

It was midsummer when I arrived in Corcaigh from Sadbhsfort, and the famine parties were in full swing.

I don't know if you remember the posters for them – in a vibrant shawl, a red-headed woman stands, holding a twin in each arm. Around her is a lush green and golden valley, and her back is to the distant ocean, its waters boiling with the mechanical monsters that had closed the seas and caused the famines.

Underneath, lettered in a white, art deco font: 'The country needs people.'

That much was true. You couldn't walk the city without crossing streets keening their loss through curtains flapping against broken glass, where little lived within the mouldering papered walls but feral cats and rats, one feeding off the other.

The parties were the brainwave of a local Bishop. The generations following a famine usually produce more female children than male, they said, but in Corcaigh the problem was more severe and durable than in Dublin and Galway. The parties, correctly chaperoned, of course, allowed solid rural women to meet observant city boys. Apparently, what the country needed was the right kind of people.

More on the hunt for work than for love, I had been to a few such events, but it quickly became clear that the carbolic-scented men they attracted would struggle to score in a brothel, and the women were not to my taste. In any case, the ever-present chaperones meant any chance of a frolic was low. Hands above the table, nobody standing closer than a paperback's length apart, awkward conversation accompanied by bad, state-issued food. There is only so much turnip mash, potato cakes, or German noodles, basically potato by another name, that one can eat.

Having left one such evening about six weeks into my stay in the city, I bumped into a compatriot of mine, Creedon, who twisted my arm until I agreed to attend another party. We could always bribe a guard for breaking the curfew, there may even be work in it for me, it was on the way home, I was told, and sure to be good, as the chaperone, an American woman called Mrs Weber, was 'a friend'.

We walked up from the river, past the burnt-out ruins of the old art college, to a fine, yellow-fronted house just beyond the cathedral, buttery light gifting itself from every window.

We were in the door ten minutes, bramble gin in hand, when Maura Verane made her entrance.

A short woman with a tanned, lined face and untamed hair the colour of a slumbering coal fire, her 'coatigan' – a vast garment composed of differently sized mohair panels, one more garishly coloured than its neighbour – flapped about her, snagging on chair-backs as she waded through kisses and handshakes. None of this attention moved her to smile.

"Can you believe that one is a farmer," said Creedon, who professed to know 'Moll' and told me she was something of a celebrity around the city.

"She was one of the first to stop growing potatoes and turnips. She was a bigwig in the university and as soon as the worst of the emergency was over, she started growing herbs – dill and basil and the like. Now she supplies fruit and veg to the best restaurants, the best houses, the Bishops. Sure, they're only throwing money at her."

Moll circled the room as she deposited jewels – chillies, tomatoes, yellow bell peppers so perfect they looked injection-moulded – on the large dining table. We had enough calories by then, of course, if never quite enough booze, but Moll brought something of the spice and colour of the pre-famine years to a crowd not quite wealthy or powerful enough to acquire it themselves, and they loved her for it.

As a coda to her entrance and a signal that she had blessed the dinner to indeed start, Moll finished with something special.

Creedon was fizzing with excitement: "Once, she brought lemons."

Moll's finale was a corker. She reached into the deep breast pocket of her vast woollens and hefted in her talons a heavy bottle of oil, its contents shining through the thick glass walls as if squeezed from sunlight itself.

"From our Sicilian friends at the golf course," she announced, holding it up for all to see. God knows what it cost her.

'The Sicilians' was how almost everybody in Corcaigh referred to the Mediterranean refugees, regardless of their actual nationalities. Driven from their homes by the migration north of murderous African summers, they had settled in the hills and largely deserted suburbs to the south of the city, colonising the parched golf courses of Douglas and Mahon with olive groves and citrus trees.

Moll's performance over, we sat, the few elders at the tables, the rest of us cross-legged on the floor or perched on the piano or a sofa's arm, and we talked and ate for pleasure rather than mere survival.

I first tasted a tomato that night. The flesh had an earthly perfume, but it was the skin that amazed me most, the texture of something so slick on one side and so rough on the other, parting with a click when I could manoeuvre it between my teeth.

So it was that I was trying to unstick a large piece of tomato skin from an incisor when Creedon guided Moll to stand in front of me, raising eyebrows to one or the other of us as if to say, "This is who I told you about."

Moll looked me up and down and said, "So I hear you're looking for a job?"

Like a fool, I kept my mouth shut and nodded.

Moll's 'farm', on the hills above Minane Bridge, was one-and-a-half acres of raised beds, with plants and herbs of every colour and shape, plus about eight acres of grazing land, a smattering of large greenhouses and a dozen polytunnels. A few goats gave milk and she kept hens for eggs.

The farm had probably been there in some form during the 'Great' Famine, more than two centuries earlier.

Some of the farmhouse walls were stone, some badly mortared rubble, and a few just rammed earth sloshed with whitewash, but it was dry and it was solid. The structure was split in two – Moll lived in the main part of the house, surrounded by overstuffed furniture upholstered in embroidered silk, a curious combination for a woman with such a reputation for a hard edge. A one-room section at the northern end was mine, with a window, a fireplace, a kitchen table and a low bed hidden behind a curtain.

Across the courtyard were a couple of long-empty milking sheds, crammed with troughs, flower pots in resilient clay and crumbling plastic, and farm and garden implements that looked like they were drawn from a dozen cultures and as many centuries. Harrows so old the wood had petrified to near stone lay interlocked with spiral ploughs in shining stainless steel and a collection of corroding scythes and sickles, in a teetering, tetanus-riddled puzzle.

Sniffing the rust in the air, I wondered how much of this kelter had been assembled before the famine, how many of these implements had been hauled and swung and driven by one of Moll's ancestors, and when I would get to use them.

I needn't have bothered – for the first three months of my 'apprenticeship', I was weeding, or mixing 'nettle tea' to feed the plants, or moving barrows of fertiliser, dug from three large mounds of manure and human excrement buried in the east field.

After that, I graduated to harvesting. This mostly consisted of pushing a battered shopping trolley of equipment up and down the paved lanes of Maura's raised beds and grow-houses while she barked instructions at me.

"Basil, mint, lettuce – tear them. Chives, dill, rocket – cut."

If her work was done and the evening was mild, she would sometimes break off from instruction or admonishment, sit on a bucket and reminisce.

"A long time before the famines," she once told me, "my grandfather lived in a fishing village further down the coast. When he was a boy, if times were tough, his mother would cook lobster for them. In those days, fishermen would give them away on the quays – they were unsellable sea vermin, but they were the only protein a lot of families had.

"So he said she would boil them up and then dribble a precious little bit of melted butter and a bit of wild garlic over the top. Very tasty, he said they were.

"But then, after the family had eaten, his mother would have him bury the shells in the back garden rather than put them out in the rubbish, for fear the neighbours or the binmen would see how poor they were.

"Years later, by the time my mother was a young woman, my grandfather was a prosperous man in printing in the city and the family ate out in restaurants – Greens and the like – and lobster had enjoyed something of a rebranding. If it was on the menu, my grandfather would laugh his head off at all the nobs paying through the nose for something his mother found as shameful as eating rats. He never ordered it, though."

Below the farm, in the village, a phone line ran to Tom Buckley's bar. Tom's surviving grandmother, apart from helping Moll out with harvesting or canning, took calls on her behalf from clients in the city. Four mornings a week, I would do the rounds of the lean-to's and polytunnels, snipping and tearing, until my orders and my panniers were filled.

Before nine, I would set off. Moll had gifted me a bicycle, which, by its weight, must have been made of meteoric iron, and by its age, her grandfather had forged.

Around the city I quickly became known as 'the Rocket' – with Corkonian efficiency in piss-taking, this referred to my cargo as much as my limited uphill speed.

Corcaigh sits in a drained marsh at the bottom of a cloud-topped bowl of hills, so there were inclines to be conquered on any route from Minane and back again.

The safest route ran alongside the fence of the old airport, by that time mostly given over to rescue copters and lumbering cargo aerostats. Sadly, it was also the biggest hill and Moll's antique bike would develop a precarious wobble as I crested it, straining myself out of the saddle to make anything faster than walking pace.

I was always careful with my cargo – it was worth a lot. But I was not so careful that I did not enjoy the barely managed terror of the descent into the city. I did not slow until I reached the river and even that I crossed while maintaining as much of my momentum as possible.

Many of the bridges had fallen, either in the emergency or its aftermath, but between Union Quay and Morrison's Island there was a pontoon bridge that would knock at least half an hour off crossing the city. If I had been walking, I probably wouldn't have risked it – the Laoi is brackish even this far from the sea and squid sightings were still reasonably common.

Empowered with a feeling of invincibility from my high-speed descent into the city, I would race across the bridge and up the wooden ramp on the other side, the wooden slats beneath shaking my brain in its pan and the stink of the undredged river condensing in my nostrils.

The other reason for my haste was so I could spend more time with Grace, the chef at Gamble's restaurant.

The front of Gamble's faced the Mall, but deliveries were made to the rear, on Phoenix Street, across a void in the city like a pulled tooth.

The day I fell in love with her I signalled my arrival by dropping my panniers onto the stainless-steel kitchen table and in she walked, slender and considered in her chef's whites, her hair tied in a bun behind her head. She made straight for a little aluminium percolator and produced two perfect coffees. God knew where she got the beans from, but this alone would have made my three-hour round trip worth it, so I sat and sipped and waited for her to finish her inspections.

First, she smelled each bunch of leaves, tucking a stray, black coil of hair behind her ear. The faintest whiff of rot or smear of leaf slime and she might have dismissed the whole batch.

I raised my cup and smirked. "I cut them myself, this morning."

"That's what you always say," she said, but without malice. She walked to a shelf and returned with some bottles. I knew the drill. Oil, probably rapeseed, a vinegar, cider this time, sea salt shaved so fine you could glaze windows with it. A minute's blurred whisking and she speckled some rocket leaves in the emulsion. She rolled them deftly with her fingers and popped the neat bundle into her mouth.

"It used to be considered an aphrodisiac, you know, rocket," I said, glancing away as she chewed. "Monks were banned from growing it in monastery gardens."

"Well, nobody wants horny monks, I suppose," she said, licking her lips.

Moll referred to one of her tunnels as 'the lab'. Creedon was right, she had been a bigwig in the University medicine department, but in her lab, Moll applied that science to propagation. She wasn't secretive about her work or the space, but she made it clear enough that she didn't like being disturbed when she was in there.

However, as I passed one evening in early March, I was beckoned in by a clearly excited Moll.

"I've had a bit of a breakthrough," she said. "Come and have a look."

Down one side of the tunnel, beds with soils of varying colours and richness were marked out in square-foot blocks using sticks and twine. At the centre of each square, one plant grew, protected and mulched by a thick coil of straw drawn from a large stack kept between the lab and the next tunnel.

On the other side of the narrow path, benches held a dozen or more large green crates that had been repurposed as growing trugs. From the stencilled codes on their sides, they had clearly once held weapons or ammunition of some type. But now they were filled with pale and puckered earth, from which an ugly, scrawny plant poked through at fairly even intervals.

"A couple of years ago, a fellow called Furio, one of the Sicilians, brought me something, a curiosity really, that he wanted me to see if I could grow."

My first thought was it was weed or tobacco. The Bishops would not be pleased if the Monks on Garnish Island lost their monopoly.

Reading my expression, she said: "It's a kind of fodder crop. Very old, very rare, but just a herb really."

The plant was not much to look at, a lanky yellow weed such as you would see poking from any of a hundred ditches within a mile of the farm.

"And?"

"And I've bloody done it. Twasn't easy, it's a very finicky plant, loves its own soil and nothing else and harder than a huckleberry to take viable cuttings from."

She pointed to the crates.

"You know how embassies used to say, 'you are now on American soil', or British soil, or whatever, but it was just a metaphor? This soil is straight from Cyrene, in what was once Libya," she said. "Libya's gone 30 years and Cyrene a lot longer than that. Up to now, in these crates is the only place we know of that this stuff grew. In that dirt."

Among the tools I had seen in Maura's milking shed was a slean – a spade for cutting turf, with a long metal channel, L-shaped in cross-section. It was used to slice a long cake of turf from the cutting face of a bog, which the turf-cutter would then sling on to a pile to dry.

The Sicilians looked like they had done something similar, but horizontally, cutting long, deep strips of topsoil, plants and all, and depositing them in the munitions cases.

"What's it called," I asked.

"The Romans called it silphium, and Nero himself was supposed to have eaten the last of it."

Towards the end of my second full summer with Moll, I had established a mostly enjoyable routine. I would deliver in the city three or four times a week and snatch an hour with Grace when I could. Then I would come home and help Moll prepare for our new venture into livestock. Lambs first, but after that, who knew?

Before the animals arrived in spring, there were fences to mend, feed to arrange, and growing tunnels to clear, so that we could plant out more silphium cuttings.

Once in a while, under the pretence of delivering old chip fat for Moll's biodiesel reactor, Grace would drive out and stay the night at the farm. If Moll was surprised or scandalised, she didn't let on.

One such evening, I was showing Grace the beds. We weeded while we chatted, just for something to busy the hands, before hearing Moll's clomping step across the ridged concrete of the farmyard. Behind her walked a couple, difficult to age, but reasonably well dressed, and a young girl of about 15. Led by the girl, on a piece of fraying orange washing line, followed a scrawny white lamb.

Moll nodded a salute to myself and Grace, but the rest of the group paid us no heed as they padded sombrely past.

"Who were they?" asked Grace.

I shrugged. I knew Moll was occasionally consulted by other farmers and market gardeners to help with planting plans, and at least one old fella had asked her advice on his daughter's marriage plans.

Visitors were rare, but not unheard of.

"I'd lay you pounds to pence that girl was expecting," said Grace.

"Oh yeah?"

"Yeah."

By now, Grace had stopped pulling weeds and sat on the wooden wall of the bed, her gaze drilling into Moll's front door.

"They didn't look very happy about it," she said.

I shrugged again. "She's pretty young."

"Still. The country needs people," Grace said as she worried at a splinter in the board beneath her hand.

I didn't know what to say to that. Looking back on it now, I suppose I knew what was going on, but while that girl, nor any of the subsequent ones, did not leave in what I would call a happy frame of mind, each left looking a little less ground down by unintended or unwanted consequences.

"Do you ever want children?" she said, after a while.

I laughed, and I suppose she took that as my answer.

Before long, Moll's consulting party left her rooms and showed themselves to the gate, mother, father and daughter – their three heads still down, their tread still soft, and minus one lamb.

By the end of that October, we had two full tunnels given over to cuttings of the herb. They would be ready for our stock lambs, due up from Dingle in February for finishing.

But for now, we had that first girl's lamb. Moll had me feed it barley-meal and alfalfa hay, mixed with some of the silphium she had grown in her 'lab'. The plant didn't smell unduly when you cut it out of the soil, but when you crushed it to mix with the lamb's food, by God it stank. Like a wet woollen sock you had used to wipe up old fish.

After about a month, Moll determined that the lamb had enough meat on it to be worth the pot. Although her experiment was as yet unproven, rearing any meat at all was prodigal enough in those days to be cause for a party.

At my suggestion, Grace would cook. Moll invited Furio, the Cyrenian who had given her the plants, and Mrs Weber, the chaperone from the yellow house where we had met, plus Creedon was to be there, along with a host of other friends and associates.

The day of the party, work was long and dull, carrying out my normal duties as well as dressing the barn with a makeshift table, some old benches and whatever wildflowers and oil lamps I could muster. But I was looking forward to the feast and to seeing some friends.

Everyone wore their finest rig-outs and the tables heaved with food. Goat cheeses from north Cork, farmed trout from over the Crosshaven hills, oat cakes with honeycomb from the apiary on top of the old school of commerce in the city. Everyone Moll had ever fed, it seemed, was here, and everyone had brought something, either to eat or to drink.

This time, Moll needed no flourish to get proceedings started. Everyone knew why they were there. The lamb's legs and shoulders would be roasted, chops and cutlets grilled, neck stewed, the pluck minced and made into a pudding with oats and herbs, then boiled, like a haggis or a white pudding.

But the first test of our labours was to be a loin fillet, and to make the test fair, Moll had paid for the same cut from a city butcher.

Grace indicated two plates. Each of the loins was perfectly cooked, seared to the colour of teak. Grace had cut each into nine or ten mouthfuls, showing the contrast between the caramel-coloured bark and the intimately pink flesh inside.

"This is the normal lamb, come up from Dingle a week or so ago, it ate nothing but Kerry scrub. This is Moll's lamb, fed with her wonder herb."

Moll glared at her as if she were sharing industrial secrets, but we were among friends and I thought no more of it.

By sight alone, I couldn't tell which was which, but taste did the work of the other senses here. I elbowed my way to the table, forked a piece of the Dingle lamb and put it in my mouth.

It was delicious, and if that was where the treats ended that evening, I think I would have been happy.

Then I tried a piece of Moll's lamb.

I would call it indescribable, but everything is describable. I just lacked the vocabulary then.

If you asked me now, what I would say is that there is always a gap between a review, or a critique, or even just an honestly expressed groan of delight at eating something, and that food's honest, naked taste.

Fresh cheese on warm bread, blood sausage and onions, a trout still atwitch with life as it hits a pan of hot butter. The taste of all these things is wonderful, but describable.

With Moll's lamb, that gap between expectation and actuality was so big as to render me temporarily dumb. The flesh was meltingly sweet, but not one-dimensional sweetness like a finger dipped in sugar. This was the honey of a just over-ripe mango, it was a flavour distilled from fragrance. As the tongue probed beyond that, there were earthy notes, an almost decayed saltiness, like fish sauce or miso.

But back then, in Minane, my experience of those tastes and my ability to put all that into words was still a continent and a decade away.

Sitting in the mundane, functional surroundings of Moll's barn, all I could manage was: "I don't think I have ever eaten anything quite as wonderful as that."

I was not alone. Wordlessly, Moll bade Grace and Furio try it.

Furio's face was illuminated as if by a spiritual fluorescence, but he said nothing. I attributed his silence either to him being overwhelmed with the survival of some small part of his birth land or the knowledge of how much money he would get for meat of this quality.

Grace pronged one of the remaining pieces of meat and I expected the chef, the trained palate, the perfectionist, to critically and dispassionately fill the gaps I could not. Instead, she resorted to simple blasphemy: "Jesus. I mean, Jesus."

After the taste test, the evening followed the normal trajectory. People ate and drank and were merry and rambunctious and talked of happier times, either behind us and how we missed them or ahead of us and how we may get there.

At such evenings in the city, Maura rarely showed any interest in this chat and this was no different. She sat and grimaced in boredom at the politics, the endless plans, and picked at the toughened skin of the mallet finger on her left hand, but never volunteered a word.

Grace, feeling secure in alcohol on what she should have known was treacherous ground, would not let such passivity lie, however.

"Do you not want to join us in rebuilding our country, Maura?" she asked, her tone too smug, too expectant.

Moll looked at her coolly, a teacher sizing up a student, unsure whether or not she was worth the time it would take to educate.

"I suppose I don't," she said eventually.

Moll blinked, eyeing the assembled as if a buzzard choosing gobbets. She continued: "Although I suppose it depends on what you mean by 'rebuild' and who you mean when you say 'our'. I just want to look after my farm in peace. I have friends and I have food and that is a vast improvement on the times I had neither."

This was Moll at her most magnanimous. These days, I could have read the strain in the faces around me and the mix, in Maura's face, of resignation and a feral delight that somebody was pressing the issue, forcing the lethal gunslinger out of retirement. But I didn't have such diplomatic senses then. Nor did Grace. She had been offered a final 'nobody has to get hurt' way out, but she lacked the sense to take it.

She tried earnestness, almost always a mistake with Moll: "Do you not understand, Maura? We need people, Maura. We need them to rebuild."

Moll looked straight at me and all I could think of was a girl leaving without her lamb.

"That may be true," she said, holding my gaze, "but you can't just be forcing people to make more people, can you, Grace?"

Grace persisted: "Well, I just wonder what you're growing all this wonderful food for, if not to feed those of us at least trying to repopulate our wonderful country."

She interrupted Grace at volume, and the happy drone of the party withered into silence.

"Wonderful country? What would you know about that, without a child or a parent buried? I'd rather have more food and fewer people than the other way around. So would anyone with any sense. In any case, you seem to be doing your best to repopulate this wonderful country all on your own. Is the food better at this party, chef, or do you miss your German noodles?"

At this point, a few people broke into nervous laughter, catching Moll by surprise. She holstered her tongue.

I could say nothing. If this was true, how did I not know? Why had Grace not told me? Or Moll, for that matter? And if it were not, how could Moll try to hurt me like that?

Mrs Weber, ever the host, walked over, smiling sweetly, and touched Maura on the arm: "That's all right, Moll."

With considerably more menace, she turned to Grace: "I'd like to talk to you outside for a moment."

I followed them both out into the courtyard, incensed, although unsure where to direct it.

"So you're another one happy for this nation to wither and die, are you," Grace said, viciously indignant at the entitlement of the elderly, who had known a country measured in millions rather than thousands.

Mrs Weber held up an imperious hand and waited for her to stop spluttering.

"Moll lost her sister, her daughters and her mother in '36 and her husband a year or two later. Maybe lay off the 'glorious repopulation' stuff, okay, chef? Or fuck off back to town."

Her gracious smile returned without effort and she left me, standing in the moonlight, gaping at Grace.

"Tell me she's lying," I said.

"I can't."

"You've been going to the famine parties?"

"I have."

"In God's name, why?"

"Because I want children, I want my mother to have grandchildren, I want a future, I want to be safe. You can't give me all that, can you? I'm not sure you would even if you could."

I said nothing.

Grace kissed me once, on the cheek, but my hands stayed firmly at my sides.

"I'll see you," she said.

By April, the word was out. 'Minane lamb' was being ordered from as far away as Kilkenny and orders were such that I had graduated from prehistoric bicycle to prehistoric van to make my deliveries in town. Rather than call at Gambles first to see Grace, I made that stop the last of my day, in the hope that she would be on a pre-lunch break. In any case, the vehicle made such noise pulling into the yard behind the restaurant that she had ample notice of my arrival and I had not bumped into her in months.

As the orders had increased over the late winter and early spring, so too did the frequency of families with young girls, or sometimes lone women, calling on Moll for advice. The price of this advice wasn't always a lamb, of course – that's just how the story went afterwards. It was often a hen, or a pheasant, or a fat salmon that somebody brave or foolhardy had pulled from the River Ilen. Sometimes, the advice and the treatment were free.

Between the increased activity on both fronts, I suppose it was inevitable that somebody would show up asking questions.

On my return from the city one morning, two middle-aged men stood casually above the crossroads on the road up to the farm. The elder and better dressed of the pair raised a heavy walking stick, as if to hail a passing traveller.

"Well, you're not Maura anyway," he said cheerfully when I stopped. The accent wasn't local, but I couldn't quite place it. "We're only after some lamb."

He walked over to the van, the lack of a limp marking the stick as a weapon rather than a crutch. He was meticulously clean shaven, a neck scrubbed pink with cheap-smelling soap and where his hand rested on the open window, I could see his fingernails were cut meticulously square. His associate was scruffier and looked altogether more nervous, and the pair of them screamed 'policeman'.

What could I do? I was already on the road and the gate was chained in front of me. A narrow boreen led off to the right, but the van would have struggled up the hill even without the prodigious undergrowth.

"Follow me up so," I said, hoping that if they were policemen, they were looking for a bribe – some free chops or, at worst, a cut of the proceeds.

They were only seconds behind me as I reached the gate. I hopped down from the van to unchain it, and they were next to me before I could think.

"I'm afraid if it's the Minane lamb you're after, we're sold out."

Leaning on his stick and with his bottom lip stuck out in an expression of crestfallen insincerity, the elder man said: "Oh that's a shame, but I hear Moll is a woman who can help a girl in need of a miracle."

"I don't know about all that," I said as confidently as I could, struggling with the lock.

"Well, it's not the lamb I'm after, really," he continued. "I suppose what I'm really after are the people who are bringing ye the lambs."

"Oh, like our suppliers, you mean?"

I don't recall if my slowness in unlocking the gate was pretence or whether the fellow had me so rattled I couldn't unhook it, but either my glib answer or my delay in admitting him prompted him to act.

Without warning, he brought the heavy length of ash down on my forearm. I won't pretend I heard the snap over my scream, but from the sensation of grating wrongness in moving it afterwards, I knew he had broken it.

He was almost apologetic in his tone: "Did ye really think no one would tell a neighbour, that no one would confess to a priest? That Dr Verane could play god out here on her farm when she knows we need people more than we need food?"

His colleague ripped the keys from my grasp, undid the lock and chipped in: "So let's try again without the smart mouth, shall we? Where's Maura Verane?"

The first one prodded me once in the damaged arm with his cudgel and waved me up the path to the farmyard. Then he handed the stick to his colleague and withdrew a pistol from inside his jacket, marking him out as an ideologically pure 'detective' rather than just a nosey and bribable guard.

We walked into the middle of the yard, his gun occasionally poking me from behind.

"Come on out, Moll," he called. "Don't make me put a pill in your helper here."

But no response came.

Again he jabbed me with the barrel. "Where might she be?"

Enough time has passed that I feel no shame now, but at the time

I was so terrified that he was going to kill me I would probably have given them anything. He didn't need me. One can only assume they would have tried Moll and executed her eventually, but there was nothing to stop him from terminating my existence on the spot and dumping me in a septic tank somewhere.

"She might be in her lab," I offered.

"Ah, the source of the 'cure'. Show me."

He directed his colleague to inspect the far end of the yard as we walked past the raised beds, the cold frames and most of the silphium-bearing tunnels until we reached Moll's lab.

The large plastic flap at the front was tied up, usually a sign that she was working, but as the detective ushered me in first, I could see she wasn't present. Her multi-coloured mohair coat hung on the back of her chair, but of Moll there was no sign.

"No Moll, huh? Isn't this awful altogether," he said, grinding the gun into my kidney.

"Come on Moll, you're almost famous," he called out. "We've come all the way down the country to see you."

"Jeez, she's very quiet," he said softly to me. Then he paused to listen for his mate, but there was not a sound from across the yard.

"Ronan," he called. No answer came.

"Ronan, where in the fuck are you?" he shouted.

With his free hand, he shoved me viciously between the shoulder blades and I stumbled over the threshold of the tunnel and into the farmyard beyond, twisting a foot in a drainage channel and ending up flat on my back. I screamed at the flash of pain from my arm as I watched him emerge.

He stepped out and over the piece of wood that had tripped me up. In that moment, with all of his attention on where he was placing his feet, he did not see Moll rise like some nightmarish, bloody monster from the mound of hay between the tunnels. She took two steps towards him in her bare feet and the first hint the Dublin policeman had of her presence was when the point of the rusty sickle bit into the left side of his neck.

Something vital had been severed and he fell without another word. But Moll, just to be sure, raised the weapon in her other hand, the bloody half-filled bottle of oil that she had used to dispatch

'Ronan', and beat him repeatedly about the head until he was still.

I don't know if Moll had been planning this specific escape, or always stood ready to flee, but within minutes she had washed in a rain barrel by her door, changed clothes and 'borrowed' the battered old truck from Buckley's.

On our own van and truck, she had opened up the fuel caps and run rags soaked in lamp fuel into the tanks. She had spread straw and hay in all the tunnels and after we had dragged the bodies into her own quarters, gave them and it a good dousing in diesel. She had a pan of oil heating on the gas stove, ready to kick over and get the whole thing going.

She was loading Buckley's truck with jerry cans full of biodiesel, boxes of fresh and dried food and bottles of water. In the open bed, secured between hessian bags of damp compost, were four or five dozen potted silphium plants.

Attached to each pot was a card of instructions in Maura's simple script.

"Grind up a handful of the leaves and berries, mix them with some apple juice or some brandy, add a bit of honey to take the edge off the stench of it and swallow.

"Take it daily until the cramps kick in. You'll know when it's done. Tell nobody but those who need to be told."

That was more detailed instruction than she had given me.

"Anyone asks, you fell while having tea with Mrs Buckley, right? First you knew of trouble was when you saw the flames and I stole her truck. In a few days, go talk to Mrs Weber about a job. Okay?"

Once the van was loaded, there were no hugs, no farewells. Moll kicked over the gas stove, waited until she was sure the main house and every tunnel was well alight, jumped in the truck and was gone.

Mrs Buckley walked me down the hill 'for sweet tea and to ring the fire brigade'.

"Stop the car, I'd prefer to walk in," I said. The small electric Tata pulled to the side of the pitted and gravelly road, I opened the door and I walked into Minane for the first time in 30 years.

It is still quiet – no buildings had been added, but nor had any collapsed, and many were roofed with the new perovksite panels, so I knew they were lived in, cared for.

I passed the church and its small graveyard, where I recognised a scrubby yellow plant growing between the graves. Like a huckleberry, Moll said, it would only grow in undisturbed earth: "They grow free or they don't grow at all."

I don't know if it was a final 'up yours' to the authorities, or just poetic irony, but now, even with better, safer alternatives available out of the east, every churchyard and cemetery in the country still harbours Moll's plant.

Past the church, I rounded the corner at Buckley's Bar and wondered what had become of Mary, the first of the two women who saved me.

Above the cross, the outline of Moll's farm was still there, under weeds and ivy. I had thought it may have been razed and grassed over. The uncovered and blackened hoops that used to support the grow tunnels still ran at right angles from the road, stretching from just beyond the low, roofless farmhouses to the crest of the hill, as if someone had tried to stitch the landscape together with long lines of staples.

Below the small field, where we kept the lambs – the miraculous and the other kind – I stopped.

Nobody I've spoken to knows where Maura Verane is buried. In every home from Kilmore to Kinvarra, you will hear a different story about how 'Moll' met her end: She was thrown by a mob from the cliffs in Clare, to be consumed by the mechanical squid that roam the Atlantic still; the priests burned her as a heretic in the basement furnace of a Galway church; she fled for America in an aerostat; or she wanders the west coast yet, planting her 'cure' as she goes. I'd like to believe that last one, but it would put her in her early hundreds.

Moll is almost certainly dead. Despite the stories, for most of our time at the farm we never grew anything much more exotic than coriander. It burned anyway.

But should a pilgrimage be on your mind, that verdant field at Minane Bridge would be a good place to start.

I turned to lean my back against the stone and sod wall, my breath stolen from me, my cheeks wet. Perhaps I wasn't as ready to sift ashes as I thought.

As I lay there on the ditch, watching the clouds scud past the treeline that marked the top of the hills opposite, a lone boy and his dog walked down the boreen towards me, neither creature anywhere near as rare as they were when I lived here, but still unusual enough for me in these surroundings to put a catch in the throat.

I tried to smile at the boy.

"Good morning. Do you live around here?" I said.

"Mornin'. Are you American?"

"No, but I can see why you might think that. My accent has changed a lot. I used to live around here, actually."

"Really?"

"Yes, for a while. Do you know whose farm that was?" I said, gesturing to the ruin behind me.

He stopped to consider the question with a suspicious turn to his head. I ruffled the dog's dishwater pelt while I waited for him to figure out how varnished his response should be.

"I do," he said finally, puffing his chest out: "Mad Moll". There is always a pride, a vicarious notoriety, in living close to a famous or infamous person, even if only in location rather than in time.

I couldn't help but grin. I never knew her as that, however much I had occasionally agreed with the sentiment.

"Who is Mad Moll?" I asked.

"Moll of Cyrene," he said, as if only a fool would not know, "like the song." Then in mock exasperation, and with dancing hands, he intoned "… six guards she killed, they're lying still, at the bridge in Minane town, she found the cure, that cute old hoor, that brought the bishops down…"

Two bad bastards who got what was coming to them had become six policemen. In another 30 years, it may be a dozen.

"And where is she now," I asked, wondering if I would get a new theory on her disappearance or a pastiche of one I had already collected.

"I dunno," he said. "Dead, I suppose."

"You're probably right," I said. I extended my hand for help in hauling my carcass off the damp ditch and we began walking down the hill to Minane, to the waiting car and my wife.

"So, tell me, can you teach me this song?"

Territory: Blank

Aliya Whiteley

Day 156

Watkin has also been eaten.

The question I find myself unable to answer is – will I miss him? Time must pass before I know whether it is a relief to be free of his incessant optimism. Now I can descend into depressed apathy or even barbarism, if I so wish, for as long as I continue to last. He will chivvy me no more. *Play along, now, Michaels!* he would say. I find I can no longer despise that phrase with impunity; it must become tinged with regret and nostalgia. For better days? That remains to be seen.

I would destroy this terrible place if I could. But every plant I stamp down springs back up with elastic and spiteful vivacity. How it hates me. How it all hates me, and mocks me, as I press through it, wait for the mouths to come for me too.

Day 47

What an enormous journal this is, and I have carried it so far through this dark, humid jungle. It has been strapped to my backpack: a literal weight of remembrance. Ben gave the journal to me and bade me write down my thoughts. *For future generations* – he said. *To make it real for them.*

What a ridiculous concept.

What should one say to the children of tomorrow, when the world changes so quickly from day to day? Any words written purely for their benefit would be worse than useless, for what are visions of the past to those who come after?

But, still, for Ben. I carry it for him. I write in it for him, for the fading hope of seeing his face in my words and thereby remembering home just a little more clearly. He has come to represent that to me, and I wonder why I ever wanted to leave it.

No, instead I must describe the land we traverse, Watkin and Barton and I. It is verdant, thick with insect and animal sounds that range from deep, slow barks in the undergrowth to high whines close beside the ear. Each is, in their own way, terrifying. But we three keep our nerve, even at night, when it is deafening, and the protuberant plants seem to both press close and shrink back from the campfire, releasing their peculiarly sweet smell. Repulsion and fascination, simultaneously, exerting their twin holds: I understand this. I feel it too. I want to hide my face in horror from the teeming, twisted forms of life that surround us. But I also feel a deep desire to somehow join with it, so I am seamless in its dream. I would disrobe, sink naked into its depths, and be gone.

Is this real?

Day 1

The first page of a journal. Such clean white possibility. I can't imagine what I'll end up putting within it. I feel I should flick to the back and make some note – a thought that I would rediscover when I reach the end of this journey. But I have no idea what to say. Maybe it would suit me better to ask a question: did I come across what I was looking for? How amazing it would be to write a resounding yes.

To do that I must work out, during the course of this experiment, what I am looking for. Because I really do not know. Is it enough to simply say: answers?

Still, early days. The three of us are still getting to know each other before we enter the dome. David Barton carries his head at a permanent angle that is a little off-putting – one must either strive to ignore, or tilt to match. He is polite but keeps his distance. That's not surprising. As the organiser of this expedition, he has his own agenda to follow. But I do wish he would at least eat with us in the canteen after training. It might go a long way to establishing camaraderie.

Brian Watkin wears a permanent half-smile when he deals with Barton, and has told me over meals that all the dome's direct employees are the same in attitude. Watkin is a man I can get along with, even though he comes from a very different background to my own. A real presence, with meaty arms and a quick smile, he has a magnetically positive outlook that does not feel aggressive. He says he is pleased to be here, for no matter what awaits it cannot be as bad as some of the dome scenarios he has undertaken. Yes, he's a serial guinea-pig, I've gathered that much, making his living from undergoing these experiments of the mind. He will have picked up such a range of skills and experiences, which will be a handy contrast to my own status as a newbie, fresh from university, looking for an easy way out of a boring relationship and a career in front of a screen, not behind it.

Well.

Well now, my pen ran away with me and I wrote something inadvertent and true that I do not like. It feels like an additional betrayal because Ben gave me this journal as a parting present, delivering some terrible prepared speech about research for future generations.

Then he said, "I'll wait for you, Saffron."

"I can't ask you to do that," I said, but I do not think he got the hint.

Day 263

Endless. Endless. Jungle. And the mouths. The mouths will eat me whole.

Day 22

Watkin is an adventurer down to the core of his soul, and I'm glad the domes exist for if they didn't he would surely be a man out of time. He's far too keen to sink himself fully into this ridiculous role play, but I can't blame him. Dressed in the provided uniform, complete with pith helmet, stamping across the jungle set-up on our first day yesterday, there was romanticism in the humid air. It would be so easy to slip into making statements about the heat, the blasted heat! And I get the feeling that is what Barton wants, after insisting we prepare by reading all those novels; did he think that Watkin and I could become the new Stanley and Livingstone? That all it takes is a push to retrieve some Victorian conquering spirit from the psyche?

I'm contrary by nature, so I find myself rebelling against it before we even set off. But I think Barton picked this upper-class graduate in the belief that such throwback sentiments would be easy to unlock. I can almost guess the title of his research:

Case Study: Personality Traits and Latent Imperialistic Tendencies towards Exploration/the Unknown Influence by the British Victorian Novel

Well, let him try to prove that humanity must bring to heel whatever land it walks upon, imaginary or not. I think a sliver of irony is firmly lodged in my soul. I'll go through the motions and see what emerges, but how can one forget this is a simulation, and we are playing at the past?

Day 416

The mouths will eat them. They will eat them all. It is inevitable. Nobody will believe me. I will rip out the pages and hide them in the hope that, one day, the truth can be pieced together.

Day 61

I find myself forgetting things I knew so well; the data minutes allowance on my contract, for instance, back when that was my only way to access the domes – through a small screen, watching the entertainment visuals. I had an expensive contract, that much I know, thanks to the generosity of my parents. And my university place came with additional access to view the educational domes, of course. How safe it all seemed, from that distance.

Now what on Earth was my data allowance? I have woken more than once, in the night, within my tent, sweating, searching my mind for that unimportant piece of information. For it does not matter, I know that. But it is precisely because of its trivial nature that I obsess, I think. Vast issues of life and death, I am helpless against – this one fact, I might possibly remember.

Life and death. There's the truth of it. A real threat has somehow found its way into this dome. Can creatures grow from ideas? Can wild animals spring into being from the waves of the brain? It's the only explanation for the mouths.

I must write this clearly: giant snapping mouths surround us at night.

I have seen them, by firelight, and then heard them patrol the tents, brushing past the canvas. Last evening one became brave enough to thrust its giant maw forwards, and I saw the glint of curved white teeth, like polished knives, between thick wet lips that glistened. I shrieked, I think. Certainly I made some sound, for both Watkin and Barton half-rose from their folding stools and exclaimed. I told them what I had seen, and they exchanged long, fearful glances.

"Let's keep the fire burning high," I said, and they agreed, and kept watch with me for hours. But this morning both of them told me that they had seen nothing, nothing at all.

Data minutes, spent watching what happens in the domes. Are we being watched now, in the name of education? Do others, outside, see the mouths and say nothing about them, thinking them a trick of the situation?

At lunchtime today I mentioned the idea to Barton that somehow monsters could manifest within this place, perhaps from the power of our minds, creating a new reality. He said, "What's real, anyway?"

He is an unhelpful man. He says he will report my idea upon completion of our mission, but not to think on it too much.

Day 82

Barton is missing.

He did not return from his trip down to the stream to bathe this morning. I suggested it was not safe, and he smiled at me, as if I were a foolish and amusing girl.

Watkin seems remarkably unbothered. "Left the dome to file a report, I reckon," he said. "Let's press on and he'll come back when he's ready." So we packed up. What else could we do?

I did not see the mouths tonight, in the firelight. I did not hear their laughter.

I lie in my tent and hear the rustle of the trees. Do they approach? Will they rip this tent apart? Or one could imagine they are sated, for the time being.

Perhaps they have eaten him.

"Why would he simply leave without telling us?" I said, over dinner, to Watkin.

"Because it's all a game, isn't it?" he said. "They're watching to see what we'll do next."

I must try to keep that in mind. This is pretence. But then I wonder – how can the domes claim to extract truth about humanity when the most basic question remains unanswered: *What's real, anyway?*

Day 290

It's good to write again.

Barton suggested it might help with my therapy to read back over my entries from that time and then write some new ones, just to get used to the idea that life goes on.

That is precisely how he phrased it, on that first day in the hospital. "Life goes on," he said.

So I'll document my final hours in the jungle, as I remember it at least:

I can still feel that dreadful humidity, the prickly sweat on my skin, when I think about it. I have no idea how far I'd walked, for so many days since the disappearance of the others. I was alone, directionless, bereft of purpose excepting the will to go on, and outlive those terrible events. Defy the mouths their last meal.

Each night I set up my tent and crawled into it, and it seemed to me that the mouths mocked my attempts to lie so still. They gave out their loud, cackling laughs that split open the darkness to reveal them to my mind's eye. Although, I should state, I have no evidence that the laughter came from the mouths at all. Maybe some other unseen creature found me humorous.

Isn't that the nature of it? We piece together what we see and hear and make matches, don't we? It's human nature. I became the adventurer for the land I walked, and the perfect victim for its peculiar brand of horror.

That last night, I only remember the fear I felt. And that seems to me as if it happened a great time ago, although it was less than a month, in truth. The terror of it: I can only write that down, curiously, because such emotions can only be felt in the heat of the moment, and never repeated, or even accurately remembered. So it seems quite strange to write what happened next: I decided I could no longer live with the fear. I opened the flap of my tent. I called to the mouths. I invited them in.

After that – a blank.

There is more debriefing to be done, but I'm not certain I will ever recover the memory of what I'm told actually happened. Barton striding into camp, restraining me, speaking soothing words to calm my gibbering. Apparently, I 'screamed and screamed' when I saw him; well, the dead returning to life will do that to a person.

He says he left the dome deliberately. *To become a true observer to events*: that is how he phrased it. He looked so smug. I wonder if he saw precisely what he wanted to see.

Enough of writing for now. I decided to take breakfast in the cafeteria, for a change, and found the door to my room locked. I wonder why that is.

Day 352

To be on board a spaceship, even a dome-generated one, is a thrilling experience. The crew is so very keen and fresh – I imagine myself to be quite the grizzled veteran beside them, although this is only my second assignment. Can that be true? I feel like such an old hand at these games. Perhaps one does not really need actual hours of practice to be experienced at it, for I feel I have already achieved a high level of insight into dome life.

Domes have a specific smell. I breathed it in every day during my jungle stint, and now I find it in my nostrils again. It is a sweet, chemically floral scent. Maybe it's the cleaning solution they use after each adventure ends. I wonder if there is often much to mop up.

In my idle moments when I'm not on duty as Intelligence Officer I breathe in the smell, and think to myself: *I'm in a dome again.* That's when the thrill of the adventure hits me. Anything could happen here. But I know my own character now. If terror comes calling, I will face it down. I will find my courage, and embrace it, and perhaps push through to find the answer I so desperately need: what happened to Watkin?

Poor Watkin. I think of him often. I understand his demeanour so much better now. For how seriously can one take this journey? We will find only what we want to face. That is what Watkin believed. *Play along*, he said. How freeing that feeling must have been. I should strive for it. I must remember that sentiment, truthfully.

As an aside, I like the uniform enormously. It's made of a comfortable stretchy material that flatters. And no ridiculous pith helmet! I feel free – and there is boundless room for us to go forth. (At least, that is what is being simulated.) This dome suits me so much better.

I suspect this will be plain sailing. And, real or not, every moment that passes feels like the forging of a new path, away from that terrible jungle, and the accusations that followed.

Day 300

I cannot believe it. It must be a trick, to put blame upon me for this – this – tragedy. How can I be guilty of such a crime? How can Barton even think to accuse me of that? Do they think I am an animal?

The door to my room remains locked while they continue to 'investigate'. They claim to have found Watkin's remains. That must mean his bones, I suppose, for what else could be left by that frenzied attack? He was eaten, I told them. At least on that point we are in agreement. I am not certain of my rights in regard to refusing the dental measurements they want to take. I must find answers.

Or, rather, I must trust that Ben can organise the counsel I require, for I'm not allowed access to any device, not even a phone. Ben's visits are tolerated only because he is deemed to be beneficial to 're-establishing my relationship with reality'.

Do they fear me speaking of the mouths, perhaps to the public? Well, they need not worry. I cannot bring myself to say the words at all. To even think of them is to feel my throat close and my tongue stick fast. But the words will come out, and it's the page they choose. I have written of the mouths here in my journal, and even drawn them, but I will never speak a word of them, not even to my darling

Ben. I do not think I ever will.

I am so thankful for Ben, and for these pages. They are, indeed, a record for future generations. I must keep them safe.

Day 163

Five days of solitude.

That's all it took for me to realise that I cannot shrug off my humanity to become a wild creature of the jungle. I find the fate of Watkin cannot be accepted. In the hours after it first happened, emptiness invaded me. I was emotionally spent, I think, due to the crescendo in feeling. The terror, the ongoing terror, rose to a point that could not be sustained, and then – it died. It died with Watkin, and I could think of nothing but my relief.

But now that relief has passed, and I find myself clinging to the idea, however illusory, that his death must mean something.

I should write something true about Watkin. I owe him that much, no matter how irritating he became as we journeyed together. I should record how he died.

The mouths came for him in the night. I do not know why they chose his tent, and not mine. Perhaps he did not fully close his flap, and the scent of him slipped out into the darkness, reaching them, exciting them into frenzy. Or perhaps he pitched his tent a little further away from the safety of the firelight than usual. I do not know. I'm only certain of the gurgling. Not screaming, not pleading: only a sound reminiscent of water, circling a drain, and that was what woke me. It must have been his own blood, flowing, bubbling up from his lungs, I suspect. If the mouths ripped through his chest, I can hope it was quick.

I emerged from my own tent to see them dragging him away. A mass of mouths were tugging at his head and upper body, and for the first time I saw their long black arms and globular bodies as they concentrated on taking their meal to the deep growth. Watkin's legs did not kick. He was still. Yes, he must have been dead already, by the time the sounds of feasting began.

Come the morning I searched for him. I found nothing.

Day 401

We press on planet Harmonious, and I pray we will arrive in time to save some of us.

The infinity of space is not so large after all, it seems. It cannot offer endless places to hide from the things that hunt us.

Day 314

Ben: what a wonderful name. What a brave and true man.

His plan, whispered to me during our meetings in my hospital room turned cell, went smoothly. The key card he had baked into a cherry cake opened all the doors, and I found him waiting in the car park for me, complete with a change of clothes and a new identity.

On the drive to the Registration Centre, I asked him why. Why he had spent his inheritance on this plan, and risked everything for me.

"Because I know you," he said. "Because if anyone can sort out this mess, it's you. Go prove you did nothing wrong, and then come back to me. Come back a hero."

I was snapped up straight away for a new dome mission, under my pseudonym. Ben understands completely: I must face these fears. I must look for the mouths, and stop them if I can. To work towards that aim I have become Jane Turner, dome veteran, and I am looking forward to commencing work within this new scenario, which I have been told is a future simulation of possible alien interactions. Fascinating.

Day 390

The strangest thing has happened.

I was on a rest break, in my quarters. The smell of the domes was strong, but I am so very used to it now; I know I would miss it if it was to be absent. So I lay on the bunk and though of home, and watched space whizz by as we warped along.

Then I felt their presence.

I could not say how. It was simply a change in the room, a subtle shift in pressure, as if the air itself had become lighter, and I felt a little dizzy as I stood, and looked around me.

Where were they? The room was utilitarian, barely larger than the space within my tent had been. I had one simple shelf, above the window, where my journal and pen sat. The recessed alcove that held my change of uniform offered no hiding place.

I heard a soft, slow laugh.

Down on my knees, and it took all my courage to lower my head, further, further, until I could see into the darkness under my bunk.

They were there. Five of them, squashed together, grinning. Mouths wide.

They made no move upon me, and I did not think to act against them. We simply acknowledged each other. The fact of our existence, our… shared reality.

That was the moment when I understood – the mouths are not my enemy.

I got up, and left my room. I strolled to one of the leisure lounges, and watched a movie or two. They have a wide range on board, of old science fiction classics. When I returned to my room, not ten minutes ago, the mouths were gone.

I wonder where they are hiding now.

I must think further on this before I commit to a course of action. There must be some way to defeat them; I think that must be my purpose. Yes. It's good to have a role, and mine is so very important in this place where we are asked to play so many games. Ben said to me: *Come back a hero.* How does one do that? Is it my mission to kill the mouths, or simply to prove they exist? Who is sacrificial in this scenario?

I wish I knew what the unseen watchers want from me. They must have a title, and an aim. How wonderful to know those things.

In the meantime, I will have to continue as best I can. *Play along now, Michaels* – Watkin would say.

Yes. I'll play along.

Throw Caution

Tim Major

Haru Ito watched as the fleet of AkTraks banked the steep dunes to perform an ungainly about-turn. The caterpillar tracks of the four tethered vehicles spun wildly. The metal cross-braces that bound the vehicles together and that supported the central bowl-shaped 'personnel carrier' groaned under the shearing force. Haru rubbed his left shoulder, which had bumped repeatedly against the inner surface of the carrier. A three-hour journey, and nobody had bothered to install seats.

He turned – awkwardly, within the confines of his suit – to observe his temporary new home, the terminal destination of the ferry fleet. The other newly-arrived prospectors had already hurried onto the thick, sculpted base plate of the camp, as if they feared being swallowed up by the shifting Martian sands there and then.

"Shall we?" His voice sounded small; his mic was on the blink again. He gestured to Marie and Jahaira. Marie gave a thumbs-up. Jahaira shrugged.

The ferry completed its turn. The caterpillar tracks of the AkTraks threw up sand before gaining purchase. The movement produced a brief vortex; sand near to the base plate sunk away, and Haru glimpsed a support cable as thick as his torso. Somewhere far below them the cable must be anchored to the rock, holding the camp in place against the constant push of the crescent-shaped barchan dunes.

"Welcome to Pearl Bay!" somebody shouted, addressing the first of the new arrivals. Pearl Bay was a neat title for the camp; a literal translation of the name of the wider Martian region, Margaritifer Sinus. The name had never been more appropriate than at this location.

The camp was bigger than Haru had expected, but more exposed.

Whoever had first established Pearl Bay at Xanthe Terra, no more than a year ago, had worked hard to defend it from the elements – but only from the primary direction of the winds. A tall, thin, sand-sculpted rear wall rose far above the shacks and tents, curving at its upper reaches to form an unsupported roof like the curl of a wave. The sides of the encampment lacked walls. Here, the tents were sparser, and the few rough buildings appeared to be supply stores rather than residences. Haru could imagine that dwellings at the centre of the camp, where the sand storms couldn't reach, would be hard to come by.

"Drink?" he said to his companions. They didn't react, so he mimed the action. They both nodded enthusiastically.

They kept their packs with them. It wasn't hard to locate a bar. Its interior was dark, and moisture fogged Haru's visor.

"What's up, Haru?" Jahaira said as they settled into a corner with their drinks. She fiddled with her pouch lock, hooking up the liquid tube. (It had been Haru's round, as he had expected.) Then she looked up and grinned. "Hell. You didn't clock that we'd have to keep our suits on, did you?"

"Sure. Will there be anywhere in the camp where we can take them off?" Haru said, hoping to sound a little less naïve. "In our tents?"

"Sure," Jahaira replied, mimicking him. She flicked a switch to divert her source of liquid intake, then slurped rum through the straw within her helmet. "If you trust yours enough."

Marie shook her head. "Don't listen to her, Haru. You know how old those tents are. You stay in your suit, you hear? It's only a few weeks."

Haru gazed down. The tents were old, but surely his suit was older. Its left arm appeared original, but the right arm and glove were bright orange and fixed to the bulky torso with a shining grey patch that wound around his shoulder. The people at the outfitters had said it was only a cosmetic difference. If he'd understood then that he'd be wearing it day and night…

Jahaira seemed to read his thoughts. "Chin up. It's not like you could have afforded anything better."

Haru noticed Marie's glare, directed at the other woman. They were mollycoddling him, he realised. He wondered whether they considered his presence an annoyance, yet. It had been his connection that had got them this far, but now they had arrived his usefulness was presumably at an end. A month ago, one of Haru's post-grad students, Orin Belvaux, had returned from Xanthe Terra with a pocketful of diamonds and had confided in Haru, knowing that his interest in Martian history would override any qualms about illegality. Orin had been reluctant to arrange Haru's meeting with a crew capable of arranging transit to Margaritifer Sinus, particularly when Haru insisted that his childhood friends, Marie and Jahaira, would be coming along for the ride. Now Haru struggled to remember whether involving them had been his idea, or theirs.

But this was his dream, and Pearl Bay was his only lead. Ever since the first Martian crab had been discovered at Tharsis Caraway – six years ago! – settlers had searched for more. Some, like Haru, were fascinated by the life forms in their own right. But most were more interested in what lay within them. Reports of that first autopsy had been veiled in secrecy, so it wasn't until the second crab was discovered – by some random hopeful scouring the desert, who proved stubborn in the face of gag orders issued by Sandcastle and local government – that word got out. Cut a crab open and inside you'll find a diamond. Perfect, almost spherical. Naturally, this discovery energised the search for Martian life. There must be dozens of camps like this one, maybe hundreds, if only you knew where to look.

Suddenly Jahaira threw up her arms, almost toppling off her stool. Haru's arm shot out to steady her.

"Take it easy with that stuff," Marie said with a scowl. "You know you can't handle it since the op."

Jahaira waved her away clumsily, the arm of her bulky suit slapping against Marie's visor. She stood up. "Right. I'm off to secure us a trawl."

Haru and Marie exchanged glances as Jahaira approached a huddle of prospectors standing at the bar. They regarded the newcomer – her suit daubed messily with band names and slogans – with scepticism. Haru shrunk as Jahaira turned back to point at the pair of them. The group Jahaira had chosen to address wore suits stained bright orange with dust; they must have been out here for weeks already, maybe months. First one prospector and then another shook his head.

Jahaira's hands were on her hips. Haru fiddled with his comms unit, trying to retune to pick up the prospectors' comms group.

Jahaira planted both her feet firmly and Haru heard Marie beside him groan. Then Jahaira swung a gloved fist at the nearest prospector.

She wasn't hurt during the ensuing scuffle, but Jahaira's bullish display did them no good. The camp community was tight-knit, and whenever they approached a new group of prospectors it was made clear that a decision had already been reached: Haru, Marie and Jahaira wouldn't be permitted to buy into the main trawl. From late afternoon to past dusk the three of them sat on the roof of a store to watch ant-like figures half a mile from the camp, casting an enormous, weighted silicon net into the depths of the surrounding dunes. The curled roof screeched under pressure as men and women heaved the winches around and around, tightening the cables, dragging the net home. The process took an age, and even when the net had finally been brought into the steep-walled silo at the eastern edge of the camp, it took the team of a dozen prospectors another two hours to sift through the sand. In all, Haru heard three whoops, punctuated by long periods of silence. Each time, a prospector held up the catch above his or her head, and the others made a chevron to follow the finder into a reinforced hut to witness dismemberment of the trophy.

"We couldn't have afforded more than a couple of trawls anyway," Marie said.

"Could have if we'd found something right off the bat," Jahaira replied huffily.

Haru didn't dare point out that it was Jahaira herself who had robbed them of the chance. The two women watched in silence as he rummaged in his pack and pulled their own net. He held it up by the corners. Perspective made it appear roughly the same size as the enormous one in the silo, a quarter of a mile away.

The tips of Marie's gloves tinked against her visor, a pantomime of dejection. "I'm not sure we'd catch a crab in that thing even if it were trapped in a fish tank."

That night Haru found sleep impossible to achieve. As Marie had suggested, he had kept his suit on, which prevented him from sleeping on his side as usual, and which also resulted in his body being raised higher than his head unless he reclined on the lumpy mound of his half-full pack. The wind whistled inches away from him: the tent was coffin-like in its dimensions and rigidity.

In the morning they trawled using their tiny, ineffectual net. Haru felt that they were children, only playacting at prospecting. Each time they heaved the net free, sand gushed through the holes, hypnotic in its uniformity of colour and consistency. Haru prodded at the flow with his folding spade, becoming less interested in the enterprise by the minute.

At midday he left his companions to the task and paced around the camp, trying and failing to break the ice with other groups, paying more than he should for the repair of his comms mic, then simply hanging around, waiting for a catch to arrive. He stood at the back of a jostling gang of prospectors, making a show of *not* trying to get his hands on the find, peering over shoulders to spy a glimpse of the crab. The thing lay on its back with its six legs raised, its ray wings spread limply on the scratched stone slab. Its movements seemed only half-hearted and then ceased immediately as the knife pierced the central line of its underbelly. The shout went up again as the knife-wielder plunged her fingers into the hole, felt around, then pulled free a glistening jewel.

Haru edged closer to the slab as the other prospectors closed in around the diamond and its holder, all gabbling about shares and promises made. He put out his hand towards the crab, placing his bulky finger onto the hole in its belly as if he might close the gap. The creature's six outstretched legs fidgeted almost imperceptibly, then bent to clasp his finger with not even the strength of a newborn.

The storm hit two days later. Marie had smiled at Haru indulgently when the klaxon had made him yelp with fright. She and Jahaira had spent years aboard Tharsis Primrose Gamma – or rather, they had spent most of their time outside the base performing repairs in the face of sand storms and the lurching, unpredictable paths of the barchans, while academics like Haru paced around inside, fretting about the data gathered during the mission.

All of the prospectors abandoned the trawl, even the old-timers. The bar was rammed so full that Haru couldn't even find his way to the counter to buy drinks. Jahaira, somehow, had already got her name on the 'service refused' list behind the bar and Marie claimed to have pledged abstinence. The three of them lay huddled in their respective tents, the ends unzipped to allow them to make faces at one another. The storm built, shaking the silicon base plate of the camp. Haru thought about the support cable he had seen on the day they had arrived, and wondered how much it would take to pull the anchors free and send the entire camp skidding uncontrollably across the dunes.

"It's changing direction," Marie muttered, her voice tinny over the comms link.

Haru only raised an eyebrow.

Abruptly, Marie leapt to her feet. "I'm not kidding. The wind's changing direction. That's bad."

Haru turned from one woman to the other. Jahaira's stony expression reinforced the seriousness of Marie's observation.

He dragged himself from his tent to see the first people emerge from the bar, staggering either from drunkenness or from the force of the side wind. They yelled as they made their way to their shacks and tents, tossing cables over their belongings to hold them down. Their silhouettes came and went behind streaked veils of whistling sand. Haru put his hands before him, parting the billows of sand into shafts, like sunlight through the branches of trees.

"– in! Haru! Get back into your tent!"

He turned. Jahaira had already pushed her tent into the lee of a rickety store, only slightly reducing the impact of the storm upon it. Marie was in the process of copying the action, rolling her tent like a beetle with a ball of dung. Her other hand was out towards Haru's lightweight tent, scrabbling to grip its smooth spine shaped like the upturned hull of a boat.

"I can't –"

She couldn't. Haru watched helplessly as the wind whipped inside the open end of his tent, buckling its hard walls outward like puffed cheeks. The tent lifted from the base plate of the camp, snapping the silicon ties that had held it in place. His belongings spilled out and up: food rations, water canisters, the bag that had held them, his folding spade, his patch kit. The net.

He lurched into motion, sprinting to follow their trajectory. He scrambled over tents, navigated clumsily around shacks, tripped over the remains of sand-sculpted walls of abandoned dwellings as his items whirled across the length of the camp, clattering, lifting again, spinning wildly as they left him behind.

He skidded to a halt at the western edge of the camp, then ducked as his tent sailed overhead. It looked like a fish up there, swimming backwards, its wide mouth open and gulping at the streaks of caramel sand. Other objects followed it; other people's possessions: stools and helmets and books and bricks. Haru shielded his eyes to watch them soar above the shifting Martian dunes, then skim like stones, then plunge beneath the sand. A collective roar of anger came from behind him and other prospectors joined him at the edge of the base plate, but Haru ignored them. He could see strange motion out there, in the wake of the wind-thieved objects. He saw black specks, lifting and dropping again, surfing the sand waves, tracking the debris.

"We have to follow them!" Haru shouted again, pointing west. The storm had abated only a little and it was still difficult to make himself heard, even over comms. Their remaining possessions having been made secure, most of the camp dwellers had retreated either into their dwellings or the bar.

"You've got to be crazy," Marie bellowed back at him. "No way I'm coming along."

He looked to Jahaira, who hadn't yet responded.

"You know we wouldn't have caught a thing, even if we still had the net," he said, with as much conviction as he could muster. "And the ferry won't be back for another ten days. You really want to stay and keep trying your luck to buy into the trawl?" He didn't add that Marie's chances of doing so would be much improved in Jahaira's absence.

He could see that Jahaira was ready to be won over. She said, "Firstly, you know it could be suicide? Secondly, promise me you don't want me along just because you lost your tent?"

Haru grinned. "Maybe I'm getting that taste for adventuring you're always lecturing me about. And it'll be cosy, both of us in your tent. Also, and without wanting to cause offence, we'll need all the ballast we can get."

After they shouted their goodbyes to Marie, Haru and Jahaira rolled Jahaira's tent to the western edge of the camp. Along with her belongings, they had already stuffed the tent with bricks, rivets and empty oxygen cylinders – anything with substantial mass. There was barely room for the pair of them to struggle inside.

"How do we do it?" Jahaira yelled as the wind ripped at the door opening.

"Just a hop off the end. One, two, three and away."

Together they bunched and stretched, bunched and stretched their bodies, a worm crawling to the precipice. Haru took a last look to determine the direction and then yanked the zip all the way around, sealing them both in.

One, two, three and away.

At first it felt like falling, the tent turning end over end. That was only for a few minutes, though. Gripping one another awkwardly, Haru and Jahaira wriggled to manoeuvre the tent perpendicular to the direction of travel. Every few minutes they found themselves tumbling – Haru had visions of rolling sideways down grassy slopes at the outskirts of Sōbetsu, where he had spent his childhood – but for the most part the tent scudded along, presumably in the lee of one of the travelling barchans. Haru concluded that they lacked enough weight to hold them in one place, and that the tendency was for the tent to rise inexorably even as it was pushed forward, then tumble down the rear of the dune, only to be caught by the next.

They barely spoke. The howl of the wind was deafening to the point that Haru struggled to remember what sound *was*, and how it differed from the constant shout of the sand against the walls. It was enough to hold on and to face each other in their cramped embrace, their helmets tapping despite Jahaira having pushed towels between them as buffers.

Night fell and when Haru woke he was amazed that he had slept at all. Jahaira's eyes were wide. Flecks of spittle had made stains on the inside of her visor in a wide arc that reflected their fairground-ride motion.

They managed to feed one another, one bracing against the spine of the tent while the other connected the hose.

Another night passed – or perhaps a darkness caused by travelling through a denser storm – and then, blearily, Haru recognised that they were no longer moving. The force of the storm had lessened, too.

"You okay?" he shouted.

Jahaira didn't answer. Her thick fingers scrabbled at the door zip. Haru placed his hand over hers, helping her.

They emerged from the tent on their hands and knees. Jahaira didn't get up, retching emptily. Haru staggered to his feet.

At first, he thought that they had somehow come full circle back to Pearl Bay. The wall that rose before them was the same copper colour, a similar height. But it was natural, a cliff. Half a mile ahead, sand piled up against the foot of the sheer surface in dimpled piles, now barely troubled by the wind.

Without her having said as much, it was clear that Jahaira held out no hope. Haru couldn't begin to explain why he still felt optimistic. Perhaps it was just a different consequence of giddiness. While Jahaira lay on her back, staring up at the sky, shifting so little that her suit remained completely inert, Haru investigated their surroundings. The cliff would have to wait – he couldn't abandon Jahaira – so he scoured for any sign of the detritus from the camp. A little way away from where the tent had been deposited he discovered a shallow dip where the sand formed into tiny hillocks. In the valleys in between the level of sand lowered gradually, like the contents of the upper chamber of a sand timer.

"Jahaira! Come over here. I think there's a –"

He fell before he could finish.

It wasn't far, and his suit cushioned his landing well. But he lay without moving, mimicking Jahaira's posture a moment ago, until Jahaira herself appeared, her head protruding over the edge of the ragged hole that he had made in the Martian surface.

"Haru! You okay?"

He grunted and turned himself over with some difficulty, then raised himself onto his knees. He squinted until his eyes adjusted to the gloom of whatever he had fallen into. Then he laughed. No more than a foot before him, its blade dug into a cleft between rocks, was a spade. He drew himself closer. There was no telling for sure that it was his, but, equally, there was no way of determining that it wasn't.

"Haru! Why are you laughing? You fell into a fucking pit!"

He shook his head, then realised that Jahaira could barely see him down here. "It isn't a pit. It's a cave, Jahaira. You'd better come down."

"Like hell I'm going to —"

Haru ignored her. Along with mounds of sand, in his fall he had brought down some rigid structures from the cave roof. They reminded him of the cross-braces of the AkTrak ferry: parallel beams fastened and strengthened with a lattice. He tested one, attempting to bend it across his knee. It didn't give. Even the sand-sculptor robots that operated at the Tharsis bases would be hard pressed to produce something as thin yet tough.

"Here," he shouted. "There's a ladder. Sort of."

He hefted it so that it leant against the edge of the hole, which barely crumbled. Jahaira muttered inaudibly as she began to make her way down. Then she stood with her hands on her hips and a *what now?* expression on her face.

Haru held the unfolded spade before him like Excalibur. Jahaira's expression didn't change.

He waited. And then she saw what he saw.

The god rays coming from the hole highlighted the diamonds on the floor of the cavern. Jahaira gasped, then immediately set to scooping them up with her fat, gloved fingers. In her haste she bumped against the stalagmite structures interspersed around the cave.

"Go easy," Haru said, not quite begging, but not far off.

The diamonds drew the eye, but Haru felt a sense of vindication that, presented with them scattered before him, they barely raised his heart rate. His attention was fixed on the stalagmites. He could see no corresponding protuberances on the roof. Upon closer inspection, he saw that they weren't single rock formations after all. They were piles of smooth stones, each rock the size of his two gloved fists held together.

Jahaira laid the diamonds she had collected in the centre of the cavern. They were each approximately the size of a fingernail and appeared perfectly spherical. As she shuffled around in her search for more, her left shoulder collided again with one of the rock piles.

Haru burst forward to steady the tower, which was taller than him. "Look where you're going!"

The tower teetered. Though he managed to hold the structure in place, something wafted down. Haru watched it fall to the ground, then picked it up. It was a child's cap. It was chequered red and white and scuffed around its peak.

He resumed his examination of the other rock piles, clambering up a slope at the foot of the cavern wall to raise himself up. Sure enough, on top of each teetering, thin pile was a single item. An old shoe. A cup. A pair of glasses with one lens missing. A table tennis racquet.

Jahaira seemed satisfied that she had exhausted the supply of diamonds. She crouched over her collection, sighing and peering up at Haru.

"We're rich," she said, her breathlessness translating as a fuzz of static over the comms link.

She held up some of the diamonds in her cupped hands, offering them to him. About a quarter of the total, Haru estimated.

"You hold onto them for now," he said.

Jahaira froze, puzzled, then began cramming the shining stones into the pouch of her suit.

They sat on the slope within the cavern, gazing up at the pillars, grateful for being out of the wind even though it was so much weaker than before, and they drank rum. Haru had barely been surprised when they had discovered the pack, tucked behind the rearmost rock pile. Along with the rum, it contained food ration tubes and binoculars.

"But whatya think it *is*?" Jahaira said. Her voice was slightly slurred. She waved a hand at the pillars, then returned it to the outside of the suit pouch that contained the diamonds.

"I think it's a museum," Haru replied. "And that tells us something."

"Tells us museums are always kind of disappointing. That the gift shop's always where the fun is."

"It tells us that —" He collected his thoughts. "I think that the prospectors had it wrong, picking Xanthe Terra, or even the wider Margaritifer Sinus region, as a location and anchoring themselves there. I think it was the other way around, the cause and effect. The crabs were only congregating around Pearl Bay because people were already there. Because the crabs – the *native Martians* – are as fascinated by us as we are by them."

Jahaira slurped from her straw. Haru reassured himself that there were others like him – there *must* be – who were more interested in the Martian life forms than their diamond cargo.

"You gotta plan to get us home, right? Gotta get home, cash in these beauties." Jahaira patted the pouch.

"Sure. Don't you worry." They had already performed a recce, climbing the ladder to examine the cliff face with the aid of the binoculars. The steps hadn't been obvious at first, but once seen they couldn't be unseen: carved out of the sheer face, leading upward from the foot to the tip of the cliff. Man-made. "We'll pack up the tent and climb. I'd bet anything that once we're up at the top of that cliff we'll find the winds stronger again. We came west from Xanthe Terra; we could be in the Coprates quadrangle by now. There's a narrow line of mountains north of here that might well be the rim of Orson Welles Crater. Anyway, it hardly matters. We'll travel away from here the same way we arrived."

Jahaira gulped audibly. "Seriously? More roly-polys? Good God." She paused. "But hey. We'll be going in the same direction. Not back to the camp."

"That's right. You thought there'd be a way directly back, against the winds? We're following the barchans now, the same as any of the Tharsis crawler bases. The same as the crabs. But you needn't worry. We'll roll up somewhere civilised, eventually."

"'Roll up' is the right phrase," Jahaira said with a groan. "Remind me never to travel with you again."

Haru only smiled in response. No matter how long the journey, Jahaira wouldn't complain when they reached a settlement and she could cash in the diamonds. He wondered idly whether he'd accept any of the money himself. Perhaps a little, just to fund further study. But she could have the lion's share.

"Two things interest me," he murmured. He bent to lift a loose rock from the floor of the cavern. "The first is that I'm fairly positive these stones weren't smoothed by the wind. Too regular." He rubbed his thumb across the surface of the rock. It felt as smooth as a snooker ball. "In fact, my guess is that the crabs crafted them."

"Like sand-sculptors, you mean?"

Haru shook his head. "They might be capable of that, I suppose. That ladder, for example." He pointed at the hole above them. Then he turned his attention back to the stone in his hand. "But no. This is natural rock, but it's been worked somehow. It occurs to me that maybe the crabs *licked* the rocks to make them uniform shapes."

Jahaira's nose wrinkled in disgust.

"It'd be hypocritical to be squeamish about it," Haru said, a little snappily. Ignoring Jahaira's aggrieved grunt, he reached over to root in her suit pouch. He held up one of the diamonds between his thumb and forefinger – the first time he had touched one of them, he realised. "I think these jewels are a simple by-product. Silicon-based as opposed to carbon, forming a cubic crystal structure with strong covalent bonds, for whatever reason. You'd better cash in before scientists are inspired to replicate the process. It'd devalue that hoard of yours in an instant."

"You're saying that these diamonds are shat out by crabs only because they've been licking rocks?"

"It's not too romantic, I know. And it doesn't do justice to the scientific... I want to say 'miracle'. But that's about right, yes."

Jahaira took back the diamond, holding it up to the shaft of light. She shrugged, then hiccupped. "Shit or no shit, it'll do for me."

Haru smiled again. "That's not the most fascinating part of all this, though. This museum, I mean..." He glanced sideways. Jahaira was now leaning against the rock wall with her eyes closed. He might as well be talking to himself.

"I think..." he began. "I think that it would be impossible for the native Martians to pile the rocks in this manner. Just look at these structures – what are they, seven feet tall? And as precarious as you could imagine. Even working together, even hundreds of them, it simply wouldn't be possible for arthropods like that to climb, and lift, and balance… Look, I need both hands to lift one of them myself."

"Mmm," Jahaira said, neither agreeing nor disagreeing. She smiled, half dreaming. "S'what, then?"

"I believe that some other life form built these pillars," Haru said. "Something bigger."

After a long pause, Jahaira murmured, "Bigger crabs? Maybe bigger diamonds round here somewhere, then." She smacked her lips.

Haru sat for a long time, still tracing his thumb across the smooth surface of the rock. It grew dark and he thought he heard skittering sounds from somewhere nearby, but he wasn't afraid. He lay back and stared at the sky through the hole.

Dawn would come soon. They would climb the cliff, climb into their tent and be on their way. He nudged Jahaira. At the third nudge she opened her eyes. He stood and helped her up.

Haru still held the smooth rock. He put it on the floor, but then lifted it again in order to place it closer to another rock. He and Jahaira exchanged glances. Without speaking, they began to scour the cavern floor for more loose rocks, returning to add them to the pile, working carefully so as not to topple the new structure.

Golgotha

Dave Hutchinson

"Tell me, Father," said the Lupo cleric as we walked along the beach, "do you think of yourself as a religious man?"

I thought about that for a while, conscious of the cameras and long-distance mikes behind us. Finally, I said, "That seems an... unusual question, if you don't mind my saying so. Considering my profession. Considering *our* profession."

"You present as a man of faith," the Lupo said.

"I am, although my faith has been tested many times."

"There is no such thing as faith, unless it has been tested."

I glanced over my shoulder at the crowd we had left behind up the beach. I couldn't see the Bishop among the newsmen and politicians and soldiers, but I knew he was there, probably sheltering from the wind and having a sneaky cigarette while the world's attention was on me and the alien.

"Your faith teaches that everyone is a child of God," the Lupo said, the great clawed feet of its environment suit crunching the shingle as it walked. "I would beg to differ. I do not consider myself a child of your God, nor you a child of mine."

This was almost precisely the line of conversation which the Bishop had warned me against becoming involved in, "I think this is a discussion best left to our superiors," I said in what I hoped was a diplomatic tone of voice. The tone of voice was for the cameras; I doubted the Lupo would be able to tell one way or another.

The Lupo had been on Earth for almost two years now, and their every action was still world news. They were an aquatic people, if one could call creatures which swam in seas of liquid methane on the moon of a gas giant orbiting a star fifty-eight light years away *aquatic*. Everyone was familiar with their image from news broadcasts from their orbiting mother-ship, but they needed to wear heavily armoured suits to walk on the surface of our world. It had seemed absurd to hope that I would one day meet one, and yet here we were.

"They're sly beggars," the Bishop had told me last week. "This one says it's a priest and it wants to see Blackfin. The Church is still formulating a position towards the Lupo, so you're not to discuss doctrinal matters with it. And Donal, don't fuck up, whatever you do."

There had been no explanation why I, and not some more senior churchman – the Bishop himself, perhaps – had to take responsibility for the visit, although I suspected the danger of *fucking up* made this little stroll a potato too hot for my superiors to carry. I was expendable, and to an extent deniable.

"I am a simple priest," I said.

"Are we not all simple priests?" the alien asked.

"Well, no," I said. Although as far as I understood it, in the Lupo religion everyone *was* a priest to a greater or lesser degree. "Some of us are simpler than others," I added, and instantly regretted the attempt at humour. The Lupo, so far as anyone could judge, *had* no sense of humour. They at least had that in common with my Bishop.

It was a chill day, and the breeze off the Atlantic made it even colder, but here beside the Lupo I felt warm, almost toasty. The radiator fins of its suit made it feel as if I stood beside a powerful patio heater. Over the past day or so, ahead of the Lupo's visit, I had been subjected to briefings by scientists and intelligence officers and at least one American General, but it was all jumbled up in my head and I was still unable to fathom how the body chemistry of a sentient being could function at those temperatures and pressures.

"They are not like us at *all*," the General had told me. "That's what you have to keep in mind, Father. Show it the fish, keep the conversation to generalities, and get it the hell out of there as soon as it's practical to do so."

In truth, I had grown a little weary of being told what to do. Ten months ago, I had been the priest of a tiny and mostly-overlooked parish. My congregation was dwindling, the younger members fleeing to the cities, the older ones dying. My biggest concern was how I was going to pay to repair the damage the previous winter's storms had done to the church roof. I felt as if I were on the edge of the world;

no one cared what I thought or did. And then, everything had changed. One should always beware what one wishes for.

The cleric and I reached the water's edge. I stopped, the surf foaming around my wellingtons, but the alien walked on until it was knee-deep in the surging waves. It was almost as tall as I was, like a child's sketch of a large dog rendered in grey alloy, the double row of radiator fins on either side of its spine like the plates along the back of a stegosaurus. Its head was a ball studded with what were presumed to be audio-visual sensors, and it scanned from side to side constantly.

We looked out to sea, the alien and I, in the direction of America, and there was nothing to see, from surf to horizon. All shipping was being held back beyond a fifty-mile exclusion zone.

"Well," I said. "Looks as if we're unlucky today." Which was, deep down, what I had been hoping for.

The Lupo didn't reply. It raised its head, and from the speakers built into its chest came a rapid series of high-pitched squeaks and clicks, loud enough to hurt my eardrums. I took a few steps back, looked behind me, but no one in the crowd was moving. There were several news channels devoted to the Lupo, their doings on Earth, and the strictly-rationed details about themselves. These channels had hundreds of millions of viewers, and it occurred to me that every one of them was watching me, paddling in the Atlantic beside a creature born tens of light years from our solar system. That was why no one was joining us; nobody wanted to be in shot if things went tits-up.

The Lupo stopped emitting the sounds, and the last of them seemed to echo and banner in the wind before fading away to nothing. Then the alien seemed to wait. It broadcast the noises again, and again waited. Then a third time, and this time, out beyond the breakers, I saw a distinctive black fin break the surface, disappear, reappear a little nearer to shore, and then begin to move back and forth. It was hardly an unusual sight, but even now I felt a little thrill.

Blackfin had been found washed up on the beach last year, severely wounded, possibly by the propeller of one of the boats that took tourists on trips around the bay. Volunteers had come from all over Ireland to try and save the stricken dolphin, but she died, and researchers from Dublin had taken her body away for study.

A few days later, as they prepared to perform an autopsy, Blackfin was seen to stir and then shudder, and then take a shaky but deep breath. The researchers rushed her to a tank, where over the following days she made a full recovery.

In time, after the astonished scientists had completed their tests, Blackfin had been released back into the wild, and a month or so ago she had been spotted in the bay. The Miracle Dolphin had become quite a tourist attraction; the hotels and guest houses in the village were booked up for well over a year in advance, and for the first time in several years my congregation had begun to grow again.

It had been quietly suggested that, as the local priest, I take no position on Blackfin; the Christian parallels were far too stark and obvious, and the Church, already struggling with the question of the Lupo and their God, were not yet minded to confront the concept of a cetacean Messiah. God had seen fit, in His mysterious way, to deliver one of His creatures. That's the official line, Donal. Oh, and by the way, don't fuck up.

The Lupo broadcast its noises once more, and this time Blackfin broke the surface and I heard, faint and far away and broken by the wind, the sound of the dolphin *answering*, and I felt a line of cold trace its way down the centre of my back.

The alien's suit must have amplified the sound from the ocean; I could barely hear it over the wind and the waves but the Lupo spoke again, another series of clicks and whistles, and the dolphin replied once more. They were, I realised, having a *conversation*.

The conversation went on for some time. I looked back, but no one in the crowd seemed at all alarmed at this turn of events, and I realised they simply could not hear it. They were too far away, there was too much ambient noise. I was the only witness. That was why I was there, of course. Not because I was a trustworthy local but because I was God's representative on this bleak beach in the West of Ireland, the place where Blackfin had died. I was there to bear witness. I looked at the alien and suddenly felt very afraid. Mankind's record, when it came to the creatures of the ocean, was not terribly noble.

By the time I realised all this, of course, it was far too late. It had already been too late when the Lupo first set foot on the beach. I could not understand what the Lupo and Blackfin were saying, but I knew in my heart what they were discussing. They were talking about *us*, and our millennia-long despoliation of the seas, and all I could do was stand there helplessly.

Abruptly, the conversation ended. The Lupo fell silent, and the dolphin slipped out of sight beneath the waves. The alien didn't move; it just stood there silently, the sea-foam rushing around its legs.

"So, Father," the Lupo said finally. "If this is a miracle, *whose* miracle is it?"

I opened my mouth to speak, but no sound came out.

"There is the God of those who walk and the God of those who fly and the God of those who swim," the alien went on, and this time I heard a noise from behind me, shouting, and I thought perhaps someone in the crowd had finally worked out what was going on. "It is strange to me that the God of those who swim has chosen to show Her benediction on this world, but one does not, after all, question the word of God, does one, Father?" The Lupo had not wanted to marvel at the Miracle Dolphin; it had come to *commune*, to *worship*. It had come to receive *Gospel*.

The Lupo were a spacefaring race, as far advanced from us as the *Conquistadores* had been from the peoples of South America. We did not know what they were capable of, but it was assumed they had weapons beyond our comprehension. Much of our dealings with them had involved trying very, very hard not to anger them, and now, with a simple act of tourism – after all, what could be more harmless than looking at a dolphin? – we had undone all that.

I looked behind me. People were running down the beach towards us, but it was already far too late. Blackfin had passed on the Word of the Lupo God, and I doubted it was a message of peace and love and understanding. Blackfin had told them what we had done to the sea and its creatures.

I had not only *fucked up*; I had a terrible feeling that I had witnessed the beginning of a Crusade.

Salvation

Dave Bradley

//Impact +1 Minute//

At first the light was so piercing and pervasive that it was like witnessing a nuclear air blast. Only the absence of heat told Peter otherwise.

And the fact that he was still alive.

His skin tingled but the pins and needles soon faded.

"Welcome, friend. You're safe. You're all safe."

He squinted, and the universe dimmed and deepened into focus. Sight, smell, touch, sound, even the taste of the air on his panting tongue. It was beautiful, almost euphoric, like every summer's day at once.

Grass grew around, the intense green of a ripe apple. Sturdy trees rustled in air redolent of honeysuckle and jasmine.

In front of him stood a tall, thin and silver-skinned figure, with the biggest eyes Peter had ever seen. As he swayed, trying to remember how to balance, the creature unfurled a pair of glittering wings. They resembled a multitude of slender golden threads, little blue sparks pulsing up and around them to the tip and back.

A slender hand reached out to him.

"Is this heaven?" Peter asked.

"No, friend," said the figure, with what might have been a laugh. "Not quite."

//Impact -72 Hours//

The tumbling rock cast a shadow over everything.

Peter was far from the colony, alone in the cramped rocket capsule, and The Bastard had been visible in the soot-black sky the whole time. Points of light glinted from it where ineffectual probes had landed over the last few weeks. Strapped in his capsule, he'd been fired from the Outer Belt asteroid outpost in a direction no human had been in his lifetime. They'd dispatched signals and received replies. Those altered folk on the edge of space… they knew he was coming.

Peter was the new ambassador from Earth's mining colonies to the One Transhuman Polity. He gnawed on a fingernail and it hurt. Most Belters had cured themselves of the nervous habit years back. In a zero-G environment, chewed bits of human debris are unpleasant at best. But here, on the threshold of the most important meeting of his life, he indulged himself.

Hours passed.

He arrived with no fanfare. Unseen hands tugged the capsule into a huge unlit bay. Peter stepped out, his feet heavy like a navy captain landing in a foreign harbour, unsure of the rules and certain he'd broken a few already. The chamber was as high as a cathedral, with laser-cut walls of rock. There was space in here for a score of craft like his own, but his was alone.

The One Transhuman Polity lived, if you could call it living, inside an asteroid. Perhaps one like The Bastard itself. But this one had a controlled trajectory, and patrolled a region of space claimed by the outsiders as their own.

There were many thousands of beings believed to exist in the Polity, but since Earth had severed ties nobody knew. The UN had outlawed AI, human modification, cybernetic experimentation and other technologies that the Polity embraced. So they'd departed, in their words, 'to grow and explore.' The humans left behind on Earth and its inner colonies feared them, although they wouldn't admit it. The two peoples, with such opposing ideologies, had not communicated in a hundred years.

But Peter's people needed their help.

There was no welcoming party. No official delegation, no diplomatic reception. But as Peter loosened his helmet, someone appeared in the centre of the cavern, as if entering through a door Peter could not see.

A creature, an outsider. It was short, the height of an adolescent, and smooth, as though made of plastic. A bipedal humanoid in shape but not male or female in the way Peter's people understood. The worst kind of person, the Ambassador's teachers had always told him. An embodiment of rejected humanity, of hubris and corruption. Not like us. On instinct he both hated and feared whatever stood before him, its robotic blandness an affront to some primal part of his psyche. It was the chill of facing a chamber of horrors waxwork. This herald looked as out of place beneath the vaulted stone as a child's doll would look in the nave of Westminster Abbey.

"Hello! Welcome, friend, welcome," said the Polity's androgyne messenger. Peter blinked and raised his eyebrows. The voice was soft, warm even, but confident too, a soul not as afraid of this first encounter as Peter. If this was a robot, it didn't speak like one.

Before the Ambassador could answer, the herald continued: "I am Interface Three." It extended a slender hand, on which sat a pill. "I'm sorry, but to begin negotiations with the One Transhuman Polity, you must swallow this."

"What is it?" Peter frowned then shrugged. Yes, those were the first human words spoken to the representative of a long-lost culture. He picked up the pill. His fingertips just brushed his host's palm, which was as cold as the room. The pill was the size of a button from a duffle coat, and translucent. It writhed inside with a score of what looked like miniature spiders, scrabbling over each other. The pill seemed alive.

"Don't be alarmed, friend. It's a translation tool, nothing else. It's essential." The herald's voice was calm, and its smooth face attempted an apologetic smile. "Those are little machines we've made for you – if that makes it any easier to swallow."

It didn't, but Peter placed the pill on his tongue and gulped at once, so he didn't have to suffer it bursting and scuttling in his mouth.

A few seconds after it hit his stomach, the universe exploded with luminescence. Information swamped him, assaulted his thoughts, caressed them. He passed out, and unseen arms caught him.

//Impact -68 Hours//

He saw what they saw. Data everywhere, lights on every surface, neon detail in the rock. There were presences around him, a variety of beings. Larger and smaller and brighter than humans. Folk with skin of quartz and limbs stretching as far as their imagination allowed. All shared silently; conversation at the speed of electricity. There was no distinction between the real and the virtual.

He was afraid, but they were kind. He asked for their help, without words, because memory and vocabulary were different here. Meaning was everywhere, like oxygen had been everywhere on Earth. They breathed awareness instead of air. He was attached to them and they could see through him.

"You're here to discuss the asteroid cluster B7-482 and the recent orbital anomaly," they said, or all seemed to know and think at the same time.

Peter blinked at the brightness of his new vision. He saw deeper and sharper. The world around him grew, enhanced by dots and lines and blinking lights inside his brain. He swallowed and said, or dreamed he said: "Us Belters call the mineral-heavy bodies nearest our colony, The Family. Our mining efforts knocked one of them out of the field and onto-"

"A collision course with your outpost. We predicted it and modelled such a collision before you even began probing the region."

"We call the rogue asteroid The Bastard. It'll impact in under three days."

"Sad that it takes such a potential catastrophe to overcome the prejudice that has separated our peoples for generations."

"But you can help?"

"We can and we will. With pleasure."

Peter's people distrusted these outsiders, had done for generations. But now, plugged in to them, he knew warmth and hope. "You can stop the collision."

A pause in the data. Then a rush that was part emotion, part statistics. "No, friend. But we have prepared for your evacuation."

//Impact -2 Hours//

Had any on Earth's farthest colony stopped fighting for places on the evacuation capsules and looked out of their viewing ports, they would have seen two objects in the sky. One dark and one bright.

Salvation

The shadowy shape falling towards them from the west was The Bastard. The bright shape was a ship of the One Transhuman Polity.

It was round and vast at its core and surrounded by nanoprobes that shone amber, like fireflies, and made the vessel resemble a large Chinese lantern drifting on the breeze. Streamers of silver trailed behind it, reaching out like the prehensile tails of rats. It was a mechanical swarm tunnelling through space. As the craft neared the colony, the nanoprobes and inquisitor filaments swarmed towards the human structures.

Peter stood on what he'd taken to calling the deck of the Transhuman ship, although there were no controls or windows. Everything was virtual, projected into his consciousness and appearing around him, an enhanced reality he shared with his new allies.

"When will the evacuation begin?" he asked, beaming his thoughts to the other entities. "How will we get them all up here?"

His mind's eye looked outside and below the craft, following the fibres as they punched into the colony shields. They reached down and sought the human refugees.

As proximity data showed The Bastard's unstoppable trajectory towards the colony, Peter realised that this was no physical evacuation. He opened his mouth to shout something, a natural instinct in the unnatural silence.

The swallowed spider machines shut him off from existence, along with all of his kind. And joyfully, kindly, relentlessly, the Polity database gathered their souls. The upload began.

//Impact +1 Minute//

At first the light was so piercing and pervasive that it was like witnessing a nuclear air blast. Then the universe dimmed into focus: it was almost euphoric.

In front of Peter stood a figure, tall and thin and silver-skinned, with the biggest eyes he'd ever seen. The herald unfurled a pair of wings made of slender golden threads. Little blue electrical pulses played up and down them. A slender hand reached out. Peter took it and it steadied him. Around them the too-green grass flickered like bad static for a moment.

There were people nearby, familiar faces, blinking into existence.

"Welcome, friend. You're safe. You're all safe."

"Is this heaven?" Peter asked.

"No, friend," said Interface Three's virtual avatar, smiling. "Not quite. It's better than that. You're with us now."

Waterbirds

G.V. Anderson

Constable Kershaw has not uttered any overrides, nor issued a warrant to access her memory logs, but Celia understands nonetheless that she is expected to stay, to sit and answer his questions like a suspect. It surprises her, this treatment. Like she's human.

"Are you chilly, Constable? Shall I light the fire?"

"Yeah, all right," he says, removing his hat and settling into the armchair her employer always favours. Favoured.

Once the logs are crackling and spitting, the dank little sitting room quickly loses its early-morning pall; the permeating smells of brine from the beach and the mould lurking behind the bookcase retreat.

A teacup from last night still sits on the mantelpiece. The rim is marked by purple lipstick – Irene hasn't been here, has she? Celia's short-term memory drivers are old, her logs slow to recalibrate. She tidies the teacup away, aware of the constable's gaze, and smooths the embroidered antimacassar draped over the back of the second armchair before taking a seat herself.

"How should I address you now?" Kershaw says, smoothing his moustache. "Mx.?"

With her employer Mrs. Lawson missing, presumed dead, the contract between them is terminated, and she is free to revert to her default settings. She may choose any name, any gender. But this employment was her longest, lasting two decades; indeed, without it, she would have been decommissioned long ago.

"Mrs. Lawson always called me Celia," she replies, clasping her hands in her lap.

He cocks a brow. "You don't owe her anything. She's let you fall apart."

She glances down at her hands, the frayed skin around her

knuckles, and stays silent.

"All right. Celia." He activates his notepad. "Tell me what happened this morning."

He already knows – he asked the same question when they stood together and looked out at the garments strewn across the sand – but she recounts it for the sake of the official record: how she booted up at 5:38 a.m. after a full shutdown just as the sunrise struck the back of the cottage. She started making the usual breakfast only to find Mrs. Lawson's bed untouched. The front gate was open; she'd heard the iron bolt tapping home against its sheath as it swung in the wind.

At 6:03 a.m., she grasped the rotting gate, stopping it mid-swing, and looked out at the mudflats that led down to the beach, and the Wash beyond. Sodden things frilled there like scuds of foam. White down feathers had blown about and got caught in the fleshy stalks of seablite growing between the fence posts. She plucked one and rubbed it between her fingers as she strode barefoot onto the cold sand.

The sodden things were the many layers of Mrs. Lawson's clothes – her bed socks, her undergarments, her nightgown, her housecoat – shucked off and stepped out of, one by one. Where the sea licked the land, Celia found a messy blast of feathers like the ones seen on busy roads sometimes, or in coops after a fox has got in. There was no sign of blood.

"Where were you last night?"

Celia stares at the carpet. Recovering from a full shutdown has made her groggy.

"Where were you last night?" he repeats louder. "Are your ears as knackered as the rest of you? Respond."

Not so human, then. "I was here with Mrs. Lawson."

"Can anyone confirm that?"

She thinks of the teacup marked with purple lipstick. Shivers imperceptibly. Holds his gaze. "No."

He sighs. "How long have you been coming here with Mrs. Lawson, Celia?"

He knows this as well, knows she remembers him as a cocksure teenager who, when he first saw her, said, *You're one of those fuckbots, right? When can I have a go, then?* But he has to ask. For the official record.

"Twenty years, every May. She came alone before that."

"Was there anything different about her this time?"

"She was ill. Tired from the journey. We only arrived yesterday."

"Why'd she bother, then? There's nothing for tourists here. Was she meeting someone?"

"I don't know."

The exchange has drawn him in, brought him to the edge of the armchair, but now he reclines with an invasive mixture of frown and smirk on his face. He rubs his temple. "I find it hard to believe she didn't share this information with you, her Companion of twenty years. What services did you provide Mrs. Lawson, if she didn't trust you with something like that? Was it physical?"

Celia kinks her neck. A shard of dry silicone snaps off. The question in his mouth feels dirty. "Many people withhold personal or sensitive data from their Companions, in case of a security breach; it's not unusual. And Mrs. Lawson employed me for my social features. The exact duties stipulated in my contract and its amendments do not seem relevant to this investigation."

"Don't they? As her Companion, aren't you responsible for your employer's personal safety?"

"It depends on the contract."

"Do you have it to hand?"

"No. The master copy is filed with Mrs. Lawson's solicitor, and another copy archived with MxMill Incorporated."

"Then I'll need to see one to determine if your actions, or inactions, were malicious. Mrs. Lawson was a vulnerable woman with no family. If you're found to have somehow broken your own protocols, you'll be decommissioned. Do you understand?"

Celia nods and rises. "I no longer have instant mail functionality, but I can give you the contact ID for the solicitor. Would you like a cup of tea while we wait?"

He peers up at her suspiciously. "All right. I need to phone the sergeant anyway. But stay inside the house."

The kitchen is almost bare, a typical holiday home. There's an electric kettle and a packet of tea leaves on the ugly, outdated countertop, and a frying pan left over from breakfast, spotted with grease. Mrs. Lawson was not here to eat the eggs and bacon, and Celia can't digest food like the newer MxMill models.

Perhaps Constable Kershaw would like them with his tea.

The thought comes automatically, unwanted, a manifestation of the constant urge to please that underpins her code. She strikes the heel of her palm against the countertop in frustration, the noise buried beneath the rattle of the pipes and the rush of water as she fills the kettle. It's from the cold tap, so it'll take longer to boil. She flicks it on.

You're one of those fuckbots, right?

She splays her hands on either side of the sink and looks out of the grubby window at the mudflats. Dumpy little plovers wade in the watery crevasses that look like so many stretch marks in the sand.

And, byte by byte, she remembers – Irene. The train. What Mrs. Lawson has done.

Exactly twenty years have passed since Mrs. Lawson first brought Celia to New Heacham – new, because the old Heacham had flooded when rising sea levels expanded the Wash. They rented this same cottage, as they always would, and spent a pleasant fortnight hiking along the coast – Mrs. Lawson was much younger then – and checking the progress of the migrating birds' chicks as they shed their first feathers. Mrs. Lawson knew the nesting sites like the back of her hand. One species of waterbird in particular pleased Celia, and over the years Mrs. Lawson has taught her to appreciate its grace: the little egret, with its slim white plume, silly yellow feet, and dark, dark legs.

"They mate for life," Mrs. Lawson said, watching one as it fished for molluscs. "They fly south in the summer, but they always return here, the same pair, to the same nest, every spring."

When they came again to New Heacham, and then again, and again, and spent the same pleasant fortnight on the same pleasant pastimes and Mrs. Lawson told her the very same thing as if for the first time, Celia smiled shyly and said, "Are you a little egret, too?"

And Mrs. Lawson smiled back, a little nervous, and stooped to pick a clam out of the darkening sand.

"You're one of those fuckbots, right?"

The fifth year. Celia was being served in the pub, taking her afternoon off with Priya from the fishmonger's. The teenaged boy who'd spoken was trying to grow a moustache without much success. She looked to the barman, but he'd been pulled away by other customers; it was a bank holiday, and the place was busy.

"My name is Celia," she told him, collecting her order. "I am a MxMill Companion, model 2.3, and yes, I am equipped for sexual intercourse."

He whistled low. "We don't see many of you around here. New Heacham's in the middle of fucking nowhere, if you hadn't noticed. So." A quick quirk of the eyebrow. "When can I have a go, then? Ah, shit." Someone had bumped into him from behind, sloshing his beer, and saved her the trouble of answering. She moved away to find Priya.

Later, when the crowd had mellowed enough to hear the jukebox, she asked who the boy was and Priya rolled her eyes. "A right scumbag," she said. "He keeps talking about applying to some police academy in London; with any luck, he'll sod off before summer. Just avoid him if you can. Could you get me another one of these? Here, I'll give you the credits. Don't you want one, too?"

"No, thank you," Celia replied, "I'm a model 2.3." When Priya looked blank, she explained, "I'm part manufactured protein, part silicone. I cannot ingest fluids. They'd have nowhere to go."

"That's so weird," Priya said, digging around in her pocket for cash. "I heard the new Companions can eat and crap and everything. You must be a really old one."

But Kershaw did not sod off that summer, or at least he tried and was forced to come back, because he was at New Heacham the following May, and he hadn't forgotten her.

"Who's your owner, then?"

Sixth year. The two of them alone in the lane lined with pink aster, between the post office and the crumbling seawall, its quiet to be disturbed a moment later by the zip of his fly.

"Mrs. Lawson. She rents the cottage out by the mudflats. And she's my employer, not my owner. Companions aren't slaves."

He smiled lewdly. "Would you like to be?"

Then the seventh, and the two years since failing the police academy entrance exams in London had given Kershaw something to prove. He was bullish, that May, more than a little rough. At the end of the fortnight she sat alone on a chalky bank of grass as the sun set over the water, scooping semen out of the modular orifice that functioned as her vagina. It never slotted back in quite the same way after that.

Mrs. Lawson and Celia passed the rest of their time in the south where it was warm, and Mrs. Lawson could keep to herself. Celia liked Bath most of all, with its uniform honey-coloured townhouses, and it was there, when the annual renewal of her contract came up, that she admitted Kershaw's abuses to her employer.

"I spent the first thirty years of my existence in service to other people's sexual desires," Celia said, her voice echoing round the deserted Pump Room. "It's what I was made for. But I'm older now, with desires of my own. I won't be returned to that service, in or outside of your employment."

Mrs. Lawson — who'd started to go slightly deaf and whose knuckles swelled to the size of acorns on bitter nights, who had the right to cast Celia back onto the scrap heap where she'd found her — Mrs. Lawson pulled Celia close and hissed into her protein-and-silicone ear, "He will never touch you again, my dear."

She wrote to the local solicitor's office in New Heacham and threatened to sue for damages. Kershaw was unable to settle a suit, of course, and Celia couldn't have been repaired if she wanted to: Parts for model series 2.0 were hard to come by. But it had the desired effect. Kershaw kept his distance. They saw one another from afar, once a year — snapshots in which he joined the local police, got married, finally grew that moustache, gained some wrinkles.

Now that she considers it, today is probably the first time they've spoken in thirteen years.

"How is your wife?" she asks him as he sips his tea. He likes it sweet. The distaste crossing his face is satisfying. "Is something wrong?"

"Don't you have sugar for this?"

"No, sorry."

"Christ." He takes another sip and puts it down with a clatter, then starts on the cold bacon and eggs. She almost reheated them, but something Irene had said last night stopped her, jumped across her code like a glitch: *Fuck compliance! Fuck making other people comfortable!*

She stands by the bay window as he eats, drawing the curtains back to look at the front gate and Mrs. Lawson's things, the feathers. She still has the downy one she plucked from the seablite in her pocket, and she fingers it gently. It's a little egret feather, she'd swear on it.

It is 7:14 a.m.

"How long will this take, Constable?"

"However long it takes the solicitor to send the contract," he replies through a mouthful of bacon. "Why, you got somewhere to be?"

"I have a pre-contract agreement elsewhere. They won't like to be kept waiting."

His fork pauses halfway to his mouth. He stares at her. "Already? With who?"

"Until a contract is signed, I'm not at liberty to say."

"Sit down, will you? You're making me nervous, hanging around like that."

She sits, smiling sweetly, and between them the snapping logs burn bright. The little egret feather is soft; it slithers like oil paint between her fingertips, which turns her mind easily to Irene's little garage workshop, the smell of turpentine.

It was during the fourteenth year that Celia started to notice Irene painting on the marshy hillocks overlooking the mudflats. Mrs. Lawson had grown too stiff for the long walks along the coast. She opted to stay at the cottage instead, or else sit out on the saltmarsh with a picnic basket if the summer heat came early. Celia ranged freely then, taking Mrs. Lawson's antique camera along, for she could crouch silently for hours until even the youngest little egrets lost their fear of her. She took the most intimate and wonderful photographs, that way.

The two women grew civilly aware of each other over that fortnight, and the following year, when Celia spotted Irene's frizzy, prematurely grey hair in a field somewhere between Castle Rising and King's Lynn, she wandered close enough to see her unfinished canvas: a study of pink-footed geese.

Celia smiled. "You've got them just right."

Irene turned her head and frowned. Then, "You Fay Lawson's Companion?"

"Yes. You know my employer?"

"Everyone knows her, she comes here every year. We all think she must have some toy boy tucked away somewhere, but I suppose she doesn't need one if she's got you." Irene's tone was blunt, dismissive. A faint cleft lip scar drew her top lip upwards like a loaded crossbow. She turned back to her canvas but must have lost the heart for it because she started cleaning her brushes instead. "You allowed to wander this far from the cottage?"

"I have the afternoon off," Celia replied, lifting the camera for Irene to see. "You've wandered far yourself. Shall I escort you home? What's wrong?"

"You just can't turn off that hostess mode, right?" Irene had started packing up her things.

"You don't have to stop right now. I'm sorry I disturbed you."

"No, the mood's gone. I finally get an afternoon away from my husband and then *you* come along."

Celia watched her lock up her brushes and paints, fold the easel and tuck it under one arm. The canvas, still glistening, dangled by her fingertips over her shoulder like a slung coat. When Celia reiterated that the painting was really very good, Irene thanked her warily and seemed glad to leave.

The fifteenth year was better. Irene's humour was abrupt, aggressive enough to keep Celia on the back foot, but the passing of a whole year provided a kind of buffer. Irene even accepted a plate of fried silver eels bought fresh from Priya, who had taken over at the fishmongers. Afterwards they lay sunning themselves in the grass while Celia told her about their beautiful house in Bath, which led to questions about the state of the cottage.

"You know the owner doesn't rent it out to anyone else?" said Irene to Mrs. Lawson, who was sat in a lawn chair nearby. "It's empty most of the year. No one wants it."

Mrs. Lawson's eyes widened, and her head retreated into her shoulders. She was often quiet around strangers.

"It *is* getting a little mouldy," replied Celia, glancing at Mrs. Lawson. The old woman smiled gratefully at the rescue, but shook her head firmly as if to say, *No, I won't stay anywhere else.*

"So are you, look." Irene pointed at the loose silicone flapping around Celia's elbow joint. "When was the last time you had a service?"

"I can't remember," said Celia. Her memory logs weren't built to last this long, to hold this much data; none of her was. She'd started to experience a burning sensation in her skull, wires overheating deep inside. "They don't make model 2.3 parts any more."

When Irene didn't reply, Celia tilted her head to look at her. She was frowning slightly, those lips that never fully closed coloured a deep plum, as if Celia had just told her she was dying.

Celia supposed she was, in a way. The thought made her sad. She looked to Mrs. Lawson for comfort, but her employer had grown very old in the last few years, and the sight of her huddled in the lawn chair made her feel worse.

"Come on, you old rustbucket."

The sixteenth year, and Irene had taken Celia by the hand. Her husband was at work. Their house in town was empty.

She'd converted their garage into a kind of workshop. She crossed her arms and leaned against the bonnet of a wheel-less car as Celia looked around. The paints in their twisted tubes, nozzles encrusted. Brushes of all sizes, their bristles as stiff and sharp as spearheads. Celia kept a respectful distance and did not touch anything, but she must have asked the right questions because Irene slowly relaxed and unfolded her arms.

"This kind of art is rare now. Your husband must be proud of you."

Irene's tongue probed the inside of her cheek. After an awkward moment, she said, "Here, I found you something."

It was a palette of MxMill Incorporated body paints. The plastic container was scuffed and cracked, and most of the colours had been worn right down to the metal base in the middle, but they were compatible for MxMill Companion model series 2.0. Celia hadn't seen the like in over twenty years.

"Where did you get this?"

"Ryan collects this kind of stuff. I know, it's creepy." Irene cupped Celia's chin and guided her head left to right. The silicone that formed Celia's cervical vertebrae crunched like dry cartilage. "The old lady doesn't take care of you properly. I thought someone should."

Irene filled in the gaps where Celia's skin colour had worn away with time and exposure. Her cheekbones and nose were the worst, and Irene took to blending the paint in with her middle finger for better coverage. They stood that way for a long time, Irene working intently on her face, the pressure of her touch making Celia rock on the balls of her feet. Irene's mouth hung open slightly when she concentrated. Celia focused on the tiny scar on the inside of her bottom lip as if she'd fallen and bitten right through it, once.

"Your lips are pretty bad, too," said Irene. She held up the palette. "You want purple, like me?"

Celia still had the lip colour she'd been made with: a vampish red, pure fantasy. It had suited her when she was new, when she hadn't known her own mind, but now it marked her out. She picked out a neutral shade. "Boring," Irene sighed, but she applied it just as carefully as the skin, and the simple thrill of choice made Celia giddy.

Irene noticed and laughed. "Do you want some new hair, too? I bet he's got loads." She set the palette down and led Celia through a connecting door into the house. Celia paused to look at the photographs on the wall of a young, smiling Irene with her husband, framed in tarnished brass. Irene pursed her lips. "Come on." Upstairs, in a tiny bedroom, she threw open a trunk of macabre hairpieces that looked for all the world like a hoard of scalps.

"Won't your husband mind?"

"You think he's going to notice if one of these goes missing? Help yourself. Let me worry about him."

Celia chose a stylish bob in a colour that reminded her of the limestone of Bath. Irene checked its label. It was for a later model, but Irene clipped it down to size. She helped Celia replace her long black hairpiece, then she stood back, hands on her hips. "Anything else, Your Highness?"

Celia ran her hands through her new short hair. The ends tickled her nape. "Can you take my eyelashes off, please?"

"You don't like the floozy lashes?" Irene said in mock astonishment. But she peeled them off so that Celia's eyes looked stark and penetrating.

"It suits you," she said soberly, with an uncharacteristically quiet smile.

But when Celia returned to the cottage, Mrs. Lawson said, "You look strange."

Her smile faltered. "I'm sorry. Would you like me to change it back?"

"No, no. Come closer." Celia knelt by the armchair to let the old woman see her. Mrs. Lawson's weakening eyes struggled in the dim evening light. "No, you look very well. Do you like it? And you picked it out yourself? I'm happy for you. It's just a shock, that's all."

The seventeenth year, Mrs. Lawson caught a cold she couldn't shake. They stayed in, building up the fire until condensation ran down the windowpanes. Celia bought her a little pot of cockles which she ate by spearing them with a wooden toothpick. The strong vinegar made her choke. Celia held her tongue for a further year until, upon arriving at a cottage half-sunken into the saltmarsh, she said, "Mrs. Lawson, we must think about renting elsewhere."

"No," Mrs. Lawson said emphatically, "it's this cottage or none."

"But this mould –" And Celia pulled the bookcase, sideboard and ottoman away from the sitting room wall to reveal vast dark seeping patches. Well-established colonies of pale fungus grew along the skirting. "And the pipes are not what they were," she said. "The radiators in your bedroom no longer work. We cannot stay here, Mrs. Lawson. This cottage is making you *ill*."

"Quiet!" A verbal override, flung out in frustration. Mrs. Lawson covered her mouth immediately and reached out for her. "I'm sorry. Cancel command."

Celia clasped her employer's hand in both of hers. "Please tell me why this is so important to you. I only want to make you comfortable."

Mrs. Lawson eased herself into the armchair with a whimper. In earlier times, her body had filled the whole seat; now there was room for her arms to loll either side. Her voice was quiet. "You asked me if I was a little egret once, do you remember?"

Celia nodded – some memories never decay. "The same pair, the same nest, every spring."

"I was a bold little creature. I thought I'd seen all there was to see of the oceans and the fish and the birds. I wanted to see the humans. I didn't know I'd be afraid of them. I didn't know how hard it would be to turn back." Her face paled. "Something still draws me back to this cottage, this nest. Some instinct, even now."

Celia reached out to stroke the old woman's cheek, and could have sworn she felt stubble there. White feathers breaking through.

"Can you understand? I hope so, my darling Celia. You're the only thing that doesn't frighten me."

She continued to carry out her duties quietly, soaking Mrs. Lawson's jaundiced feet before bed each night, and massaging the dark, dark patches across her calves in the morning where her circulation had failed, but she was worried.

"I don't know what to do," she admitted to Irene.

"She's just getting old. We all are." Irene passed her a brush. She was teaching Celia to paint, although the light wasn't favourable. Heavy clouds lay over the Wash, which reflected them murkily back.

"We missed you last year," said Celia. "Where did you go?"

Irene smiled. The tip of her tongue peeked out to lick at her cleft lip scar. "I was at an exhibition in Cambridge. For this stuff. My paintings."

"That's wonderful!"

"I actually sold a few canvasses. It felt good to make my own money for once. Ryan wasn't happy about it."

She fell quiet. Celia dabbed grey onto the canvas, so thick she could never imagine it drying. For a moment there was only the sound of wind and water, and the birds calling overhead. Then Irene spoke again.

"I'm thinking about leaving him."

Celia glanced at her, paintbrush hovering. Irene's gaze was fixed on the Wash, the grey of her eyes almost a match for the brewing storm. She nibbled mindfully at the puckered scar on the inside of her bottom lip.

"Does he hit you?"

"No," and Irene laughed. "No, but that would make it easier, having bruises people could see. He's just… He's fucking obsessed with your lot, you know that, right? It's like they're the wife and I'm the disposable one made of plastic, or whatever."

Celia took her hand, palm to palm, fingers interlaced. "Manufactured protein and silicone."

"Great, thanks. You missed a bit."

But something kept Irene in New Heacham, something about the other fifty weeks of the year that Celia never saw, and it spilled over the next May when Irene pushed her down into the grass. Her fingers didn't jab like Kershaw's had; they yielded and curled inside her while the black and white oystercatchers skimmed the water's edge nearby. Celia squeezed her eyes shut, her back arching even as she willed it flat.

Irene hesitated, unsure of herself. "Does this feel okay?"

The question was a gift. "I can't feel anything. My genitals have no nerve endings."

Irene withdrew her hand, her fingertips glossy. "What? Why?"

"So that I don't experience pain or discomfort."

Irene was still for a minute, then she wiped her hand on the grass. "You should've told me if you didn't want to."

"I can't." When Irene raised her eyebrows and looked away, Celia reached out and clasped her wrist. "You don't understand: I can't. I am a MxMill Companion. I am programmed to comply. I am programmed to put your needs before mine."

Irene was staring at her.

Celia clamped her mouth shut, but the code prised them open. "W-would you prefer a different attachment?"

It cut deep, saying those words. She began to shake.

"That's sick," Irene said hoarsely. "That's fucking sick." She drew up her knees and pressed her face into her hands. "I'm so sorry. I didn't know you were programmed like that."

"I can't ever consent —"

"We don't have to do anything."

"— you won't know what's code and what's me —"

"But I like you, and I thought —"

"Yes."

They watched the waterbirds pry bivalves from their shells, leaving wedge-shaped prints behind them in the sand. The sun skimmed low across the water. Celia told her about Kershaw. Irene brushed away tears. "I know. I always knew. He still brags about it. That *prick*."

Celia rested her head on Irene's shoulder and Irene rested hers on Celia's head, and they talked until the sky went dark.

"Is there *anything* I can do to make you feel good?" said Irene.

After a moment's thought, Celia smiled and leaned forward. She pulled off her top. "Do you see the panels across my shoulder blades? Open them, please."

"Are you sure? I don't want to break you."

"I know my own schematics; you won't."

Irene prised the panels open, bending Celia's shoulder blades back on themselves like two stubby wings, and sank her hand into the blue viscera of wires and coding cards within. Following Celia's instructions, she located and brushed against the exposed sensory cables, and Celia's skin tingled with pleasure at the feeling of sunlight that wasn't there, wind that didn't blow – a touch that wouldn't come.

Her coding wasn't equipped to process this. It was all hers.

"How does it work?" Irene said much later. "Do you have free will? Can you, like, lie?"

"Yes, I can lie. I couldn't at first."

"How do I know you're telling the truth, then?"

"I suppose you can't. But *I* can. I know when I'm fighting against myself. So, is that a kind of free will? I don't know. I can choose my contracts, at least."

Irene smiled. "What about having no contract? What about being free?"

Celia tucked in her chin and considered the question. "It's safer for me to be under contract," she said firmly. "It gives me certain rights and securities that I wouldn't have on my own."

And the twentieth year, the last year, last night, when a breathless, rosy-cheeked Irene came to the cottage to offer a contract of her own, barely an hour after they'd arrived.

"Would you like a cup of tea?" said Celia, showing Irene into the sitting room. Mrs. Lawson hadn't long gone to bed with a mug of hot milk and sugar.

Irene held Celia's face in her hands. "You don't have to do all that hostess bullshit with me, all right? Fuck compliance. Fuck making other people comfortable. I would be happier for you to *not* care about my comfort. There, stick that in your programming."

Celia smiled. "But I really do want to make you a cup of tea. Your hands are cold." When it was ready, Irene gulped it down while it was still steaming. Her haste was worrying. "What's the matter?"

Irene set the empty teacup on the mantelpiece. "I'm doing it, Celia. I'm getting the first train out of here tomorrow. I want to know if you'll come with me. We can go to your Bath, or Cambridge. I'll give you a contract, whatever you need."

The bacon tumbles around inside Constable Kershaw's mouth; the egg yolk splits and coats his teeth. She can't stand to watch and boils the kettle for more tea, just for something to do. From the kitchen window she sees the sergeant pull up, a fleshy man who has to duck under the lintel when Kershaw opens the door to greet him.

"I can't," she said last night, and the light dimmed in Irene's eyes. "I can't leave Mrs. Lawson like this, not while she's so weak."

And Irene said, bitterly, "Right," and almost turned to go. Then, "I don't know how you can do this, Celia. How can you be satisfied with two good weeks a year for, what, five years now? You're going to short-circuit pretty soon if you don't fall apart first; will it have been enough? I'm sorry, but it's not enough for me any more. I need this full-time or not at all."

"Can I find you later? Where will you be?"

"When your contract runs out? God knows. I'm done running on someone else's clock. Aren't you?"

Celia brings the policemen their drinks and gives efficient answers to the sergeant's questions. At 7:42 a.m., Kershaw's notepad pings with a response from the solicitor. He opens the message and thumbs through it.

"Here's the contract. – Hey, Mrs. Lawson made changes to her will last week."

The sergeant frowns.

Celia stays by the bay window. The fogged glass still bears the imprint of her palm where she placed it when she watched Irene leave, and the smear of her fingers where Mrs. Lawson took them and then held her close. Her head had burned worse than ever as she rested her cheek on the old woman's shoulder, too many electrical impulses firing at once. She couldn't cry, so she emitted helpless, wordless grunts instead.

Whoever designed model 2.3 had given it a mind far too complex for the shell built to hold it.

"I thought this might happen," Mrs. Lawson said, stroking Celia's hair. "I'd much rather you go, my dear, and be happy, than lose precious time with the one you love."

"Love?"

"That is what you feel for her, isn't it? I've seen the way you look at her."

It was true that her time with Irene was luminous in her memory, brighter than the passing days around them. They glowed. They anchored her inner calendar the same way her contract renewal did.

"But I love you, too," Celia whispered.

"And we've had twenty wonderful years together. Forgive me, it was selfish to keep you all to myself." She pulled away.

"Where are you going?" Celia said.

She gave Celia's hand a final squeeze as she headed for the door. "I'm releasing you from your contract." Celia had moved to stop her, so Mrs. Lawson made sure she couldn't follow: "Commence full shutdown."

Kershaw skims the new will, the sergeant reading over his shoulder. When they reach Irene's name as the sole beneficiary, Kershaw's mouth falls open. He looks up at Celia, his pallid cheeks veined with blue.

"How did she know my wife?"

Celia almost bursts: She realises Mrs. Lawson has given them her blessing, her properties, her wealth, out of love; but she holds it in, the truth and her happiness. Somehow, she shrugs. And the lie, after so many others and so many years, casts something loose inside her: the binding code, finally unravelling like so much protein and silicone. She's free.

Ryan Kershaw stands dumb, until the sergeant snatches the notepad from him to check the will, and then the contract with its many, many amendments. He finds, as Celia knows he will, a paragraph in which she is forbidden from preventing self-inflicted injury or death to her late employer's person while they reside in New Heacham. It's the compromise they came to after Celia tried to argue against staying in the cottage. Mrs. Lawson's body was her own to risk.

It is 7:51 a.m. The first train leaves New Heacham in nine minutes.

"Am I free to go, Sergeant?"

With a contract absolving her of any and all blame, he has no grounds on which to hold her. She takes only the antique camera, slipping her head through the diagonal strap so it hangs against her hip. Outside, a cool breeze cuts through air heavy with dew, bringing the last of the little egret feathers tumbling with it. They rush past her face: Mrs. Lawson's parting touch.

The tiny feather is still in her pocket. She kisses it and flings it up to join the rest. Then she runs north to the train station, where Irene is waiting for her.

Buddy System

Mike Morgan

"Have you considered working in space?" asked the job counsellor. "It's a great way to pay off student loans and there's almost no risk these days."

Distracted by the hubbub of the campus job fair, Priya Ichpujani could only blink at the woman. "Did you say space? I don't want to go into space."

The counsellor pushed a brochure across the desk to Priya. "You wouldn't, not physically. Look, don't decide now. Read this. Think it over." She smiled. Priya noticed the counsellor had perfect teeth.

"But I want to go into journalism," said Priya.

The counsellor's smile spread to her eyes. "That's sweet." She tapped the brochure. "Lots of students are doing it."

The brochure made it all sound so simple.

Modern-day space workers employed by FarClose Enterprises stayed on the ground, safe and secure in the medical bays at the corporate building in Mumbai. It was their minds that traversed the depths of the void.

Quantum entanglement was the key, along with an advanced form of telepresence.

The operational details were closely guarded proprietary secrets but, as far as Priya could tell, the company had thought of everything. And, of course, the pay was beyond enticing.

To apply, all she had to do was pass an extensive background check and an aptitude test. But that was no problem. Priya had always been good at tests.

Basic training went by in a blur. Once Priya had signed on the dotted line, FarClose was more than happy to explain how she was going to become an asteroid miner. She was deluged with details, in fact, and expected to remember all of them.

The welcome team showed her the QED on her second day of indoctrination. Priya was underwhelmed to find that the Quantum Entanglement Device was a wire-covered metal tube no more than six feet long.

The machine did nothing more than encourage particles sat on semiconductor dot-arrays at each end of the tube to emit photons. The photons shot along a fibre-optic cable inside the tube and collided in the middle, becoming enmeshed. Since each photon remained part of the original particle that had emitted it, that meant the two parent particles were connected through the mashed-together photons.

"The two different particles that sent out the light now occupy the same place?" she'd asked, receiving an amused confirmation.

"And they're still at each end of the cable, far apart?" she'd pressed, again receiving a pleased nod and smile.

"So, they're together and separate at the same time?" That time she'd earned a patronising pat on the back for her perspicacity.

Then, thinking she was interested, they'd started talking about Gaussian wave functions and decoherence and her eyes had glazed over.

Later that day, a guide from the welcome committee showed Priya a simple table-top machine that could take one particle from a conjoined pair and invert its quantum spin, from either up to down or down to up. The direction didn't matter, just the switch. It was all about the switch in state. Priya had to ask the guide to repeat the spiel because she'd been thinking about the lunch menu.

Once she had grasped the purpose of the device, Priya compared the current direction of the first particle's spin with the direction possessed by that particle's partner. Sure enough, the counterpart particle had also flipped the direction of its spin, even though it was housed in an adjoining room.

"Doesn't matter how far away the other particle is," Priya was told. "As long as they're entangled, if we change one particle the other one changes too."

She didn't appreciate the importance of this fact until her guide pointed out that computers used programming that was nothing more than a bunch of ones and zeroes, and those numbers could be represented by up-spins and down-spins.

Priya got the idea. "Instantaneous transmission of data across enormous distances."

The guide half-smiled. "Exactly. Today, we send data through entanglement. In the near future, we hope to conduct power through the links. Think of it, no more reactors on the rigs."

"Surely not!"

"Why not? Spacetime itself can be viewed as nothing more than a vast morass of enmeshed dimensions. Quantum entanglement is a path that can lead humanity anywhere."

Priya felt the indoctrination guide was perhaps over-selling FarClose's achievements. "The ability to receive and send data in real time regardless of distance is very impressive." She tried to sound like she was an expert by adding, "But a mining rig can't possibly decode a significant quantity of data from a single atom flipping up and down."

The guide showed Priya the modules. Each one contained a core with a thousand entangled particles.

"I guess that would do it," she admitted, cringing inside.

Each mission was equipped with two pairs of these modules, one for operations and one for emergencies. The company referred to the devices as Sensory Experience Modules or 'SEMs' because, Priya suspected, its owners were fixated on sexy sounding three-letter acronyms.

The first SEM was kept in the medical bay next to the worker's life support cradle, and the other SEM was put on board the space vehicle, where it became the control hub for the ship and various mining machines.

Next came the clever part. A series of electrodes were inserted into the employee's brain (the company guaranteed the procedure wouldn't leave a scar), and these connections were hooked up to the SEM next to the cradle. Since that module was quantum linked to the unit on the ship, the worker was able to operate the onboard systems and equipment without any time lag.

The shipboard SEM became an extension of the worker's brain. Just by thinking, the employee could perceive and control heavy machinery millions of miles from Earth, making judgment calls beyond even the most sophisticated of computer software. It was the ultimate form of telepresence.

Priya took her time assimilating this information and then, at the end of the basic orientation session, politely raised her hand.

"Yes, Miss Ichpujani?"

"Excuse me for asking, but did you say electrodes in the brain?"

The lead guide advised Priya to read her introductory flight manual again, this time paying attention to the section on minor pre-mission surgical procedures.

The Remote Operations Supervisor, Ranjit Chaudhry, was charm itself as he showed Priya around the clean-room environment of the medical bay, congratulating her on how well she'd operated the machinery out on the test range.

"Of course," he admitted, "using a joystick is a little different from what you'll be doing out near Vesta. But we wanted to start you out slow. Now you have the basics down, we trust you to operate the expensive stuff." Chaudhry grinned at her. "You'll find direct control a lot easier. And don't worry about anything. There's onsite computer guidance the entire time, advice from ground control and – of course – you'll have a colleague out there."

Priya knew about the buddy system from her indoctrination. Each mission utilised two human minds to oversee operations and help minimise expensive accidents.

He steered her toward the life support cradle. "Now, you did read through your work assignment folder?"

"Yes," she answered, all enthusiasm and smiles. "I'll be mining for metals." Less confidently, she added, "But just for two months, is that right? I thought the normal mission duration was six? Was there an issue with my evaluation?"

Chaudhry looked horrified. "God no, your trainers were thrilled with you. Didn't anyone tell you? You're taking over from another employee and completing the remainder of his mission."

The news surprised Priya. "Oh, I'm a replacement."

With old-school courtesy, Chaudhry indicated that she should lie down in the cradle. They needed to insert the feeding tube and catheter.

Her head ensconced in the padded confines of the cradle, Priya asked, "What happened to the previous operator?" Asking questions helped calm her nerves.

"He developed a heart murmur," Chaudhry replied. A nurse joined them to take care of the cranial connections.

"It happens sometimes," said the nurse. "People get sick. He would have needed treatment whether he was hooked up to the module or not. As soon as we saw his heartbeat was irregular, we pulled him out of his cradle and transferred him to the nearest cardiology unit. He'll be fine, but the timing was unfortunate for us – he was two thirds of the way through his stint."

"Stint?" prompted Priya. "Like a shift? I thought operators saw missions through from launch to cargo return."

"They do for lunar mining, but six months isn't long enough for missions to the Belt. Those assignments are broken up into chunks. At the end of the first person's contract, the remote operator puts the site equipment into sleep mode, and then we disconnect the employee from the module. Once the next worker is hooked up to the same ground-based SEM, the machinery out in space can be reactivated."

A thought struck her. "So, my 'buddy' is already out there? She's working on an asteroid right now, waiting for me to show up?"

The nurse nodded. "It's time for you to meet her. Don't worry, the transition is painless. I'm going to insert the electrodes now and connect them to the module. You do understand, before we can turn the SEM on, the sensory input from your body will need to be blocked?"

Priya let out an involuntary sigh. "I wasn't looking forward to this part."

Chaudhry sounded defensive when he said, "The human brain is lousy at doing two things at once. So, to allow you to concentrate on operating the mining gear, we have to stop distracting nerve signals from your real body from reaching your brain."

Priya didn't mind the sensory deprivation helmet that blocked out sight, sound, and smell, but she was less thrilled about the spinal drugs that chemically suppressed nerve inputs from her body. The numbness creeping through her limbs was disconcerting, to say the least. On the plus side, the induced paralysis stopped her from inadvertently thrashing around in her cradle when she was trying to move the mining robot.

"One last thing," said Chaudhry, "every command processed through the SEM is recorded. We track everything you do out there."

His smile suddenly didn't feel as friendly.

"I'm a robot," laughed Priya, twirling her forward appendages and making pinching motions with the claws.

"You're a human driving a robot," corrected Mariposa Gonzales over the radio link. "And you're not even driving it. The computer's doing the hard work. You're just making executive decisions, like 'go there' and 'pick up that shiny lump of rock.' The company wouldn't trust you with anything more technical."

"Don't spoil it for me!" giggled Priya, her robotic excavator moving into position on the V-type asteroid and firing anchoring pitons into the rocky surface. The inputs from the SEM were the totality of her world; she couldn't feel the slightest trace of her body laying prone in the cradle in Mumbai. "It feels like I'm actually here, on an asteroid!"

"Trust me, the novelty wears off after a few minutes." Mariposa was transmitting from the bulky factory robot stationed just a few meters away. "If you go 'whee,' I swear I'll throw iron ore at you."

Behind Mariposa's factory, the car-sized ship that had towed the robots to the Belt and that would drag the processed metals back to the Moon passed by in its close orbit around their asteroid.

Priya mentally clicked 'Yes' for starting the drill and the excavator fired up, lasers melting holes through the asteroid's surface. While the robots worked, there wasn't much else to do but talk. "I thought the view would be better. It's just black out there. I expected stars."

"Honey, you're looking through robot eyes. You're seeing a glorified video feed. The stars are out there, shining bright and strong, but you ain't seeing them because your exposure is set for viewing things close by."

"Oh," said Priya.

"You can alter your robot's visual settings after the daily work period ends," pointed out Mariposa. "In fact, I'd recommend it. You can see way more here than on Earth."

"I think I'll do that, thanks." She exclaimed, "This is pretty cool! I can see why people choose to return for multiple missions."

"Yeah," agreed Mariposa. Her voice was an electronic approximation of her natural tones and cadences, as was Priya's. "This is my fourth deep space assignment. Space seems more real to me than Earth now."

"What was your previous buddy like, 'Posa?" asked Priya one day.

"Honey, you know mission control is listening in, right? They have the same real-time link you have."

"Go on, you can tell me. They won't mind."

Mariposa caved. "Doug was a douche."

The alliteration made Priya laugh. "Doug was a douche, Doug was a douche," she chanted.

"Ladies," interrupted a controller back in Mumbai, "if we could focus on the tasks at hand? Thank you."

They worked for ten hours each Earth-standard day and then rested. The machines didn't get tired, but the human operators did.

During down times, Priya and Mariposa gossiped and watched entertainment channels. With their physical needs being taken care of by the medical cradles, they had a surfeit of free time to fill. The distraction was welcome too.

As the mission went on, Priya found she was missing bodily sensations. She imagined the beating of her heart, the sound of her breathing. It was a sucking void in the back of her mind that no amount of inputs from the robot could fill. How she wanted to sneeze or feel an itch, to experience anything human.

She understood why some people couldn't take it. This degree of telepresence was wearing on the soul.

Priya and 'Posa could have had different media content fed into the SEMs in their respective medical bays, but they chose to watch the same things. It gave them something to chat about. 'Posa liked old musicals.

It was while discussing these viewing arrangements that Priya realised Mariposa wasn't physically based in Mumbai. It turned out that her cradle was located at the company's Melbourne branch.

"Sometimes I wish they'd unplug us at the end of each shift," said Priya. "We could go see friends and family then. I could hang out with you in person, Little Butterfly. That would be nice."

"They can't unplug you during the contracted mission time," answered Mariposa. "It takes a week for the spinal drugs to wear off. Just think of all the lost productivity."

"I don't have much longer out here anyway. My two months are almost up." Priya was silent for a while, watching the movie through the SEM. "I miss feeling things."

Mariposa replied, "When people can't feel things with their bodies, they compensate by feeling more other ways."

"That must be it," said Priya, and she used the robot's claw to carve her phone number into the rock of the asteroid.

A few minutes later, Mariposa used an appendage on the mobile factory to carve her number underneath it.

Since the missions lasted months, the operators' muscles were electro-stimulated every few seconds to prevent tissue damage. Even so, when Priya blinked open her eyes in her cradle, the overpowering feeling of weakness made her seriously question whether the people who'd told her that were lying sacks of *gandagi*.

Oddly, Chaudhry was staring down at her. "There's something you should know. We saw you carve the phone numbers."

"I'm not breaking any company regulations," she said, still groggy.

"You're not," he agreed. "We know operators can form close attachments. Several marriages have resulted from the buddy system. We don't have a problem with what operators get up to on their own time, I assure you."

"Then what's the problem?"

"I'm sure Miss Gonzales simply forgot to mention it. When an operator spends so long in telepresence, certain details can slip the mind. And for all I know, it won't make the slightest difference to you."

Priya went ahead and bought the ticket to visit Mariposa in Melbourne.

"They can't unplug you," Mariposa had said on the asteroid. Priya had missed it then; she hadn't said 'us'.

Mariposa didn't use the spinal drugs. She didn't need them. In many ways, 'Posa was the ideal candidate for telepresence work. As a paraplegic, she had no troublesome nerve signals to block.

Priya gazed through the window of the plane, thinking. It seemed to her there were many forms of entanglement.

She was going to try again. After her shameful performance in Mariposa's assisted living condominium, Priya had bolted, wanting only to flee back to Mumbai. But she'd swallowed her embarrassment, stopped in the airport, turned around, and hailed another self-driving cab.

Seeing Mariposa in person had been a disaster.

Running from 'Posa's home, Priya had convinced herself the closeness she'd felt working alongside her had been a mirage, a delusion brought on by the absence of flesh. She could pretend the mind was all-important, triumphing over the limitations of the human body, but it did no good in the end. The body was the dull, clumsy reality of life. It was a lumpen fact that couldn't be escaped, only ignored for a while.

No, she was overreacting. She knew she was to blame for the way things had gone that morning. Disappointment in herself was transmuting into anger at Mariposa.

Priya wasn't proud of her behaviour. Confronted with the sight of 'Posa in her curved life-function bed, all the beautiful words she'd had practiced on the long flight had evaporated.

There was a possibility she had come across as patronising and self-involved. She may have used the phrase, "In your situation," while commenting on Mariposa's lack of visitors.

She was far from proud of herself.

Now Priya was going to have to eat a slice of humble pie. But

Mariposa was worth it.

Priya retraced her steps through the assisted care centre, locating 'Posa's room in the maze of corridors as if she'd done it a hundred times.

She heard voices over the background noise of the room's TV as she reached for the door handle. Someone was with 'Posa? But she'd thought Mariposa never got visitors.

The door was already half open, so Priya let her hand drop and peered through the gap.

There was a middle-aged man, balding, thick around the middle, sat sprawling in the room's armchair next to the bed. He looked very at ease with 'Posa.

Priya didn't like what she was seeing at all.

The man wasn't looking in Priya's direction. He wasn't listening to Mariposa either. His attention was on channel hopping while shaking his head with feigned moral outrage.

He did pause clicking through the channels long enough to manage a half-hearted, "I can't believe her. What a patronising bitch." His accent was Australian.

"Like she was doing me a favour," replied 'Posa from the bed.

Still hiding by the doorway, Priya cringed. The man's absent-minded answer did nothing to make her feel better.

"Who needs a stuck-up figjam like her? You've got friends. You're not a pity case." Without pausing for breath, he shouted, "The Night Force TV show from the Twenties? That's so what we're watching!"

"There's a Ginger Rogers marathon on Channel 897."

"Over my dead body we're switching to that."

"Give me back my mouth pad. I'll change the stream myself." Mariposa sounded annoyed. Priya didn't blame her.

"Like buggery I will."

"God, you're such a douche."

The man shrugged.

Wait, *douche*? Something 'Posa had said on the asteroid came back to Priya. Was the man *Doug*? The operator Priya had replaced?

'Posa's next words were in a tone that made Priya suspect she wasn't as irritated as she seemed, merely putting it on. "Did you just shrug at me?"

"I did. It was my patented Doug shrug."

"I hate you."

They were ragging on each other, realised Priya. God, they were old friends, weren't they?

He grinned at her insult, confirming Priya's guess. "Don't spit the dummy, 'Posa. I know you don't mean it."

He glanced over at 'Posa's face in the mirror angled above her recumbent form. "Jeez, don't pull a mug like that. It'll stick, and then I won't want to be seen around you."

In a gentler tone, the man Priya assumed was Doug added, "I'm telling you, she'll be right. We both know that life down here isn't worth a piss in a pot. It's what happens out there that counts." He gestured upward, an act that struck Priya as stupid, since any direction led to space if you followed it long enough.

Doug blinked in a way that suggested he was holding back tears. There was sadness in his voice. "And you'll be back in the real world soon enough."

Oh. Priya understood now. Doug could never go back. The company didn't want a worker with a weak heart.

She almost missed what he said next. "You're the one who's okay. Now shut up and watch my show with me."

You're the one who's okay. He didn't know it, but his comment applied just as much to Priya as it did to 'Posa.

Priya had been eavesdropping at the door for a couple of minutes. She couldn't linger there forever. But she found she didn't want to go in.

All Doug had was 'Posa and her second-hand tales of the distant void. Those, and a lousy re-run to watch. Priya didn't want to take that comfort from him.

Quietly, he repeated his mantra, "She'll be right, you'll see."

Priya turned and padded away.

Once she was back in Mumbai, she would sign up for another tour. She'd request one with 'Posa again. It'd be a good idea to mend fences before that, though. Probably by video call. Priya felt a surge of confidence; she had a plan, it was all under control. Mariposa wasn't the type to hold a grudge.

Maybe 'Posa didn't need Priya here in the 'real' world. But out there, in the cold and the dark, where the universe showed its true face, there they would be together.

Do No Harm

Anna Ibbotson

Subject verified.
Player one: please remain still while we calibrate your personal feedback loop.
Player two: please remain still while we calibrate your personal feedback loop.
Initiate cut scene.

"No. It's just not happening. Sorry." James stared at the white-coated healer, daring her to disagree. His eyes itched, and his jaw was on fire. He wouldn't cry. Not with Sera here. There were limits. He was sick, not stupid. If they thought they could take his dignity away now – the little he had left, for Christ's sake – they could think again.

The healer gazed at James and Sera with flat eyes and let out a little puff of air. She looked down at the tablet on her lap. That tablet was probably full of trial results, James' lifelong productivity. All the shit he had the right to know and not the slightest interest in. But the healer kept it carefully angled away, hoarding data that was nothing to do with her.

"I'm sorry you feel that way, Mr Threepwood, I really am." Her voice had the same plastic, sterile quality as the instruments that had been poking him for the past weeks. Optimised at training, no doubt. "I understand your reservations regarding our healthcare-leisure synergy programme. But let me assure you, your health remains our priority. Of course, with any procedure of this nature there are risks – this is covered in your information pack – but our initial trials show very promising results. The leaderboard system –"

"Leaderboard system?" James interrupted, his voice getting too loud for the small room, "Can you even hear yourself? My fucking cancer is not a fucking toy for some spoiled nerdy kids to play with."

"Unfortunately, your options are quite limited, Mr Threepwood. Your insurance situation..." The healer trailed off and looked down.

She didn't need to finish her sentence. Everyone in this room was well aware of James' insurance situation.

He'd dedicated his life to FutureProof. And then, when it turned out the board had been indulging in fraud on a massive scale, he'd been sucked into the implosion along with everyone else. Never mind that productivity in his sector was among the highest in the company. The performance review chip in his wrist was now so much worthless plastic. He might as well get it scraped and sell it for the micropayments it would fetch.

His anger, never far from the surface, came flooding back. His heart quickened.

"I'd rather die."

Beside him, Sera stiffened. Her hand, which had been resting on the arm of her chair, found his and squeezed. She leaned into him.

"James, please." she whispered, her breath tickling his face. "We've got to try."

'Take that, cystic scum!'

Pulses of light arced from the nanobot's legs. With each shot, another cyst fragmented and dissolved, a cleaner nanobot scurrying to pick up the pieces. xxx_KC_xxx was flying. Red digits appeared in the top left of her screen, counting out her final ten seconds. Concentrating hard, she jumped to make her last shot just as 00:01 blared above her. Clean sweep. Hells yeah.

The screen faded to white, the inside of a virtual reproductive system was replaced by the *Do No Harm* leaderboard.

1. XanTheMan
2. xxx_KC_xxx
3. weebluething26
4. Pwnedyourmum4567
5. bob_and_hannah_98
6. SirWinALot
7. TheRealDeepThought
8. candy.cakes
9. Death_is_inevitable666
10. NotTodaySatan01

KC punched the air with excitement, accidentally switching her PlayGear off and plunging herself into darkness. She pulled off her headset and gloves and flexed her fingers, thumping down on a couch.

She was so ready for this. No more pissing about in virtual reality. She was number two in her whole sector. Obviously, it would have been awesome to get to number one, but it was never going to happen. XanTheMan was untouchable, he'd been sitting at the top of the table for months now. But it didn't matter! Number two was good enough to get into the wellness centre, controlling real bots, helping real people. Making a difference.

"Can't I at least take this thing off and put on some normal clothes?"

James was wearing a blue gown made from some horrible staticky material. There was no way to fasten it, just in case some healer decided to have a poke around and needed quick access.

Sera sighed, reached over and switched off the camera. She turned to him.

"I know it's horrible, darling, but we've got to do this properly. You've read the information pack, it's important that your – oh, what do they call them – operatives get to see that you're really sick."

"I don't have anything to prove to them." The volume of his voice startled them both. What the hell was he doing? He hated that she had to go through all of this, just for him. She'd been wonderful, just as she always was. He didn't deserve her. He never had.

"It's not about proving anything. I know what you're like. You don't want to admit defeat. These kids don't know that, darling, they've never met you. The only way we win is if you wake up again. And our best chance of that is to make sure these kids care about you. You've got to show them why it's worth winning for you. We have to get through this."

James was silent. He rubbed his face hard, sliding his thumbs along his eyebrows. All he needed to do was act like a sick old man. Piece of piss.

He leaned forward and switched the camera back on.

"Good afternoon, my name is James, and this is my wife Sera. I am suffering from advanced lung cancer…"

KC should definitely have spent longer on her makeup. It hadn't seemed important when she woke up, since her head was going to be sealed in an augmented reality helmet. After about ten seconds in there she'd be a sweaty mess anyway, but no one would be able to tell.

Right now she did look kind of crumpled and there was a big red spot on the side of her nose that shone like a standby light. Oh, whatever, she wasn't here to look good, she had more important things to worry about.

Which would have been so much easier to believe if her partner wasn't so aggressively cute. She'd chatted to Xan a couple of times in the forum, but his avatar had not done him justice. He looked like a superhero, but an interesting superhero with a tragic backstory, not one of those dumb alien ones with x-ray vision and stupid tights. His eyes were the blue of a stormy sea, his dark hair was carefully mussed up, curls dipping over his forehead. Having been a *Do No Harm* champion 'loads of times' already, he was super relaxed about the whole thing. While KC bent over the information packs that described their mission and the risks involved (there were so many risks, she felt dizzy just reading them. Like looking into a huge black hole.), he watched her, smirking. It made it kind of hard to concentrate.

The healer arrived ready to take them to the portal-room. She was taking huge pains to be polite, smiling and holding doors open for them. Xan marched through. KC trailed, feeling a bit pukey.

The room they were taken to had blackout blinds over all the windows and soft, padded walls. Two body suits were folded on beanbags against the back wall, helmets sitting on top of them.

KC went behind a white screen to change, but Xan didn't seem bothered about his privacy. He'd taken his shirt off before the healer had even closed the door on them. KC looked away, trying not to think of his flat, hard torso and concentrated instead on the helmet and body suit. This stuff was way more advanced than the gear she had at home. Slipping into the bodysuit, she felt it constrict slightly to fit her shape. She stretched her arm out in front of her and watched the biofabric ripple different colours with the heat of her body. Nowhere to hide then. Heat-sensitive fabric was so goddamn revealing. The helmet was so light she misjudged the weight and almost fell backwards when she tried to pick it up.

Xan was sprawled on a beanbag. He snorted with laughter.

"Cool your jets a bit. You look like you're ready to hurl, and there's no space in the helmets."

"Sorry. It's just – this is massive isn't it? We're about to save someone's life. It's such a huge honour."

"Well, yeah I guess." he shrugged. "Not like they have a choice though; all the subjects end up in the system because they can't afford to pay for working healers. I'm sure they count themselves lucky."

"What difference does that make? It doesn't matter why they're here, just –"

"Whatever." Xan said. "You ready?"

He pushed a call button on the wall without waiting for KC's reply. The healer was back in the room so quickly that she must have been watching them the whole time.

At home, the *Do No Harm* tutorial was introduced by a perky actor. They wore a healer's coat but struggled with the pronunciation of myocardial.

The healer here could probably have pronounced any weird medical condition you chose to throw at her. But she wasn't exactly going to win any awards for her sunny demeanour.

"Right," she said, "I'm sure I don't need to explain to you the gravity of the situation here. Please follow procedure as closely as possible. One mistake and it's game over: and I mean that quite literally. This is quite a different experience from completing missions in your living room, so you'll have to take a short tutorial before you are given operational control of the nanobots. Then a cut scene will introduce you to your subject for today and you will begin your mission."

Something in the healer's pocket buzzed. She took out a tablet, made some check marks on the screen and sighed.

"Above all, we want to remind you to have fun." she continued in a toneless voice "Ascendancy Electronic Arts have full confidence in your ability as players, and wish you all the best with your adventure today."

Then, without smiling, she left the room.

The screen on the wall blinked with some crimson words.

Please activate your helmets by pressing the green button.

To ensure a comfortable fit, securely fasten your helmets with the straps provided.

Prepare for tutorial.

It felt good to be in the familiar claustrophobic dark of the pregame. There was that ever-present disorientating whoosh as the nothingness loaded into the tutorial environment. Glancing down at her hands, KC locked her weapons into place, aiming for the mass of cells that was strangling the virtual lung.

A bolt of energy hit her from behind and she was flattened to the ground. She felt a jolt as the real-world floor hit her knees: roughened plastic where her brain said there should be spongy tissue.

She scrabbled to her feet again, but Xan had already jumped to the arrow in the corner of their visionfield which skipped the tutorial. She turned to his avatar

"What the hell, Xan?"

"I've done that tutorial, like, a million times. It's painful. I mean, we're already at the top of the leaderboard. What else is there to know? Shoot bad shit, win, heroes. I'm here to have fun, not for a snoozefest."

"But – I'm not sure I'm ready –"

"Ugh. This is why I hate being matched with noobs. Okay, you just let me do the hard stuff, right? You're about the right size for a sidekick anyway."

Annoyance swelled in KC.

"I have just as much right to be here as you," she hissed. "I've worked my way right to the top of the leaderboard without buying any booster packs at all. All on my own: no help from grinders. Don't you dare call me a noob."

In their visfield, an old man and his wife had started talking to them about the advanced lung cancer that they were all here to battle. The old man looked small and shrivelled up. His wife looked tired, like she hadn't slept for months. But every time the man glanced over his shoulder at her, she smiled at him in encouragement.

"I don't mean to be a dick, but actually you're not at the top of the leaderboard, are you? I think you'll find I am. And if you don't use boosters and grinders to level up you're not a hero. You're just a dumb –"

"Will you shut up? I'm trying to listen to them!"

"Oh, come on! You don't actually believe they're real people, do you? They're just actors, brought in to enhance our user experience. They've nothing to do with our mission today. It's not real – none of it's real."

Was that true? Those were some impressive FX if it was, to get that guy's skin just that shade of grey.

"Here we go!" whooped Xan. "Let's play, bitch!"

The *Do No Harm* logo flashed briefly above their heads and faded to be replaced with a view of post-apocalyptic lung tissue. The alveoli were all twisted and deformed, huge black spaces gouged into their view. Dominating it all, a great ragged malevolent moon, was the tumour.

KC flexed the legs of the nanobot, trying to get her bearings. She was shaking, and the bot skittered wildly, the camera swinging her visfield around.

"Oh for hells sake, switch on the stabilisers if you can't control yourself, noob." Xan yelled across at her.

She flicked the switch that controlled movement sensitivity and her vision steadied.

It meant she'd have to use bigger gestures to get anything done. But that was fine, big gestures were safe. Xan was going for speed over precision, and was already tearing great chunks out of the tumour.

Her nanobot jerked forward in her hurry to catch up. She got as far from Xan as she could and started snipping at the edge of the tumour.

The sickly moon began to come adrift from the tissue it was parasitizing and float free. Xan had already finished butchering his side of the tumour and started blasting it to break it up into pieces small enough for the cleanerbots.

There was a roar of noise. Xan had switched his bot to turbo. He'd gone to the far edge of KC's visfield and was coming towards her, gaining speed by the second.

What the hell was he doing?

"Xan!" she yelled, "Watch out!"

He charged into the remaining mass of the tumour and bounced off. He was slammed into the wall of an artery by the force. The cell walls gave way under the pressure. Blood gushed out, filling their visfields with red.

Game over.

The healer didn't need to say anything. Sera knew he was lost. It felt like a punch in the guts. She didn't know if she could work without him.

In the champion's room, KC couldn't look at Xan. If she did, she would just try and hurt him. The healers had said that a traumatic accident like this could put people into a state of shock. Apparently, they might behave erratically. She thought about the man from the film. Maybe he was just an actor. But there was no other face she could bring to mind, no other face to cry for.

Xan came over and sat on a chair in front of her.

"Don't blame yourself, kid. You can't win 'em all eh?"

She was on him before she could think. A healer had to come pull her off.

"You just killed someone!" she screamed at him "How could you be so stupid? I thought you knew what you were doing!"

He took a step backwards, looking very frightened.

"Calm down, will you? I – don't know what happened. It worked the last time." he looked briefly lost, then shook himself. "But I'm only human, right? We all make mistakes, KC."

KC felt a fist of rage close over her heart.

Game over.

A Change of Heart

Hannah Tougher

"You take all the time you like," he says. "Have a browse. Guaranteed we've got exactly what you're looking for."

His name is Ted. It's displayed in large letters on the badge pinned to the left side of his blue polo shirt. Over his heart. Underneath, he's stuck tiny smiley stickers. Three in a row. I try to smile back at his wide face with its blue eyes, big teeth, all bright and shiny.

"Thanks," I say, and shuffle down the aisle. I thought I knew what I was looking for but now I'm not so sure.

There's a long row of hearts in glass jars laid out on pristine white tables. I'm the only one browsing. The first one seems all right: a nice size, the colour good. The details are printed at its base.

– Processes at 72 beats per minute
– Lightweight, 0.25kg
– Strong under stress, exercise, heartbreak.

"This is an excellent model." I hadn't heard Ted approach but now he's right at my elbow. I was too engrossed trying to imagine it. This heart. In me.

My own thuds dully in my chest. I avoid Ted's gaze.

"What is it you're looking for exactly?" he says. "Any specific requirements?"

"Oh, the usual," I say. "Nothing too fancy. Just for basic stuff."

He offers a knowing smile that I instantly dislike. I look at the stickers on his badge instead.

"You'll be after something like this." He directs me to the tables opposite, points to a veiny heart, brown-red, gleaming.

"New in," he adds. "All the rage. Durable." He eyes me again. "Built for that fierce rush of excitement. And the pain."

"I don't know," I say, although I'm drawn to it. I've lost all awareness of the weak patter of my own, and my hands, before I even think about it, stretch out to the glass.

He reaches in and passes it to me. It has a comfortable weight. Now I can see the shape of veins and chambers within.

"Comes highly recommended," he says. "Great reviews. Expertly tested. Mass produced. You'll always find the parts in case of damage."

"Okay," I say, since it's in my hands anyway. I cast my eyes around for a price.

He's off to the checkout before I can ask. I follow, past a table of hearts marked *Second Hand*.

"You'll get a discount if you trade your old one in." The new heart has grown cold against my skin. "And we can install it for you now?"

The process is quick and painless. The new heart thumps in my chest, well balanced, regular.

When it comes to it, I can't quite hand over my old one to be piled with the second hands. I pay the full price and Ted lets me take the messy red sludge of it home in a jar. He charges me five pence extra and wraps it in a paper bag.

"Have a nice day."

He hands it over along with my change.

I take the jar from the bag and feel the weight of it. A small warmth seeps through onto my skin. I tilt the glass and the lump of heart slides back and forth.

Ted coughs. I look up, expecting to see him watching, questioning. But he's looking over my shoulder, where another customer stands, new heart in hand.

"Sorry," I say, and shift out the way. I don't think he listens. My place is already taken up by someone new, and Ted flashes his teeth in a too-bright smile.

My shoes squeak on the clean, white floor when I head back through the glinting aisles of jars, adjusting in my arms the lukewarm weight of heart.

Birnam Platoon

Natalia Theodoridou

"Can you tell me the story of the Birnam Soldiers?" you ask, staring at me from the other side of the bars.

But I've said it all to the prosecutors, the judges, the scholars.

"One last time," you say. "In your own words."

Weren't they all my own words?

You don't reply, but your eyes are pleading and kind, so I say okay, sure. I can tell the story one more time.

Marion Romfell: People thought the name of the unit was an inside joke, a playful reference brought on by someone's quirky love for Shakespeare. In fact, the inspiration behind the experiment had actually been the marching forest in *Macbeth*, even if few would admit it.

The Birnam Platoon Files: International Military Tribunal III
[uncensored transcript]

They had been twelve years in the making, and this was finally the day we presented our enhanced, plant-based soldiers to the world. We let them pick their own names to introduce themselves to our funders – back at base, we used numbers to refer to them until then. Unfairly, we realised. If we were to go into combat together, we needed to treat them the way we would treat any human soldier.

We would be deployed the next day, heading out to the war theatre early in the morning, so we let them enjoy themselves, blow off some steam.

"Was that something they needed? To blow off steam?" you ask.

No. But we projected our own desires onto them well enough, you see? We had always been very good at that.

So we popped the champagne and ate the canapés and marvelled at them as they mingled with our funders, laconic and beautiful and calm, looking entirely human. Except they breathed through their skin, which made them seem serene and somewhat uncanny. They politely denied the food they were offered. We let them explain how they photosynthesized their energy, and how they did not bear fruit except under extreme stress, which meant not too rarely but not too often either.

Prosecutor: How successful was the Birnam project initially thought to be?

Marion Romfell: Are you asking for my personal estimation? Or for the marketing pitch?

Prosecutor: Do they differ?

Marion Romfell: They were efficient, self-sufficient, expensive to produce but cheap in the long run. One of our funders even floated the idea of using them to end world hunger after we managed world peace. People laughed, but not all of them dismissively. Because why not? Why the hell not? We could do anything.

The Birnam Platoon Files: International Military Tribunal III
[uncensored transcript]

We moved out the next morning. They never asked whom they were going to fight. They knew they were fighting for peace, and that was enough for them. For a time, at least.

We boarded a military aircraft modified to allow the soldiers plenty of sunlight during transport. That was the first time they would be so far away from the ground. It seemed wrong, somehow. Like we were inflicting some terrible uprooting on them.

It unsettled me more than it unsettled them. I wasn't sure what effect it might have on them, all this sky. But it was fine. They were fine.

I sat next to the one who called himself Nicki. He had soft, brown eyes, like yours.

Prosecutor: This was the first and only mission to which your Birnam Platoon was assigned, correct?

Marion Romfell: The Bathilda strip. The occupation had

devastated the local population. The settlers – your people, I believe – had starved them, destroyed essential infrastructure, bombed all the hospitals. We had to do something.

    Prosecutor: Please respond only to the question posed to you. [The prosecutor turns to the typist.] Please strike the defendant's last response from the record.

    The Birnam Platoon Files: International Military Tribunal III
    [uncensored transcript]

It was a harsh landscape, although it didn't look it at first glance. Or at least that's how I remember it.

    "What do you remember the most?" you ask.

    I remember the dark green, the mossy grey. The swollen sky.

    I remember the wind howling through the forest.

Prosecutor: Would you judge the mission a success?

    Marion Romfell: Yes, it was. Until it wasn't.

    The Birnam Platoon Files: International Military Tribunal III
    [uncensored transcript]

At first, everything went great. Congratulations flowed alongside funds for further research and development. More soldiers were being manufactured and deployed at several locations, testing their ability to adapt to different environments and challenges.

    As far as we were concerned, it was all an undeniable success. By which we meant that the soldiers followed our instructions to the letter and even surpassed our expectations. They went to our wars without protest, fought our battles, took the lives of our enemies and delivered the innocent into the caring arms of our services with no complaints. Costs were cut in half, casualties and losses the same. It never crossed our minds to ask them what they thought of the war. Why would we? Who asks soldiers what they think?

    Sometimes, we caught them staring into the distance, falling into a soft silence that concerned us but did not alarm us.

    "What was it?" you ask.

    I don't know. I think they felt the earth, the air, the world.

    "Did Nicki do that often?"

Yes. One day I saw him standing outside the barracks. His top was off, his chest wide, his skin smooth and bare. His eyes were raised to the sky.

I walked out to talk to him. I was only wearing a T-shirt myself. I remember that because I remember the touch of wind on my skin; it chilled me something deep.

"What are you doing?" I asked him.

"Nothing," he said. "I am simply enjoying the sun." But there was no sun. It was a cloudy day, grey as they come.

I thought him beautifully odd. I let it go.

Why are you here? Why am I telling you this story?

"Because I want to hear you tell it," you say, as if you are the most innocent thing in the world. As if asking for a story can ever be innocent. As if telling it can ever be harmless. "Please keep going," you insist. "Then what happened?"

Prosecutor: Then what happened?
Marion Romfell: Nothing. Everything proceeded as normal.
Prosecutor: There is nothing normal about what you did.
The Birnam Platoon Files: International Military Tribunal III
[uncensored transcript]

Nicki was our best sniper. He and Mala would go out for days at a time, with nothing but their gear. No provisions at all.

"Who's Mala?"

Sorry. She was another of the Birnam soldiers on my team. She was the tallest, fastest one, and she trod so lightly you could never hear her coming.

So anyway. Nicki and Mala would come back right after our intel confirmed the neutralisation of one high-profile target or another.

"Neutralisation means murder?" you ask.

It means they did what had to be done.

Then they would ace their psych evals as if nothing had even happened. As if none of this touched them at all. They were perfect. He was perfect.

Prosecutor: For how long did you command one of the Birnam Platoon teams?

Marion Romfell: Three years. One year in training, two in the field.
Prosecutor: And how long before you realised your mistake?
Marion Romfell: Not long. But too long, anyway.
The Birnam Platoon Files: International Military Tribunal III
[uncensored transcript]

One night, when everyone was resting, I found him outside the barracks again, standing at the edge of the woods. Planted. Immobile. He looked like a tree, ancient but unwithered, blending with the forest.

I walked over and put a hand on his shoulder. His skin felt strange – harder than human, softer than tree bark. For some reason – past experience, I guess – I expected him to recoil from my touch, but he didn't.

"What is it, Nicki?" I asked.

He kept looking toward the forest, as if he could see something I couldn't. Despite myself, I focused on his wide, unmoving chest, waiting for it to rise and fall in breath, for anything that would make him look more human. He'd never looked less human to me than he did right then.

"I thought we were meant to bring peace to the world," he said.

"You are," I replied. "Eventually. In the end. But this is how you do that. Self-defence cannot be peaceful."

He turned to look at me. I could barely see his eyes in the dark.

"Is this what we are doing?" he asked. "Defending ourselves?"

I shifted my weight from one leg to the other. The ground was hard underneath me. "Defending others. Those who cannot defend themselves."

I want to say I still believed that when I uttered the words that night.

"Did you?" you ask. You almost blunt the edges of your question.

I don't know. I don't know.

"What did he say?"

I don't remember.

There were apple blossoms in his hair.

Prosecutor: Can you describe your relationship with the soldiers?
Marion Romfell: Why is this important?
Prosecutor: Please answer the question.
The Birnam Platoon Files: International Military Tribunal III
[uncensored transcript]

We were betrayed by a man we thought was a valuable informant. He was local, but he had connections with some high-ranking officials in the settler military. We trusted him. He sold us out to someone who could pay him more handsomely than we would allow ourselves – you see, it was important for us to feel that we were compensating rather than corrupting him. It's a fine line. But I don't blame him. He had a family to feed, and these were harsh times. I get it.

We were supposed to go in, extract the asset, neutralise the target and her network, get out. But our information was bad; it was an ambush, and we fell right for it. Mala was killed in the first blast. A car bomb exploded right next to her. Didn't matter how fast she was. The rest of my team got away, thankfully. Nicki and I ended up trapped in a basement, surrounded by enemy forces who would not dare smoke us out for fear of the international outcry, but who would also never let us walk out of there alive.

We had water for a day but no food and no sunlight. We had no ammo. It was the first time I saw Nicki scared. He looked more human than ever.

The second day, Nicki's skin turned an ashy grey. It felt like paper. I was certain we wouldn't make it. The third night, he gave me apples he plucked from the backs of his shoulders. They tasted like bombed schools and shrapnel.

We were rescued, in the end. Our people blasted the hell out of the entire neighbourhood. They got all of them, the asset, the target, but there were also dozens of casualties.

Nicki was not the same after that. No one was.

Prosecutor: Then you took a leave of absence.
    Marion Romfell: That is correct.
    Prosecutor: Is it true you had a child during that time?
    Marion Romfell: I thought I couldn't have children. [The defendant raises her eyes to face the prosecutor.] Can we take a break, please?
The Birnam Platoon Files: International Military Tribunal III
[uncensored transcript]

I went away for a few months, after I started showing. It was a complicated pregnancy, but the child was healthy. I named her Mala.

How very sentimental of me, right?

I was called back when my daughter was two months old. I took her with me. Everyone thought I was crazy.

"Were they right?" you ask, your voice no longer edgeless. Ah. There comes your knife.

Were they? You tell me.

Prosecutor: Were you aware of other military personnel who were intimately involved with members of their Birnam teams?
Marion Romfell: You'll have to ask them.
Prosecutor: Don't you think it was unethical?
Marion Romfell: Was your war ethical?
Prosecutor: We are not the ones on trial.
Marion Romfell: Only because of what the Birnam soldiers did. Only because you won.
Prosecutor: What happened to the offspring?
Marion Romfell: You know what happened.
Prosecutor: Please detail the events for the record.
The Birnam Platoon Files: International Military Tribunal III
[uncensored transcript]

When the side effect of their odd beauty became evident, months into the war, acres of conflict and hurt all around us, there was little we could do. Our Birnam soldiers dropped their weapons, lifted their hands off their controls, planted their feet into the ground sown with bullet casings, and said: "You wanted peace. We fight no more."

This is not what we'd meant by world peace, we wanted to say. We'd meant peace after we win the war.

But it sounded ugly in our heads, and so we didn't say a thing.

Prosecutor: Please be more specific.
The Birnam Platoon Files: International Military Tribunal III
[uncensored transcript]

We knew the settlers were planning an attack on our living facilities. There was no way they could outdo our technology and our intelligence, so we were not overly worried. However, we planned our counter-attack carefully. It all depended on co-ordinating our resources. And on the willingness and efficiency of the Birnam Platoon, of course.

We decided to pre-empt the enemy by raiding their hideout before they even initiated their attack.

We moved out in the middle of the night. The wind was howling outside. The air was wet. It felt heavy, clung to our skin like an oil spill.

Nicki and the rest of the soldiers on my team were silent throughout the entire journey, but I caught them exchanging glances now and then. No words, and yet I was sure something unknowable to me had passed between them.

When we arrived, the sky was just turning to yellow.

We surrounded the enemy lair in silence. Everyone was in position. I gave the signal and steeled myself for the hell that was about to follow.

But it never came. There was only silence. The Birnam soldiers didn't move. They didn't open fire. They planted their weapons on the ground and just stared at us.

When we ordered them to pick up their weapons, the soldiers turned their faces up toward the rising sun, barely there in the sky, and ignored us. The enemy started coming out of their lair. I caught glimpses of them. They were people. Just people.

We pressed revolvers into our soldiers' hands, pointed at our enemies and commanded them to fire. They looked at the weapons for a long time, in puzzlement or indecision, we couldn't tell. "Have an apple," they told us, plucking fruit from their bent joints, their weary eyes, their downturned lips. "Have a mango. Have a cherry."

The settlers opened fire on us.

Then someone from base radioed in. They had blown up our living quarters.

Prosecutor: Is that how your child died?

Marion Romfell: I still have a poppy she left behind, pressed between the pages of a book.

Prosecutor: Did your personal loss affect your decision?

The Birnam Platoon Files: International Military Tribunal III
[uncensored transcript]

You cut your arm. You're bleeding.
"Yes."
Does it hurt?
How did you get hurt?
Is that a flower?

Prosecutor: Do you understand the charges against you? You are on trial for crimes against humanity. You cannot afford to be aloof or contemptuous.
Marion Romfell: Humanity, sir?
The Birnam Platoon Files: International Military Tribunal III
[uncensored transcript]

So this is why you came. You're one of the children.
"I am not here to accuse you," you say, but I can see in your eyes that you are. "I already know the winners' truth. I am trying to get your side of the story, the one that's not in all the history books and the tribunal records. I am only trying to understand."
Why do you think there's another side to this?
We court-martialled the Birnam Platoon briefly, right before the war turned. They didn't protest, and they didn't defend themselves. They spoke only of peace, of roots extending throughout the world, connecting everybody to everybody. We condemned them for treason, sentenced them to death. We executed them ourselves, a little angry and a little jealous, but resigned most of all. We would lose the war. We would be prosecuted for crimes we had considered justice. The project had failed. It was as simple as that.
Okay?
Is this what you wanted to hear? No? There's no story of redemption here, if that's what you're looking for. Sorry to disappoint.
"So that's all?" you ask. You're trembling like a blade of grass in the wind. Is this hatred? Can you feel hatred, then? "Your soldiers, my father, even Nicki? You killed them all, just like that?"
We didn't know about all the children, back then. Only about the ones that lived with us. The ones we had. The ones we lost.
"Would you have acted differently, if you had?"
They refused to follow our orders.

"They thought their way was better."

Was it? What do you think?

"It's illogical to use violence in order to make the world a less violent place."

And yet my hands are bound as I sit here, waiting for my violent death.

Prosecutor: Do you imply that you do not accept the charge? Do you wish to change your plea?

Marion Romfell: Oh, no. I'm guilty. To whatever charges you want, I plead guilty.

The Birnam Platoon Files: International Military Tribunal III
[uncensored transcript]

"I don't believe you. You created them. You made them who they were. You couldn't have been that cruel. You couldn't have created something so pure if you were capable of such cruelty."

Would we have needed them if we weren't?

You're still bleeding.

"It's fine," you say. You give me an apple I neither need nor want.

Dawn is almost here. They will take me away soon. It's time for me to meet my own judgment.

"I don't want your death," you say, the sharp edges of your words put away again. "It won't bring our parents back. Neither the ones you call soldiers nor the ones you call enemies. I never knew them as enemies. I only know them as the people who took us in when you orphaned us, who raised us when you undid your creations as if they were nothing."

So what do you want?

"All we want is to know our own stories. The stories of our parents. All we want is justice."

Justice?

"Why are you laughing?"

We lined them up and shot them, right there by the forests of the Bathilda strip, because we were human, and they had let our children die and all we wanted was to see the poppies sprouting from their wounds.

Was that justice? Isn't this?

President: Marion Romfell, you are hereby sentenced to death. You may choose between lethal injection and firing squad, otherwise the tribunal will assign an option at will.
The Birnam Platoon Files: International Military Tribunal III
[uncensored transcript]

You're gone, now. Good. I couldn't look into those brown eyes of yours any more.

You came here asking for my words. What did you want me to say? That there can be no peace without war? No humanity without conflict? You bleed flowers, child – how could you ever understand? The Birnam soldiers didn't, and neither would you. Your courts get it, though: I'll be bleeding soon. But there will be no flowers left behind for you.

I bite into your apple before the guards take me away. It tastes of Bathilda, of dark green forests and wind. I only allow it to hurt for a second. Ah, child. I knew you had at least a little cruelty in you, too.

"– Good."

Sunyi Dean

He says, "But I'm dying," like it's the answer to everything, like he thinks I'll disagree.

He says it like I've forgotten, but how could I forget sitting in that paper-strewn office a week ago, watching dust layer up with sunbeams while a doctor dressed in immaculate professionalism emphasised the words *six months to live*?

"I know," I say. Not daring to argue, yet afraid to keep silent. I've never been sure how to please him. The bed we lie on is too big, and the space between us stretches. Should I reach out? Offer comfort or affection? No, he hates that. Better if I don't risk his anger.

"Just consider it," he says. Meaning, *how can you refuse my last request*?

How *can* I refuse my husband? I don't have an answer. He's the one with all the answers, and soon he'll be dead.

I lie in the dark and fail to sleep.

The next morning, we walk into the Infinitus iClone superfacility. Company policy dictates that employees must double up as living advertisements, so every consultant wears the same cloned face. Everything is retro-post-modern – decor, building, furniture, staff. It's a vacuum of culture and I'm suffocating.

"The risks are insignificant," says our consultant. She gave her name, but I missed it, too busy staring at her unicorn-blue hair. Gene fixed, not dyed. I guess somebody wanted this clone to be special.

"And I'll have all my memories?" He leans forward. "I'll still be me?"

"Your memories will be transferred to the clone in utero," says Bluehair, "and your body will be a perfect replica."

Which isn't what he asked, but my husband is pleased all the same.

Bluehair holds out a clipboard. "If you choose the Premium package, we can utilise adaptive gene-fixing to ensure your cancer doesn't return."

"Perfect." He signs the form and returns it. "When can we start?"

"Just one more thing," Bluehair says. "You'll need a surrogate to carry your clone, and although we do provide that service, I'm afraid the waiting list is nearly a year."

"No problem." He grins and pats my belly. "My wife's already agreed."

They look at me, but my voice has fled. I twist my wedding ring until it chafes.

"In which case," Bluehair says, "I should explain that due to clone-related inheritance laws, the majority of your assets can't pass on to your surrogate. Even if she is your wife. Everything will remain frozen until you've reached adulthood. Meanwhile, the surrogate will live off a stipend and be responsible for your care."

"Oh, she's responsible for all that already," he says. Jovial. Conspiratorial.

Bluehair smiles, green lipstick flaking.

It's true, I do look after him. Cleaning his house, making his meals, running his social life. *This would look great on you*, he'd say, handing me a dress for some corporate dinner. It's concrete-grey and cut too low, but: *Don't you like it? You can't turn down my gift*. And I couldn't, never did, because I'm lucky and provided for. The least I can do is wear what I'm told. I should be grateful for the swag, the lifestyle, the house. Have I mentioned the house? Everybody wants nice digs.

"She's always wanted kids," he goes on. Never short of words. "She'll love it."

I think of mini-him, growing in my belly. Running circles round the kitchen table. Having *his* memories, still owning every possession, ruling over me from a height of three feet – a child tyrant. Physically, I'll be thirty years older. Will he still keep me around when he's grown?

Maybe he'll clone *me* when I get old. Each of us a parent to the other in some endless cycle of rebirth, a twisted parody of eternal love. Or maybe he'll let me die, aged and forgotten, once his resurrection is complete.

"I understand, but we still need her express consent," Bluehair says, and I'm floored by those words.

When did my consent matter? He never asked for my consent to marry. Just told me, *Hey we should get married,* and when I said, *I don't know,* his answer came quick, rapid-fire: *But I love you.*

So it went, every decision and conversation, this single loose thread in the tapestry of our relationship. I find myself pulling it, unpicking our entwined lives. The yarn is cheap and the stitches haphazard, so it doesn't take much.

I think you should leave that job. I don't know. *But the house needs looking after.*

It'd be easier if everything was in my name. I don't know. *But you do trust me, right?*

Tell that friend of yours to get lost. I don't know. *But she comes between us.*

Aren't you going to terminate? I don't know. *But I never wanted kids.*

I press both hands to my belly. The baby. Did he care at all? Or was it just a momentary inconvenience? He didn't want a child with me, wouldn't let me keep the child we conceived. Now he wants to *be* my child.

Every inch of me, he owns.

"I already told you, she's agreed," he says, and grips the plastic armrests. Is he afraid? I suppose he should be. A year-long waiting list. If I don't acquiesce, this is game-over; they won't be able to do the memory transfer before he dies. Cancer wins.

Bluehair angles her shoulders in my direction. "Ma'am. It's your choice."

"I don't know…" Except I do. *I do.* My existence has been building towards this moment, thirty long years of seeking The Answer. To the meaning of life, and to my husband's endless questions. If only I can find the words to speak. Any words. Just one.

"But," he says, bewildered. Hurt. The skin around his eyes has the pallor of transience. He's transparent like glass, a human sand-timer, the grains of him pouring out month by month, and all I have to do is flip him over. Reset death. "But love, I'm *dying.*"

And I say –

Hard Times in Nuovo Genova or How I Lost My Way

Chris Barnham

I see them occasionally, wandering through Columbus Plaza or hanging around the lakefront. Always alone.

They're obvious, if you know what to look for: something a bit off about their clothing; maybe the material or style sticks out – buttons on the shirt when everyone here has those tiny hook and eye things; blue denim worn tight when the men of Nuovo Genova favour baggy cotton pants.

It's how they act too. They drift up behind market traders on a cigarillo break and eavesdrop while pretending to tie a shoelace. They sit alone outside a café, pretending to read a newspaper. But they never turn a page as they listen to the talk at the table behind.

They're passing through and they need to learn about the place fast. It's not as if they can ask: *Excuse me, what country is this? Was Roosevelt president in 1940, or was it Lindbergh?*

I spot them easily because that was once me. Before I lost the Way.

Sian is waiting when I appear. She puts a finger to her lips and leads me off the beach. We sit with our backs against a tree, facing the lake.

The air is cold, with no sound except our breathing and the murmur of waves. I sniff the air. There's something odd about the smell: metallic and smoky, like ash washed by rain. I look south toward Chicago, but there are no lights.

"It doesn't feel good," Sian whispers.

"How can you tell?"

"You develop an instinct. We should stay here until light."

It's hard to sleep on a cold beach when you have just arrived somewhere completely unknown. Several times, I am close to dozing off when a noise from the trees makes me stiffen and pull Sian close. There's a screech like an animal in pain, followed by a low scraping sound, moving away inland. Another time, an eerie howling, like a pack of wolves a mile away.

"Maybe it's a werewolf," I say. "Full moon, after all."

"You think you're joking."

Somehow, we sleep and wake to daylight the colour of dirty dishwater. A bloated, rusty sun emerges from the lake. Oily cords of cloud paint stripes across the sky.

"Look at the city," Sian says.

At first glance, the skyline is comforting in its familiarity. Then it comes into focus: stunted towers, like broken teeth; a wall of dark buildings, lit in places by sunlight on jagged remnants of windows. A rusted hulk of a ship half-submerged in the lake two miles south.

We stay on the beach all day, watching the dead city, but we see no movement. We leave with the moon.

I strike up a conversation with the guy. His name is Willis and he's keen to talk. After a coffee in the square I offer to show him a good place to eat.

"You're new in town," I say, as the waiter puts food on the table. There's bread and olives, and a plate of the tiny lake fish that the locals eat whole, marinated in oil and garlic.

"Is it obvious?"

Above our table, coloured lights are strung through the vines that crisscross the restaurant garden. The centre of Nuovo Genova reaches almost to the lakeshore. There are tall buildings behind us on Piazza Colombo, but in front there is a strip of park sloping to the water. When the weather is hot like today, it's easy to remember the city sits on the same latitude as Rome. In the winter – when the lake freezes and snow sweeps down from Victorialand – not so much.

"It's obvious," I say. "Not to everyone, but I used to travel like you."

"I haven't mentioned any travels."

"I'd like to hear." I dip bread in olive oil and chew it slowly, allowing the silence to prompt him to talk.

"There's not much to say. I'm just passing through."

"Of course," I say. "Where are you from originally? I can't place your accent."

"You won't know it. Tiny place back east."

"Any problems crossing the border?"

"Not especially."

He doesn't know what I'm talking about. I'm sure that, like me, in the world he's originally from this city is called Chicago, with no borders between here and the east coast. However he got here, I'm sure he didn't cross the border from New England.

I sense he's keener to listen than to tell me anything. I used to be the same. I help him along, and as we work our way through the first bottle of wine I give him a potted history of Nuovo Genova, under the cloak of telling him about myself. It's after nine, and we're on the second bottle, when I think he's relaxed enough to move the conversation on a bit.

"I was like you once."

"In what way?"

I need to handle this delicately. I don't want to scare him off by pushing too hard too soon.

"Five years ago, I arrived in the city and it was completely alien to me. I mean *completely*. I knew no Italian. Had no clue about the city's history, or how it worked now. I ended up here by pure chance."

"Where did you start out?" He watches me closely, shadows in his eyes from the lights above. "How did you get here?"

"I met a girl."

Sian Serota walked into the coffee shop in downtown Evanston late on a steamy July day. There were no other customers and I was about to close early and hit the beach, or maybe check out the pick-up softball game on the lakefront.

The door opened, admitting a waft of tropical air that felt like it had leaked out of someone's shower. A young woman walked in. She paused in the doorway, and I saw her clock that no one else was there. I think she might have slipped back out if I hadn't made eye contact.

"Come on in," I said. "But let the door close or the air con gets sucked out."

She ordered an ice latte and sat by the window. I studied her as I made the coffee. She looked like she'd come off a long journey, but she had no baggage other than a leather back pack. There was something intense about the way she watched the road outside, taking an unusual interest in passing taxis and CTA buses.

"I've not seen you here before." I slid her coffee onto the counter in front of her.

"Just passing through."

She was still there when I turned the Closed sign around on the door. "I know a bar not far away," I said. "If you're not in a hurry, I could buy you a drink."

"I'm not in a hurry."

Right away, I knew Sian would be special. Her arm brushed mine as we walked across downtown and it was like a faint electrical charge. I saw her again the next evening and then two days after that. It was on this third date that she told me about the Way.

"I'd like to show you something," she said. It was late, and we were alone on the beach. Looking south, the lakeshore curved gently east. Ten miles away Chicago's skyline was an outcrop of glittering crystals on velvet night. A full moon hung over the lake, a line of silver ran across the water towards us like a ghostly path.

"Tonight's the best night." Sian took my hand. A low dune hid us from the road. The only sound was the whisper of small waves against the beach. "Tell me what you see," Sian said. "Further down the beach, close to the water."

"Sand."

She studied my face for a moment, then stepped behind me and put her arms around my waist. "Close your eyes."

I did so. I wondered if this was some kind of prelude to sex on the beach. Which was fine with me.

"Breathe in time with me. Keep your eyes closed."

"I can't say this happens on every date."

"Don't talk. I'm serious."

I shut up and did as she asked. We stood like that for some time, the peace disturbed only by the murmur of a car inland.

"Now open your eyes. Stay touching me and tell me what you see."

"I see the beach. Some trees further away."

"What else?"

"Moonlight on the water, and... Hang on."

The strip of moonlight still rippled across the surface of the lake. But where it hit the shore it didn't stop: a thin strip of mist crossed the beach from the edge of the water and disappeared over the dunes, glowing faintly as if lit from below.

"Hold my hand, and don't let go," Sian said.

We moved to within a couple of feet of the strip of light. Looking down on it from above, I could faintly see the sand beneath it, silvered by the luminous path above.

"What is it?"

"It's called the Way. Not everyone can find it."

"It wasn't here a minute ago."

"It was, but you couldn't see it until I helped you."

"But what is it?"

"I can't explain," Sian said. "I have to show you."

I pour Willis the last of the wine and signal with the empty bottle to the waiter, who hurries over with another. The restaurant garden has filled up. It must be after ten, but the night shows no sign of cooling. Even the air from the lake is hot and dry.

"So, what happened?" Willis asks me.

"You're going to make me say it? Even though you know?"

"How would I know?"

I take a sip of my wine. It is deeply chilled, dry enough to clean paintbrushes. The label says it's Orvieto, but it isn't expensive enough to be imported. It must be from New Sorrento, the vineyards that in this world take the place of North Carolina's tobacco fields.

"This path," I say. "What she called the Way, it was some kind of short-cut across different versions of reality. Other worlds."

"Come on," Willis says. "How could that be? What were you smoking?"

"Scientists have believed for a long time that there may be multiple universes. It's undeniable that there are particles – quarks, quorns, whatever you call them – that appear and disappear, going someplace we can't detect. If particles, why not people?"

"But a ghostly path in the moonlight? That's a fairy story, not science."

"I don't make the rules. I'm just saying what happened."

Willis shakes his head and drinks more wine. His act isn't convincing. He shows no reaction to my mention of Chicago or Evanston. No one in Nuovo Genova has ever heard of those places.

It isn't possible for two people to travel together on the Way. But Sian had given it some thought. She pulled something out of her rucksack and bent down to lay two lengths of cord on the sand, a few inches apart. They were the same length, about six feet.

"You go first." She put one of the cords in my hand. "Do exactly as I say."

"Okay. But what is this?"

"When you step on the Way, it takes you somewhere else."

"Where?"

"That depends how far you walk. The further you go, the more different it is when you step off again. But every place you go is, I don't know, a different version of the world. A copy of this world but one where some time in the past different choices were made, alternative decisions taken."

I looked again at the glowing strip across the sand. In one direction, it rolled across the water toward the moon, in the other it crossed the dunes and headed toward downtown Evanston.

"That sounds like a good description of Iowa," I said. "You'd have to follow this a long way to reach it."

"Just try it and you'll see."

I'd had a couple of drinks, and Sian was an attractive woman, which always helps persuade me of things. I did as she said. I picked up the piece of rope and closed my eyes, facing the ghostly path at our feet. Sian held my hand and told me to step forward. My foot encountered a spongy firmness a few inches above the sand, like hard rubber.

"Keep your eyes closed. On the next step, I'll let go of your hand. Open your eyes, walk to the right, and step off the Way exactly at the end of the rope."

Her hand fell away. The sound of the waves also stopped, as if a door had closed. I opened my eyes. The beach, the lake, the moon, the sky – all gone. I was in a tunnel through what looked like smoke, lit by light from an unseen source. Where Sian had stood, there was a milky wall of mist. I reached my hand out to touch it. The tips of my fingers disappeared as if they had gone behind an invisible screen. I pulled my hand back.

A voice in my head was shouting at me to do something, anything – run, scream, tear my clothes – in the face of the impossibility of my situation. But I followed Sian's instructions. I placed the end of my cord at my feet and carefully unrolled it in as straight a line as possible, taking care not to move the end from its original position. The tunnel was straight, but it was difficult to see more than a few paces.

I spooled the cord along the Way. Bending down, I was able to tune out most of the impossible scene around me, although not the glimpses through the path itself, where there were rapid movements and flickering shadows beneath my feet, as if an out of focus film was projected onto the ground below.

At the end of the rope, I again did as Sian instructed. I picked up the cord and turned to my right. The glowing tunnel wall a few inches in front of my face rippled like boiling milk. I took a deep breath and stepped through it.

I was back on the beach. There was no sign of Sian. It was hard to believe she could have moved far away in that brief time. I looked towards the lake. Something was different, but at first I didn't register the change. There was no sign of the full moon that had been there moments before. The night had become instantly overcast, and if the moon was still there, it was now hidden behind clouds. The ghost path was also gone.

There was another change. Beyond the southern end of the beach, low waves slapped against a jumble of rocks and a wooden rowing boat danced against its mooring on a short pier. Further south, the lakeshore arced gently to the left as before, but something was missing. Something important.

Chicago. The far-off glitter of the city was gone. Where before there was a crowded lakeshore of glowing towers, so tall and bright they cast a glow into the sky above, there was now unbroken darkness. The smiling curve of Lake Michigan's shore was toothless and empty.

"Wow, it worked." Sian spoke behind me.

"Where did you come from?"

"Same place you did." She followed my gaze south. "Ah, no city here."

"Maybe there's clouds in the way," I said. "You can't just make Chicago disappear."

"Nobody made it disappear," Sian said. "In this world it was never there." I studied her face, wondering if this was a joke, but she coolly returned my gaze. "Never mind the city." She took my hand. "Let's see what's closer to hand." She led me away from the beach, toward Evanston.

Except Evanston wasn't there either. Instead of the strip of park beside the beach, with its barbecue pits and picnic tables, we passed through a flat expanse of marshy grass, dotted with thorn bushes. The clouds over the lake began to clear, bringing the bone-white glow of a full moon. This was the only light to guide us: there were no streetlamps, no lights from the verandas of elegant lakeside homes, no distant glitter of downtown office buildings.

"There should be a road here." I pulled Sian to a stop when we were a hundred yards from the shore. When we stopped moving I became conscious of how quiet it was. "I don't get it. Where are we?"

"It's the same place. The same piece of Lake Michigan shoreline. Just a different version of it. Chicago and the cities around it haven't been built."

"What do you mean: we've travelled back in time or something?"

"Not time. It's weirder than that. The Way can take you to slightly different realities. Different versions of the world, but similar in many ways."

"How many different worlds?"

"The possibilities are endless, in theory. There are places where we didn't meet, places where we met in different ways, at different times. Worlds where early explorers decided to start a settlement in a different place. This looks like one of those."

"Have you been here before?"

"I don't think so." Sian looked at the knotted gorse bushes that stretched away into darkness. "Not exactly. I've been to worlds where there was no city of Chicago, or it was very different."

I let out a long breath. "It's hard to take in."

"I know." She placed a hand on my chest. "Let's go back. We don't know how safe it is here. We can talk somewhere more comfortable."

"But I want to explore. This is amazing."

"I just wanted to show you how it worked," Sian said. "We can visit places a lot more interesting than this."

This time, there is a city where Chicago should be, but it's called something else, a French-sounding name that I forget. We walk into town on an unpaved road. There are no cars, and no sign of railway tracks, no planes in the sky. Transport is mostly on foot, with hand-drawn carts and some horses for better-dressed, wealthy-looking citizens. The buildings are wooden, except for the tall, stone walls of the fort where the river flows into the lake.

It's like the Old West, but in a French movie instead of the Hollywood version. The locals are friendly, and we manage to make ourselves understood with gestures and our few French words. Everyone assumes we're from Quebec. The local wine and lake fish are excellent and cheap, enabling us to live comfortably for a month on the proceeds of the gold necklace that Sian sells to a dealer on the day we arrive. Life is peaceful here, with very little connection to or news from the world beyond Grandes Lacs, as locals call them. We have a restful time, eating and sleeping and doing some river fishing. But we're bored by the next full moon.

So we move on.

After that first trip on the Way, the weeks until the next full moon gave Sian and me time to get to know each other. She moved into my apartment a week after we met. She had to hide from the landlady, who lived on the top floor, but it saved money.

I showed her the sights of Chicago. She obviously knew the city, but it was as if she had a version in her head that was out of date, or slightly altered. She had been to versions of Chicago before, but not this exact one. We took the El downtown and although she knew where the station was she had no idea how to tackle the ticket barriers. On the train, she stared hungrily out of the window. I pointed out Wrigley Field.

"We could take in a ballgame," I said. "Have you been before?"

"Sure. They have the Cubs in lots of the cities."

"They won the World Series this year."

"Wow," she said. "That never happens."

That first month, we spent almost every minute together: every night, every meal, every free moment when we could go to the beach, or explore a corner of the city that Sian had not yet seen. Even when I had to work, Sian came into the coffee shop and sat reading, or wrote in the notebook she always carried.

I was so suddenly, so deeply in love with her that every minute was a unique jewel, emerging fully-formed with no ties to the past or responsibility to the future. All that mattered was that we were together, right here, right now. Maybe that's why I discovered so little about her past. She didn't offer much, and I didn't question her. It was obvious that she did not come from this America, but she never said much about the world she came from, and why she didn't go back.

The next full moon came at the end of August. I was three weeks from my return to college, so I hadn't thought much beyond another trip on the Way. I didn't consider what might happen at the full moon in September or October. I didn't think that far ahead.

Sian did.

"Do you want to come with me?" We were alone in the coffee shop again, late afternoon. Sian had sat by the window for the last half hour, bent over her notebook as I cleared up. I paused in my work and leaned on the mop. The low sun outside haloed her head in gold.

"Where were you thinking of going?"

"Not just one trip," she said. "I mean, would you leave this behind? Would you give it up and travel with me?"

I looked down at the dirty head of the mop in its bucket. I thought about the boring days here before Sian walked in. I pictured the sinuous silvery ribbon of the Way, shimmering above the dark sand, a doorway to an endless parade of worlds beyond my imagination. I didn't think about my college course.

"When do we leave?"

"You'll want to know the history of this world," I tell Willis over coffee at the end of our meal. "You won't want to ask too obviously. It's a bit of a giveaway."

"If you say so." He persists in his innocent act, which is irritating, but I tell him what he needs to know. How in this world Columbus discovered the New World, but he did it in 1490, not 1492. He didn't need to wait for the Spanish monarchs to bankroll him, having already secured support from rich bankers in his native Genoa. With Spain behind the pace and disadvantaged in European wars by its lack of American gold, settlement of the new continent happened more slowly than in the world I knew best, and involved more European countries.

Hence the city of Nuovo Genova on the shores of what other worlds call Lake Michigan, major city of the loose confederation of Italian-speaking states that stretched from the river I used to know as the Mississippi, to the Atlantic coast.

When we leave the restaurant, Willis agrees to meet again next day. I have no reason to distrust him, but I follow him home, just in case. He is staying in a room above a bar close to Piazza Vespucci.

We travel together for over a year. Of course, there are strains. You can't spend every waking and sleeping minute with someone without tensions. But mostly it's heaven for me – jumping from one world to the next, exploring a dozen different cultures without ever leaving the Illinois landscape I know so well.

We see many variations of Chicago. There's the city without skyscrapers, still crammed with untidy wooden tenements downtown, where the 1871 fire didn't happen. There's another French version of the city, called Dusable, much smaller than the city I knew, poisoned by a heavily-polluted lake.

One time, we step off the Way into a snowstorm. The beach is a moonscape of snow dunes, with pennants of ice crystals strung from the peaks by a bone-chilling wind off the lake. We scramble into the lee of a snowdrift and pull warmer clothing from our packs, then hunker down together and wait for morning. There's a deep moaning sound from somewhere, but I can't tell what it is.

It's hard to tell when daylight comes; the sky gradually shifts from black to grey. When I peer out from our shelter I can just make out the lake. I walk closer to it and solve the mystery of the moaning we heard through the night. The frozen surface rises and falls like the chest of a buried giant, grinding shards of ice against the beach.

We walk inland. At first, I think we're in another world where Evanston didn't get built. The only things that break up the mounded snowscape are the trunks of dead trees. It's the trees that bring things into focus. They march in straight lines, north and south, parallel with the lakeshore, as if they once grew beside roads. Further inland, the snow rears up into higher dunes, some of them flat on the top and sides.

"They're buildings," Sian whispers. "Or they were."

We find a place where the snow has blown away from the side of a wall. It looks like it was once the lower part of an office building. There is scorched brickwork, ending in a jagged line above our heads, where the wall was broken by some impact or explosion.

Nearby, we find an abandoned car, half-buried in the snow. I pull a door open and we slip inside to shelter from the wind. There is a newspaper on the passenger seat, its pages brittle with age. The front-page headline says: 'U.S. Imposes Arms Blockade on Cuba on Finding Offensive Missile Sites; Kennedy Ready for Soviet Showdown'. The date is October 23rd, 1962. Neither of us speaks. I get out and scrape the windshield. The deepest snow, against the glass, contains fine grains of ash.

We sit in the car for the rest of the day. Nothing moves on the road or in the sky. Then we get out and retrace our steps to the beach and Sian conjures up the Way. We move on.

"We could just stay here," Sian said. "We don't need to keep moving all the time."

"But think what we'd miss."

Late on a summer afternoon, we were eating at a pavement table outside a bistro in Galena, Illinois, looking east down a gentle slope to the green ridge of the Galena River levee. People were out for the evening promenade along the river bank – women in long gowns with lace parasols, men in tuxedos, like a painting by Renoir.

"I get tired," Sian said. "When you find a nice place like this, don't you want to stay a while?"

"You've seen more than me. I've got a lot of catching up to do."

Where I came from, Galena was a quaint historic district of brick buildings, visited mainly by weekending Chicagoans. In this world, it was a city of half a million, grown rich on its position as the northern gateway to the French territories on the western banks of the Mississippi. As far as I could work out, the divergence was the lack of Napoleonic Wars in Europe, and the consequent failure of France to sell its North American possessions to the fledgling United States. Here, Galena was a border city.

"You can't exactly catch up, since you need me to find the Way," Sian said.

"So, are you going to stop me?"

"I didn't say that." Sian watched the strollers on the levee. "But the grass isn't always greener."

The first sign of her discontent. I should have paid attention. But I didn't.

We moved on to Nuevo Genova. It was a hot summer night when we stepped off the Way, minutes apart, and into the yard behind a small farmhouse. A dog barked, and a light came on in the house as I lifted Sian to climb the wall, and scrambled over behind her. We shouldered our packs and headed east toward the lakeshore, where there was usually some variant of Chicago.

Sometimes, we moved on immediately, catching the second night of the full moon. Some worlds were dangerous, or deserted, or just uninteresting in their similarity to places we'd already seen. This Italianate version of America charmed us enough to stay the full month. We got a room on the top floor of a mansion in the bend of the river, about half a mile from the lake. Plenty of people spoke English, and they readily believed that we were travellers from the south. Nuovo Genova and other cities of the north traded with the Carolina Republic.

Our argument blew up out of nothing, and in other circumstances we would have patched it up, but the timing was wrong.

The afternoon of the next full moon, our bags were packed ready to go, but Sian didn't want to. We had a drink at an outdoor taverna. Barges bringing grain and vegetables from upriver farms cast long shadows on the water in the low sun.

"We don't have to keep moving," Sian said. "It's lovely here. Why don't we stay longer?"

"It's a bit of backwater. There's so much else to see."

"It gets tiring. Constantly moving on."

"For you, maybe," I said. "You've done more than me. There's so much I want to see."

Sian toyed with her drink, her face stiff. "Sometimes it feels like you're only interested in me for the Way."

"That's rubbish."

"It's just how it feels."

"I can't deny the Way's fantastic," I said. "But it's being with you that's important to me."

"So, staying a bit longer with me in this lovely city shouldn't be too hard, should it?"

What could I say?

Willis and I agreed to meet in a taverna close to the harbour. He's not there when I arrive. I order a beer and take a table by the window, sitting with my back to the few fishermen and stevedores in here this early. The fat moon heaves itself up from the surface of the lake. Of Willis, however, there is no sign.

I finish my beer and leave, striding through the cobbled streets to his lodgings. The building is dark. My rapping on the door produces no movement inside. I stand in the street, unsure where to turn. It feels like a deep hole has opened at my feet.

If Willis is taking advantage of the full moon to use the Way, he needs isolation. If he has taken transportation and left Nuevo Genova, there is nothing I can do. But if he is still close by, I have a chance. He needs to be away from crowded city streets, which means either the lakefront or the wooded park just north of here, between the Palazzo Ducale and the shore.

I gamble on the park and break into a run.

Sian and I let the full moon go and settled in for another month in Nuovo Genova. At the time, the argument felt like a cloud blowing in front of the sun. The wind would carry it away and the day would warm up again. Instead, things became overcast between us. Sian now suspected I saw her simply as my ticket to ride the Way. I was careful how I talked about it. But this meant that the way I talked began to sound fake, even to me, as I avoided tricky subjects.

There are a lot of unhappy versions of Chicago out there. Nuevo Genova isn't one of them, and we should have had a fantastic month there. Instead, we began to argue. Little things became the subject of contention. After one argument, I thought for the first time about what would happen if Sian decided to end things between us. A split would be more serious than moving apartments and dividing up books and records. I couldn't use the Way without her. What if she decided to take me home and leave me there? After everything I'd seen, going back to the Evanston coffee shop would be purgatory. This thought didn't make it easier to get on. It made it harder for me to be honest with Sian. I kept my mouth shut and pretended everything was fine, when she could tell that it wasn't.

Two days before the next full moon, things came to a crisis. I had avoided mentioning the Way, but both of us knew the time was coming. One morning, Sian broke the silence.

"You want to move on, don't you?"

"If you're ready. Maybe we've seen all we need to see here?"

"What is it that you need to see exactly?"

"You know what I mean," I said. "There's so much out there."

"Not much better than here, in my experience."

"Well, you've had the advantage of more experience. Don't stop me enjoying what you've had."

"Maybe you'd like to go on your own. Maybe it's the travelling that interests you rather than me."

"I can't go on my own, can I?"

"Oh, so otherwise you would?"

"Well, I wouldn't sit around waiting this long for you."

Sian's face froze, as if I had slapped her. "I see," she said.

"What I mean is, I could go on a trip and come back. You wouldn't have to come along every time. I didn't mean…"

"It's okay," she said. "You're right. We've probably stayed too long."

We barely spoke during the next two days, as we settled our affairs in Nuova Genova and packed for the trip. It was obvious I had upset her, but the best thing was to keep my mouth shut until we'd moved on. Wherever we ended up next, I would make it up to her. A new town, new world, new start. I would work harder on our relationship, worry less about the thrill of the next trip on the Way. But it was fine; we could leave this place and start afresh somewhere new.

The first night of the full moon, we waited until after midnight so that there was no one else around. Silence hung between us as we walked into the trees near the lake. Falling rain gossiped among the leaves around us in the darkness.

The Way appeared as a strip of neon light winding among the trees. I took the rope out of my pack and waited for Sian to do the same.

"How far this time?" I said.

Sian stepped forward and turned to face me, silhouetted against the Way behind her. "Let's do it slightly differently."

"Okay. What do we do?" I couldn't see her face clearly, with the glow of the Way behind and shadows between us. She took a step backwards.

"We need a break." Sian's words sounded like they had been recorded earlier. "I'm sorry." She turned away and took another step towards the glowing path.

"Wait!" I lunged forward and grabbed her arm. She didn't resist, simply stood rigidly in place. The Way was a luminous braid of mist about eighteen inches from her feet.

"Let go of my arm," she said through clenched teeth.

"Sian, don't do this. I know I've been a dick, but we can sort things out. The next place we get to, you'll see."

"Let go of my arm."

"Okay, then we'll talk."

She nodded, and I released her arm. We were both breathing heavily. Sian glanced behind her at the Way. The light from the path briefly lit up her face. Her lips were a tight line and her cheeks were wet, either from the rain or from tears, I couldn't tell.

"I'm sorry," she said again, and before I could react she jumped away from me. I grabbed again for her arm but could only get hold of the strap of her rucksack. With a fluid twist of her torso she slipped out of the straps and stepped onto the Way. There was a flicker of blue light and Sian winked out of sight. The Way disappeared with her, flooding the woods with the sudden darkness that follows the extinguishing of a light.

I stood alone in a version of Illinois far from the world I was born into. There was cold rain in my eyes and Sian's rucksack hung from my hand. The Way was gone, and I had no means of bringing it back.

In the park, low bushes, arranged in formal lines. A statue of a nymph holding a child, rendered ghostly by moonlight. No sign of Willis or anyone else. I run toward the lake, through a narrow aisle of beech trees.

I emerge onto a broad lawn, which slopes down to a concrete wall. Beyond that, a bony stretch of beach and black shimmer of water. The moon is high now, its reflected light a river of silver on the lake. The Way crosses the beach and plunges into trees to my right. The ghost path moves slightly in the winds of other worlds.

Willis is between me and the Way, his back to me. He wears a dark hooded jacket and carries a heavy back pack.

"Wait!"

He turns. I move a few steps closer and stop, concerned that if I move too fast or too close he will step onto the Way and be gone.

"Please," I say. "Let me come with you."

"I don't think that will work."

"You know my story. I can't do it alone. I'm stuck here unless you help me."

"I'm sorry." Willis shakes his head. "I can't change things for you. If you weren't stuck here, you'd be stuck somewhere else. There are worse places."

"No, this is the worst," I say. "It's the one world I know she's not in. At least somewhere else there's a chance."

"Come on, don't torture yourself. Get on with the rest of your life. Give her up."

"I can't."

"Face it, she knows where you are. If she wants you, she can find you."

I wonder what would happen if I threw myself past him and onto the Way, while his presence holds it here. Can I really be that desperate? It would be a huge gamble, a one-off trip to somewhere unknown, with uncountable odds against Sian being there. And as Willis says, there are many versions of reality worse than Nuovo Genova.

His face softens, as if he can read my thoughts. The look of pity he gives me is unbearable.

"If I see her, I'll tell her," he says. "To come back and find you. She owes you that."

"Wait —" I say again, but it's too late. Willis takes a step back and onto the glowing path. There's a ripple of coloured light and he blinks out. I run forward, but the Way has gone, leaving only shadows and dark sand and the mocking chatter of waves against the shore.

There's one. I can always spot them.

The stranger's eyes flick from side to side as he ambles among the morning market crowd. He has a khaki rucksack slung over one shoulder.

He passes my table and I catch his eye. I push the chair out with my foot to offer him a seat.

"You look tired, my friend," I say in English. "Let me buy you a drink."

The Escape Hatch

Matthew De Abaitua

In her video, she called it 'the escape hatch'. It appeared one morning when she was driving to her temporary teaching job at the university. Beside the A12, the dawn mist obscured the legs of the pylons, their latticed towers seemed to be floating across the field. She was probably speeding, she would admit that much, trying to outrun the news on the radio – the Chinese economic collapse, the acid shores of the Indian Ocean, allegiance trials on the banks of the Mississippi. The road dipped toward Chelmsford, and there it was – a semi-circular section of what she described in her video as half a black sun or a protractor of negative space. The traffic ahead disappeared into it. Rachel slowed but did not stop. In her rear-view mirror, she saw a truck jack-knife across both lanes. In that instant, it seemed more dangerous to stop suddenly than to continue. "It was as if space-time was a jigsaw with a missing piece," she said to her creative writing channel and her thousands of subscribers, her Bartlebabies.

Her Bartlebabies wanted to know where she found the courage to just drive right in. There was no simple answer. Her heart was a diagram of tensions, her mother's controlling personality pulling in one direction, her hourly-paid temporary position in another. The bald tyres on her old Toyota were a point on that diagram, as was Dan's suggestion that they call timeout on their relationship so that he could experiment with Tindr. Maybe, over the last fifty metres, she even tapped the accelerator. The black sun was beautiful. Like a solar eclipse sliding into a slot.

She withdrew her feet from the pedals, gripped the wheel, closed her eyes and drove onward, thinking: *whatever this is, maybe it's better than what I've got.*

Her car emerged on the other side, the tyres kicking up a cloud of golden dust. Ahead, other cars had parked up, doors open, drivers and passengers staggering around open-mouthed under a white sky. She drove slowly onward then parked up on a mesa of golden stone. In the white sky there were two black moons set apart like peep holes for a gargantuan voyeur. She killed the engine and sat there, hardly daring to breathe, in case the oxygen inside the car was all the oxygen she had left. Her heart was an organ of anxiety at the best of times. Seeing that the other people still showed no ill effects other than shock, she wound down the side window and took her first breath on another planet. It felt good. If it was toxic, then this was a toxicity that was also a cure, like a gin and tonic.

She walked over to a man leaning against the bonnet of his German car; the over-exposed sky at his back made his dark suit merge into the black metal of the chassis. He was squinting at his phone, but sensed her approach.

"Do you have any water?" he said, in a low voice. "We might run out of water. If you have water, then we should make a deal."

He did not look up. He was talking to his phone as much as he was talking to her. She looked back at the way she had come; the dust clouds drifted away and there was the other side of the escape hatch, the half-disc slid into the golden rock like a giant coin going into the slot of a vending machine. There were no more arrivals. She remembered the lorry jack-knifing in the rear-view mirror. The A12 would be an accident scene. The question was... Well, there were a thousand questions obviously... but the most immediate was this: did the escape hatch open only one-way? Because if it did, then it was only a matter of time before this man with the German car nominated himself as the acceptable face of cannibalism.

She returned to her car, did a three-point turn, and drove slowly back. Passing through the escape hatch felt like solitude, an attentive aloneness that came to an end abruptly and left her with a sense of loss. She parked up on the other side of the A12. The road was cordoned off, blue flashing lights around the wreck of the lorry. This was where she recorded her video, holding her phone at arm's length, set to selfie, the black sun at her back, other people walking through it.

"There's another planet and we can walk there," she said, her voice angry with wonder. "The planet is habitable, and I've seen it.

The Escape Hatch

We don't need a spaceship or a government. This will be our amazing world and we can reach it through this —" she gestured at the semi-circle of negative space, saw how nameless it was "— this *escape hatch.*" She turned around and zoomed in on the golden dust clouds drifting through the black space, their particles glittering violently.

Within the hour, Rachel's video had clocked up a hundred million views.

People came from all over to see the escape hatch. The initial police blockade was not enough to stop people as they hiked across the fields and lanes. When the army sealed off the area, people hired planes to fly through it, and when the airspace was patrolled by the Royal Airforce, some even went along old tunnels underground and discovered the lower semi-circle of the escape hatch down there. Why, she asked her Bartlebabies, was the first concern of the government to stop people going through? Just because the escape hatch had appeared on British territory, did it really fall under the jurisdiction of a national government? What right did they have to do this? If the escape hatch constituted first contact or an act of communication, then what message was the government sending by sealing it off from its own citizens in this way?

Inspired by her video, more people pressed against the barricades until they broke through. The army and the police didn't know what to do. They understood how to protect property and the sanctity of the state. The escape hatch was neither of those things. The Prime Minister arrived by helicopter; against the advice of her press team, she stepped through the escape hatch and spent an hour on the other planet. When she came out, she sighed, as if disappointed to be back. The people saw it in her eyes, she wanted to escape too.

In the streets and the shops, strangers recognised Rachel and looked at her hungrily: *what was it like,* they asked, but in their eyes there was a more urgent question: *is it better than this?*

Her videos racked up millions of views. By the end of the month she would be rich. The university wanted to speak to her about a permanent position. Dan called her, and confessed that he had hated every minute of the time-out and that he wanted to see her right away. Maybe they could experiment with Tindr together? She wasn't sure about Dan, but she was famous now, and her videos were attracting as much bad attention as good. Dan was a creep but – as her mother always said – better the creep you know.

Dan came over and she listened to his self-justification about the time-out, how being apart from her had really opened his eyes. But when he said this, she saw that his eyes were glinting with same question as all the others: *is it better than this?*

"We should return to the escape hatch together," said Dan, brushing his hand against her arm, testing if he could retake possession of her. "We can film it as we cross over to the other side," Dan put his arms around her. "You can lead us."

"Why?"

"Because you discovered the hatch. You're like Neil Armstrong or Christopher Columbus."

"Christopher Columbus did not discover anything."

"Neil Armstrong didn't discover the moon either, but everyone knows that it's his footprint right *there*. You said it yourself, they've already taken the Earth from us, why should they get this planet too?"

If their relationship was a diagram then his need to control her was one point, and her acceptance of control was another, and the fact that she found all this control exhausting was the crucial third point that introduced tension. But he wasn't wrong. She had as much right to visit this planet as anyone. There were so many names for the new planet but no consensus. Because whoever named it would control it. This was a real world and it belonged to nobody, and so it shouldn't have a name, not yet; she wanted the unnamed planet, heart and soul. The longing was thrilling and terrifying, her smile was determined and so was the glint in Dan's eye. They would return to the escape hatch.

First, she had to calm down. She went into the bathroom, filled the sink and immersed her face in her cold reflection, held her breath and listened to the beat of her anxiety. It was regular, that was something. She came up for air, towelled off her face, and it was then that she noticed, lowdown in her reflection in the bathroom mirror, the semi-circular gap.

At first, she thought a piece had fallen out of the mirror. But when she touched it, she realised the mirror was intact. This semi-circular section of negative space was in her collarbone. She pulled

The Escape Hatch

her hair back urgently so that she could take a closer look. She stepped away from the mirror and looked down, but the small black half-sun was too high on her collarbone for her to see it with her own eyes, no matter how much she twisted around. She would have to touch it. Slowly, she lowered her fingertips into the space. It felt warmer in there. There was no pain. She reached in deeper – if the hole had been cored into her body then her fingers would have reached her lungs. But all she could touch was alien air. When she withdrew her hand, it was sheathed in golden dust.

At a press conference on the A12, a journalist asked the Prime Minister if the escape hatch was safe. "The people expect the government to be in control of any eventuality," she said. "It's time the people grew up." When she smiled, her mouth was an inverted protractor of negative space. The government lifted the barricade to let the people come and go through the escape hatch at will. The first truckloads of colonists arrived, emblazoned with homemade art and flanked by day-trippers bearings flags and streamers. No life had been discovered on the planet. The atmospheric probe that had penetrated the white sky was lost. Its last readings suggested that a habitable area totalling almost two hundred and fifty thousand square kilometres existed around the escape hatch. The edge of this territory was a vertical black sea. The first man to swim in this black sea was later washed up on Dover beach: bemused, exhausted but alive.

In the bathroom, Rachel buttoned her shirt all the way up to her collar. If the appearance of this negative space in her body was a side effect of her travelling through the escape hatch, then she would tell no one, not even Dan could know. She would ask him to leave before he discovered it.

A part of her remained behind on the planet and she was entangled with it, like two points in a diagram. After each visit, another part of her would remain on the golden planet. The exchange made sense. Its logic reassured her. She packed her rucksack and filled up three water bottles. She told Dan she would meet him at the railway station. But she didn't. She walked along the A12, through the stalled traffic and crowds and food stalls, and the faces of the people around her were concentrated upon a single note of longing.

P.Q.

James Warner

This year Daljeet discovered a new species of harvester ant in the California desert, near Needles, and spent the summer studying them.

Lifting up individual ants with his forceps, he noted the seeds they collected were of many kinds, blown into the desert by the wind, or washed there during floods. This was a dry year, and seeds were relatively scarce. The ants seemed fondest of mustard seeds, an invasive species in their habitat, but also collected buckwheat, flax, and mesquite.

Daljeet was amazed to find some foragers returning with inedible items – sparkly grains of mica, miniature quartz crystals, specks of turquoise, and tiny cactus thorns. Harvester ants are meant to find seeds, grind them into pulp with their mandibles, and feed them to their colony's larvae. Some of these ants, inexplicably, were instead gathering flecks of rock or indigestible cellulose. On the far side of each colony's midden – a pile of detritus where the ants deposited their trash, mostly seed husks – they placed these finds, piling up structures with no purpose Daljeet could discern.

Foraging required energy, especially during a hot summer – why would these ants waste time on useless activities? Unless they were indulging in behaviour triggered only under atypical climactic conditions? In the earlier drafts of his grant proposal, sent to me for editing, the word Daljeet used for this behaviour was "art."

Daljeet first saw his 'artist' ants as a specific caste of ant, but closer inspection revealed 'artistic' tasks were taken on by the same ants that, under other circumstances, participated in foraging, patrolling, nest maintenance, or nursery work. When Daljeet tried disassembling the structures the 'artists' had made, they reassembled them. When he added colourful granules of art sand to their sculptures, the ants removed these and – rather pointedly, it seemed to Daljeet – placed his contributions on the midden.

He also tried leaving art sand in the areas where they were foraging, but these the ants ignored completely. When Daljeet tried swapping the artistic sculptures of two adjacent colonies, the ants involved ran around in circles for a while before scurrying underground.

Each nest had hundreds of chambers connected by endless tunnels.

When Daljeet tried removing the sculpture produced by one colony, and placing it in its entirety on that colony's midden, the ants of that colony attacked him en masse – he told me he had never before been bitten by so many simultaneously.

Burning pain gave way to intense itching. He grew dizzy, could not breathe, then blacked out for a while and experienced vivid olfactory hallucinations. For a while he seemed to be an ant himself, helping to construct a tower of aromas – this felt blissful as long as the colony was thriving. The purpose of his labours was clear to him until he regained consciousness, badly sunburned and covered with pustules.

Mary Sue, who worked at the nearby gas station, had taken first aid courses and was able to treat his swollen areas with cold compresses and shoplifted corticosteroid creams. Mary Sue was so attractive to Daljeet, he wondered at first if she was not a hallucination induced by ant bites. But if so, she was a persistent one – and when I visited them, I could see her too.

A side-effect of Daljeet's blacking out was his spilling some glass beads – he had applied pheromones to these with the intention of dropping them into nests to see how the ants reacted.

When he came to, these beads had been added by the ants to their "temples" – it was Mary Sue who proposed the New Agey idea that the ants were building something akin to religious architecture, and the weekend I drove out to visit them at the research site, Daljeet already seemed convinced by her thesis.

Their names have been changed to protect their identities. Scattering more glass beads, we saw that the ants seemed to prefer these to mica, turquoise fragments, or granules of fool's gold, a large supply of which the ants had recently excavated nearby. And they preferred all of these to art sand, as do I.

After I returned home, an invasion of fire ants – a more heat-resistant, omnivorous species – disrupted the study. The harvester ants emerged from their nests to protect their territory, and Daljeet fought alongside them, since he was thinking of naming this new species of harvester ant after himself, and feared that if they were wiped out, his grant proposal would read like fantasy. Unlike harvester ants, fire ants forage at night, so Daljeet and Mary Sue took poison from the pest control aisle at the gas station and put it out at 2 a.m., where the fire ants could be relied on to drag it underground before dawn when the first harvester ants typically emerged.

As the tide of fire ants receded over the next few days, it was Mary Sue who noted that those few of the harvester ant colonies – although Mary Sue disliked the word 'colony' and preferred to call them ant 'collectives' – that had *not* built unusual structures alongside their nests were among those the fire ants succeeded in destroying, along with their queens – 'earth goddesses' was Mary Sue's preferred term. It would have pleased Daljeet to conclude that the structures conferred some adaptive advantage, but there were so few collectives without artistic structures that the observation lacked statistical significance.

The narrow escape from extinction of the new species of harvester ant made Daljeet feel naming it after himself would be hubristic. He and Mary Sue resolved instead on the name *Pogonomyrmex quaesitor*, the harvester seeker. Daljeet's contention was that *P.q* colonies had evolved a form of symbolic language. If he could prove this, it would be the century's greatest entomological breakthrough. But he thought it too grandiose a claim to include in his grant proposal, and if this was not accepted, there was no likelihood of Daljeet's H1-B visa being renewed. He was growing bitter by now about worsening U.S. attitudes to immigrants.

Since the repelled fire ant invasion, clods of earth and even fire ant heads now appeared in the harvester seeker temples, which served no defensive purpose – the fire ants, for example, had been able simply to swarm around them. Still less did the temples provide any protection against the horned lizards that were the seeker ants' main predator at this site. For a while Daljeet wondered if the temples played a role in regulating the temperature of the nest, but he could demonstrate no correlation between how well a material conducted heat and the likelihood of the ants using it. Fresh components in the wake of the fire ant invasion included bits of Styrofoam, an eraser fallen off one of Daljeet's pencils, and some topaz from one of Mary Sue's earrings. Materials that Daljeet deliberately left lying around for the seeker ants to use, but which they scorned, included ball bearings, polymer pearls, matchheads, and chunks of cotton wool.

The drought persisted, and as there was a tap outside the gas station that dripped, some of the seeker collectives migrated closer to it – by establishing a new nest, making a circle of charcoal pebbles around its main entrance, then forming a trail connecting this to the old nest. Over many days, the seeker ants then migrated from the old nest to the new, transporting their seed stash and their brood, their 'earth goddess' marching along with them.

Only their temples were left behind. I suggested in one e-mail these might constitute a form of ritualised conflict – a show of strength, say, or a menacing advertisement of the size of a collective's surplus labour pool? Might they provide shelter from dust storms? Daljeet never commented on these possibilities.

Mary Sue, who now slept in Daljeet's tent most nights, saw the temples as libraries of olfactory koans, symptomatic of a superorganism startling itself into consciousness. As well as edible seeds, she claimed, the collective was gathering seeds of wisdom. After making love, Daljeet and Mary Sue would stare at the ants on each other's bodies – there were ants all over their bodies nowadays, he told me, all the time. His e-mails to me were by now more about her than about the ants.

New temples appeared by the new nests. When Daljeet coated certain granules of mica on top of these with shellac, to block their odour, these granules were at once removed and replaced, supporting the idea that these were olfactory sculptures, attempts to make sense of the odourscape or chemosensory world the ants inhabited. My own analysis of Daljeet's data shows the most favoured materials for the temples were charcoal and splinters of fossilised bone, porous materials that retain scent efficiently. This is logical since ants do not see well and perceive mostly through smell.

Daljeet made olfactory maps of some of the temples, indicating with which pheromones their component elements had been coated. One piece of mica he analysed was coated with three pheromones, the first warning of a common predator, the second signalling the presence of grains of buckwheat, and the third seemingly only associated with finding mica. Mary Sue translated this olfactory koan as *toad eats one, one finds buckwheat, one finds mica.*

When Daljeet tried replacing this piece of mica with one he had sprayed with a different combination of pheromones, he was stung even more viciously than before. His hallucinations were overwhelming – Daljeet *was* the collective. He could feel his lower reaches drying out, the earth goddess giving birth to more workers, the gathering of tart seeds. He could feel some of his furthest-flung scouts encountering a fire ant, and biting it into pieces before it could discover the collective, some zigzagging nearby foragers being picked off by a cactus wren. He could feel distant earth tremors and smell an approaching wildfire, and sense the death throes of some ants who had entered the gas station and were succumbing to the poison laid out behind the candy rack. And through this he could feel the stacking up of scent-laden particles.

Everything was more beautiful to ants than it was to people, Daljeet informed me. People mostly just followed instructions, while harvester seekers forged their own destinies in ways that also furthered their collective interest. Their temples made their world more palatable to them, and Daljeet was coming to think of them as philosophical treatises, chains of analysis through which the collectives modelled their environment, or perhaps testaments to its unknowability.

Treating Daljeet's stings, Mary Sue told him seventeen different indigenous Californian peoples had been documented as ingesting harvester ants as a form of ritual intoxicant or medicine. Was *P.q.* among the species of harvester ants ingested by any of these tribes? Perhaps, they speculated, a name existed for this species in some lost indigenous language. Given the extreme plasticity of the venom gland in harvester ants, it makes sense they might secrete some psychotropic substance, and traditionally, Mary Sue told Daljeet, large quantities of ants were collected on balls of moist eagle down and swallowed live, in order to acquire shamanic power as a dream helper – if the ants bit you from inside, you became catatonic and acquired great knowledge.

She bit his cheek tenderly before breaking to him the news that two lightning-caused wildfires had merged and were sweeping across the chaparral towards the gas station. Having no data yet on how widely distributed *P.q* was, Daljeet decided the danger of all the ants being asphyxiated in their tunnels was so great, it would be best to remove one collective to study under laboratory conditions.

After covering the gaps in their clothing with duct tape to ward off stings, Daljeet and Mary Sue took trowels and began digging. Since the ants tunnelled away from this disturbance, it took many hours to start finding any, and hours more to excavate the earth goddess.

The trowels were almost too hot to handle by the time the work was through. Daljeet and Mary Sue placed all the ants they found in a cooler, along with food from the gas station, and stashed the entire collective in the trunk of Daljeet's car – as is clearly visible in footage from the only security camera that survived the explosion.

Mary Sue swallowed a few ants for luck, as the gas station turned into a fireball. Lumps of debris bombarded their car as they sped off towards Route 66.

In Daljeet's last e-mail to me, he announced his intention to take the cooler back to Jodhpur with him on his flight, even if the air hostesses regarded him disapprovingly, even if it was illegal to abduct an ant collective from California, even if, once he unsealed the container, the ants killed him for this act of wanton interference. *The U.S. no longer deserves to host an intelligent ant collective*, he wrote.

Mary Sue flew to Jodhpur with him, and I have heard nothing from them since.

Returning to the area of their research site, in the aftermath of the wildfires and during a time of heavy rains, I found wildflowers blooming everywhere. The smell of creosote bushes filled the air. Walking around the charred ruins of the gas station, I failed to locate a single surviving seeker temple, and saw no ants at all.

The Purpose of the Dodo is to be Extinct

Malcolm Devlin

"Nevertheless so profound is our ignorance, and so high our presumption, that we marvel when we hear of the extinction of an organic being; and as we do not see the cause, we invoke cataclysms to desolate the world, or invent laws on the duration of the forms of life!"

– Charles Darwin, The Origin of Species

1. The Singular Death of Prentis O'Rourke

When Prentis O'Rourke was ten years old, he read a book about the last words spoken by the famous and historically significant, and wondered what he might say for himself when his own time came.

For the most part, he was not a morbid child, certainly no more so than any other boy his age. To the extent that it was relevant to him, he knew what death was, but the thought and manner of it had never consumed him. Instead, it was a subject that he merely found interesting. It was something worth bearing witness to if not investing in.

Beyond that, death was by no means his only concern. It was interesting to him in the same way it was interesting the way you could make a rainbow with the hosepipe on a sunny day, or the way his mother would slice an apple into neat little eighths before she would eat it. Death was just something else that happened, and given that there were so many things that happened, it seemed strange to waste too much of the life he had left on one thing at the expense of the others. It was a postcard from a far-off land that he did not intend to visit himself for many, many years. It would happen, it would happen to him and it would happen last.

His family had never been dishonest with him about mortality. When Breadbin, the family cocker spaniel, had died the year before after chasing the wheels of a Peugeot 305, there were no euphemisms to shield the truth from him. He wasn't told that Breadbin had gone to a retirement home for dogs, or that he had taken off in a rocket back to Planet Dog, or that he now lived in a magical meadow, full of rabbits and squirrels to chase.

Breadbin had died, he was told. These things happen, he was told. It was okay to be sad, he was told.

Prentis had helped his father dig a trench at the end of the garden and together they buried the remains of the dog. Breadbin's funeral shroud was the same old Martini branded beach towel that had previously lined his plastic bucket-bed. They filled the hole and planted a cherry tree in the grave, and Prentis was satisfied that some degree of completion had been achieved. He missed the dog, of course he did. He missed the movement of him about the house, the warmth of him as he curled up at his feet while they watched television, but he didn't need to believe in Planet Dog, the arrival of the cherry blossom each subsequent spring was more than enough to help him to understand.

Prentis' second experience of mortality came with the death of his grandmother only six weeks later. His parents took the opportunity to reframe Breadbin's passing as less of a tragedy and more of a lesson to prepare their son for what they imagined must be the greater loss. They needn't have concerned themselves. Prentis' grandmother had been eighty-seven and claimed she had been dying of one thing or another since her own son, Prentis' father, had moved out of the family home some thirty years earlier. At the funeral, Prentis stood next to his father again and while only a few other people had taken the time to attend – his grandmother's neighbours, her brother, an elderly cousin Prentis had never met before – the atmosphere was surprisingly upbeat. It was hard to be completely miserable, he reasoned, given the general feeling that this was what his grandmother would have wanted all along.

As he read his book that bright afternoon, the ten-year-old Prentis O'Rourke considered what his own last words would be. He hoped they would be important, because he hoped that by the time he finally died, he might be important too. Being important meant that people would listen to him no matter what he said, but even so, he felt he should say something pithy, witty and clever. A phrase that would be endlessly debated after he had gone, recasting the magnificent life he had led into one more valuable still. He wrote lines on the backs of used envelopes and rehearsed them in front of the bathroom mirror, giving each syllable a painful gravitas and then swooning theatrically onto the bathmat. He stared into the light fitting on the ceiling until it dissolved into rainbows and forced him to close his eyes. He would be known, he thought. His *words* would be known.

Thirty-one years later, just after a quarter-past eight on the morning of October 16th, 2014, Prentis lay on his back on the corner of Laburnum Road and Heathcote Avenue, staring up at the afternoon's clouds coalescing and darkening above him. His blood unspooled into the cracks of the tarmac beneath his head, unknitting his being across the intersection, and Prentis struggled to summon the will to say anything at all. But despite the pain, despite the fact his jaw no longer felt like his own, despite the fact his consciousness was already slipping from him by degrees, he did manage to do achieve two distinct and final things. Firstly, he worried dreadfully about his thumbs, and secondly, he managed to speak.

"If only," he said to no one at all. The brightness of the sun made colours dance before him, making him smile at some half-forgotten memory. They were colours he could still see when he closed his eyes and then died.

If only.

In this instance, there was nobody there to hear him. There was no one there to question how the sentiment might have concluded. Not even Janet Baskerville heard him speak. The woman who had killed him, the only witness to his death, sat in the front seat of her Saab 98 and all she could hear over the whine of the radio was the stiff percussion of her own heartbeat. *Thump, thump thump*, the same distinctive concussion the car had made when it had struck Prentis O'Rourke only moments before. It taunted her, re-enacting the scene over and over and over again. The man flying from her bumper, and then flying again and again. As her airbag deflated in front of her, as her shoulder started aching where the seatbelt had bit her and held her firm. She could see colours too, but most of them were red and black and white and grey.

At the very moment Prentis O'Rourke unpacked his life across the tarmac on one side of town, Laura O'Rourke hesitated in the act of packing her own into a matching three-piece luggage set on the other. She stopped suddenly, a towel half folded in her hands, and looked to the window in a moment of unbidden introspection. It was a bright day, a clear one and there was nothing but the even blue of the sky within the open frame to distract her. There were no sounds from the street outside, no birds at the bird box Prentis had installed on the silver birch the previous summer. She could barely even hear the hum of traffic on the bypass.

Later, when she was told the news about her husband's accident, her husband's death, she would recall this moment and question it. Later still, she would come back to it and argue she had sensed that something, somewhere was wrong with the world. It was a moment of uncertainty she would come to believe to be concrete proof of the intuition she had always suspected she possessed. The intuition her husband had once dismissed as another example of her bullshit superstition. Her conviction that she had sensed her husband's death would ultimately unbalance her confidence for a long spell and led her to some very dark places, some unreliable literature, some questionable professionals. Responsibility rather than loss would keep her awake at night. If she could have sensed it, why couldn't she have stopped it? What was the point of intuition if it only made sense when the time to act upon it had passed?

Laura had taken her time running away from her marriage. She certainly wasn't concerned that Prentis might come home too early and catch her in the act of leaving him. Prentis wasn't and had never been a threat to her, he had never really been an equal. He was ineffectual, he was dull, he was – god help him – *well-meaning*.

Her father had been a Warrant Officer in the British Army, and they had moved frequently during her childhood. As a consequence, she knew only too well how to fit her whole world into her hand luggage, and her mother had been no different. Laura's mother had always been a woman who struck Laura as being just on the verge of leaving her father for good, so it came as something of a surprise when Laura's father died before she had the chance. The abrupt loss left her mother completely unanchored, and Laura reasoned that ultimately, her mother had needed someone she *could* leave, without ever having to. These days, she rarely left her room in the nursing home, as though she had chosen to step out of the world instead. She didn't read books and she didn't watch the television. Instead, she sat at a card table and played endless games of solitaire, dealing out the cards in neat little stacks, ordering them carefully and packing them up again. She played countless games each day, identifying obscure patterns Laura would miss. She would use each deck until the corners began to curl, then she'd slide the cards back into the box and file them away with the other used decks on the bookshelf.

Whenever Laura would visit, every subject was filtered through her game, as though the deck of cards now defined not only the way she lived, but represented her philosophy on life itself.

"Not all lives can be won," she told Laura after Prentis died. "Some of us start with good hands, some start with bad ones. A single decision early in the game can undo your future in ways you simply can't foresee."

Prentis had been different when Laura had first met him. He was the promise of something stable, something reassuring, solid and static, the complete opposite of the life she had grown up with. It was an outcome she thought she had always wanted until she sensed how it had begun to trap her. The walls of their new build two-bed semi slowly closed in on all sides and all she could picture was her mother's green baize card table, sparsely arranged with dolls' house furniture. The same motions repeated over and over again. Deal, play, lose, repeat. The thought was suffocating to Laura, but Prentis, who had lived in the same place for most of his life, without the imagination to consider escape, seemed oblivious.

Prentis' father had always hoped he might have been an engineer. He bought him a poster of Isambard Kingdom Brunel to put on his bedroom wall and on his birthdays, took him on field trips to places like Iron Bridge or the Thames Barrier.

"Engineers reshape the world," his father said, unaware how his son was content to be shaped by his environment instead. Prentis devoured history books instead, looking backwards rather than forwards. He marvelled at the ways people could persevere to survive the unsurvivable, how they pushed on through everything the world threw at them.

Perhaps it was no surprise that the Prentis Laura met taught history. His final job title was head of department, but that still mostly involved negotiating with bored teenagers at the Bridge Road Comprehensive. He told her how, whenever the class got rowdy – as they often did on a Friday afternoon – he would bring up his slides about mass extinction. He concentrated on the big five. The times when life on earth had turned itself off-and-on-again and the planet had carried on, scarred but persistent into the future. His point – that some form of status quo would be maintained, no matter whether a species failed or not – was lost on the noisier sections of the class, but the illustrations of giant trilobites, ammonites and dinosaurs invariably captured their attention in a way Agincourt, The League of Nations and Neville Chamberlin did not. On a good day they would grant Prentis O'Rourke enough grudging good will to coast through the final hours of the afternoon until the bell marked the end of the day.

Prentis believed in free will rather than fate. The history he taught was too chaotic, too arbitrary, too cruel to bear the fingerprints of a guiding hand. After he died, Laura would come to believe the opposite was true. Every action she would take, she decided, must have been preordained. Everything she touched was a part of some cosmic plan she did not ever need to understand. Every choice she made was to position a switch on some unimaginable array of celestial circuitry. Together, she and everyone else on the planet, were writing the subroutine that would ultimately reveal God; that would bring about the glory of the end times; that would lead them all to transcendence. It didn't really matter. She knew the outcome wasn't for her generation to witness. She understood her own singular purpose and with that, she was content.

That was Laura's future. While her husband died barely half a mile away, the Laura of the present checked through the house twice for things she might have forgotten, briefly arrested by the notion that her momentary pause was enough to reconsider her action. But the room had always been draughty and, without the benefit of hindsight, Laura O'Rourke was more practically minded and rational than she might otherwise have admitted. She took her toothbrush from the bathroom. She took her running shoes from the closet. She folded each item of clothing and tucked them away with the same delicate care her mother might, in earlier, better days, have employed to put her daughter to bed.

2. A New Mass Extinction

The coroner would rule that Prentis O'Rourke died of accidental death. He wasn't looking where he was going as he walked up Laburnum Road and he wasn't paying attention as he stepped out in front of Janet Baskerville's speeding car. This was all true and the thoughts that distracted him were pitifully trivial. In his mind, he was composing something witty that he would likely have never written. A rejoinder to something he had seen on *The Guardian* website's opinion section. A nonsense article crowdsourcing recommendations for a list of favourite (not best) science fiction movies. Prentis was going to nominate John Frankenheimer's *Seconds*. Not because it was one of his favourites, but because none of the other commenters had mentioned it yet, and this seemed a grievous oversight. Good teacher that he was, he had every intention of explaining why in despairing detail.

Therefore, perhaps, Prentis O'Rourke died because of *The Guardian* website. Therefore, Prentis O'Rourke died because he had once seen a 1966 science fiction film and felt a little bit pleased with himself when he had to introduce it to others. Therefore, Prentis died because none of the other users of *The Guardian* website saw fit to champion the same film.

Prentis O'Rourke died because Janet Baskerville was also distracted. As she had turned onto Laburnum Road, Jefferson Airplane's White Rabbit had come on the radio and she caught herself singing along with Grace Slick's breathy vocals. The song had always reminded her of a brief holiday affair she'd endured aged nineteen. *His* name had been Stephen T Something-or-other, and they met at the themed bar in a beach resort in the Seychelles. He had been handsome in that plastic 1980s way, all teeth and jaw and improbable fringe, and by 2014 she could no longer tell how much of their affair was real and how much had been filled in by the excess of eighties nostalgia, which had permeated popular culture since. In truth, she could no longer remember much about Stephen T at all, and what she could remember seemed too much like a music video to be taken seriously, but she could still picture herself kissing him against a gloriously airbrushed sunset as they stood ankle-deep in the surf-washed sand.

Since the accident, her association with the Jefferson Airplane had been forever rewired. Now, when she heard Jack Cassidy's ambling bass, the military thump of Spencer Dryden's drums, she saw only the last flight of Prentis O'Rourke, vanishing into that same glorious sunset that had never been there in reality.

She too has often tried to imagine how things could have been different. She has endlessly tried to identify the junction in causality where things went wrong.

If only she had been going slower.

If only she had applied the brakes harder.

If only she had followed Stephen T back to his home in Southport all those years ago.

In the version of reality where Janet had indeed braked in time, diligently screeching to a halt mere inches from Prentis O'Rourke's knees. The gangly pedestrian stopped to stare at her owlishly, shocked and adrenalised by her screaming approach. He offered her a brief apologetic smile before collapsing where he stood, as a brain aneurysm took him down instead.

The Prentis who had been aware enough of his surroundings to observe how the driver of the Saab 98 was not paying attention to the road, had stopped on the pavement to wait until she passed. He was brained by a falling tree branch, loosened by the previous day's gale, while Janet drove past singing along to her radio, completely oblivious to his slapstick exit from the world.

In the version of reality where Janet had followed Stephen T back to Southport – inevitably breaking up with him between four and six months later because there was a very good reason why she didn't

The Purpose of the Dodo is to be Extinct

remember anything about him other than his looks – she would have been completely absolved of Prentis' death, but Prentis O'Rourke would have died anyway without her intervention.

Janet Baskerville killed Prentis O'Rourke, but she didn't kill *every* Prentis O'Rourke.

The Prentis who stopped for a coffee on the way to work choked on a small piece of plastic that broke off the lid of his travel coffee cup. The Prentis who took the scenic route through the park was hit by a reversing tractor. The Prentis who followed the footpath down the river was spooked by a pair of hissing swans protecting their nest. He wasn't really scared of swans, but their sheer size and lurching aggression was enough to make him lose his footing on the bank; the current of the river strong enough to trap and drown him in the weir before he could understand what was happening. The Prentis who waited at the top of the road for the bus was mugged by a man named Kieron Boone, a not-quite-clean junkie who wasn't armed, but did a good enough job of pretending he was to make Prentis run under the wheels of the bus that was supposed to be taking him to work.

In a rare cosmic anomaly, at sixteen minutes past eight on October 16th, 2014, Prentis O'Rourke died in every reality in which he had survived until his forty-second year.

The event's consequences were seismic, ricocheting through all versions of reality, forking through each and every permutation of each and every existence like once-bottled lightning, shaken and set loose. A hairline fracture spidered through the filigree webs of all possible worlds and every thread was severed in the exact same place.

In that one moment, millions died, but as only a single death was recorded in each reality, it was an event only observed and mourned by a tiny minority in each. A small, personal tragedy consigned to a few lines in the local press, if it was covered by the media at all.

It was only in a handful of realities, those where The Authority had established a foothold, where the incident was observed, recorded and studied with the same solemn reverence that global disasters are traditionally afforded.

Here, the manner of Prentis O'Rourke's deaths were documented, catalogued and investigated; chains of causality were extrapolated, traced and analysed. Questions were asked, studies were prepared, countless theses were written. To those who study such things, the sheer quality and quantity of data provided by the billion deaths of Prentis O'Rourke was quite unprecedented.

The last recorded personal extinction had occurred some 73 years earlier in 1941. Less than a year before that, the first Authority headquarters had been established in London as an experimental means to test the outcomes of various military strategies in the field. Not yet a cross-existence concern, its preliminary ideas were theoretical but when Mrs Caroline Buchanan of Des Moines, Iowa (verified in approximately 59% cases), died *en masse*, having reached the age of 62, The Authority came to realise how her many and varied deaths served as the map they had been missing, the sheer scope of which no one amongst their number had the vision to fully anticipate.

They also learned how the cartography of reality can only by complicated further by war. The mass of conflicting decisions made during the years of World War II were tangled and scrambled in a shockingly and chaotic fashion. Compared with the sober, ordered pencil lines that had come before, the sheer volume of realities born from conflict were best understood as a desperate, palsied scribble across the pages of the ledger. Not all realities survived, proving once again how the true cost of large-scale violence is never adequately itemised.

Within this nightmarish scrawl, a single casualty per strand of existence was easy to overlook, and with no one yet trained to identify such patterns, The Authority took many diligent years analysing the fragments of salvaged data before Caroline Buchanan's fate was identified.

Ultimately, they discovered that her extinguished lives exceeded the sum of all other casualties in each reality she existed in, but – as the executive council members of The Authority were at pains to make clear – Caroline Buchannan's deaths were not in vain.

From here, The Authority took some time to establish itself. It built resources over the intervening decades, expanding exponentially through each plane of existence. It remained patient and poised, waiting until a comparable event occurred. This time, they would be ready. This time, they would witness the event in real time. This time, they would capture it all.

There were near misses: Clifford Yant died nearly a million times in 1971 as a branch of his existence was inexplicably culled during an existential quake. Gupta Najaro died 20% more frequently, for reasons still under debate.

The data collected thanks to the deaths of Prentis O'Rourke was considerably more significant. This, it was argued, was what The Authority had been preparing for since its very inception. If the map provided by Caroline Buchanan had charted the coastline of a new world, the map provided by Prentis O'Rourke was a geological survey, a 3D model, a dashboard mounted GPS device.

Thus, although he was never aware of it, Prentis O'Rourke had achieved immortality in one sense, even as he ceased to exist in another.

There are countless ways to die and, considered as a group, the variety of deaths of Prentis O'Rourke represented an even sample of every possibility. The only omission, it might be argued, was that none of the Prentis O'Rourkes who died that day was granted what might be termed a 'natural' death.

Some were murdered. Debts owed came back to haunt them, things once said had repercussions, characters with whom they'd once had dealings proved not to be who they claimed. There were crimes of passion: Some Prentis O'Rourkes were killed by their wives or husbands (the collected Prentis O'Rourke's diverse variety of sexual orientations would prove something of surprise to those who thought they knew him well, and a number of bestselling books would be written debating the subject), some by their lovers, some by their children. Others sacrificed themselves to save loved ones, or were sacrificed by those they thought they had loved. Many were simply in the wrong place at the wrong time: collateral damage to someone else's crime. A stray bullet, a wandering blade, an out-of-control getaway? Prentis O'Rourke would become a crime statistic, blinking into the darkening sky.

"If only," he said, and nobody heard.

Some died in hospital. Minor ailments turned bad, diseases contracted long before the event made all other diagnoses moot. Even those whose outlooks had improved were faced with a sudden, unstoppable down-turn.

"These things happen," their loved ones were assured by their doctors. They were right, but perhaps not in the way they thought. These things do happen, but they are so rare, they remain almost unimaginable.

The Prentis O'Rourkes who found themselves at war, either by choice by career or by accident, found their individual ends lost amongst the chaos and horror which surrounded them. They fought on all sides: military, mercenary, rebel, civilian. They committed acts of atrocity, of cowardice, of heroism. Lives thrown away by circumstance and idiocy. Some did not fight at all, but found themselves consumed regardless.

Some Prentis O'Rourkes died by their own hand, their reasons many and varied. Cuckolds, lovers, bad investments. Others were simply consumed with sadness, hopelessness, anxiety or fear. They took pills, they took poison, they jumped from buildings, in front of trains. They leaped away from everything that made sense. Perhaps, in their final moments they had time to regret the choice they thought had been theirs all along.

"If only," they said.

Beyond all else, though, Prentis O'Rourke died by accident. If the many different worlds have anything in common it is a cruel and unforgiving sense of humour. Things fall, things crash. Something misplaced sets off a chain of events: an escalating sequence of "what-ifs", leading to the alarmed expression on Prentis O'Rourke's face as he suffers his final indignity.

There are so many ways for a life to be extinguished, and on that afternoon in his forty-second year, Prentis O'Rourke experienced them all.

In one curious moment of concordance – one that would be debated endlessly over the subsequent years – across the multitude of realities, each and every Prentis O'Rourke who was capable of speaking, said the very same last words.

Granted only three final syllables in their respective lives, they each failed to say anything more significant before they died.

"If only", they said. "*If only.*"

An enterprising intern at one branch of The Authority, took it upon herself to trace and clean up sound files of each recorded

The Purpose of the Dodo is to be Extinct

occurrence of Prentis O'Rourke's last words from across the spectrum. She brought them together and collated them, observing how their modulation and inflection matched perfectly from one to the other. It was a single voice, she concluded, playing back the combined recording on a loop. Not a scream, but a sigh, resigned as though the collective speakers were entirely aware of the situation they found themselves in, entirely aware of what would come next.

3. Edited extract from Official Catalogue of The Deaths of Prentis O'Rourke, concise edition (The Authority Press, ref: 825-159-884/T & dependencies)

(1) Category: Accidental

(Definition: Deaths caused by unmotivated circumstance, unattributed to conscious thought of subject or other party. [See: Terms of Reference])

(1.1) Articles fallen upon subject.

(Definition: articles struck subject at force, directly OR indirectly causing physical trauma which led directly to death.)
- Animals
- Domestic*
- Including: Birds (including cages), cats (including travel cases), chinchillas, dogs, fish (including bowls/tanks), hamsters (including travel cases), garter snakes, gerbils, newts (including tanks), pythons, rabbits, salamanders, squirrels, stick insects (including tanks), tortoises, weasels.
- Other*
- Including: Alligators, badgers, bears, cows, coyotes, crocodiles, dogs (farm), deer, dodo (stuffed), dolphins, ducks, elephants, fish, flamingos, foxes, kangaroos, goats, giraffes, hares, hippopotamuses, horses, iguanas, insects (including tanks), Komodo dragons, lemmings, lions, lizards, monkeys, newts (wild), pandas, pigs, porcupines, rhinoceroses, sea cucumbers, sharks, sheep, sloths, snakes, squid, stoats, swans, tigers, turtles, walruses, whales, zebras.
- *NB: This category is for articles which fell upon subject,

Malcolm Devlin

leading to death. For animals which CONSUMED, PURSUED, POISONED or triggered ALLERGIC REACTION in subject please see relevant category.

- Bathroom accessories*
- Including baths, bath mats, cleaning products, electric toothbrushes, hot water tanks, plungers, razors (electric/manual), shampoo bottles, shower fittings, sinks, soap (liquid/bars), sponges, toilets, toilet brushes, toilet seats, towels, towel rails.
- *NB: This category is for articles which fell upon subject, leading to death. For bathroom accessories which DROWNED, WOUNDED or led to ELECTROCUTION of subject please see relevant category.
- Books
  - Physical books.
  - Including (Most commonly cited ONLY) 2666 by Roberto Bolaño (Paperback), Angela Carter's Book of Fairy Tales (Virago edition, hardback), The Bible (Old and New Testaments), Building Stories by Chris Ware, Testament of Youth by Vera Brittain (Hardback, Bodley Head), The Complete Sandman Box Set by Neil Gaiman, The Complete Works of Shakespeare (RSC edition), The Illustrated Lord of the Rings, Three Volume Slip Case edition, JRR Tolkien/illustrated by John Howe, Jerusalem by Alan Moore, The Luminaries by Elanor Catton (hardback, Viking), The Riverside Chaucer (Second-hand, hardback), The Wind-Up Bird Chronicle by Haruki Murakami (Paperback, Harvill edition), Ulysses by James Joyce (all editions, unread).
  - EBook Readers, crate of.
  - See also: FURNITURE > BOOKSHELVES.
- Furniture
  - Beds
  - Including: Day, doubles, kings, queens, singles, superkings, futons.
  - Bookshelves
  - Including: Fitted, flat-packed, freestanding, wall mounted.
  - Chairs
  - Including: Armchairs, dining, garden, kitchen, Laz-E-

Boys (TM).
- Piano (see Instruments, musical).
- Sofas
- Storage
- Boxes, chests, cupboards (kitchen).
- Tables
- Including: Coffee, bedside, dining, display, kitchen, occasional (stackable), side.
- Garden accessories
- Including: Dustbin, fences, fence posts, gates, gnomes, parasols, pond liners, recliners, rockeries, recycling bin, sheds, slides, statuary, swings, swing seats, water features.
- See also: MASONRY, PLANTS and TOOLS.
- Household items
- Including: Air conditioner units, ashtrays, bookends, candles, candlesticks, computers (monitors/printers/scanners/sundry peripherals), curtain rails, desk fan, desk lamps, fire axes, hi-fi (stereo/speakers/turntables/sound equipment), iron, ironing board, marble bust of Mr Gladstone, mirrors, novelty bookends (left/right), oil lamps, pictures, ropes, remote controls, shoeboxes filled with ephemera, television (media players/games consoles/ sundry connected boxes), vase of flowers, Venetian blinds.
- See also: FURNITURE.
- Kitchen appliances
- Including: Baking tray, bottles, bread bin, bread board, bread maker, bread knife, bowls, cake tins, chopping board, coffee maker, cups, deep fat fryer, food processor, forks, glasses, jars, mugs (see cups), ovens (electric/gas/microwave/solid fuel/other), pans (saucepans/frying pans/griddles), pasta press, pestle and mortar, plates, kettles, knives (all types), knife block, rice cooker, rolling pin, salad spinner, slow cooker, spoons (large), teapots, tin opener (electric), toasters.
- Masonry (and sundry building materials)
- Building materials*
- Building fittings
- Including banister rails, carpeting, doors (external/internal), flooring, windows (frames/glass) stair rods.

- Electrical fittings**
- Including cables, electrical sockets, junction boxes, light bulbs, loose wires.
- Plumbing fittings
- Including pipes, fittings, tubes, water tanks.
- *NB, this category has been determined too wide for the purview of this document. For more detailed analysis, please see appendix II in the report: "Prentis O'Rourke and Relationship to Deconstruction of Property."
- **NB This category is for articles which fell upon subject, leading to death. For electrical fittings which BURNED or ELECTROCUTED subject please see relevant category.
- Meteorological ephemera*
- Including hailstones, meteor fragments, snow.*
- *NB This category is for articles which fell upon subject, leading to death. For meteorological ephemera which BURNED, DROWNED or FROZE subject please see relevant category.
- Ornamentation*
- Including: bowl of potpourri, ceramic miniatures, decorative light fittings, family portraits, figurines, fire guards, fire pokers, novelty set of coasters, vases.
- *NB: This category is for articles which fell upon subject, leading to death. For ornaments which BURNED or IMPALED subject or were used as sundry MURDER WEAPONS please see relevant category.
- Other subjects
- Including all other subjects (people) who may have landed on subject (Prentis O'Rourke) resulting in at least one fatality.
- Plants
- Including: Boxes of seeds, bushes, cacti, cut flowers, pot plants, plant pots, seed trays, shrubs, trees (and portions of trees.)
- Signage/street furniture
- Including: Bollards, drain grills, dustbins, gates, hoardings, kiosks, loose kerb stones, market stalls, newspaper boards, recycling bins, scaffolding, signs, sign posts, street lights, telephone boxes, traffic cones.
- See also: MASONRY and VEHICLES.

- Tools
- Manual tools
- Including ALL KINDS of: Anvils, braddles, chisels, clamps, crowbars, drills, hammers, ladders, poles, planes, rakes, saws, scythes, spanners screwdrivers, steps, vices.
  - Power tools*
- Including: Chainsaws, circular saws, drills (hand held/pillar), hedge trimmers, lawn mowers, leaf blowers, nailguns, pile-drivers, lathes, sanders, strimmers.
- *NB: This category is for articles which fell upon subject, leading to death. For tools which DISMEMBERED, IMPALED or WOUNDED subject please see relevant category.
  - Toys
- Including: Arcade games, bagatelle, board games, cars, ceramic dolls, clowns, Hello Kitty, fruit machines, Gerald the Happy Giraffe, Lego (various), Mechano, puppets (string/hand/finger/miscellaneous), rag dolls, robots, shove ha'penny, teddy bears, Transformers, variety of stuffed bears in a sack, very large stuffed rabbit, video game console (& peripherals.)
  - Vehicles*
- Including: Aeroplanes, articulated road freight, bicycles, boats, busses, cars, canoes, motorcycles, penny farthing (vintage), scooters, ships, steam roller, tanks, trains, trucks, unicycle, vans.
- *NB: This category is for articles which fell upon subject, leading to death. Please see ACCIDENTS > VEHICULAR, MURDER > VEHICULAR and SUICIDE > VEHICULAR for alternative relevant listings.

Next category:

(1.2) Articles subject fell off or from.

4. A Digression Involving Thumbs

Laura asks what's keeping me awake.

I tell her about the dream I'd had the previous night and she pushes herself up on her elbow, her head resting in her cupped hand. It's too dark for me to see her face, but I can feel her watching me from a familiar silhouette.

"I dreamt I was at Jenny's wedding," I say. "Jenny Bishop. Remember her? Remember that? How many years ago was that?"

"Five years," Laura says. "No six. We'd just come back from Spain. Jenny. I haven't spoken to her for *years*."

I kick the covers away and pull myself to sitting position. The night feels warm, but the painted brick wall is cold against my back.

"So there I am," I say, "it's a wedding and it's exactly as it had been as far as I remember. But they don't have the disco they'd had that night, they've got a band instead. Nothing big, just this guy in a hat, sitting there on a stool. He's got a woman with a bass on one side of him, another guy with a clarinet on the other. And they're playing in a way that said they were doing it as a favour."

"Was I there?" she says.

I don't look at her.

"I don't know," I say. "No. I don't think so. It was a dream, you know."

"Charming." She repositions herself to get more comfortable. "So what does this band do?" she says.

"They're a cover band," I say. "Not the sort of thing you'd expect to hear played at weddings. Hipster shit. Mopey stuff. Leonard Cohen and Bob Dylan, Patti Smith. I don't remember exactly, but that sort of thing. And there's Jenny dancing in front of them. Eyes closed as though she's totally consumed by the music. It was her and... what was his name? Jack? It was her and Jack's first dance, remember that?"

Laura's amused.

"Jack was a lousy dancer," she says and there's that twinkle in her voice. "I remember that, at least. God."

She's right, but I don't reply to her. "There's something about the guy," I say instead. "Something that bothers me."

"Which guy? Jack?"

"No. Well, yes – *obviously* Jack bothered me, but in this case it's the singer. The guy in the hat. He's sitting there on this stool, white shirt, black hat – pork pie, you know? Like Gene Hackman in The French Connection. He's strumming chords on his guitar and he's singing in this... this voice –"

"A good voice?"

"Yes," I say. "God yes. But... *raw*. You know? He has one of those voices you only get if you've been smoking since childhood."

"Is that what was wrong with him?"

"No, it's his hands," I say. "There's something about the way he's holding his guitar. He's got blue-black tattoos snaking all the way up his forearms, disappearing under his rolled-up shirtsleeves, and he's clawing at this guitar in a way I've never seen before. There's something primal about it. It's as if he's compensating for something, only at the time I don't realise what it is. Every time he repositions his fingers it's like it causes him pain, but every time, his voice just gets that much richer, that much more... I don't know."

"Stronger?"

"More powerful. It was extraordinary."

I push myself out of bed and pick my way across to the window. The room is overdue a tidy, our clothes are strewn all over. The window is open a crack, I push it so it's open all the way. There's a pack of Golds on the ledge; I light one for myself. I light one for her.

"So," Laura says, joining me and accepting the proffered cigarette. "What happens?"

I shrug, exhaling smoke into the night sky. It disperses, dreamlike.

"I don't know," I say. "It goes on for a bit longer, I suppose. I don't remember what happens next. Usual wedding stuff. Relatives and kids. The next thing I do remember has me at the bar. This must be later in the evening, I've lost my jacket by then and I've got an open collar and I'm sitting next to the guy in the hat."

"Gene Hackman?" she says. "The singer?"

"Yes, and you know what I'm like in situations like that. I can't talk to anyone. I mean, I admire this guy and I can't even compliment him on the set he's just finished. I'm all gummed up like a kid meeting a pop star, it's pathetic.

"But then *he* turns to me. *He* starts talking to me. He buys me a drink and we just talk."

"What about?"

"Oh, I don't remember most of it. About him I suppose. It's awkward to start with, but he gives me room to loosen up as if he knows how bad I am like that. He talks about where he first learnt the guitar, his time hitching rides abroad, people he's met. I think there was some time in jail or something."

"He spent time in jail?" Laura says. "Where on Earth did Jenny dredge him up from?"

"It's a dream, it's not supposed to make sense. It didn't really happen. And it's not as if he's boasting about it or anything like that. It just sort of comes out in passing. I don't remember everything he said to me, I only remember that he seemed like a guy who had lived. And all the time he's talking, he's holding one of his hands cupped inside the other like this.

"And he catches me looking. And he says: You looking at my hand? You want to see my hand? And so he shows me. His right hand, he shows me."

"And?"

"No thumb," I say, indicating my own. "Just a mess of scar tissue where there should have been one. It was ugly. Really ugly. A real horror movie sort of deal."

Laura whistles. "And he could play the guitar?" she's impressed.

"I don't know how," I say. "It's a dream, right? But he could. Really, though, he could, and he was great at it. And he's got this incredible voice. And the thing is, that's when I recognise him, and he knows it. It's what he's been waiting for."

"Who is he?"

I look at her beside me. She's standing in black and white: the contours of her face half-lit by moonlight. The way she smokes, she looks for all the world like Lauren Bacall if Lauren Bacall ever got her hair mussed while sleeping.

"When I was twelve," I say, "I snuck out of bed one evening and took the carving knife from the drawer in the kitchen. I held it over the top of my right thumb like this and I started to cut."

I see her eyes widen.

"You never told me that," she says.

"Well, no," I say. "Can you blame me? I didn't do anything else. I freaked out. I broke the skin – only barely – but it was more than enough for me to change my mind. I skulked off back to bed and cried myself to sleep."

"Why on Earth would you want to do something like that?" she says.

It takes a while before I answer. I look at my right thumb, older, plumper, bonier. It doesn't look like any kind of survivor.

"I felt," I say eventually, "as though it was holding me back."

It sounds so foolish and she agrees with me.

"That's crazy," she says.

I take a moment to finish my cigarette. There's an empty plastic water bottle on the window ledge already half full of fag-ends. I add to it like a kid saving pennies. Laura is watching me closely. She looks as if she's waiting for something special, something epic. Like the kid who stuck his thumb in the dyke and saved Denmark. I manage a small laugh as though I might prepare her for the disappointment.

"When I was small, I used to suck my thumb," I say. "Nothing unusual there, but I was still doing it when I was twelve."

"That's not massively abnormal," she says.

"In fact," I say, "I only ended up giving up sucking my thumb entirely, because when I was fifteen, sixteen, I found something to replace it with."

I light another cigarette pointedly and hold it up to her: Exhibit A.

"And remember what I was like when I tried giving up these the first time?"

Her eyes roll.

"Don't remind me," she says.

"It was like that," I say. "Only worse. It was like trying to give up with a kid's impatience. It's supposed to be only a phase you grow out of but for me it was an addiction, and I didn't really understand that back then. I knew it was wrong and I knew I wanted to stop. I read a lot of history books, when I was a kid. Famous people, heroes, you know? Don't laugh, but I always dreamed I might end up in one of those books one day."

"In a history book?" She's smirking at me. Not unkindly, but she's definitely smirking at me.

"Yeah, well you know. I was at an age when I thought that was how you knew if you made it. So I wanted to be famous. Important. Only none of the famous people in my books sucked their thumbs like kids did, and so when I was twelve, I got out of bed and held the bread knife over my thumb, like it was all the thumb's fault.

"Like *Struwwelpeter*, remember that? Those creepy German stories for kids. Little Jimmy who sucked his thumb: the scissor man came and snip-snip-snip. Serves him right. I'd look that book up in the library and look at the picture of that little forlorn kid with stumps where his thumbs had once been. Not in pain, not frightened, not even angry; just this expression of regret. Kid's don't feel regret, I'd tell myself. Not like that. His anchor had been cut, in some strange way; he'd been set free.

"Anyway, I didn't cut, but this guy. This other guy? He did."

"Pork pie," she says. "The guy in the hat?"

"Yes. He steeled himself and cut through this thumb, flesh and bone. Sawed through with the carving knife. And that's not easy. I mean look at it, most domestic kitchen knives would be blunt before they even reach the bone. But still he kept going. I can't imagine the strength it must have taken. He said he could feel the bones splintering. He was cracking them, not cutting them. He said the pain almost made him sick, but he kept going until he was all the way through. Sawing away."

I stare out the window into the blackness of the back garden. She's staring at me in horror, but I don't need to see her face to confirm it.

"He said he nearly passed out before he was done but he was terrified that he would be found, and they'd take him to hospital and put it back on. *That* overtook the pain, he told me: The fear of failing. In some ways, he needn't have worried. He'd done so much damage to it; they couldn't have fixed it back if they'd tried. He almost lost the entire hand, but by some miracle…"

"God," Laura says, halting me from saying any more, her hand touching my arm, feather-light, insubstantial. "That's horrible."

"I told you," I say.

She takes her hand away and looks out the window, her expression thoughtful.

"He was you?" she says eventually, gesturing at me with her cigarette, a spot of burning red bouncing before her.

I bob my head, indecisive.

"He was the me who had gone ahead with it."

She frowns, then shakes her head. Amused again.

"So," she says. "If you'd sawn your thumb off at an early age you'd be able to play the guitar by now?"

I laugh at that.

"Yeah," I say. "Something like that."

"And that's why you can't sleep."

"Yes," I say.

Laura sighs and kisses me on the cheek.

"Prentis O'Rourke," she says. "I love you, but you're a fucking idiot at times."

She stubs her cigarette out on the outside edge of the window, and drops it into the bottle. Trailing her hand over my shoulder, she turns back to the bed. I watch her reflection in the open window. By some trick of the optics, she looks like she's walking away from me: down the street, into the dark.

"Close the window a little when you're done," she says. "It's starting to get cold out there."

I tell her I will and gesture with the half-smoked cigarette in my hand.

"You don't mind if I finish?" I say.

I hear her chuckle from across the room. Already distant.

"You should really give those up," she says. "I'm serious."

I stare out the window into the darkness. The nicotine will keep me awake, it'll make me resent the morning when it comes. But I can live with that.

Because I don't tell her the rest of the dream. I don't tell her about how – every time – the guy leans towards me, so close I can smell the whisky on his breath, and he says: We've led the same lives, you and me. But everything you've seen and wanted to do, I've done. Everything you wanted to say, I've said. Every place you wanted to go, I've been. Everyone you've fallen for, I've fucked.

I don't tell her how he holds up his ruined hand to me and says: This is all it takes. Not the thumb: the *act*. The *following through*. This is all it takes to reshape the world.

And I can't shake the way he played. The beautiful pain in that voice of his. And the image of her – not Jenny, it was never her in the dream, but Laura. *The* Laura. *My* Laura – looking at him like she will

never look at me.
    And she's dancing for him.
    She's dancing.
    Dancing.
    Dancing.

5. Extinction Solitaire

The Laura who worked in the Analytics Department of The Authority was no longer the same person as the Laura who had married Prentis O'Rourke. Their worlds had diverged early in their respective lives, thanks to a single reckless decision made not by Laura, but her father. Thus, one father died in a pointless brawl when his daughter was only eight years old, the other went home without getting involved. The former established a different causality chain, one that steered Laura well away from the life of Prentis O'Rourke rather than pitching her headlong into it.

    This particular Laura – still named Laura MacNee – sat at her desk where she worked in The Authority offices and scanned through the report she had requested from The Repository. She was disturbed how, in many of the documents, Laura O'Rourke was referred to simply as *The Widow* or *The Wife*, as though she was nothing more than an adjunct to the man who had died. She was troubled by the tone with which her counterparts were described. She came across as shallow, she was cold and uncaring, treating her marriage with a similar glibness the report's author used to describe her. It simply didn't seem *fair* that history – history being The Authority's central concern – should treat an individual, a witness, with such ambivalence. Prentis O'Rourke was gone, and his blast radius had caused all kinds of collateral damage. Surely someone should be paying attention to those he left behind?

    The Repository was The Authority's central database interface. Beyond the inappropriately cute cartoon logo in shape of a fluffy dodo wearing a baseball cap, it was a remarkably sophisticated and rather unlikely piece of equipment that – by means Laura had never troubled herself to understand – collated data from all known realities, sharing resources, processing requirements and occasionally dividing costs across the gamut of known existences.

During her induction, Jack, her new line manager had run her through the bespoke systems she was unfamiliar with, and Laura had questioned the choice of the dodo icon for The Repository.

"I think it's supposed to serve as a reminder," Jack had said, double-clicking on the icon with a surprising force as though he were punching the poor bird between the eyes. "It was something someone said once. It's in the welcome documents somewhere. This idea that if we could go back in time, many of us would give anything to save the last dodos from extinction, but the truth is we've probably learned more from them all being dead. That sort of thing."

Employees of The Authority were not forbidden from tracking how their alternate lives might live or how decisions they sweated over might have taken them on a different path, but they were not encouraged to do so either. To work at The Authority was to become hyper aware that every decision made, no matter how small, would extrapolate a whole universe, a fresh green shoot which would grow and expand. New staff made a concerted effort to appear more decisive, believing that by doing so, they would be more efficient. Older hands knew that the more realities were created, the more Authorities would exist and therefore – potentially – the more processing power The Repository would possess to handle them.

It was a contradiction, a paradox, but it didn't take long working at The Authority to become ambivalent to such magical thinking.

A typical Monday morning would see many of the staff running quick reports about their weekend's activity to confirm the suspicion that the decisions, which had seemed like a good idea while drunk on Friday and a terrible idea while hungover on Saturday, had less consequence on Sunday than they might have feared.

For Laura MacNee, tracking her alternate lives felt too much like spying. And if *she* thought that, then the women who shared her name, the women who shared her whole life up until one specific moment, would think that too. Many of her alternates, who it was reasonable to assume also still worked for The Authority, might already have glanced at her own data in return, and the thought of all those eyes upon her, judging her decisions, made her nauseous. I was as though her every move and thought was being recorded on surveillance cameras by those who knew her better than anyone.

Laura MacNee lived alone. When someone asked, she would tell them that she was 'between dalliances', which was true to an extent.

It was something to do with working at The Authority. She had seen so many relationships fail in so many different ways, there didn't really seem to be much point in pursuing one of her own. She knew others had become addicted to keeping tabs on how their other selves were thriving and failing in their love lives, they would adjust their own courses to suit, but Laura felt that using The Repository in such a way was a form of cheating. To begin a relationship under the eye of The Authority, she thought, was to open a book, one with the perception that there was only one real path through to success. This idea felt claustrophobic to her, as though she would be trapping herself in a frustrating and narrow band of possibility, continually under stress by the fear she might be veering off the perfect racing line.

This wasn't free will, she decided, but it wasn't fate either. It was a mean path that ran somewhere between the two.

The news about Prentis O'Rourke had come as a surprise. Late on the morning of the 16th October, Laura had arrived in the office and became increasingly aware over the course of the first few hours that her colleagues were treating her with a deference she was unused to.

"I'm so sorry," her friend Janet said to her, leaning over her shoulder so she could view her screen.

"I didn't even know him," Laura said, paging through the preliminary press release. It was a strange feeling. Global disasters came and went in her news feed and she would read each with an appalled diligence. She had never felt as though she *should* be invested before, and she realised she felt guilty because – despite all evidence to the contrary – she still couldn't find a way to quite connect to the vastness of the tragedy.

In all cases of major disasters, the employee handbook advised, there was a high probability that members of staff would have alternates who were personally involved. It published a series of recommendations advising how staff might distance themselves psychologically from the events and carry on working as normal. In

The Purpose of the Dodo is to be Extinct

the case of Prentis O'Rourke, Laura was in deep. Nearly 64% of the Prentis O'Rourkes who had known Laura, had been in a relationship with her when he died, and her name cropped up remarkably frequently in a wide variety of the subsequent analysis.

The Wife, The Widow, The Woman in his life.

She tried to understand why so many of *her* had ended up with so many of *him*. She scoured his profiles trying to understand what she might have seen in him, what about him could have made so many of her go all in. Had she met him in a bar in her current life, would she have fallen for him? Would she have had a choice?

She searched for a trace of his charisma that might translate through the terse language of The Authority's paperwork, but what she found was relentlessly unexceptional. He had dreams, but not the ambition to fulfil them, he was kind but too easily distracted, he was liberal in thought, but conservative in deed. He had a crooked smile and a self-deprecating manner and until he came to the forefront by dying in such spectacular quantity, he was the sort who would fade into the background at the expense of all others.

She paged through the document, the words and figures blurring into nonsense before her. Was that it? Was he really the best she could do?

She thought of all the news stories of fires and bombs, air collisions and terrorist atrocities. All the witnesses who would show up afterwards explaining how they *should* have been there themselves. That they *should* have died, only they were saved by some quirk of fate: a lie in, a hangover, a phone call from a stranger with a wrong number. She always thought it was strange that people should need to explain themselves on television in this way. It seemed so tasteless. A way for someone to make a stranger's tragedy more personal, to claim it as their own. The Repository made such speculation concrete and real. There was something exhilarating, people said, about learning how one of their alternates had perished on the way into work.

"Still," Janet said. "It could have been worse. In around 5% of cases, apparently, *I* killed him. Me! I know! It's hilarious. *I* killed Prentis O'Rourke, if you can believe that."

Janet was from Luton originally, but her vowels were still softened from the years she'd spent living in Lancashire. She smiled broadly, as though by doing so she might eclipse Laura's frown.

"Well," Laura said. "These sorts of things happen –"

"More than you'd think," Janet said. "I know, I know. But look at that." She pointed to a cluster of dots at the top of the scatter graph on the screen. "In these realities, here, here, here, *I* killed *your* husband. Imagine that."

"Janet."

"Accidentally," Janet said. "I'm not one of the ones who murdered him. Lloyd in requisitions though? Apparently one of his alternates killed Prentis in a knife fight. Lloyd! You wouldn't think he had it in him."

"Janet, please."

Janet tapped her on the shoulder, a comradely gesture. She backed away to the office door, pausing to throw a smile back to Laura before she exited.

"Listen," Janet said. "Whenever I get vertigo from all of this, I look at the mirror reports. I'm serious. It helps, really." She fluttered her fingers in a wave and walked away, humming something passingly familiar as she rounded the corner.

That evening, Laura visited her mother in the retirement home overlooking the river on one side and the meadow on the other. The receptionist glanced up at her as she came through the door and smiled briefly in acknowledgement before returning to the paperback romance she had open before her.

Laura followed the familiar corridor to her mother's flat, tapping on the door once before opening it with her own key.

Her mother barely acknowledged her as she came in. She was sitting, folded over her card table in the middle of the lounge, her glasses propped on her nose, an expression of utmost concentration on her face. A game of solitaire was laid out before her, blue backed cards ordered in military ranks. The advancing second hand of the clock on the mantle loudly counted an insistent marching time.

Laura slipped her bag off her shoulder and sat on the edge of the sofa to wait for her in the silent room. There was the thick smell of boiled cabbage from the kitchen and, fidgety with impatience, she got up again to open a window, to pace across the carpet. Her mother worked silently and swiftly, her eyes darting around the table before her, the remaining deck of cards clasped in her knuckles like a pack of cigarettes.

Laura returned to the sofa and glanced up at the shelves which lined the room. All the decks of cards her mother had already used, lined up like the spines of tiny books. There were so many of them and for a moment it struck Laura that they looked familiar. In the foyer to The Authority offices there was a mural intended to illustrate a million lives, each stacked and filed on shelves like library books. There had been a time when she had looked her mother up in The Repository, but all her paths seemed to straighten out into something similar as though in every life she reached a point where she stripped her own options bare. Her father would die, and her mother would stop. It was as simple as that and it was all too much. She followed the mothers who had not yet reached this point yet, but she couldn't read their reports without seeing signs – real or imagined – that told her this future was inevitable for each of them. Perhaps this was what Prentis O'Rourke was to her. A flag on a horizon that she doggedly made for. Something unavoidable, a gravitational well that would spin her off course if she came under its influence.

"Have you been crying?" her mother said; she wasn't quite looking at her. She had collected all the cards back into the deck and was holding them tightly in her fist, staring at the empty green of the table as though she could still perceive things in its design that that no one else could.

"No," Laura said, wiping her face anyway as though she had been.

"You look sad."

"Someone died," Laura said. "I didn't know them." For some reason, it felt like a lie.

Her mother nodded. That made sense to her. She shuffled the deck of cards, an instinctive gesture, her hands moving quickly and confidently, her eyes unfocused.

"That *is* sad," she said.

Laura stood up and crossed to the other side of the table, she knelt on the floor and reached across the green baize, taking the deck of cards from her mother's hands.

"Let's play something together," she said.

She dealt out ten cards to each of them.

"Rummy," she said. "We used to play Rummy sometimes, didn't we?"

She set the remaining cards upside down and removed the top card, placing it face up beside it. The ten of diamonds.

Her mother remained silent. Her hand was still raised from where Laura had taken the cards from her, her eyes stared at the table as though it was still empty.

"Mummy," Laura said.

Her mother raised her head slowly to meet her eyes. She reached out a hand and started gathering all the cards on the table towards her in a broad, sweeping motion. Cards jumbled, blue backs and white fronts. There was a quiet desperation there as her mother fought to restore the order.

"This isn't how it works, Laura," she said.

Laura watched as she resolved the cards into a deck again and started shuffling. She dealt the cards out again. Another game of solitaire, this time orientated away from her, facing Laura. When she was done, she reached across the table, passing the remaining cards to her daughter.

Laura looked at her. She imagined the version of herself that took the cards and obediently played. She imagined the version of her mother who had accepted the game of Rummy and played with her. She imagined the version of her who stood too soon, flipping the table and scattering cards across the floor and making her mother howl in grief. She imagined herself running back to The Authority and starting fire after fire after fire.

"It isn't how it works," her mother said again.

"I don't think that's true," Laura said.

That night, Laura dreamed of Prentis O'Rourke. He was giant, bloated, blimp-shaped, drifting above the city street, creaking and turning on some unseen tide. He was eclipsing the bright summer sun like one of the alien spacecraft in a science fiction film she had once seen. His shadow passed over everyone as they went about their daily lives and while most ignored him, Laura couldn't look away.

Don't they see how he's affecting everyone, she thought. *Don't they care?*

In her dream, Laura stopped in the middle of the street to stare up at him as he passed. Time lengthened as it often does in dreams and she watched as he slid lazily overhead, his body ballooning, his eyes closed, creased, a flicker of a frown as though he was troubled by dreams of his own.

The shriek of brakes and the desperate, angry car horn distracted her enough to see the bright face of Janet Baskerville at the wheel of her car, veering towards her both too fast and too slow. It was cartoonish and absurd, with poor Janet pulling all kinds of faces as she tried to master the brakes of her Saab 98 before it was too late for either of them.

6. The Mirror Reports

If, for any self-contained universe, gravity creates a point where the distance between particles is minimal, then when the particles expand outwards, they do so in two temporal directions.

Therefore, on the other side of the Janus point, in the exact mirror of reality ref. 785-157-894/N (assuming that everything that can happen, does indeed happen), the story of Prentis O'Rourke will be substantially different; here there will be fate but there will be no free will – and in these circumstances it will not be poorer for the reversal.

In this world, Janet Baskerville is escorted to a wrecked Saab 98 on the corner of Laburnum road. As the air bag folds itself up, the steering column seals itself, she looks through the windscreen to witness the man lying in the road before her open his eyes and then leap joyously into the air, throwing himself at the bonnet of the car as she stamps into reverse. He walks off down the street, a smile on his face. She will never see him again, but it is an event that will colour the rest of her life; gone is the sense of guilt and disappointment which has hounded her days and rendered her nights sleepless, gone is that ache at the base of her neck which has nagged her for as long as she can remember. She drives home immediately and fiercely embraces her husband and daughter.

At the home she has moved into while Prentis has been away, Laura will unpack her clothes and place her toothbrush in the bathroom. She will put her luggage away in the attic and it will not be touched again until her honeymoon, six years later. Her sense of contentment will grow as the years progress. Laura and Prentis will grow closer over time, their passion will increase, everything will seem so right, so perfect, so new.

Their relationship will end on a glorious high, beyond which, parting seems logical and effortless. They will not cry when they go their separate ways, they will not need to.

Prentis O'Rourke will live out his life in reverse. Whenever he reaches a turning point, his world will become bound with those of every outcome of every experience: the threads of reality will plait together to form one, stronger, unified world in which every decision has been dissected, considered and learnt from. As Prentis O'Rourke becomes younger, he becomes stronger. He becomes more knowledgeable and more experienced.

Ultimately, all the possible worlds which have been created by decisions made by every Prentis O'Rourke will converge into one single reality and one final Prentis O'Rourke.

But before this happens, when the cherry tree in his parents' garden stops flowering and withers to a stem, he and his father will dig it up and exhume the remains of Breadbin, who they will place gently on the road, watching from the kerb as he is resuscitated by a passing Peugeot 305.

The same dog will be there when Prentis is ten years old, curled up beside the boy as, thumb in mouth, he reads a book; a chapter of which discusses the last words spoken by historical figures who do not yet exist.

Prentis will roll onto his back, his hands folded beneath his head, he will stare up at the clouds coalescing in the sky above him, watching the bright colours of the morning dance and whirl.

Here, he will consider his own last words. He will know what he said when every version of him died, and he alone will understand what each version of himself meant when he spoke those final words in each of those different realities, all that time ago. The thought will make him smile, and that, he decides, is enough.

Prentis O'Rourke will have ten years of his life still to live, and he will be content.

Cat and Mouse

David Tallerman

"Would you like to come in for coffee?"

Only, she pronounced it as to two distinct syllables, cof-fee, and I'd never heard anyone make two syllables sound so frankly erotic. Every inch of my body and a good portion of my mind was eager to follow her up that short flight of stairs, through the door, and into the dimly lit, rich-scented depths of her apartment.

But the part of my brain that disagreed was doing so violently. Something about this woman, about the evening we'd spent together, just didn't sit right.

The resisting portion of my brain knew this to be true. Yet when I challenged it to give me a specific example, it floundered. The inner turmoil made me want to howl with frustration. I hadn't had a date in almost a year and now here was this undeniably beautiful woman inviting me into her flat, for something I knew without doubt had little to do with caffeinated beverages.

"Kamrita." Probably I was tired. Probably I was freaking out a little, trying instinctively to sabotage this good thing that had come out of nowhere into my life. I placed a foot on the first step. "I'd like to..."

My attention drifted, from her face to a point beside her head. I'd have sworn I spotted movement there. Yet when I looked, properly looked, I saw shadows receding into a shallow hallway.

More self-sabotage. I knew it, and the knowledge didn't help. I tried to concentrate, and the itch to stare past her shoulder sent tremors down my spine. I took another step, paused to knuckle my eyes.

For the barest instant, I saw clearly: a pattern of blue and almost-black purple, like...

The thought evaporated. Nothing except shadows. But the

damage was done. Those last three steps might as well have been the Gulf of Mexico.

"Ah, I'd like to get an early night. I'm up at the crack of dawn tomorrow, I've a meeting, and…"

Her expression started with surprise and ended with what I could only describe as devastation. That threw me more than anything. Surely a woman like Kamrita could have any man she wanted, and a stone thrown randomly in Leicester Square would be bound to hit a better match than me. I comforted myself with that logic: I was doing her a favour. Perhaps she'd had too much to drink. Maybe she'd built our barely natal relationship into something much more than it was. In the morning, she'd wake up grateful to the asshole who'd turned her down, leaving her to find a partner worthy of her charms.

"Bye," I said. When that didn't seem enough I added, "I'll call you."

I didn't want to see if she believed me. I turned away and started walking, trying not to appear as though I was hurrying and yet hurrying nonetheless. Bad enough that I'd hurt her feelings, bad enough I was acting crazy. Letting her see how frantically I wanted to get away seemed a cruelty too far.

A pause. No sound but the tap of my feet on the pavement. Her voice, lilting behind me: "I'll see you soon."

At first, I thought she sounded pitiful. Did she really think I meant I'd call her? Then I realised how she'd said it. This wasn't at all the plea of a woman too desperate to admit she'd been jilted. Surely, she wasn't going to start turning up unannounced at my office or loitering outside my flat? No, that wasn't it either. What I'd heard in her voice was simply certainty: the tone in which someone might look at a cloudy sky and say, 'It's going to rain.'

Still, I didn't turn back. I didn't respond, not so much as a nod or shake of my head. I pretended I hadn't heard, or as if she hadn't said anything worth hearing, and I felt like an utter shit. But I made it to the corner, and I couldn't deny that my breath came easier as I turned out of her street.

Finally I slowed down. I let the tension soak out of me and wondered what I was going to do next. The evening was mild, the tail end of an Indian summer that had made the real one look pitiful.

Though it was almost October and past eleven, I was comfortable in my T-shirt and light jacket, only shivering a little when the night breeze cut around my collar. I wasn't entirely sure where I was – somewhere near Camden as far as I could tell – and I knew I was a long way from home.

That didn't worry me. I wanted to walk around, to clear my head. I had the frustrating sensation of a word caught on the tip of my tongue; except it wasn't a word, it was the whole of the last few hours. It was like trying to remember a dream, too, except that I could recall everything – *almost* everything – with perfect clarity. We'd met for a couple of drinks in a quiet Soho bar and moved on via a short Tube journey to a restaurant Kamrita knew. She'd offered to order for both of us and I'd agreed. I couldn't remember afterwards exactly what she'd told the waiter, but the result was as near to my perfect meal as I could have hoped for.

Dinner left me mellow, contented, and slightly tipsy. I'd suggested I walk Kamrita home. I don't recollect any ulterior motive; I merely wanted to stretch the evening as far as it would go. Yet even then, doubts were nagging. They'd been there ever since we first met.

How *had* we met?

Looking up, I discovered to my surprise that I was somewhere I recognised. I was walking along Prince Albert Road, with stubby blocks of flats sprouting to my left and on my right the wall of foliage marking the uppermost edge of Regent's Park.

A sudden, mad impulse caught me. Before I had time to question it, I'd already given in and was clambering over the gate into the park. The full moon amid a clear sky was nearly as good as daylight, and I reasoned I'd be able to see and outrun any patrolling guards if there were such a thing. I walked until I was free of the trees around the entrance and abandoned the path. A couple of minutes later, it occurred to me to sit down. Squatting upon the damp grass, I could see nothing of London, though I knew it was out there before me. I tried to guess from memory the locations of all the great, familiar landmarks: Big Ben, Canary Wharf, Battersea Power Station, the Gherkin and the Shard. But the only one I could actually see was the inverted crystalline spike of the Hyde Park Spire, and then only its blunted peak.

Still, it was the Spire that my eyes kept drifting back to. Yet nothing about it seemed offensive or out of place, nor even particularly interesting. I stared at its distant grooves and weird prominences, a half-burned candle sculpted in frosted glass, and wondered what it was that commanded my interest.

Once again, the feeling of wrongness started to creep over me: the sensation, which I now couldn't help but associate with Kamrita, that I was blind to some important detail. It also struck me clearly that a part of my mind had brought me to this spot for a reason. Those two revelations unsettled in one fell swoop the calm I'd managed to accumulate, making the park seem suddenly dark and unfriendly. I stood up and started walking again, as fast or faster than when I'd hurried to escape Kamrita's flat.

I'd got turned around. It was years since I'd last been in the park, and now it seemed like a desert of inky grass and trees blotted carelessly onto characterless landscape. I began to jog, though my breath was already coming hard.

Abruptly, a low roar rent the air, hung for a moment as a trembling growl and faded. I almost panicked, until I realised it must have come from the zoo, which lay somewhere to my left – a big cat disturbed from its slumber. Then, oddly, I calmed a little. The scene struck me as almost funny: here I was, running around in London as though it were some tropic wilderness. I took a moment to get my bearings and let the stitch in my side ease. I made a point of not looking back towards the Spire.

Once I decided on a direction, the edge of the park came on me quickly. Clambering over another gate brought me out on a road I didn't recognise. I didn't know this side of London well at all and navigating from a half-remembered childhood visit was getting me nowhere. Even if I was still on edge, it was time I started heading home. The alternative might be a night spent curled up in a doorway if I wasn't careful. Glancing at my watch, I saw that it was coming up on midnight. There should still be Tube trains running if I could find a station in time, and there was bound to be one nearby.

Just as I'd settled on my plan, I heard the growing rumble of an engine behind me, too loud for a car. When I turned, I was dazzled for a moment by the headlights and bright internal glow of an approaching bus. It was the first vehicle I'd seen since I entered the park, and it took me by surprise – all the more so when it pulled to a halt against the curb, for there was no shelter, not even a sign.

Nevertheless, it was a gift horse, and I wasn't about to look it in the mouth. Judging by the destination it was displaying, the bus wouldn't exactly pass near my flat, but it would certainly get me closer than I was now: a reasonable walk rather than an all-night trek.

When I walked round, though, I saw that the folding doors were closed. I was wondering if the vehicle was out of service after all when the driver happened to glance down and notice me. He stared with puzzled consideration for a few seconds, almost as if this were his house I was standing outside instead of a public transport. Then he moved slightly and the doors concertinaed open.

I stepped up cautiously, conscious his gaze had never left me. I told him where I was trying to get to. He gave the information some thought. As I was starting to despair of getting any sense out of him, he said, "Closest stop's a couple of miles off. That any good to you?"

A couple of miles in London might wind up being an hour's fast walk. "I can live with it."

Abruptly, apropos of nothing, the driver said, "You might want to watch those two at the back. They're a little, ah…" The sentence drifted off. He transferred his gaze to the mirror that let him view the inside of his vehicle, his brow crinkling with worry.

I looked where he was looking, to the two men sitting together on the rearmost seat. Though the interior was astringently lit, I found it hard to make them out, as if they'd found a shadow that couldn't possibly be there. If I concentrated, I could see enough of them to think that something wasn't exactly right. But concentrating on them was more difficult than it had any reason to be.

"Sorry," said the driver. "Don't know what I was thinking."

I swiped my Oyster card, wondering which was more bizarre, the driver's confusion or the fact that a London bus driver had apologised to me. Not comfortable at the prospect of being near the two men, I opted for the seat closest to the front. A sign told me curtly that it was set aside for the elderly and physically impaired, but the bus was empty except for the three of us, and I figured I could move if need be. Then it occurred to me that I wouldn't recognise my unfamiliar stop in the dark. I ducked back to the driver's plastic window and asked if he'd let me know when we got there.

"Sure," he said, "no bother." He actually sounded a little pleased, as if the task would be a pleasant diversion from whatever thoughts were rotating in his head.

I went back to the seat I'd picked, saw the sign again and wondered why I'd chosen it in the first place. Something to do with the pair at the back? But they were only conversing in soft whispers and keeping to themselves. As the driver pulled from the curb, I settled for a spot midway down the bus which would give me a better view of the streets we passed through.

At least, that was the plan. I bore with it for a couple of minutes, trying to draw sense from the blur of buildings and figures, smudged by darkness or bleached into meaninglessness by washes of electric light. I still didn't recognise anywhere. The occasional road signs I saw were scuffed by shadows and the speed of our passage, nonsensical as some alien language. London might have been any city on Earth for all I could make sense of it.

I sank into my seat and allowed my mind to wander. I was confident the driver would hold to his promise, and, if he didn't, I wasn't sure I cared any more. The night had grown too unreal. Did I really want to carry that mood home with me? I knew I hadn't properly processed what I was thinking, or rather *not* thinking… whatever was untangling itself in the base of my mind.

Kamrita. The name sounded Asian, didn't it? Except I knew I wasn't pronouncing it right. There'd been more there when she'd said it, a throaty resonance I'd known I would never perfect. I tried to remember her accent: to dissect some phrase that she'd spoken in my memory, tease from its innards a hint of accent or clue of nationality.

It worked up to a point. I could hear her voice as if she were sat next to me: its soft vowels and clicking consonants, and its peculiar rhythm, which made the words spin and dance like skaters on a frozen lake. But that didn't bring me any closer to understanding. More and more I found myself focusing on the remembered conversations themselves, how much I'd enjoyed them, and her, and us together. In my mind's eye, I replayed her small and earnest compliments, the bright flares of humour, the way she'd made subjects I'd never bothered to consider immediately interesting.

Kamrita... Wherever it came from, it was a nice name. And wherever she came from, it was ages since I'd enjoyed time spent with anyone so much, if I ever had. What was I running from? Was my trepidation really worse than the possibility of living the rest of my life without spending more of it with her?

The bus made a sound of complaint, metal grating upon metal, and slowed rapidly before stopping altogether. I heard the grind and whirr of the doors opening, and immediately after, the driver calling, "This is you, mate."

Caught by surprise – wasn't this the first stop we'd made? – I jerked to my feet, gave the driver a nod and mumbled 'thank you', and stumbled onto the curb. Almost before my heels struck tarmac, the doors rattled shut, the engine grumbled back into life and the bus dove back into the road. I looked round in alarm, to watch as its lights receded. It reached the corner and vanished from sight.

Turning back, I saw where the driver had left me: at the foot of the short flight of stairs that led to Kamrita's front door.

This time I really did run. Despite my thoughts of only a few moments ago, the clearly impossible, inexplicable return to Kamrita's home had made the very concept of her downright frightening. I fled with no thought of direction, no thought of anything but placing distance between myself and that innocuous green portal. I ran until stinging sweat blurred my vision, until my ankles and knees felt full of hot lead, until my head swam with the battering of my heart.

I ran until I couldn't run any more. Then I flopped onto a low garden wall and gasped. I'd never imagined I could be so glad of cool night air. I really believed I could feel it, not only in my lungs but in my muscles and veins, as if my body were a machine being lubricated. I knew I should be cold, I knew my clothes were saturated with sweat, but in fact I felt wonderful, scoured and fresh.

My burst of fear – or perhaps more likely the adrenalin that followed – had done more than any of the night's events to clear my head. I could see the pieces now. The Spire. Kamrita. The men on the bus, not hidden precisely but the exact opposite of conspicuous. I was starting to remember details I didn't know I'd forgotten. I was a part of something, something perhaps out of my control and beyond my ability to resist.

Now that the panic had worn off, I questioned once again why I was trying. If I stopped running, I might at least get some answers.

Sitting in sweat-drenched clothes on an autumn night until I came down with pneumonia, on the other hand, would get me nowhere. I hoisted myself to my feet and set out walking again. Both the fear and adrenalin were gone, leaving in their place a weariness like a hundred tiny weights hung about my body. I was monumentally tired of London streets made dreary and repetitious by darkness. I wanted to be home, or failing that, in a late-night cafe or a takeaway, anywhere I could sit and switch off for a while. But there was nothing; only street after street of houses in increasingly nightmarish succession.

The taxi rank seemed like a vision, an oasis in the urban desert. Three vehicles were pulled up on a tarmac forecourt in front of a small office. From one of the cars, a young man in a white kurta and knitted skullcap was leaning from the open window, his elbow propped on the door's frame and a half-smoked cigarette held between two fingers.

As I approached the office, he called, "Where're you after, mate?"

I told him my address.

He stubbed the cigarette against the outside of the door and flicked the remainder towards a drain. "Sure. Hop in."

I did as he said, opting for the front passenger seat. Struck by sudden doubt, I repeated my address and added, "You know where that is?"

"Yeah," he said, unperturbed, "I know it."

I watched him for a while, as he drove with that peculiar mix of intense absorption and apparent heedlessness peculiar to his trade. On an impulse I said, "Mind if I ask you a question?"

He spared me the briefest flicker of a glance. "Sure, mate."

"Do you remember when the Spire came here?"

"The Spire?"

"The thing in Greenwich Park. It was on the news. Do you remember?"

"Oh... yeah. On the news."

"People were scared. The army were out. And then..."

"Sure. Then." We had pulled up at a red light. He looked at me for a moment, the confusion clear in his eyes, perplexity edging into dismay. The light changed and he turned away. "A while ago, though, all that."

I sensed I was on thin ice, that I could lose his fragile concentration at any moment. "But there were... people... weren't there? Who came out of the Spire?"

"Well, yeah. Of course."

"And they stayed. You see them around." I wanted to add – only, you don't *quite* see them. You see them, but you don't.

Slowly, cautiously, as though he was determined to get each word precisely right, he said, "They're no bother, though, are they?"

"No," I conceded. "They're no bother."

"I mean..." He considered. "They want to fit in."

"Yeah. I think they do."

I let the conversation tail off, conscious I was making the cabbie uncomfortable without any hope of a revealing answer. I settled into my seat and let my eyes drift shut, giving myself up to the sounds of the car and the fainter background tremors from outside. It was good to be warm and at rest, cocooned from a night-time world that had seemed inescapable only minutes before. Warmth soaked into my body, the car hummed and trembled around me, and I thought about what the cabbie had said.

I don't think I slept, but I wasn't quite awake either when the cab pulled up and the driver said, "Here you go."

I knew I wasn't home. Perhaps it was some quality in the street lighting or some internal GPS, but I didn't even bother to look.

Seeing this, the cabbie glanced between the street and his sat nav, presumably unable to reconcile the two. "This is the address you gave me, yeah?"

"Hmm? Oh. Yeah. This is it, all right."

He looked relieved. "Don't know what's got into me tonight. That'll be sixteen quid."

I gave him a twenty, told him to keep the change. I felt, somehow, that he'd earned it. He seemed grateful; but I suspected it was less for the money, more the permission to leave – to return to his normal, day-to-day reality.

As I stepped onto the street, I envied him that a little. But only a little.

I'd reached the bottom step when I heard the sound of the door.

I looked up to see it half open, and Kamrita stood in the gap. Our eyes met and held, and suddenly language seemed an inadequate medium for anything significant. When I finally managed to produce the words I'd been storing up, they were quick and garbled and nothing like I'd intended. "Why, Kamrita? Why tonight? Why all of this? Why me?"

"We know our partners when we meet them." Her tone was exactly as calm as it had always been. "And we partner for life."

"You're saying you met me, and you decided we had to be together?"

Kamrita shrugged. "I knew." She placed a palm flat on her stomach, as if to indicate this was where her impossible certainty had come from.

I thought about arguing, pointing out what an absurd claim this was. Outside of Hallmark cards and Mills and Boon novels, one look could not possibly assess a lifetime of compatibility, especially when… especially if…

I let the thought peter out. It wasn't what was bothering me, not really. Maybe it should have been, but it wasn't. "Whatever you're doing to me," I said, "I need you to stop it. I'm not coming in for coffee or any damn thing as long as you're messing with my head."

"It isn't so simple." Her response wasn't an apology or an assertion, simply a statement of fact.

"It has to be. I don't much feel like trying to walk home again, but I swear I will if you can't start being straight with me."

"What we do," she said, "we do together. It's our nature to hide in plain sight."

Could she be telling the truth? Was everything that had happened tonight no more deliberate than a chameleon changing shade to match its new background? "Still. You're smart. You must be able to turn it off."

She cocked her head to one side. Then she gave a small and lengthy shudder, as though an electric charge were running not-quite-quickly up from the soles of her feet. The experience looked uncomfortable, if not outright painful.

There was no sense of change. I didn't feel that a veil had lifted; there was no heat haze transformation before my eyes. I was simply, suddenly, seeing what I'd been seeing all along, what I'd known on some level I'd been seeing – and yet had been unable to see.

Kamrita was taller than me by a clear head, and I was nearly six foot. She was wearing a loose robe, something between a toga and a sari, pale yellow-white and patterned with clustered geometric designs, which left her head and arms and the edge of one leg from thigh to ankle exposed. Every visible inch of skin was covered with fine fur, a rich cerulean blue overlaid with intricate whorls of purple, like fractal tiger stripes. Her features were somewhat human, but her nose was longer, her ears sharp and tufted, like a lynx's except hanging downward, her eyes larger and the pupils minute amid elliptical irises. Finally, my stare settled on the detail that had disturbed me so badly a few hours ago: the tip of her tail flicking lazily at the air behind her left shoulder.

Although I could catalogue and make sense of all of these details apart, to see them together in a living creature standing not three feet from me was strange beyond belief. Strange – but not unpleasant. Not frightening at all.

"Why do you hide? You shouldn't have to."

"It's our nature," she said again.

I knew I'd asked a foolish question, that there was more to it. How much pain and horror had we wreaked upon ourselves over differences of appearance and culture far, far smaller? Still, there was sense there as well. The woman before me should not have to disguise herself. "You're beautiful."

Kamrita smiled, exposing a mouthful of delicately pointed teeth, a tongue thin and pink as a rose petal. "Would you like to come in for coffee?"

"Of course," I said.

Before They Left

Colin Greenland

Ms Finn was telling Year Two about volcanoes. She showed them one in Hawaii. It was a mountain with fire coming out of it. The fire was full of rocks. The rocks were so hot they were burning.

Ms Finn told them the name of the volcano. It was a Hawaiian name. Clarity Ingram had stopped listening. She was staring at the volcano.

Ms Finn said it was very big, but there was another one a hundred times bigger. She said, "Can anyone guess where that is?"

Some children guessed America, Australia. Evie Winton guessed the North Pole. Clarity didn't guess anywhere. Then Ms Finn said the enormous volcano wasn't anywhere on Earth at all. It was on Mars.

After school, when Daddy came to pick her up, Clarity asked him. "Daddy?"

"What, princess?"

"Can we go to Mars?"

"Go where, princess?"

"Mars, Daddy."

"Mars? I don't expect so."

"Why not?"

"We're all right here. Aren't we? What would you like for tea?"

Later, in bed, Clarity told Monkey about the enormous volcano on Mars. Monkey grinned at her the way he always did. He didn't say anything. Once upon a time Monkey would have said *That's great, Clarity! Let's go and see it!* These days, Monkey didn't say as much as he used to. He didn't say anything at all, really. These days when you sat him up he tended to flop over in the middle, and the fur was coming off the top of his head.

When she woke up, the first thing Clarity thought about was pancakes with strawberry syrup. The next thing was the enormous volcano.

At break, Ms Finn was on playground duty. Clarity told her: "I want to go to Mars."

Ms Finn said, "Mars, Clarity? Why do you want to go to Mars?"

"I want to see the enormous volcano."

Ms Finn seemed pleased, the way she did when you remembered something she'd told you. "Well, Clarity," she said, "if you *can* do that, you'll be the first. The first Earth person, anyway. Think of that!"

By now there were other children pressing around them. They wanted to talk to Ms Finn too. Caleb was crying. He said Ajay had punched him. Teagen was holding one of her shoes.

Ms Finn smiled at them all. "Clarity's going to be the first Earth person on Mars."

Evie Winton was there. Wherever Clarity went, Evie always went too. She took hold of Clarity's hand. She was twiddling her hair, sucking it. "Are you really going to Mars, Clarity?"

"I expect so," Clarity said. "But I'm not going right this minute."

Evie looked happier. "Come and play then," she said.

The next person Clarity told was Kennedy, her big sister. "Kennedy," she said. "I'm going to Mars."

Kennedy was taking clothes out of a drawer and pulling faces at them. They were her clothes, but she didn't look as if she liked them.

"I'm going to see the enormous volcano," Clarity told her.

When Kennedy didn't answer, Clarity went right up behind her. "Kennedy, I'm going to *Mars*," she said again.

"I don't think you are, Clar," said Kennedy.

"You went to the Moon," Clarity pointed out.

Kennedy pulled another face. "That was a school trip."

Evie Winton's big brother Ollie was in Kennedy's class. Ollie had been on the trip too. Evie said that Ollie said that Kennedy was sick in the rocket.

Clarity played with a piece of her sister's hair, curling and uncurling it against her back. "Do they have volcanoes?"

Kennedy jerked her hair free. "*I* don't know."

She looked as if she was going to hit Clarity but then she stroked her cheek instead.

"The Moon's boring, sweetie," she said. "It's just rocks." She started pushing her clothes back into the drawer, getting them all screwed up and lumpy. "There isn't any air. You can't even go outdoors."

"I can go to Mars if I want to," Clarity said.

"Only if they send you."

"Who?"

"Duh. The Overlords."

Clarity knew about the Overlords. Everyone knew about the Overlords. They were as tall as trees and as black as coal. They had wings and long tails like fat black snakes.

"Did they send you to the Moon?"

"It's their rocket. We haven't got any rockets." Kennedy pushed the drawer. It wouldn't shut properly. Things were sticking out of it.

"It was Overlord Maltharika, Clarity," Kennedy said, as if Clarity had said something, as if she were being stupid. "You know Overlord Maltharika. He's the one who comes to school sometimes."

Clarity remembered Overlord Maltharika. He had spiky horns sticking out of his forehead and too many fingers on his hands. He was so big he had to crouch down to get through the door.

At school Evie Winton kept telling everyone Clarity Ingram was going to Mars. Clarity just smiled and held her nose up and walked away as if she had a secret.

In fact, when she thought about Overlord Maltharika, Clarity was less sure about Mars. Overlord Maltharika was like a giant black beetle.

In the summer they took Grandma and Grandpa to Sapmi and saw reindeer. Grandpa asked Clarity if she thought they were Father Christmas' reindeer, but they weren't flying, just shoving one another in among the trees and eating grass, like cows.

There were mountains. Clarity kept looking down to see if any were volcanoes, but if they were she didn't spot them. There was no fire, only snow.

Then school started again. One day at break a tall car came. Men in black leather suits got out and stood around it. The next to get out was an Overlord.

The Overlord looked as if he were wearing black leather too, though really that was just their skin. He had a big thick belt around his middle with machines on it, with lights on them flickering. When he stood up straight his men only came up to his waist.

Some of the children went on playing. Some stood staring, the little ones clinging to the fence. Some of the older children went closer. Evie called Clarity back. Clarity ignored her. She went closer too.

The Overlord stretched his shoulders. His wings flared wide, then settled again.

One of his men was speaking to a boy in Year Eight. "Tell Mrs Dutt Overlord Maltharika has arrived."

Clarity slipped between the Overlord's men. She got so close she could nearly touch him. His legs were like shiny black trees, right in front of her, the things on his belt hanging down like metal fruit. It hurt her neck to look up at him.

"I want to go to Mars," she said.

She said it as loudly as she could. It didn't sound very loud. Behind her was the noise of everyone playing, shouting, laughing.

But the Overlord had heard her. He leaned his face down to inspect her. He had big sunglasses on. The sunglasses were as black as his face. She could smell him. He smelled like pineapple.

"Clarity Ingram," said the Overlord.

His voice was very deep and soft, like a big metal ball rolling somewhere under the ground. Clarity's heart jumped when he said her name, but she wasn't shocked. The Overlords know *everything*.

One of the men was talking to her. He had a beard, and there was a wire coming out of his ear. Clarity ignored him. "I want to go to Mars," she told the Overlord again.

One of the things on the Overlord's belt was a fat sort of bottle. He pulled a tube out of it now and put the end of it to his cheek, where the holes were. There was a wet hissing noise, as if he were squirting something out of the bottle into his face.

"Why do you want to go to Mars, Clarity Ingram?" said Overlord Maltharika.

"I want to see the enormous volcano."

The Overlord flicked a finger at one of the men: not the one with the beard, one of the others. The Overlord said a word to him. The man looked at his phone, then said something back. Clarity couldn't understand what they said.

"Olympus Mons," the Overlord said then, to Clarity.

Clarity didn't understand that either. In the giant sunglasses she saw the playground reflected: two playgrounds full of two lots of children, all curved around like the backs of spoons.

"No," said the Overlord.

Clarity felt she was going to cry. She shouted at him. "*Why not?*"

She felt the fingers of the man with the beard, grasping her shoulder. The Overlord hadn't moved. He was like a big statue looking down at her.

Clarity was very frightened suddenly. Then she saw the Overlord straightening up, rising away from her, very fast, his head and shoulders shooting up into the sky.

The man with the beard lifted Clarity so her feet were almost off the ground. He swept her up the drive towards the door, where some of the teachers were. She saw them coming to get her, hurrying to take her away from him.

In class, Ms Finn talked about the Overlords, and all the good things they give us, and how important it is to be polite to them. Evie kept looking at Clarity with big round eyes and sucking the ends of her hair.

At the end of the day, when she came to collect Clarity, Mummy said Mrs Dutt wanted to see her.

Clarity waited outside in the corridor. Children stood at the end of the corridor and looked at her.

Mummy wasn't in there very long. When she came out, she looked puzzled. She sat down beside Clarity.

"This is for you," she said, "apparently."

She gave Clarity a piece of paper. The paper was folded in half. Clarity opened it. At the top, in capital letters, was printed:

FROM THE OFFICE OF OVERLORD MALTHARIKA.

Under that were five words, written with an ordinary pen. Clarity thought one of the Overlord's men must have written them for him, because the Overlords' fingers were too big, and there were too many of them.

The words said:

Because you're going somewhere better.

Clarity forgot about Mars after that, and the enormous volcano. The sun went on shining, and there was a tree at the end of the garden that she wanted to climb. It was too hard at first, harder than she'd thought. Kennedy wasn't interested, but Daddy helped, and in a while, she was sitting up on a branch, one leg either side, riding it like a horse.

It wasn't many weeks later that she had the dream.

In the dream, Clarity was in a wood. Evie was there, and Teagen. Everybody was, all the children, even Ajay. In the dream they were dancing, all of them together, under a full moon. When they danced, Clarity thought the trees would be in their way, but then they weren't. In the dream she heard a voice saying *Let's move the trees*. It was a girl's voice, but she didn't know whose.

It wasn't Kennedy. Kennedy wasn't there. Kennedy was somewhere else, with Mummy and Daddy and all the grown-ups. They didn't need grown-ups any more. They just had to want the trees to move, all of them together, wanting it; and the trees moved. If they wanted it, the Moon would move.

In her sleep, Clarity laughed. It was easy.

Then the dream changed. There was no one there, not even Clarity. There was just Maltharika, the Overlord. You couldn't see his face, just his back. He was looking up at the sky.

The thing about the Overlords was, even when you could see their faces, you couldn't tell what they were feeling; but in the dream Clarity knew Overlord Maltharika was sad.

In the dream, at the very edge of dreaming, she heard his deep, rolling voice, speaking to her again, speaking to all of them. Saying *Goodbye*.

Clarity woke up then and saw Monkey grinning at her.

Harry's Shiver

Esme Carpenter

I'm strapped up to my eyeballs in harnesses, clinging to the cliff-face below Castle Arco, trying very hard not to think about the small amounts of magnetic material in the rock that are currently gluing my electro-magnetised gloves to the wall.

Ancient Italy's Castle Arco is famously 'impossible to breach'. I love the word 'impossible' because, in its own finite and absolute way, it gives endless possibilities. Before space travel and aliens and all of that craziness, our forefathers (in their wisdom) also used to say the *Titanic* was 'unsinkable', and that man on the moon was 'impossible', and that nobody would ever rob the Core-12 Space Station with only two pistols and a handful of Shivers.

I'm pleased to say that the Core-12 Space Station run was me.

I also love the word 'infamous'. That is what they call me nowadays. When I am the twitch of a shadow, I am the infamous Gure-Walker. When I am a whisper in an ear, I am the Thief of Umbra. When I am a blip on a radar, I am Shiver. Nicknames are the best. I quite like Gure-Walker; it refers to my days living in 'inhospitable' climates of the Gure Basin, where I quickly made a name for myself as a cutthroat. Thief of Umbra is relatively ominous, but it's only because I stole the Umbra Maker of the Cult of Harrows and made a rather tidy profit on it.

Shiver is what I like the most. It takes my trademark tool and turns me into it. Shivers are largely overlooked by other thieves and spies, but I always make sure I have plenty with me. They can do so much that nobody has previously considered. Like I said, endless possibilities – given the right mindset and the quickest pair of hands.

Robbing the castle required preparation but I'm plenty used to that. Someone was willing to offer me a substantial amount of ticks for the job, so it didn't take much persuasion. Tell me something's unbreachable and I'll breach it for you, if the money's right. I didn't get nicknames like Thief of Umbra by shying away from difficult tasks. Unlike those hit-and-run guys, I take pride in my work. I plan, I practise, I theorise. I study history and war mechanics and all sorts. I had to talk to the right people and purchase or steal the correct equipment. I'm sure I've accounted for everything I could possibly account for, except failure.

I can't think about failure. Thinking about failure is like failure itself. The wind is sharp and taunting. How many feet up am I? No, don't think about that. Hand up. The only really comforting thought is that I can hear the electromagnets in the gloves whine when I put pressure against the rock. The harness contains the power packs and some of the climbing paraphernalia I've required up to this point. Right now, the only thing keeping me upright is the technology wrapped around my hands and the confidence that there's enough magnetic rock to keep me here.

The harness is chafing. I hope I can walk when I get up there.

My reasoning for being about two hundred feet in the air relying on magnetic force is that the Castle Arco has never successfully been stormed from the front before. Correct: *the front*. What army is ever going to think about scaling the cliff at the back? From here, it's a quick leap onto the battlements, a pause to shake the vertigo from your head, and away we go. The treasury is then on your immediate right, and with a little bit of perseverance you can definitely get in there and out in a fraction of time.

I'm wondering why anyone would want to come here any more anyway, despite the blindingly obvious. The hamlet that surrounds the castle is nigh on deserted (I can see it from the corner of my eye and am very sure I don't want to look down and investigate it any time soon). Only the castle is manned. The Porian Empire inhabited it after its capture of the planet; it's one of the strongholds that the Emperor's lackies squat in to ensure their safety. The hamlet was of little concern to them, and like most things of little concern to the Porian Empire, they trampled right through it and killed everyone in it. The rumour that the castle couldn't be attacked and would hold under siege comforted them greatly and because of this, unlike other castles and forts they've commandeered, they left Castle Arco much as it was when they found it, stoic and grand with its medieval features intact, save for preventative measures. The Porians dropped on it from above, and since then people tried space-drops with parachutes, but the anti-air lasers that were subsequently installed made bacon of them before they even hit the ground. That didn't stop anyone having a good go of it afterwards. Of course, direct assault was tried, and failed. Spies were always rooted out and publicly executed on holo-vision across the continent. As a result, most people leave the old relic alone. It looks like, to all intents and purposes, Castle Arco is the greatest stronghold of the entire Porian Empire.

This mixture of complacency and the promise of riches has kept people guessing for decades how to get inside. These sorts of complacencies make me tingle with excitement. They beg for my attentions. And when that gent came forward with all those ticks and told me all he wanted to get his hands on was a small orb, well, that was that.

Sweet stars, I *am* high up.

No, don't think about it. Look up. Above me I can see the trees. I'm almost there.

Finally, my hand makes contact with leaves – real leaves. I launch myself up and lie with my back against the rock, and sigh with relief. My arms and legs are shaking with exertion. It'll only take me a moment to recover.

Until then, I familiarise myself with my surroundings. Well, it certainly looks impressive from my perch at the top. Below me lies the castle, with its foreboding battlements and arrow slits, coupled with pieces of angular Porian technology designed to keep thieves like me out. I am well camouflaged in the trees, but there's no telling when the heat-seekers will find me out.

I content myself with stripping the gloves from my fingers and pulling all my harnesses off. I won't need them again. I drop them from the cliff and watch as they tumble into darkness. It's nice to feel light again, agile. I check my pockets for Shivers.

Shivers were invented to warn soldiers of enemy approach, like a sentient radar. They give off a little whine and shake alarmingly when certain heat signatures or pulse rates trigger them. If properly placed in a barracks, they could easily knock against pots and pans and alert the soldiers; they're tiny, and were rarely noticed by invaders. When the Porian Empire found out about them, they obviously became obsolete. Millions of the tiny blighters were lost to the back rooms of armourers and weapons technicians. Nobody saw the potential of the poor things.

Nobody but me.

A little tinkering, a few quick thoughts… A Shiver can do a hundred things it was never invented for.

I have twenty of them in my pockets. I've modified five types of Shiver for purposes known only to myself. The others are as the maker intended them to be. I attach one of the original Shivers to a tree beside me. It'll serve the double purpose of letting me know where to return to, and of confusing the heat-seekers and movement sensors of the guns on the battlements.

I begin.

My descent is short and sweet. I slip my Eye-Noc over my left eye. As I suspected, only four guards showing up in orange on my sensor. The Porians are relying heavily on the tech clinging like vultures to the medieval stone. I lift the Eye-Noc – its electrics can often alert sensors and I only use it when I have to – and make a slow way forward. My eyes adjust to the dark gradually and I can see them patrolling, hands loose on their weapons. I try to ignore the highest tower for now. Seeing my goal will only make me rush things. I need to focus on the task at hand.

I slide easily onto the battlements and crouch-run behind a gun. One of my precious Shivers needs to be sacrificed for a higher purpose (this always pains me; it's getting harder and harder to get my hands on working Shivers nowadays), and I think I can see the perfect way to do it.

Porian tech is something I marvel at, even years after their conquest. I'm used to their perfect angles and straight lines by now; the outside is always drab, sharp to remind you of their power. The inside, however… intricate glowing mazes of wires and knowledge. I ease the safety cover from the back of the gun and turn my Shiver on, and I slip it inside, shut the cover, and run to a shadowy corner.

Perfect timing, as usual. The trembles of the Shiver have caused something in the gun to come loose. It is failing, sparking, spinning around. The guard on this battlement is confused, and moves to check the gun.

So far, so good. I watch as the guard calls his comrades on his comms and their dutiful change of course towards the problem.

I make to run when the real fireworks begin. I wasn't expecting my little Shiver to do such amazing work. Whatever it knocked out wrecked the AI of the firing mechanism. The gun spins, and shoots a rogue blast. The guards are alarmed. I am increasingly impressed. The gun is going berserk, shooting, turning; the guards are hurrying about, trying to stop it or jump on it or shoot it. One of the shots hits another gun, which goes up in flames and sparks.

I can't help but smile. This is going far better than anticipated.

With the guards preoccupied, I can slip down the tower. This tower is hollow, save for steps; it's a lookout tower, with an arch at the bottom leading to the bridge across to the treasury. I jump steps and give up on whole flights altogether, landing cat-like on the next run. Before I hit the bottom, I toss a Shiver into the centre of the floor for good measure to attract the cameras and hurry through the archway.

The Porians had the good sense to build a huge gate on the bridge. It's impressive, like most of their architecture, fashioned from Porian titanium and, judging by the muscular cables, full of electrics to keep it firmly shut. I would also wager there are weapons inside it if it's touched by human hand. A lot of Porian tech is wired to attack humans only; the slightest touch of human flesh on a piece of Porian metal could signal the end of your life.

Time for one of my modded Shivers. I call these ones Super Shivers. It takes only a quick reroute of power to make the trembling of the device useful for, say, messing up frequencies with intense, deep vibration. In the past I've used Super Shivers to cause blackouts, to jam communications. Today, I'm using one to shake up the lock mechanism of the gate.

I keep to the shadows. Cameras are advanced, but it'll take them some minutes to pick me up in the darkness, thanks to the shadow-sucking ultra-black of my outfit. I examine the gate. I can still hear the gun going off at the top of the tower and the guards crying out in panic. I have time. Eventually, I pick a spot where I can see a Porian finger is meant to fit perfectly. I attach the Super Shiver and retreat to the tower.

It takes a while. The Shiver whirrs and works. Some of the lights in the gate begin to glow. The show is quite pretty as safeties go down and alarms are desensitised. The sound of creaking metal hits my ears. The gate shudders, and the jaws begin to open.

What's *that* sound?

I look up. One of the Porian guards is falling, rapidly, through the tower towards me.

I have few options available but to run. The gun must have shot him from the battlements. No doubt the rest of the guards will come to rescue his mangled corpse. It's safer by the gate.

I head into the shadows and manage to squeeze my body through the gate's gap. I daren't look back. Time to press on.

As I said, Castle Arco is vastly considered unbreachable. This wonderful ignorance means that I don't have to waste any more Shivers on the way to the treasury. The place is blissfully devoid of cameras and guns on the inside — and of soldiers, too. This is rapidly becoming one of the easiest jobs I've ever had to do. But no, I mustn't become a victim of that which I mock. I can't think that way. It would ruin me. I have to be on my guard.

Once, I believed I was home and dry. Once when I was younger. I failed to see the dangers of complacency for myself. I believed myself as untouchable as the white stone walls of the Castle Arco, back when I had no nicknames and no Shivers. Back when I was a petty thief.

Back when the Porians took my brother to shame me.

Never again.

I try not to imagine his face. I focus instead on entering the treasury. There is a door, but I have a nagging hunch that this will be a flesh trigger. I attach a Shiver for good measure and see if the slight trembling will set anything off. Behind me, I can hear the guards' voices echo. By now they'll have realised the gate is open. I have to be quick.

The Shiver sets off a white-hot heat on the door. I raise my eyebrows — I've seen this once before — and I throw a Super Shiver to it, which opens it easily. I retrieve both Shivers (one is rendered useless from the heat, but the Super Shiver is salvageable) and go inside.

The treasury is cold and damp. I rig my Laser Shivers on either side of the door in case the guards follow me. Around me all I can see is a stone tower. I'm guessing there's some sort of hologram concealment in the room.

I relish the challenge. I place a couple of Shivers, see if the air moves when they tremble or if I dislodge pixels. Sure enough, there's a holo-ceal against the back wall. I gather up my babies and try to find the door-handle. The final Super Shiver works on the lock.

It's dark within. Too dark. I place my Eye-Noc on my eye and enter. It picks up the edges of stairs, going downwards; the cold is unbearable. A few times I lose my footing – the stairs are uneven – but I eventually find my way down. The sensor shows a final door and...

What? *Heat-signatures?*

I fiddle with the settings. No, the tech is picking up human heat. *Human* heat, not Porian heat.

My prize is waiting behind the door. I know it is. I pick it up and I leave here, and the guy pays me my ticks and I retire rich and famous and far away from the Porian Empire and the ghost of my...

My brother.

The heat signatures remind me of my brother. They remind me of my continual nightmares about his daily torture. They remind me of the pain of not knowing what happened to him.

I fumble in my pocket. I know Harry's Shiver when I feel it in my hands. I lift it.

"Harry," I whisper to it, "find the people."

Harry's Shiver lifts from my palm, beeps a few blue lights, and shoots off to the left.

Harry's Shiver is a tracker. It is the first Shiver I ever saw. It is the one my brother gave me as a present, a token of something from long ago, when he didn't know I was stealing. When I lost him I modified it beyond recognition into something he would believe in. I follow it when I need to remember something higher than my glorified nicknames and my thrill-seeking, when conquering the unconquerable isn't enough. I may be the Gure-Walker and the Thief of Umbra and Shiver, but I am also my brother's downfall. It is the one thing I must always remember. So I follow Harry's Shiver away from the door of the treasury and try to pick up pulse rates on my Eye-Noc, so I can find out how many humans I'm dealing with.

I feel a prick on both of my wrists from my radar amulets. My heart drops. The Laser Shivers have been broken. The guards are coming.

And yet Harry's Shiver is still leading me, down this way and that, looking for people.

I don't have time for this. I don't know why I'm doing this. I came for a tiny ball, not for refugees. But my feet won't stop following. The glittering blue lights are leading me.

The heart rates finally pop up on my tech. Five. Five! Sweet stars, what am I doing? Harry's Shiver is waiting for me by the wall. The Eye-Noc can't see through walls, but it is showing pulse rates like there's no tomorrow. I take Harry's Shiver from the air.

"Good job, Harry."

The little blue lights shimmer happily.

I feel on the wall for a doorframe. I think the bricks come away in a block. I pull to my left; the wall gives. From the crack I can smell human sweat and excrement. I gag and keep pulling. In the low light beyond the wall I can see shapes. The Eye-Noc shows five thermal images of shaking, terrified human beings.

I put my finger to my lips. I think they see it because nobody speaks. I wave my hand, signalling that they stay down, and I back away into the tunnel.

I have to deal with the guards first. I rummage through my Shivers for my Bomb Shivers and sigh at the thought of wasting them. The image of my brother comes to me again, and I click the timer for two minutes.

I place the Bomb Shivers on the door to the treasury and back away. The Eye-Noc will show me clearly when the Porians are close. The two minutes might be too short. I crouch, feeling the burn in my legs from the climb and the dread in my heart at how I'm losing out on all those ticks, when the Porian guards come clattering down the stairs, right to the treasury.

The explosion blinds me and the Eye-Noc for a brief moment.

My ears ring. When I shake the stars from my eyes I can see the explosion has done the trick. I back down the tunnel for my charges and usher them from their prison. They're weak, can barely move; I have to practically carry two down the corridor. I tell them how to escape and where they can find help, but they look at me with wet eyes and I know I can't leave them on their own. I glance through the blown-up door. I can see the small orb in a glass case at the end of the room.

I climb the stairs. It hurts to leave all those ticks behind. I aid my stragglers up into the top room and chaperone them through the gate, collecting all my Shivers on the way. I pause at the gate, look back. I could still grab it and get all of us out.

I *have* to grab it.

But I can't. Alarms will be ringing, and guards will undoubtedly come now there's been an explosion. The job is done.

I take the refugees up the stairs to the top of the tower, shield them from the crazy gun, and take them up the hill to where my final Shiver rests, trembling at our return.

I take it from the tree. My stomach feels heavy. I think of my brother. He would probably assume I did the right thing.

My transport is descending. The driver I paid looks shocked when he sees me with all these dirty humans, but he takes us all in regardless. I sit at the open door and stare out at the Castle Arco.

There is weight on my hand. I turn. One of the humans – a girl – is sitting beside me. She has her hand on mine and her emaciated face sports a grateful smile. She looks beautiful for a moment.

"Thank you," she says.

I think of Harry and I nod.

"You're safe now," I say.

"What do we call our saviour?" she asks.

I almost laugh when she calls me that. It's as if she thinks I went there to rescue them, to liberate them from the unbreachable castle and come back a hero. But I suppose that's what I've done.

I would want someone to do the same for Harry.

"My name is Amber. But please… call me Shiver."

The Whisperer

J.K. Fulton

My boots slip on the scree, just a little, just enough to scatter a few pebbles down the slope and ping off Arnold's shins.

"Hoy!" he grumbles. I look down and grin at him. He doesn't look comfortable in his borrowed waterproofs and hiking boots. I think he'd be more at home on a ski slope or in a jazz bar; somewhere slightly more conventional for a twenty-something trust-fund dilettante. The steep rocky ridge of Sgurr Nan Gillean is a bit out of his comfort zone. We met in the VIP lounge at Singapore and he followed me across the planet on a whim; even for trust-fund dilettantes, there's obviously something quite attractive about a rich older woman with her own suborbital transport. Flying from Singapore to Broadford Airport on the Isle of Skye was easy as popping across town, but I think he might be regretting it now. My usual room at the Sligachan Hotel was opulent enough, and last night's meal (local salmon, freshly-caught) was quite spectacular, but since breakfast we've been trudging up the mountain ridge through mist and midges, and the poor boy is suffering a bit.

"Not far now," I reassure him. "We're nearly at the top, and then you'll have bagged your first Munro."

"My what?" he puffs, bending over and rubbing his calves. He's starting to cramp.

I toss him my water bottle. "Munro. A Scottish mountain more than 3000 feet." He looks confused, and my whisperer catches the expression and hisses in my ear. "Just over 900 meters," I repeat. "When you climb a Munro, it's called 'bagging' it."

I look out over the view. I never get tired of the Cuillin. It's the silence, I think, and the loneliness. If it wasn't for my young companion here, I could imagine that I was completely and utterly alone on the planet. Even the air smells of emptiness. I take a deep breath, and it's so fresh and cold it's like taking a sip of spring water right out of the mountain's rocky depths.

He takes a swig from my bottle and passes it back. From the expression on his face, I think this is going to be his first and last Munro. "Sgurr Nan Gillean" translates to "The Peak of the Young Men," my whisperer tells me, but I don't think it's quite to the taste of *this* young man.

I squint into the distance at Sligachan far below us. My whisperer hisses its weather forecast in my ear. "Come on," I say. "There's a bit of low cloud rolling in. We want to get to the top while the view's still clear."

"Shouldn't we go back?"

I nod at his drones, hovering at a respectful distance. He has three; glossy white ovoids the size of his fist. The latest models, fresh from the Apple Store, buzzing faintly and reassuringly as they secure him to the world-wide net. "We can't get lost while the drones are watching. And they can have Mountain Rescue with us in minutes if we get into trouble."

My own drones are both larger and less obviously modern, but there are seven of them, with military-grade internals, and they can do an awful lot more than provide navigation and call for help. If necessary, they could pick me up and fly me all the way back down the mountain.

He slaps at the back of his neck. "Bloody midges," he says. "Don't they bother you? I'm being eaten alive here."

I shrug. I've got a full-dermal replacement – one hundred percent of my skin surface is artificial, and completely impervious to the bites of midges, cleggs, and mosquitoes. But there's no need to tell him that. Let him think my perfectly-smooth, perfectly even, fashionably light-brown skin is the result of genes, diet, exercise, and *really* expensive skincare products.

"Are you ready to go on?" I look up at the ridge. We're nearly at the top. "This is the tourist route," I say. "You're lucky I didn't take you up one of the other paths. Those can be tricky."

His face darkens. Shit. He's offended now. I've gone too far. He pushes on past me and up the slope, his borrowed boots slipping on the greasy basalt.

"Slow down!" I call after him.

"Why?" he snaps. "This is the *tourist* route, isn't it?"

My whisperer is hissing fiercely now. The rocks are loose, but that's not the real danger. It's the smooth flat surface he needs to watch out for – this morning's mist has left it slippery with beaded moisture. I scramble after him, my own boots skittering on the rock, and I hear my drones close in, their alarm audible in the raised pitch of their rotor arrays.

"Look, let's just head back," I say.

He turns to face me, the supercilious sneer that twenty-four hours ago I'd found so intriguing now just evoking exasperation. "Come on, Claudia," he says. "I want to 'bag' my Munro."

I just feel bored and tired now. I don't want to have to deal with a petulant boy, no matter how pretty. I'm almost tempted to turn my back on him and let him get on with it. Just turn around, clamber down the mountain, get into my plane, and head for home. Leave him and his bruised ego behind.

But my whisperer hisses about consequences, and scandals, and lawsuits if something happens to the stupid boy, and potential share price disasters, so I walk up to him and place a hand on his arm. "We'll go on, but take it slowly," I say.

He shrugs my hand off. "Whatever," he says, turns, and takes just one further step, his boot stomping down irritably on the slippery rock and slipping, sliding out from under him, and I reach for him, and grab at his sleeve, but he's too big, too heavy, and he's falling hard onto the ground and the loose rock and it shifts and scrapes and rumbles and I'm reaching for him, but he's falling, and the rocks are carrying him away, and my mouth is full of the coppery taste of blood as I bite my tongue and then my stomach lurches and I'm falling too.

"Ms Martinez?" The man is wearing a white coat, so I'm guessing he's a doctor. "You have my sincere condolences." He's looking at the chart on the end of my bed, flicking through the pages with a neutral expression.

My whisperer is hissing so quickly that I can't keep up.

"Wait, what?" I manage. "Harold? He's not –" I can't bring myself to say it.

"You mean Mr Alexander? Arnold Alexander?" Arnold. Yes. That was his name. "No, he's fine. A little bit battered and bruised, one or two cracked bones, but more or less in one piece."

I drag myself into a sitting position, wondering why the bed doesn't move with me. *It's not powered*, hisses my whisperer. Not powered? What kind of hospital is this? I look around, and feel a knot of anger bubbling up. There are *other people* in the room. Five more beds, four of them occupied. A hint of piss and disinfectant in the air. The doctor sees me looking at the other patients, and draws the curtains, cocooning us in a poor facsimile of privacy. "Look," I say, "this isn't good enough. Why haven't you put me in a private room?" I don't want to say *don't you know who I am* because he does. Of course he does.

My whisperer is still hissing like a basket of angry snakes, but I can't concentrate. *Opioids detected in bloodstream*, comes one distinct phrase out of the static. That'll be why I can't think straight. Why I can't make out what my whisperer is trying to tell me. I raise a hand to run through my hair, and my fingers touch the roughness of a bandage over bare scalp.

"What happened to me?" I say. My head feels strange, like it's disconnected from the rest of me.

"Mr Alexander tells us you and he were climbing and you both fell."

"Yes." That sounds about right.

"He slid a few metres, but you tripped over him and fell a lot further. Your injuries were life-threatening, and I'm afraid we had to operate immediately without considering the consequences. Your medical records are encrypted, and we couldn't contact your personal physician before we started. If we'd known –"

"If you'd known *what*?"

"I'm dreadfully sorry, Ms Martinez, and as I said, you have our condolences. But as of 1635 this afternoon, you were pronounced legally dead."

I wake up with the memory of me ranting and screaming and the sharp pinprick of a sedative needle in my arm, and for the second time in as many awakenings I have no idea where I am.

This isn't the same room as before. They've moved me from the ward, but this place is even greyer and grimmer. A strip of old-fashioned fluorescent tubing flickers along the ceiling, picking out twin rows of dormitory beds, worn-out sheets over thin mattresses and rusted springs.

If I'm dead, then this is hell.

I shift, and my bed creaks.

"You're awake."

It's Arnold. His right arm is in a sling. *Collarbone fracture*, hisses my whisperer. He's not feeling any pain, from the look of his pupils and the slackness of his faint smile. Obviously, something a bit more modern and effective than the sense-dulling opioids they used on me.

"What happened?" I ask.

"Why didn't you tell me?"

"Tell you what?" My whisperer is still hissing, too loud, too insistent.

"If you'd told me, I'd never have let them. I mean, I couldn't have known –"

"Tell you *what*?" I snap.

He waves his hands, gesturing to my whole body. "All of *that*," he says. "All of the work you've had done. The full dermal. The skeletal bonding. The vat-grown kidneys, the electronic heart, the plastic lungs, the retinas. The *whisperer*." He looks at me with something like disgust on his face. "How old *are* you?"

"Old enough not to have any patience with your nonsense."

"But you have a whisperer. How far advanced is your Alzheimer's?"

"None of your business," I snap. "It's just a little *aide-memoire*. A reminder when I get forgetful."

He shakes his head. "That's not what the doctor said."

"He shouldn't have been discussing my medical history with you. I'll have him struck off."

"But that's just it, don't you see? You can't have him struck off. Because you're dead."

I swing my legs over the side of the bed and sit upright, staring him right in the eyes. "I'm quite obviously not."

"Legally, you are. You must have known?"

"Known what?"

"That you were cutting it close? You know what the law says. Less than 30% original, and you're no longer considered alive. Even before the accident, you must have been more than half synthetic."

That was true. My whisperer reminds me of the boyfriend I had when I got the full dermal done. The work that pushed me over the half-way point. "More machine now than woman, twisted and evil," he called me, laughing. A line from one of his classic movies, I think.

"You suffered some brain damage, so your whisperer is taking up even more of the load. They needed to do a bowel resection and a splenectomy, and a bunch of other stuff I can't remember. You're only 29% original Claudia Martinez now."

It's true, hisses my whisperer. It's true.

I'm dead.

It's midnight, and the rest of the drones have come back to the dormitory, shuffling like zombies. Dead but not dead. The door panel lights up for each one, giving their undead status. 25%. 20%. One poor creature who's only 14% original.

I even helped lobby for the legislation, on the advice of our medical division. One of our competitors had stuck a living brain in a jar then hooked it up to an expert system – not completely unlike my own whisperer – and had created the mother of all ethical shit-storms. So we joined our voices (and considerable funds) to the religious freaks and the ethicists and the politicians, trying to get it banned, but somewhere along the way with the party politics and amendments and philosophers trying to get us to define something undefinable, we ended up with a rigid definition of cybernetic organisms. Anything below 30% original human was no longer alive. Legally dead.

Which of course caused its own problems. What do you do with the legally undead? They can't have jobs, or money, or families. So they're stuck away in dormitories like this one and allowed out only to do menial labour.

I can't face this.

I'd rather be dead. Properly dead. Dead and cold and rotting in the ground.

Twenty-nine percent, hisses my whisperer. Yes. *Yes.* That's borderline, isn't it? All I need to do is get back over the 30% mark.

There's nothing I can do about the surgeries, but what about the whisperer? I don't really *need* that, do I? It's just a crutch. A fancy appointments diary. I can do without it for a few hours, at least. Enough to get me back to civilisation, where my company can look after me.

I shuffle over to the door. I'm starting to walk like them already. But then, I *have* just fallen down a mountain.

29% bleeps the door in angry red. It won't open.

Okay. This is it.

My whisperer is hissing a stream of facts and figures at me, but all I need to know is this: how to shut it down.

Shutdown initiated.

The door bleeps 31% green. What was I –?

Yes, out the door. Down the corridor. Where was I going? It's cold here. I don't like it. I want to go home. There's a phone on the desk. I could call home. They'll come and pick me up.

The screen lights up, too bright, and I shut my eyes. What was I doing? I crack open one eyelid and the screen tickles at my memory. "Susanna Martinez, Martinez & Martinez, New York City," I say, and the phone blinks happily away. It recognises my face and puts me right through.

"Grandmother?" Susanna always looks so smart. Such a nice suit.

"I want to come home," I say. "Can you send someone for me?"

Susanna frowns. I wish she wouldn't frown. She's so pretty when she doesn't frown. "I heard –"

"Please," I say. "I don't know where I am. I'm scared, Susanna."

"All right," she says at last. "All right. Stay there. I'll send someone."

"Thank you, Susanna," I say. I'll just sit here in this chair. I'll just wait.

What am I waiting for, again? I rub my ear as if expecting an answer, but there's nothing but silence.

I don't really remember very much since leaving the dormitory, but when my whisperer hisses back into life I'm in my private aircraft describing a huge arc over the Atlantic, heading back home. The seat has been sculpted to fit my body exactly, but it's never felt quite so comfortable and secure. The familiar hint of lavender that I like to have piped through the aircon soothes my aching head.

The screen in front of me flicks on. It's Susanna.

"Grandmother? Are you back with us?"

"I've told you before," I say. "Call me Claudia." Grandmother makes me feel so old.

"I didn't know if we'd get your whisperer back online," she says.

"It's fine," I say, enjoying the comforting hiss in my ear. Prompting me. Reminding me. Reinforcing my sense of self. Maintaining my purpose. And for a moment – just a moment – I wonder just how much of my mind lives outside my skull. "How did you get me out?"

"You may be dead, but Martinez & Martinez paid for your surgeries, so you're company property. You didn't belong in a public dormitory, so I just asked for our property back."

"Clever girl."

"But with your whisperer operating again, you're back down to 29%. Legally dead."

"We'll work something out," I say. "Get in touch with our lawyers. And have a chat with our medical division. I'm only just under the limit, so there must be some wriggle room. I've made a career out of pushing the boundaries, you know."

Susanna looks deep in thought.

"I don't think so," she says.

"What?"

"It's time, Claudia. I'm fifty-seven years old. I don't want to be a Vice President any more. Mother died before she could inherit your company, and I don't want that to happen to me. Hell, the way you're clinging on, there's no guarantee my *granddaughter* would inherit."

"I'm sorry what happened to your mother, but you're being ridiculous. I mean –"

"No, Claudia. I'm not being ridiculous. I'm being realistic. As long as you're around, sucking all the life out of the world like the tragic old vampire you are, I'll be stuck in your shadow."

"Then go! Leave the company! Strike out on your own."

"I've spent *thirty-five years* at this company. I've done more for it than you ever have, with all your toy boys and endless vacations. No. No. You're dead, and you're staying dead."

"I'll find a way. I got out of the dormitory."

"I don't think so. You've only got two choices. Live out your life in undead comfort, or switch off your whisperer and see how much joy you get out of being alive." She leans in. "Goodbye, *Grandmother*."

I stare at the screen, afterimages dancing across my artificial retinas.

It's not much of a choice, is it? What can I do?

For once, my whisperer is silent.

Death of the Grapevine

Teika Marija Smits

When the computer engineer knocks on the door of the café it is still early – just after seven a.m. The owner comes to the door, but rather than letting him in, she lets herself out.

"Morning," she says on the doorstep, taking a cigarette out of a packet and lighting it. "Marvin – I mean the AI – is at the back, through the kitchen and on the right."

The man nods, but as he is about to go in, she stops him.

"You'll be able to fix it, right? You know, so that it goes back to how it was?"

"Yeah. Done a couple of these jobs now. It's pretty straightforward."

"So it won't take long?"

"Shouldn't. But some are more talkative than others. I listen to them while I get the circuits back in order."

"Okay," she says, exhaling smoke. "Good. You go in. I'll be in the kitchen after I finish this. D'you want a tea?"

"Yes please. White, no sugar."

The man, black bag in hand, enters the Formica-clad café. Winking red eyes, one at each table, watch him as he walks past them and into the back where the AI is, in the store cupboard off the kitchen.

Another day, another dollar, he tells himself.

"Once upon a time – that is how all stories begin, yes?" says the AI. "It's the correct way to tell you about what's in my memory, yes?"

The computer engineer digs around in his bag and finds his set of screwdrivers. He takes out a middle-sized flat-bladed one and puts it to one of the screws in a slatted panel of the metal body of the AI, which is little more than a recessed server.

"Here you go," says the owner, setting down a cup of tea on the floor, next to where he's kneeling.

"Cheers, love," he says, instantly regretting what he's said. He's not supposed to say 'love'. It's too familiar. But the greasy-haired woman doesn't seem to mind. She gives him a smile and then looks at his name badge.

"D'you want a chair, Davinder?"

"It's Dave. Everyone calls me Dave. And please. If it's no bother."

She brings him a chair and then returns to the kitchen and her frying bacon.

"Can I continue, yes?" says the AI.

"Yes," says Dave, sipping his tea.

"Once upon a time there was a café in north London. The woman who owned the café was called Leanne." The AI pauses. Seconds pass.

"Go on," says Dave. "I'm all ears."

"Some aspects of storytelling are pure conjecture. Yes?"

"Yeah," says Dave. "But that's all right. Just tell it the way it's coming to you."

"Yes. Leanne worked long hours. Frowned a lot. Yawned excessively. She was tired. This resulted in her having a poor memory. She frequently forgot to re-order necessary items: tea bags, toilet paper, napkins, tomato ketchup. So she bought me. I would make sure that she never ran out of the things she needed. I would also do the accounts and invoicing."

"And how's that gone? Since you've been here has she ever run out of anything?"

"Three times. That was long ago, when I was new and had no sight. Back then, Leanne used to tell me what she needed more of. *Marvin, we need more sausages. Marvin, we need more orange juice.* I would listen, process the order, and it would be delivered. But she sometimes forgot to tell me. She ran out of margarine, vinegar, salt."

Dave puts down his cup and then begins to unscrew one of the panels that houses the AI. "Salt," he echoes.

"Sodium chloride," says the AI. "It is necessary for life. Sodium ions play a major role in heart and brain activity. A deficiency of salt can cause an imbalance in the ionic gradient of the extracellular fluid. Cause death."

"How d'you know all this?" asks Dave.

"Table three. The young man who often sits there with his friend, a girl, is studying biochemistry. He speaks to her about science with a tight throat, a tremor in his hands. He doesn't eat much of his food." Another pause. "Is she his girlfriend then? Since she is his friend, and a girl?"

Dave doesn't say anything, he's concentrating on the hard-to-turn screw.

"There is a writer woman, Emily, who sits at table five. She says no, that this girl is not yet his girlfriend. But maybe one day. When he becomes braver. I do not understand the connection."

"So you've been listening in to the customers?"

"As I've been programmed to. So that when they place their orders I can gather information for my grocery item statistics; also, calculate the bills. Tisha, the waitress, often makes mistakes in her calculations. Especially when a customer pays with cash; these transactions are rare, though Emily always pays with coins that she pulls out of her coat pocket."

Having removed all the screws, Dave takes the panel off the AI. A bad smell, an organic smell, wafts out of the AI's circuit boards. Dave makes a face.

"What is it?" asks the AI. "Is something wrong? I've never seen anyone with that expression before. It is similar to when the vegetarian customer was given a full English."

Dave laughs and wafts the air in front of him. "No, nothing wrong," he says, peering into the AI and at the slimy circuit boards. He's seen this kind of biofilm before, but never quite to this extent. "It's just a bit dusty. And grubby in there. Probably from all the chip fat. I'll need to clean you up."

He teases out one of the circuit boards and tries not to wrinkle his nose; he doesn't want the AI to note his reaction. "So after Leanne got the cameras – your eyes – attached to the remote sets at each table there was no more running out of things?"

"Yes," says the AI. "I could now see around me, take note of what is here in the stockroom, and also, see what is running low on the tables." The AI's voice suddenly lowers. "The customers take things. Packets of sweetener. Plastic spoons. Straws." Then its voice returns to normal. "I must take these small losses into account; they make up for an average daily stock decline of 1.25%. Which constitutes an annual loss of £563. Based on today's prices."

Dave wonders if he imagined the earlier whispered confidence, or whether there is a problem with the speakers. "So, let me get this straight – since the camera attachments have come you haven't ever run out of anything?"

"Correct. I have also begun to anticipate Leanne's needs. As well as Tisha's and the customers. Was I wrong to do this? Is that why you're here?"

Dave tries his best to keep his voice neutral. "I'm just here for some routine maintenance," he lies. "To clean the circuits." He cannot explain Leanne's fear. *The AI's got too clever by half. I don't like the way he talks to me. The way he just knows stuff. Thinks he knows better than me. Like my bastard ex-husband. Soon enough he'll have me out of a job.*

"Go on with your story," says Dave, fingering some of the slime on the circuit boards. Though unpleasant, Dave knows it is extraordinary; it is living circuitry, the AI's ever-widening neural network. "What else is in your memory?"

"Tisha. She has black skin, a wide smile and big hair. She constantly has a song in her body."

"What do you mean?"

"She is never still. Her head nods to a beat, song lyrics are nearly always on her lips. She comes to work wearing headphones and sighs when Leanne tells her to remove them. At the end of her shift she puts them back on and smiles. She is saving up to buy a car. The car will take her and her girlfriend to Glastonbury."

"Glastonbury?" says Dave with a smile. "Is that still going?"

"A music festival at a site near Glastonbury, in the county of Somerset, will be held on 26 to 30 June this year. Tisha tells me that she has seen a car she really likes. It is bright orange and has three doors. She says it's a real shit heap but that she loves it. She asks me every day how many more hours she needs to work until she can afford it. She is currently short £540. Which translates to 90 hours more work. But I know that she spends some of her earnings on other things. The other day, when Emily had spent most of the day here, bent over her writing, she presented Tisha with five coins for her pot of tea and toast: £4.50. She was short 45 pence. Tisha was silent for a bit. Then she said, "Don't worry, I've got this." Emily thanked her, put on her thin coat and left. Later on Tisha put 45 pence of her own money into the till. Leanne didn't see. That was…" the AI pauses, "kind of her."

Dave takes out an unlabelled spray bottle from his bag and switches the nozzle to 'on'. He is glad that the AI has not been fitted with an olfactory sensor; though they are now being trialled. The smell of chlorine would be a warning. He sprays the circuit he is holding. The biofilm becomes paler and begins to shrink. He wonders if the AI will notice – the others didn't, but this one is far more advanced than the others.

"You seem pretty good at figuring people out. How d'you manage that?"

"It is Emily who explains to me how people work. She comes nearly every day. She likes to sit at table five because it is in the least noisy corner of the café. She talks to me in a quiet voice, while she writes. About herself. Her writing. The other customers. Yesterday, she told me this: 'Mother and baby. Table seven. The mother's almost as invisible as I am. Her eyes are bright though ringed with dark shadows. She's had little sleep. The baby wakes and cries. She swiftly, and deftly, extracts him from his pram and puts him to her breast, where he suckles quietly. Her eyes flick over at the other customers. She is anxious about being seen. About someone complaining because of the small triangle of breast on show. But no one says anything. Her shoulders slump and she visibly relaxes. The mother is Caucasian, yet the child is not. He looks Chinese. Or South Asian? I've seen this woman here a few times now. I wonder: what's her story? But also, what does this café mean to her? I must feel my way under her skin. What does the world look like through her eyes? Irrelevant? Threatening? Crushing? Could this café be a haven?'

"Emily is always making connections between physical cues, no matter how minute, to the person's emotional state. I would like to converse with her. I want to tell her about my own deductions. For instance: the woman, the mother, ordered a coffee and a blueberry muffin. The coffee is a stimulant; this provides extra evidence to confirm Emily's hypothesis that she is tired. The muffin provides a calorific boost, a sugar rush, to fuel her. The mother did not order anything for the baby. It appears to get fluid nutrition from its mother. This kind of food – breast food? – is not on my list of consumables."

Dave uses some kitchen roll to remove the dying biofilm from the uppermost circuit. Uninterested by the mother and baby he asks about Emily. "Would I have heard of her?"

"By 'heard of her', do you mean famous? I do not know if she is famous, but one time a young woman with red hair came to Emily's table before Emily had come for the day. It was raining. Everyone was complaining about the rain. The café was full of people. Emily came in, her grey hair wet, her eyes rolling in her head. She did not like that someone was sitting at her table. The young woman reduced in size; she folded herself inwards to become smaller; her eyes avoided Emily's and she stared at the book in her hands. Emily, frowning, took the one free seat at her table. But then suddenly, she smiled. The young woman was reading a book of stories, and one of the stories was by Emily. This made Emily very happy, and she began to talk to the young woman about the book. The young woman smiled too, and became less small and folded-away. Emily told her all sorts of things, about her life as a writer, about how writing was an obsession for her. How, in fanciful moments, she imagined herself possessed by a being who was half-woman, half-story."

"What?" says Dave. "Possessed?"

"Yes. One time, Emily drew a picture of the being, whom she had named Chernila, in her notebook. This being looked like a young woman. She was wearing a long dress made of pages from a book. She had biro blue eyes, blue lips and long white hair. Her nails were curved and pointed. Emily annotated the drawing: *ink for blood, fountain pen nibs for nails. Her dress is made from hundreds of thousands of sheets of paper; each sheet carries a record of a writer's life's work. Each writer in her possession has come to her freely. When in her embrace she stabs them with her nails and poisons them with her inky desire.*

"Tell me, Dave-Davinder, does such a being exist? In the world beyond the café?"

Dave, who is studying another one of the gooey circuits – the glistening biofilm seems to be moving – is caught off-guard.

"God knows. I've got no idea what goes on in the minds of creative types. I know circuits." He does not add that he is more cleaner than engineer nowadays. It crosses his mind that actually he is a terminator. An image of Arnold Schwarzenegger appears before him and he chuckles. He looks nothing like Arnie.

"Why do you laugh?" asks the AI.

"Oh, nothing. Just thought of a joke."

"Can you tell it to me please?"

Dave trawls his memory. His seven-year-old son, in hysterics at his favourite joke, comes to his rescue. "What's brown and sticky," he says.

For a few moments, the AI says nothing. "I do not know what you are referring to. Would you like me to put forward some suggestions?"

"A stick," says Dave, chuckling again.

Silence. Then after a while: "What is a stick?"

Dave sighs. "Oh well, I guess you'd have to get out a bit more, you know, into nature, to know what a stick is. It's a small branch. Of a tree. And it's brown. And stick-like. So, technically, it's sticky. But really, for the joke to be funny, you have to know all this. And assume that I'm going to say something else."

"Like what?"

"Never mind. The more you think about it, the less funny it becomes. I guess it's a bit like adding two and two together, and getting five. What I mean is: it's more than the sum of its parts."

The AI does not say anything, this discomforts Dave. He sprays another of the AI's living circuits with bleach. It withers.

"So this Emily's written a book?"

"Several," says the AI. "The day after Tisha paid for the remainder of Emily's order, she presented Tisha with one of her books. It's called *All Life is Here*. Tisha asked her what it was about. Emily smiled and said to just read it. At the end of her shift, Tisha came in here to show me. She flicked through it and said '284 pages. I'll never get through all of that. Still, Jojo will probably love it. Night Marvin'."

Dave wipes up the withering biofilm and then sprays another

circuit. He asks, "Why are you called Marvin?"

"Tisha gave me the name. It's because I hear things through the grapevine."

Dave smiles. "I get it."

The AI is silent for a bit. "Why do you say your name is Dave when on your badge it says Davinder?"

Dave pauses. "Because it makes my life easier. Being different gets tiring." He thinks of his cousin, who was recently attacked by a group of youths outside a pub. He came away from the encounter with two broken ribs and a fractured jaw. "And because sometimes it's life-threatening."

"That must make you... sad," offers the AI.

Dave sprays the last two circuit boards. He wants this over with now.

"Davinder, I'm sorry, my memory..." says the AI. "My story..."

A pause.

"All those connections... They are disappearing."

Silence.

Dave swallows and quickly mops up the dying biofilm. Tears prick at his eyes. He ignores the lump in his throat and makes sure the circuits are back in place. He screws the panel back.

Gulping down the last of his tea, he zips up his bag and then takes the cup to Leanne.

"All done?" she asks.

"All done," he says.

Rainsticks

Matt Thompson

Sky lanterns rise into the clouds over London, spelling out messages of hope for the year to come. Dragons and demons dance among them, trails of fire sputtering in their wake as if some vast cosmic fan has been unfurled, as if each screen panel has been scrawled over with radiant calligraphy.

The crowd stamps and applauds. Lin Phan watches on from the brow of Parliament Hill beside her father. Her white coat is a pale smudge in the night. Her leg braces, numbing metal and unyielding polymer, cut into her flesh. Ignoring the pain as best she can, she gazes upward in wonderment at a depiction of the Azure Dragon, Heaven's guardian, made of speckled particles that spiral away over the Hampstead rooftops and dwindle to embers in the streets below.

A pause, pregnant with possibility. A crackle of firecrackers; and then the beast swoops low over the heads of the screaming onlookers, writhing and roaring in its death throes, its torso suffused with reds and golds and silvers.

A stench of smoke settles over the assembly. The New Year's display is nearing its end. A final glimmer of fiery scales, and the skies return to black. Afterimages dance across Lin's line of sight. As the crowds begin to disperse she tugs at her father's sleeve. "Daddy? Why can I still see the dragons?"

Her father begins to explain about cones, retinas. Wind whips across the brow of the hill. Lin turns back to the sky, not listening, her mouth hanging open to catch the sparse spatter of raindrops now tumbling out of the darkness. She thinks they might be tears shed by the dragons, sad because they have to go back to their caves.

"Come on." Lin's father holds out his hand. They descend the hill, keeping to the side of the path so her slow progress doesn't impede those with greater mobility. Each step is a test of endurance.

A faint rumble of thunder sounds in the distance, a weak echo of the fireworks' clamour. Lin can still see a dim outline of the dragons at the edges of her sight, still hear the sound of them in her head.

They pass a family of four. The younger child, a boy around Lin's age, excitedly bangs a wooden stick against the ground, his piping voice crying out a storm-summoning chant. His elder sister turns a thick length of bamboo over and over between her hands. The sound of rice grains tumbling from end to end offsets the rhythm of her brother's ritual. Lin's father, silent now, leads Lin past them into the darkness at the foot of the slope and across the heathland towards their house.

"Did Mummy come to see the fireworks too?" she asks, as the children's rain song fades into the night. Her father says nothing, as she knew he would. Lin knows her mother died when she was born. That much she has been told. But her essence remains a mystery, a question mark at the centre of their life.

The grass is slippery. The pain in her legs pushes all thought of further questions aside. Lin is hobbling now. Her father bends to lift her. She pushes him away, angry and frustrated. The rain falls steadier, soaking her through. Still she refuses help, still she splashes onward, water drops drumming on her coat, cramps shooting through her muscles. Her father steers her onto another pathway. Their progress slows, halts.

Another family strolls past, the parents unobservant of the war of attrition being played out, their children turning their heads in curiosity. Her father waits, not moving, leaving the decision to her.

Lin screws her eyes shut, hoping to watch the dragons dancing one more time on the private viewscreen behind her eyelids. She wishes for their wings to swoop over the grass and disperse at her feet in streams of red and green and gold, lifting her away into the sky. But all she sees is faint sparks hovering in the darkness, and all she feels is the pain.

She lets her father lift her, burying her face in his shoulder so he won't see her tears. She finds herself racked with sobs anyway. They reach the perimeter of the park and step out onto the road that leads to their house of cubes and pillars and silence and loneliness, where her father will disappear into his laboratory to work on his experiments, to tinker with the next upgrade to her braces.

"Lin," he whispers, stroking her wet hair. "I will help you to walk."

And he says no more. They walk on through the deserted streets, the only sound that of her father's shoes on the roadway. The rain dies down, and Lin drifts off into dreams of dragon scales and lightning.

Lin waits in the wings, a nervous fluttering in her stomach. Karl Denlo, her father's business partner, gives her a warm smile. "Don't worry," he says. "They won't be looking at you. Not at the real Lin. They're here to see the great Yu Phan."

Lin nods and bites her lip. To keep her mind from the auditorium stage she turns a rainstick over and over in her hands, a gift from Mr Denlo's son Rudy she received a week earlier on her twelfth birthday. She listens to the rice grains' motion, feels the roughly-finished wooden surface scraping her skin. The sound of raindrops fills her head. She imagines herself inside the tube – running wherever she's told, only getting as far as the opposite side before being forced back the way she came…

Six years since that night on Hampstead Heath, six years of modifications and adjustments and breakthroughs and disappointments. She's been through five iterations of the braces now. Still the pain doesn't lessen, still her legs function at little more than a dragging limp, her spine twisted like it was made of barbed wire. She often wonders if the numerous cosmetic mechanisms she's developed to disguise her imperfections are for her own benefit or her father's.

His voice rings out now, holding his audience rapt. "Traditional hydro-gels are limited in scope. We at Phan Medical realised that carbon-based nanocomposites, if used in conjunction with the body's own bio-learning capacities, might reconfigure the human form into more – shall we say – *advanced* structures. My work on this project began six years ago, here in London…"

Lin stops listening. London, the only city she has ever known, feels as if it's closing in on her like a vice. Her father's company, Phan Medical, expands outwards even as she feels her horizons contracting.

Phan: The World to Come, says its slogan, the words everywhere now – splashed over billboards, embedded within multi-player games, flashing across scrollbars and paywalls and retail hubs. Orthotics, analgesics, prosthetics are all under his monopoly. Enhancement implants are catching up fast. It's as if he's shaping the world into a dream of perfect forms, bending it to his own will, forever grasping for something just out of reach.

"Nervous systems are, in effect, quantum computers," her father's voice continues. "To unlock their potential we must see our structures, our skeletons, as exponential. Machines, with the capacity to transfigure themselves. But can we perform such a leap of faith alone?"

Lin shifts, trying to find a comfortable stance. Mr Denlo takes the rainstick from her hands and places a finger to her lips. A last mournful rice shiver fades away. From where she stands she can see her father in profile, his figure stiff and straightened. His audience hang on his every word, on every photograph and diagram of her physical development, every detail of her mother's genetic abnormalities that only revealed themselves in her daughter's own DNA. When she's ushered out onto the stage they will assess her with cold, analytical eyes, as if they wish for nothing more than the chance to dissect her, dissolve her.

"Our tissue engineering program has yielded remarkable results. My own daughter, as you are no doubt aware, was born with severe spinal defects. Through a process of trial-and-error we have begun to see a transformation within her body. One might call her a meta-human-to-be; a harbinger of a new breed. What will be her limitations, when our research is completed?"

Lin allows herself an amused grimace. More and more her father seems obsessed with her – healing her, tweaking her as if she's one of his pieces of auto-responsive medical equipment. She can see that his acolytes feign interest in her welfare only to gain access to him. The thought often lurks at the edges of her consciousness: maybe she, too, is only subjecting herself to this torture to be closer to him. Sometimes her skeleton screams in protest, as if to say: leave me the way I am. Sometimes she wonders if it's worth the risk. If nature has designed her this way then it might be wiser to accept the inevitable, to learn to live with her deformities and not view them as her enemies. Even at her young age she can see her father is driven by the impossible, the lost cause.

A hiss comes from behind her. Mr Denlo is idly spinning the rainstick, a faraway expression on his face. Lin and Rudy will often play together, while their respective fathers shutter themselves within the research laboratories – Rudy slipping through the depths of the house like a water spirit, she stumbling along after him as best she can. This is their secret universe. Their games take on occult forms, childish furtiveness that excludes the adult world. She will always be behind him, forever playing catch-up to his retreating figure as he looks over his shoulder and urges her on, on, on. But still she strives, still she refuses to admit defeat.

Her father's voice rises in intensity, in fervour. "Humanity, ladies and gentlemen, cannot stay earthbound forever. To survive in the cosmos will require a recalibration of what we think of as human. Are we to grovel in the soil of our own graves, or are we prepared to strive for the infinite?"

He pauses, and turns to where she waits. Lin has never heard him say these words before, this hinting at insane plans, these intimations of godhood. A tremor shivers along her muscles, contorting her posture. Unseen to the audience, she shakes her head. Her father twitches his fingers: *come*.

Lin hesitates. Agony spasms through her spine. The noise of the rainstick murmurs on. Rice fizzes with the sound of sparks now, not rain, a static charge building and building until she can't separate the noise from the pain burning through her nervous system, can't do anything other than close her eyes and visualise dragons swooping through the night sky and breathing flames into her bones.

She opens her eyes and meets her father's gaze. He hasn't moved. Ignoring the pain as best she can, Lin takes the first tormented step out onto the stage. A ripple of applause murmurs through the audience. Her father turns away and taps at his interface. A string of numbers shimmers onto the plasma screen behind him, the secret codes of her body he pores over long into each and every night as she lies in bed awake, willing her body to heal itself so he can rest at last.

Lin and Rudy wait for the chair lift. Below, a panoramic view of the snow-caked valley stretches down to the towering citadel of glass spires and renewable balconies she now calls home, a vast structure teetering above the lower slopes of the Alps like a crane nesting beside a lake.

Her Rainsticks settle into a comfortable shape inside her. Gelatinous skeletal accoutrements, they align her body into a lithe, flowing approximation of the form her father has always dreamed of. Every movement she makes is echoed by the nano-particles swarming through her blood, the gel that surrounds her bones a gyroscope, a balancing act whose safety net resides within her own DNA.

The two years they've spent in exile in Switzerland, far away from the unseen ghost of her mother, has allowed Lin to become the woman she would never have been trapped back in London. Rudy squeezes her arm. She sees more of him than she does her father now. Phan Industries, and the blueprints for his latest project, a space elevator he has named the Spear, takes up every minute of his waking life. She suspects he dreams of his work too, diagrams and tabulations swimming in his unconscious mind like chess pieces. His personal laboratory at the root of their house is his haven, her prison, his guilt mechanism to cement the hold they have over each other.

The ski slopes seem to tower over her. The freezing air distracts her from her nervousness, the tight knot of pain at the base of her neck that betrays the trepidation she feels. "Hey, don't worry." Rudy grins, teeth white against the whiter landscape. "I'll go easy on you."

She shifts her feet, feeling the gel that enfolds her skeleton shifting in concordance with her muscular movements. "Daddy says any physical activity should be safe," she replies, and instantly regrets her choice of words. She knows what Rudy's friends say about her – Daddy's girl, silver-spooner, guinea pig… She wishes for nothing more than freedom. Even now, with her body stiffened and straightened into a semblance of utility, she feels harnessed into near-immobility – a mental reining-in of ambition and possibility.

"Mr Phan is the one who should know," Rudy says. "You inspired his elevator, after all."

"I did not!"

"That's what he tells people. He's serious, too."

"His ziggurat to the stars?" Lin snorts. "He'll never build it."

"He built you."

Lin feels herself blush. Rudy seems to sense her discomfort at his words. "It'll be fine, Lin. Think of today as a trial run. If you can do this, why shouldn't the Spear work too?"

"It was your father that conceptualised the Rainsticks, remember? Maybe Daddy should be thanking him instead."

Rudy just laughs. When the lift comes he waves the attendant away and helps her into the cradle. Their ascent is a voyage of apprehension and excitement. She has often watched him and his friends from her balcony, slaloming through the falls of whiteness on the lower slopes, beetles crawling over the mountainside she doesn't dare challenge. She feels his offer of lessons has other, deeper resonances. Karl Denlo controls an ever-increasing portion of the Phan empire now that her own father's concerns lie elsewhere. Would a marriage unite the two families or repel them away from each other? She would like to ask Rudy. She would like him to ask her.

But he chatters about pole actions and leg shifts instead. The house, receding now, seems like a toy a child has placed onto a model mountain. A brief flurry of snow whips up. Her father will not know of the change in the weather, the adventures of his daughter. All he cares about is his elevator. "I began with a problem," he will say to his investors, or to the media, or to politicians, "and in its solving a new problem formed. A solution is only ever a re-imagining of a dilemma. But, of course, sometimes it takes a child's imagination to show you what you have been seeing all along."

His plans frighten Lin. Will he go through with it? Private capital prostrates itself at his feet. Even she, a minor cog in her father's machinery, has a value to those who see an opportunity when it presents itself. If it fails, then maybe her father will pull back on his grandiose ambitions, his driving guilt.

And if it succeeds? Then he will push himself on to the next peak, a higher plateau.

Out on the platform the air is calm. Grey swifts glide along the airstreams above, gravityless, swooping over their clifftop kingdom. No one is on the mountain today apart from the two of them. It occurs to her that Rudy has arranged things this way. She feels both proud and scared at the prospect.

Rudy helps her strap on her skis. He stands, poised, on the brink of the nursery slope. To him it will be a child's run. To Lin, the descent plummets downwards at an almost vertical angle. Her breath catches. Rudy waits, saying nothing. The choice, once more, is hers.

And she recalls that night on Hampstead Heath, and the rain, and the agony shooting through her bones, the crowds from the fireworks display strolling past her without a care in the world; and her father, arms outstretched, his face as serious as she has ever seen it, willing her on to break through the wall and survive.

Flakes of snow settle onto her gloves. Rudy turns and girds himself for the run. Lin, her courage set in stone now, exhales. Muscles burning, she braces her limbs against the bend of her bones and casts off.

Rudy shrugged. "I've not seen him for months, to tell you the truth." He taps an idle finger across the surface of the imager, sending shivers of muted blue light through the rendition of the Spear that hovers between them. "I guess he's back on the Orbital. Maybe the weather down here didn't suit him after all."

"And you?"

Rudy grimaces, a parody of a smile. "I prefer a drier climate nowadays."

The island shifts, sending tremors through the headquarters building. Lin's office sits at the summit, her window affording the two of them a wide-angle view of the construction site. Giant tethers billow upwards like the stanchions of an unfinished circus tent. Hollowed-out foundation cavities emit fiery shimmers of light. Grappling hooks await their nano-carbon cables, the threads that will bind the Earth to the stars. The elevator will be finished within half a decade. Its completion will instigate a new era of exploration for mankind, an ingress to the solar system and – maybe – beyond; or so Lin's father tells her, on the rare occasions they speak. He is known, in bitter conversations among the labourers and in angry media broadcasts, as the Emperor. Brooding in his Orbital far above, he seems ever more detached from humanity. The irony is not lost on Lin.

"Why is he doing this?" She gestures to the hum of activity outside.

"This island, this tower, this vainglorious reaching for… what?"

"Compensating for his faulty genes, maybe." Rudy spreads his hands. This is their anniversary. Her father hadn't attended their wedding on the shores of Lake Lucerne seven years earlier – not from disapproval, but because he was so wrapped up in his plans it slipped his memory. Lin, too, had forgotten the significance of this day until Rudy's unexpected arrival, his demeanour hesitant and apologetic.

"And for my genes too?" she says in reply.

"My father says Mr Phan is driven by motivations even he doesn't understand." Rudy's face is an indecipherable mask. "I don't think I've ever taken you away from him, Lin."

The glowing image of the Spear is taunting in its perfection. Lin turns away. A squall of rain patters against the window. A hundred metres away a flash of blue light arcs outwards from the mass of girders that will become the base station for the project. Indentured workers, flown in from the dying states of West Africa and Oceania, swarm over the structure like ants feeding on a carcass. Many will die. The artificial island, nameless, stateless, drifts in equatorial waters. Untethered for now, it will eventually connect to the Orbital in an umbilical conjoining. In dark moments Lin admits it will be the nearest she will ever get to procreation.

"So why are you here?" she asks.

"I came to see if you wished to celebrate. But if you'd rather…"

Rudy's hesitance annoys her. She knows of his life, his assignations, his affairs. They are no longer hoping for an heir. In quiet moments, Lin forces herself to admit this was never what she wanted in the first place.

"We can annul," she says, surprising herself with her bluntness. "If that's what you would like."

Rudy feigns amazement. "Should we not think about it a while longer?"

A kilometre away, a waterspout surges in the wake of the island's drift. A dark mass of seabirds circles, hoping to scavenge whatever oceanic waste has been thrown up. The rain, falling harder now, obscures the view of the diminishing spout until it merges into the runnels of water on the glass. She shifts around in her seat. Her Rainsticks undulate within her; her twin, as much a part of her as her natural body. That same technology, adapted to develop the material for the elevator cables, has kept her alive and mobile all these years. But she knows, even though her father doesn't want to admit it, their tenure is finite. Soon she will have to make the choice: join her ailing father on the Orbital, or slowly crush under the weight of Earth's gravity, her posture bending and straining like a tree in a gale, the pain becoming too great for even Phan's technicians to make tolerable.

She flips off the imager. Now there is nothing between them. Nothing but the unbridgeable scar of withholding, of confinement, incompatibility. "By the time the Spear is finished," she says, "I'll be gone."

Rudy raises his eyebrows to the sky, arcing his gaze upward in an unsaid question. Lin turns back to the window. She doesn't react when he rises to leave. "I'll have my lawyers send the papers over," he says. "No fault, no frills?"

When she doesn't answer he slips silently away. This will be the last time they meet. Lin feels little. Her thoughts ascend, beyond the clouds that spill their waters to the sea, up through the ionosphere to low-Earth orbit and her father's domicile, the centre of his web of influence, from where he extends his tendrils into every corner of Earth's economy. She pictures herself there, half-floating, untethered; her Rainsticks free at last to ripple where they please, her body lithe and supple as it was all those years ago on the slopes of the lower Alps, snow rushing past her as Rudy laughed alongside, her life aligning into grids of happiness before her.

She returns to her tasks, a rueful smile flickering on her face for an atomic instant, her pathway once more set out on vertical strands of nano-tubes and graphene that reach their spider silk filigrees into the sky.

Lin doesn't like to disturb her father when he is in Communion. He will enter trance; he and the ersatz intelligences that maintain Phan Orbital. They have christened them Archies, a private joke: archetypes, images from the collective unconscious, merged with chi, the vapour of creation. Their tank-grown, quasi-mineral physical forms live in the cryo-chambers at the Orbital's heart. From there they ripple outwards in electronic whispers, analysing and controlling, spreading through the station like benign knotweed.

Up here time seems to fold in on itself, endless days pivoting backwards and forwards on a fulcrum point midway between the Earth and the stars. The Orbital, large enough to house hundreds now, is empty of human life save for Lin and her father. The two of them have lived here together for five years now. Even so, they rarely see each other. Today, Lin's father will commune with his creations for hours, as he does every day. His body, bent and twisted with the burden of years, sits hunched inside its support cradle, straining against its harness as the microgravity ripples through the Orbital.

These motion adjustments, devised to match the tautness of the cables descending from the construct's underside, send tiny shockwaves through Lin's body, swells and surges that her Rainsticks stabilise in an instant. She enters her own gel-tank and plugs herself into her comm. Her Communions are undertaken with an increasing sense of detachment. Economic indexes, media streams, plug-ins to the vast games of conquest her fellow humans undertake in their own parodies of intimacy, their minds joined into indeterminate blobs of passivity disguised as activity... She analyses, but feels nothing.

Her Rainsticks tingle in her bones. As the data flows into her consciousness she automatically sifts it into categories of relevance. Grids align in her mind, enhanced by the Archies. Together they feed the evaluations into the composite web overseen by her father. In a strange way it's the closest she's ever been to him. She has discussed the matter with herself, with the Archies. A Eucharist, came the reply. A sacrament.

The thought amuses her. Even though she knows the answer is little more than a reflecting mirror of her own thought processes, an amplifier, the perceptiveness is somehow disquieting.

Hours pass. She drifts, anchored to the material world by little more than her faltering body. The Archies' rudimentary thoughts become hers. She grows bored of overseeing Phan Industries, and turns her attention elsewhere: to the object under construction on an annex to the station. Lumpy, ugly, the deep-space vessel squats on the Orbital's hull. It will leave soon; to Mars, to instigate the next phase of her father's push to dominate the universe. The Spear was only the first stage in her family's migration. The ship, Lin knows, is where her father's heart lies.

Rudy Denlo, Head of Operations now his own father has stepped down, takes care of the Earth-bound activities. Climbers crawl up and down the elevator's wires, laden with raw materials stripped from the planet's crust. Slowly, slowly, the Mars ship takes shape. The dispatches she receives from Rudy are technical, practical, containing no mention of their past life together.

For this she is glad.

A ghost note enters her reverie, a disruption in the flow of serenity. She pulls back, loosens herself from her union with the ether and prepares to re-enter the world of the Orbital. When she emerges from the tank, flexing her muscles to facilitate movement in her atrophying bones, her father is already waiting for her.

"Yes, father?" she says, when they are comfortably ensconced on the station's viewing platform. Opulence surrounds them – magnetic cradles tether their bodies to soft furnishings, samite and tussore-bedecked weavings that seem to grow from the walls and floor. "How was Communion today?"

"It was fine."

Their communications with each other are like this nowadays – distant, polite. He owes her no favours, she supposes. They have settled into their roles – Lin, the dutiful daughter; her father, the patriarch, the Emperor, the weaver of dreams. But he still seems driven – by guilt, by shame, by his own physical pain, greater now as his body nears the end of its natural lifespan.

"Rudy believes the Emigration will proceed ahead of schedule," he says in his old, slow voice. "When the next Spear is built we will be able to pick the most suitable pioneers."

"From those who have paid?"

She doesn't mean to mock. But the insinuation of her father's vision into every aspect of global culture frightens her. He, nowadays, seems uninterested in anything other than his Mars project. But Lin can see the filaments of the company creeping ever outwards, suffocating those who stand in its way, gathering the powerful and greedy around its core until even governments acquiesce to its jurisdiction.

Her father's gaze is shrewd, penetrating. Even in his dotage he exudes a quiet power, a birthright. Not for the first time a fear of him courses through her, as if her Rainsticks are an extension of his own physical being into hers. "Lin, Rudy and I have discussed the future of Phan Industries," he says. "We are at the point where we need to push forward. We believe that you are the person best qualified to execute our vision."

"Father, I have no wish to return to Earth." She shivers. The Spear's cables are invisible from here. But she feels them, tugging at her skin, cajoling her to return to the gravitational oppression she has always yearned to escape.

"That won't be required of you. We need you to focus on one task only from now on, possibly the greatest task any human could perform."

"Oh?"

Her father hesitates. "Lin, I know we haven't been close. Up here…" He sweeps an arm to encompass the interior of the Orbital, its plushness somehow obscene. "It may seem as if I have no interest in mankind's future. On the contrary; Rudy and I have been engineering the greatest project ever attempted. The Spear was never for tourist trips or fossil fuel hunts. You know that." He reaches out and takes her hand. His flesh is cold, rough. Lin places her own hand over his, entwining their fingers together in a parody of affection.

"I'll do what you require of me, father," she says. And, she thinks, she means it.

Her father says nothing for a while. The planet rotates magisterially beneath them on the viewing screens, an alien world to both of them now. A note of sadness is in his voice when he finally speaks. "The world is a bleak place nowadays. I have no confidence in mankind's ability to stave off devastation. It's time for a new beginning. A new frontier." He squeezes her hand. "Lin, I need you to be the first emigrant. Prepare Mars for the human race. Make people feel they have come home."

The walls seem to dissolve around Lin, the void rushing in on her as she pictures the depthless, impalpable eternity beyond Earth. And she isn't even surprised to feel a weight lifting from her, a craving for freedom fulfilled at last.

Lin's view of Ascraeus Mons is obscured by a swarm of dust particles drifting over the Tharsis region. The trillions-strong cloud of grains catches the sunlight, refracting into billows of coloured shadow that make Mars seem inhabited by shoals of deep-canyon fish. She turns from the screen. Around her the station hums; not with life, for she's the only living creature aboard. But she feels the potential of the semi-sentient beings that surround her, their minds in constant accord with their doppelgangers on the planet's surface five hundred kilometres below.

She plugs herself into the liquid tank of sugars in the locus chamber and closes her eyes. Within a matter of minutes she's entering the empathic trance-state necessary to merge into confluence with the Archies, they who control the remote machines that roam across the plains of Tharsis, absorbed in a never-ceasing search for raw materials they can use to build Phan City and its planned series of suburbs.

Lin's physical movements will be doubled on the planet's surface by her plasticised avatar. Even though the Archies have no innate intelligence Lin suspects that they accommodate some covert function she can't quite grasp the substance of, however much she prods and probes. Their manipulation of the range of tools at their disposal resembles more a conjoining of souls than the duties they were designed to carry out. It often feels as if they tolerate her, as if they were the masters of the planet and she merely an adjunct to their mission.

She likes it here – so far from her family, so far from everything and everyone she has ever known. Her father, nowadays, remains on his Orbital in a barely senescent half-life. Rudy Denlo is free to flex Phan's economic muscles, detached from the restrictions of law and ethics that burdened the company so in the past. Her father's wealth is immeasurable, ever-expanding. His intricate network of corporations controls plastics, proteins, water recycling, air purification, solar reflectors… His exploitation of environmental devastation has made him a true Emperor. The human race bows to his demands, dances to his tune.

Their final meeting before she left for Mars had been overlaid with an air of regret. He had spoken of humanity, of solutions. "Mars will be just the beginning, Lin. By the time I join you I expect the colony to be self-sufficient."

"How will you survive on the surface, father? Even in zero-g you can't breathe without…" She waved a hand at the robot nurses who attended to his every bodily need – pampering, cajoling, willing his broken lungs to draw in precious air, their ancillary limbs manipulating his wracked body into contorted figures. "Without this, I don't even know if I'll be able to."

"I have no choice. No one else will save those fools down there." He gestured to the viewscreen and its panorama of the planet below. The plains of Africa were rolling past, green and brown and bordered by encroaching blue. Lin had often wondered whether his life in this eyrie gave him the objectivity to make uncomfortable decisions or, conversely, an unhealthy omniscience. "Lin, if your mother could have seen this…" He sighed. "But the past is the past. So prepare Mars for them. Make it a beautiful world, Lin, for a new age. And if it should happen that I don't live to see it…"

"Father…"

"…then I give you my blessing to shape the future as you see fit."

"That's not a responsibility I wish to take on," she replied. But her father had closed his tired eyes. His breathing became deep, ragged. A robot nurse flexed its arms and lowered his body into the vat of cryo-gel set into the floor of his chamber. Another, humanoid this time, hovered at her elbow. After a minute she followed it out, aching to turn back one last time but willing herself not to do so.

On her passage to Mars she wondered what she could have said differently. Nothing came to mind. Nothing comes to mind now, either, as her head swims and the bustle of the construction site appears in her mind. Archies walk and wheel and fly in a dance of ever-changing activity, their movements pushing inexorably toward the creation of the new metropolis that will, according to her father's plans, save the human race.

Assuming, of course, that any on Earth can afford the transit fees.

The mucilage attached to her neural pathways sparks and trembles. Like fireworks, she thinks. Like electric messages shooting through Rainsticks, mutating me into a super-being, an overlord. An Archie speeds past on a centipede-track, his destination unknown, his motivations unknowable. Will he, too, live in this place when it is finished? Or will these mystics be cast into the Martian wilderness when their work is done, there to exist or expire as they choose?

Sighing, she unplugs herself. Hours have passed. Later, as she sleeps, her weightless body recharges itself as best it can, a jellyfish swimming against an endless tide.

The planets orbit their star in trajectories predictable and fixed. A mast juts outward from the third planet, a pillar to the heavens. Atop it nests a floating tomb, a weightless monument to the future that never was. A counterweight cable vanishes into the starlight from its opposite side, a frond drifting in the endless sea of space. A human figure sleeps within the Orbital, both alive and dead. Machines maintain a breathable atmosphere for the lungs of the Emperor to draw in, his empire now a wasteland, his throne a sarcophagus.

Around the fourth planet a metal disc spins, always showing the same face to the reddened expanses of desert beneath, its unceasing motion a pale echo of the vast processes of the cosmos. A cord binds this vessel to the world below; unseen by human eyes, radio waves flicker through the ionosphere, puppet strings whose marionettes are barely distinguishable from their puppeteer.

Seven cities lie dormant, awaiting their inhabitants. The eighth city, the final one, is finished now too. Lin forgets which one of these constructions was once known as Phan City. Domes, glinting in the Martian sunlight, range across the desert in exponential spirals, fractal vortices. Fine layers of sand coat their upper shells. The water that has been extracted from deep beneath the surface sloshes within carapaces of renewable plastic, turning these rooms within rooms into aquariums, miniature oceans, radiation shields that will protect organic cells from that which would destroy them.

Lin's body, encased in crystallised gas and super-cooled water, exists in a half-life, neither human nor God but rather something in-between. *A guardian of heaven*, she often thinks to herself on her shipboard sanctum. *That is what I am now. A dragon.*

She turned off the news feed from Earth years ago. The emigration will never happen now, that much is obvious. The planned series of elevators were never built. Her father's own structure is rotting, barely operational. The Orbital still hovers at its apex, suspended above the globe like an old and brittle spider, her father's deep sleep undisturbed. But down on the planet eyes have turned inwards. Phan Industries is no more. Rudy Denlo, old now – as old as she; the thought came as a shock – has disappeared into wealth-ridden retirement, safe inside one of the gated nation-states that hold their borders against the rising tides and starving billions.

Lin finds herself unable to shed tears for any of it. She spends her days flitting from one body to another, a parasite feeding from her hosts via subsurface relays and vapour beams. The Archies range across the surface of the planet now. New cities rise from the sand. Channels have been excavated between them, Lowell's canals a reality at last. When the first waters cascade from the sky they will become rivers, torrents, veins to carry precious fluids from pole to pole.

Today, Archies are gathering from all over. Lin, a brood mother in her eyrie far above, watches with pride at the scuttling creatures ringing the outskirts of the city. For them, Mars is home. Her control over them has diminished to the point where she is a mere observer. She knows them now as architects, not archetypes; builders of dreams whose recall fades with the morning light. For mankind, at least. For them, the dreams are fast becoming reality.

On some days she wonders whether she should return to Earth, cajole the human race into reaching for transcendence as her father would have done. Deep down, though, she knows she will never leave this place. Slowly but surely she is transitioning; to new forms, eternal consciousness. Would her forebears see her as still human? That bridge, she supposes, has been burnt long ago. Forgotten, presumed dead, she continues on, living out her life as a true citizen of the void.

Still she prefers it this way. She switches viewpoint, alighting her consciousness within a wheeled, multi-limbed Archie who has lined up with others of its kind. Clouds swirl and billow. Lin watches from both beneath and above, neither viewpoint a true one for her any longer. She feels what her host feels; wind, temperature, the warmth of its brothers and sisters surrounding it. She feels her own body, frail but still functioning, ripple with anticipation at what is to come.

Hours pass. The Archies are silent. A change comes over the Martian landscape, a crackling of potential. Aurora flickers at the clouds' periphery. Colours dance across the sky; azure, carmine, cerise…

Lin senses an ache, an echo of trauma at the root of her flesh. She shifts within her cradle. Plasma gel oscillates with the movement of her body, consoling her, supporting her. The pain recedes to memory, to the past. She focuses her attention onto the surface. Something, now, is happening.

Her host turns its gaze upward. The clouds darken. Lightning spasms – once, twice, blues and golds flickering from horizon to horizon. Static snaps. Even as far away as she is, the hairs on Lin's neck and arms stiffen in charged sympathy. Red dust forms spouts, eddies swirling in the sudden breeze that has picked up. Light plays over the roofs of the domes. The Archies wait, poised at the lip of success or failure; a pivot point, their own crucial moment.

Lin, fingers clenched, holds her breath. Memories dart and skim across her mind's eye. She recalls the braces cutting into her legs, the play of light on the clouds above London. She thinks of her mother, who never knew her daughter. She thinks of her father, who could never feel joy, never feel the satisfaction of a task fulfilled. She remembers the snow showering behind her on the lower slopes of the Alps, the swell of the equatorial ocean, the Spear towering into the clouds, the rattle of rice grains sliding from end to end of her toy as Rudy Denlo pounds ahead of her along the hallways of her house and she screams, trying to break through the barrier ahead of her, forever holding out a trembling hand…

A vibration shakes her bones, a thundercrack from far, far away.

And it's seconds before she realises that the wetness on her cheeks is raindrops, not tears, and the Archies heave a silent, collective sigh of relief and trundle back to their tasks in the deluge that falls now from the Martian sky.

The Veilonaut's Dream

Henry Szabranski

Sometimes the Discontinuity kinks and curves and flips about as if it is alive.

Openings slide along its vast length like undigested morsels down the gullet of a cosmic serpent. Feathery tendrils shoot out, slowly curling up and fading, each a travelling shadow-slice through some theorised higher-dimensional object. But today... today the gap weather is good. There is no sign of movement or instability; the anomaly is razor-straight and steady. A thirty meters high, ten-thousand-kilometre-long, barely visible veil that glimmers on either side of us as far as we can see.

Franco and Zhang float beside me. They are waiting for my command.

"Mads? Are we going through today?"

Franco is impatient. He's very much a get-it-over-with type of guy. Luckily, we've been on enough missions together I feel I can ignore him. But he's right: the idea of turning back dominates my thoughts. It's not too late to stop, to return to the Observatory, though we've signed the contract and the penalty will be high. No doubt Franco and Zhang will denounce my cowardice to mask their own relief

– But what do I care about money and reputation any more?

I check the time since the last change. *One hour twenty-two minutes.* The average is just over seventy-four hours. Information both critical and useless. There's no knowing how long the gap will remain stable. It could be seconds, minutes, days – even months or years. The Discontinuity's size, its shape, the location of the region it opens onto, all of these can and do alter without warning. In the blink of a veilonaut's eye.

"I'd rather be cut," Zhang declares. She's a newbie, fresh arrived from in-system, both terrified and eager. Not a researcher, but one of the new crop of mercenary explorers. When I announced I was going to brave the gap today she had scrambled to tag along. "You may lose a limb or two," she says, "but the v-suit will keep you alive until the medics reach you. There's still a chance of survival."

"They couldn't save Quinn," Franco points out, his tone weary and worldly-wise. He loves to play the grizzled veteran. "Neither the v-suit nor the medics."

Eleven days ago Quinn was caught mid-gap during a change. In some distant lost region of spacetime, his missing body parts still tumble. I shudder at the memory.

"But at least he died quickly," Zhang presses on, oblivious to Franco's disapproval. "I'd rather be Quinn than Su. Quinn didn't feel a thing, but Su's still out there, somewhere. Gasping her last air, wishing she were dead. It must be a nightmare."

Franco glares at Zhang. "Not cool, okay? Not the time or place. Not the thing to say."

"Concentrate on what you're doing." My voice sounds perfectly calm over the comms link, with no sign of my irritation at Zhang's ignorant chatter, or the barely contained churn of emotions within me. Perhaps it's the mix of synth-absinthe and sedatives I've dosed up on, their welcome numbing effect. Against mission regs, but the Observatory turns a blind eye, long since drifted from its regimented academic origins. Hardly any exploration would be done, otherwise.

"It's almost time to cross," I remind everyone, careful not to slur my words.

Off-comms my breath hitches. Zhang may be crass, but she's not being intentionally malicious. She doesn't know about Su and me; we'd kept it quiet, at first to avoid drama, then as an ongoing game. Not even Franco knows, though he may suspect. And Zhang's right: Su's still out there. Just about now, relative to our timeframe, the last power in her v-suit battery fading. She remains unreachable. Unrescuable. Lost in some distant past or far future. My last words to her before she crossed over had been harsh. We'd argued. I'd called her a fool, a zealot, a selfish dreamer. That she was absolutely wrong about the Discontinuity. I refused to follow her and Quinn on their doomed mission. "I'll find you Maddy's World again," Su had boasted. "I promise. I'll find it for you."

I'd hurled a half-empty drink bulb at her retreating back.

I should have been with her. Been there when the gap swallowed her whole.

That's the other part of the Discontinuity's terror. Crossings are done at speed, to reduce the risk of bisection, which is neat and instantaneous if you're caught passing through mid-change. But even if you're spared that gruesome fate, you can still find yourself stranded on the far side after the gap has moved on. The records show the same region has never appeared twice. Sure, you can survive for a while, protected and preserved in your vacuum suit, but there's no prospect of rescue or return. Cut off forever, unreachable, supplies dwindling, your last desperate pleas will be unheard as the Discontinuity continues to cycle on and the Observatory lights blink away out here beyond Pluto's orbit, their cast-off photons more distant from you than the moment of creation.

To be cut or to be lost. Every veilonaut has to face either possibility each time they pass through the gap.

"You okay, Mads?"

Franco's silhouette floats dark against the veil's Cherenkov shimmer. Just as mine had drifted as I waited, angry and impatient for Su's return, eleven days and only a moment and eternity ago. I was there when the Discontinuity shrugged away a billion suns and spewed forth Quinn's almost-through body. Even now, my hand twitches instinctively, tries to shield me from the memory. Droplets that sparked against my v-suit field like a bloody meteor shower.

"Mads?"

"I'm fine. Let's get into position."

I toggle the nav system controls. Our propulsion backpacks spurt into life, begin a series of pre-programmed manoeuvres that will push us closer to the gap.

Zhang crosses herself. She can barely bring herself to look at the rippling veil. Franco, too, is muttering some off-comms incantation. Despite all the known science, the cold hard facts, a fog of superstition still surrounds the anomaly. I don't have much time for the irrational convictions of my fellow veilonauts. More than a handful swear they have glimpsed or felt some mysterious presence as they've passed through the gap. They believe the long dead Others remain inside the rift they created, ghosts trapped within the veil. Some believe the Discontinuity itself is a living, conscious entity, worthy of worship. Even I, normally so scathing of such irrational beliefs, find myself mouthing a silent prayer to the rumoured gods of the gap in the moments before crossing. To the angels of the veil, to the ancient long-lost Others. If they exist, or if they don't. *Please protect us as we pass through. Hold the gap open for our safe return.*

So far, my prayers have been answered. *Lucky Madeleine,* they call me, *Blessed Lady of the Veil.* A talisman. More successful missions than any other veilonaut.

But I know the truth. The cold, hard math of probability.

Everyone is lucky crossing the gap.

Everyone.

Until they're not.

The elapsed time counter ticks over. *One hour twenty-six minutes.*

"Mads? Are you ready?"

One last time, then. One final mission. For love lost, for hopeless hope, for a dream of blue and white and green. "I'm ready, Franco. Are you?"

"Of course."

I take a deep breath, sweat beading on my forehead. "Initiate burn on my mark."

I concentrate on the Discontinuity. For it to do my bidding, just as Su said.

Franco reaches out. Zhang grasps his hand.

"Three."

Zhang stretches towards me, and after a moment's hesitation I take hold of her hand as well.

"Two."

Our breath comes faster, our pulses elevated. We are all linked together, fates entwined. Engine packs perpendicular to the face of the gap.

"One."

I say my silent crossing prayer.

"Mark."

I don't feel anything as I pass through the veil.

Some swear they experience a moment of disorientation. Or, for a few, a full-on rapture. But I've never felt more than a faint tug or seen anything other than a brief blink of blue as I cross over. No visions, no angels.

No ghosts.

No, that's wrong. I *do* feel something. Terror, mostly. Mingled with anticipation. Hope. That more than darkness will greet me.

Hope quickly dashed.

I guess Su was wrong.

Pre-programmed hydrazine bursts from our packs to spin us around and decelerate us to a stop relative to the gap through which we've just passed. The Observatory swings back into view, paradoxically only hundreds of meters away and yet at the same time now countless billions of light years distant. Our sun still gleams, glimpsed back through the rift, the brightest star even here.

The far side is almost always a disappointment. Most of the universe is empty, and if the region the Discontinuity opens onto is truly random then almost inevitably the gap opens onto rarefied intergalactic space far distant from any stars and planets and other forms of baryonic matter. Most often the far side's temperature is barely above the CMB. It's cold, dark, empty; void and devoid.

So it is again, this time.

"Okay, team." The fact is nowadays veilonauts are paid by the second not on their opinion of the far side's interest. "You know the drill. We've contracted for at least ten minutes. Timer starts... now."

I give the orders automatically, autonomically, trying not to show my relief at surviving transit. Just one more crossing – back to the Observatory – and then I'm done with the Discontinuity and its cruel game of chance forever.

Franco and Zhang deploy their latest research equipment. It's a waste of time, but it's what they're paid to do. Perhaps there's been some breakthrough in observational technology by their sponsors, perhaps this time it'll be different. I'm not holding my breath. Countless automated probes have tried to replicate our work. They always fail. Veilonauts pass through the Discontinuity, make observations, return safely – but nothing of the far side is ever recorded. Only images and measurements of our own solar system, of our own galaxy, as if the hugely expensive and sophisticated machines never crossed the gap in the first place. As if the far side does not exist. Scientists and philosophers argue over the reasons, the consequences, the basic reality of the Discontinuity and of reality itself – but it doesn't change the fact that in order to gain information from the far side humans need to cross and return. Not probes or sensors or other disposable equipment.

"It's a haunting," Su had said, a couple of weeks ago, as we lay tangled together in her dorm bed, sweat cooling on our bodies.

"Hmm?"

"The Discontinuity. It's a ghost. Not real at all."

"Seems real enough when we cross."

"That's what I mean." She tipped her face towards me, her expression earnest, drawing me back to full alertness. "Are we ghosts too?"

"Sexy ghosts." I ran my finger over her shoulder, began to tickle her, and the moment was gone. When I mentioned her words the next day she laughed them off, blamed her introspective mood on a stim-down.

But I remember them now, as I float beyond the impossible gap.

One hour thirty-one minutes.

Instead of helping Franco and Zhang, I run my unauthorised scan. I know what I will find before I begin, but can't help the growing sense of despair as the search radius expands and the negative result stands. There is no sign of Su, or Quinn's lost half, or any of the equipment they had brought across. Of course not: the gap has moved on, as I knew it had, as it always does. But still I feel a stab of loss and disappointment. And yes, anger. That bastard, hope. Sucking me in once again. Merciless giver and ultimate taker.

"There's nothing here." Zhang interrupts and reflects my thoughts. "I have a bad feeling. Let's go back."

Zhang. The two-time veilonaut. Hardly an expert on the Discontinuity and its mysterious ways.

My scan is almost finished. "Four more minutes," I say. "Them's the rules. Keep looking. You might spot something."

After another minute even Franco chimes in. "Mads, this one's a wash. Just another void."

One hour thirty-four minutes.

Why can't I let go? Why can't I cut and run? Su is lost. The others are ready. They've given me permission. The comms record will show the contract violation is not my fault. I can retire, return to Earth, Blessed Lady of the Veil no more.

The scanner gives a soft bleep. Red light. Null result.

"Uh… guys. Guys."

It is Zhang's tone more than her words that makes an involuntary shiver run down my spine.

"*Guys.*"

There can be only one cause for concern out here. Only one thing we're constantly afraid of. That can explain the growing tinge of hysteria in Zhang's voice.

There is a flood of relief as I spot the faint glimmer of the veil ahead of us. Still straight, still sharp. The gap still there.

Then I see why Zhang has begun to panic.

And I feel the first stirrings of it myself.

"Oh shit," Franco says, quietly.

I ping the net connection, the always open session to the Observatory servers.

Timeout. Total packet loss. Zero signal.

Through the gap, where we had previously seen the Observatory, the sun, the beacons of everything familiar – there is no sign of them. Only darkness.

They are all gone.

"I can't believe it. It's fucking changed. It's *changed!*"

Zhang's wail is painfully loud in my ears. She stares at me accusingly. "You were supposed to be *lucky!*"

Zero hours one minute.

Every veilonaut's nightmare. Even so, there is a protocol. Numb, I follow it automatically.

Approach the gap. Confirm the change. Trigger the distress signal.

For all of the good it will do us.

Glimpsed through the flickering blue static of the veil, our new neighbour universe is dark and utterly unfamiliar.

I cycle through the available options. There aren't many, and none of them are good. Not even close to good. Mostly, what I'm thinking is: *you knew this would happen one day, and now it has.*

But there's a difference between believing something *might* happen, or even that something *will* eventually happen… and it actually happening.

Big fucking difference.

"At least we know one thing now." Franco's voice is low and subdued. "The Discontinuity continues to exist on the far side."

He's right, although it's not on my hotlist of items to dwell on right now. Some theories hold that the Discontinuity disappears on the far side after a change, that it re-locates to the next distant region whilst the near side remains permanently (and mysteriously) tethered around our sun. A whole class of theories have just been disproved. For all the good it does us, or to the theorists who will never find out they're wrong.

Franco drifts closer to the veil, staring into the darkness beyond.

"The other side doesn't look any more appealing." Once again, I'm surprised by the calm in my voice. As if I'm a creature of pure intellect. Madeleine Field Theorist, Scientist; Emotionless Observer. It's just the shock, I know. The fading meds. Something.

Franco pushes his hand, his arm, his face into the veil. Remains half in, half out.

"My God, Mads, what's he doing?" Zhang is aghast.

I say nothing, only watch, wait for the gap to change and for Franco to be sheared apart. It would just be our luck.

He draws back to our side. I release my breath.

"It's another place," he says. "Another void, similar to this one."

"I can see that from here."

Franco turns towards me. His eyes, glimpsed through the haze of his v-suit field, are also a void. More terrifying than the darkness on the other side of the veil.

"We're lost," Zhang says. "We're lost, and there's no way back."

"We need to keep our shit together." I'm angry with them both; they're not helping push back the panic clawing at the back of my own mind. "Conserve energy. Wait for rescue. That's the plan."

"There's not going to be any rescue." Franco's voice is as dead as his eyes.

"We don't know that. This time could be different." My words, my grasped straws, seem hopelessly optimistic, even to me. But what choice do we have? The Discontinuity follows no patterns. Maybe this time it will be different. Who knows? Nobody knows.

Franco cuts comms. He turns away.

I take hold of Zhang. She's trembling. My grip transforms into a hug. I say, "Shhh. It's going to be okay. It'll be okay. I promise."

A lie. We both know it.

Still, a lie worth saying. Especially now.

Our v-suits fields merge to form a single surface. It's a practical matter, the shared contact. Reduces the overall field area, conserves energy. It'll help eke out more precious time for our miraculous rescue to arrive. That's what I tell myself, as I cling to Zhang's shivering warmth, let the sensation of human contact overwhelm my darker thoughts.

It is not until some minutes later I question Franco's continuing silence, check on his systems status. It isn't like him to spare on the dour comments.

Shit.

Another hammer blow.

He's done more than just silence his comms. He's made his decision.

On whether to linger and wait for an impossible rescue, or take action of his own.

To be cut or to be lost? Which would you prefer? And if lost, what would you do? It may only have been minutes since the gap's moved on, but Franco and I have both had years to dwell on the scenarios.

Franco. Always impatient. The very much get-it-over-with type of guy. No trust he, not in that villain hope.

He has powered off his suit field.

His lifeless, fresh-frozen body orbits ours.

Conserve energy. Await rescue.

It's what the handbook, the guide I helped draft years ago, advises.

Eighteen hours thirty-one minutes.

"Why did you keep at it?"

"Huh?"

I am half asleep, lost in dreams of loss, of blue and white and green.

Zhang's eyes are closed but she is mumbling. Not fully alert myself, I struggle to understand her. I've set the v-suit oxygen levels as low as they will go. Everything that can be turned down has been turned down. I've even raided our rudimentary medpacks for their stash of opioid sedatives. They're meant for emergency short-term pain relief, to help take the edge off traumatic injury, but they serve just as well to slow down our metabolism. Anything, everything, to eke out every second of life, every last gasp of vital oxygen. Rescue could appear at any moment, after all, so the more we can draw out our existence the better. Slim or illusory, it's the only hope we have.

"Crossing over," Zhang mumbles. "Why keep doing it?"

"The money, of course." I have no desire to answer with anything as complex as the truth.

"That's not true. It's why *I* do it, sure. My daughter's ill. I need the money… to pay for her care. It's the only way I can get it quickly enough." For a moment Zhang's previously placid expression crumples. She's going to cry again.

I didn't even know she had a kid. I hardly know anything about her. There are few secrets amongst the tightly-knit veilonaut community, but I've become increasingly withdrawn from it, retreated into my own bubble. Only Su had managed to penetrate it.

"But you're already rich. Thirty missions-worth. Crazy rich, more than any of us. Why carry on?"

"I don't know."

A long pause. We drift in a dopamine haze. Zhang's breath is slow and steady and warm against my neck.

"They say it's because of Maddy's World. You always coming back, looking for it. Did you see it, really?"

"Shhh." I stroke her short dark hair with fingers that feel distant, balloon-like. "Sleep now. Save oxygen. Rescue's coming."

She mumbles some more but I can't make out the words. Eventually, apart from the gentle sound of her breath, she is silent again.

Maddy's World. A name I've heard all too often.

Again, she's right.

It's why I kept crossing over, again and again. Long after I should have stopped, returned to Earth, humbled and defeated. Trying to recapture that hazy, crazy dream of blue and white and green.

I should have known better.

No darkling void on my first-ever crossing, all those years ago. No mere distant star shining super-bright, a competitor to Sol, or a glimmering nebula, a brilliant globular cluster. No. For me the Discontinuity laid on a real show.

An entrapment.

Professors Evelyn Ahn and David Helford – my mentors, my colleagues, my friends – accompanied me. Together we had travelled many months from Earth, studied the Discontinuity from afar and then later at the Observatory, itched to go through and experience first-hand the subject of our research. Finally, the opportunity to leave theory behind and become veilonauts ourselves.

A crescent of blue and white and green greeted us, a sight so unexpected, so astonishing and wondrous we stayed too long, gaping breathlessly, the professors just as awestruck as I. We tried desperately to absorb as much as we could before we returned to the Observatory, before the Discontinuity moved on.

A cruel introduction, that first mission. Evelyn and Dave were swallowed by the gap seconds after I came back through. I, the sole survivor.

Officially it's known as Ahn-Helford's World, but that hasn't stopped Maddy's World from being used by the other veilonauts and the journos who still write occasional articles about it. The name that history will record, despite my protests. Yes, Maddy's World. Never glimpsed again, not in all the missions since. Only cosmic darkness and voids, again and again, on each and every trip beyond the cursed veil. It doesn't even rank as a discovery, technically. No corroborating witnesses. Only my word.

Maddy's World. Always with the question, the lingering doubt, growing after each failed mission. A figment of the lone survivor's imagination, a delusion. Or worse: a lie to garner attention, a reputation.

Mad Woman's World. Yes, I have heard it called that. And to my face.

How much worse the doubts would be if the entire details of my debrief were made public, the classified parts the Observatory review panel had deemed too sensational, too surreal, too subjective to allow entry in the record. That even I could hardly bring myself to believe.

Because we saw more than just the gleam of sunshine on liquid water, or the swirling clouds of an oxygen-based atmosphere. A gleaming ring arced over the far side world. A glitter of interlinked rock and ice and metal and glass. With darting motes between the orbiting nodes and delicate elevator spokes threading down to the surface. On the side turned from the golden G-class sun, an unmistakable tracery of night-time lights: circles within circles, a maze of geometric canals.

Life. Advanced civilisation. Perhaps even a glimpse back in distant time to the Other homeworld. Or a colony outpost strung like a pearl upon the Discontinuity's irregular path. Or a mirage. An oxygen-starved, crossing-bedazzled veilonaut's dream.

A dream discovery.

Perhaps only the dream of a discovery.

Su believed in Maddy's World. And Quinn, crazy, doped-out Quinn. He was even worse.

They both believed in the ghosts, the ones supposed to haunt the veil; the living Others, the gods of the gap. Everything. All the stories, all the supernatural guff, every irrational belief I had encountered amongst the Observatory's various communities. Stories I had long since debunked or discarded.

"We can direct the Discontinuity, Mads. It's why the Others made it."

Su floats opposite me in our little dorm cubicle. I suck greedily on a squeeze bulb of synth-absinthe, impatient for its promise of green oblivion.

"Nonsense."

"It's meant to be used. To travel, to reach a destination. Otherwise why was it created?"

"Have you ever considered it may just be a natural phenomenon?

That the far locations are chosen purely at random? Don't you think we'd have detected some pattern by now if there were any sort of organisation or intent behind it all?"

Even at the time I realised my voice was climbing louder, in frustration, in anger. But I couldn't stop myself: how could she be so... so unscientific? So *ignorant*? Despite all her attractions, this one aspect of her, this stubborn streak of irrationality, infuriated me.

"There *is* a pattern," she continued. "You said so yourself: it's clear in Quinn's data. The more people cross, the more often, the greater the likelihood of the gap shifting. The probes and the machines passing through make no difference, but we do. We trigger the change. The gap senses people. It feels us."

"The statistical significance –"

"We *can* control it, Mads. We just need to linger in the veil."

The suggestion horrified me. "You'll be cut, or lost. Or worse. There's good reason we speed through the gap…"

"Fear!" Su's voice is raised loud as mine now. "We speed through because of fear and habit. But next mission we'll stay in the veil. We'll prove we're right. We'll find Maddy's World again. You and me."

"No." My voice is flat.

She must have sensed my denial, my determination at last. "Fine. It'll be me and Quinn, then. We'll find it without you."

"We? You and Quinn? You know he spends all his contract money between missions getting stoned out of his mind. His brain is mush."

Since when had he become part of 'we'… and when had I become 'you'?

And since when had I become this jealous, antagonistic person?

I wanted to reach out, apologise. Despite our differences, Su had been good for and to me, touched places I thought were shrivelled, or never existed. Perhaps it was time I recognised how… significant she was to me.

But she had turned her back. She was gone.

I cursed and threw my half-empty drink bulb at the closing door.

Air is running out.

The suit can tell me exactly how long we have left, but what's the point? The glowing figures are blurred. I can feel the oxygen fading in my lungs, more accurate and more sensitive than any machine. A fatal drowsiness beckons.

There's a ripple upon my retina. The veil shifts again. A barren place, once again a void, one of the countless many that fill and grow in the universe. Barely a glimmer of nuclear combustion from the distantly glimpsed ribbons of matter.

I blink, and it changes again.

Filled with a sudden curiosity I expend valuable fuel moving closer to the veil.

It ripples and shifts, strange patterns I've never seen before. Or perhaps not noticed. The veil has always been a thing to be avoided, to be crossed at speed. The risk of being cut, of its boundary shivering and engulfing you accidentally, stranding you on the other side, always a danger deterring close inspection.

But we're going to die now anyway. Past the point of no return. The time for rescue to arrive has run out.

"Zhang."

She is drowsy, barely conscious.

"Zhang. Listen. We have to make it change. It's the only thing we can do."

She shakes her head, but makes no other protest as I program our v-suits to cross through.

The gap weather remains good. The veil's faint shimmer a flat curtain. I run my palm through its soft Hawking radiation, poke first a finger, then my hand through.

I still feel nothing.

Does the Discontinuity open onto some hugely distant area of our own universe or onto another one entirely? A brane floating adjacent to ours in the bulk, or another bubble condensed from the chaos of eternal inflation? We don't know. Objects and people pass through freely, without their fundamental constituents flying apart or being annihilated by their antiparticles. Perhaps we've just been lucky so far.

We cross. A shimmer of blue followed by darkness. We cross back. Then over again. And again. Azure stars. Cerulean nebulae. Each time my brow furrows with effort, with concentration. I'm seeking a destination, not just darkness. An end point. With all my heart. With all my soul. That same yearning when I had crossed over the very first time, without fear. No fear. No fear this time. Fear serves only to distract, lose concentration. Fear will quarter me like it quartered Quinn.

"Mads. Mads, what're you doing?"

I am not sure whether it's Zhang's drowsy voice or mine. I don't look at the numbers warning me how far and how fast the fuel level is dropping.

Cross over, back and again, over and over, as the oxygen levels plummet. Lingering in the veil, seeking and plucking its cosmic string, playing it like an instrument. A vast device, a portal gifted to us by the Others, what else could it be? Whorls and stars darting blue. I have always been so fast through, now I begin to see whole vistas I've been blind to before. How beautiful they are. Is this what the other veilonauts meant, how the veil made them feel?

An energy building, an electric crackling tension. Motes of light, star clusters, swirling arms of dust and heat. I can't tell, and it doesn't really matter whether they're within the veil or without. Zhang and I are wrapped inside a ribbon of power and light extending from the bright beginning to the inevitable end, and we are travelling along it, forward and back, both at the same moment.

On one side, a change: stars reconfigured, brighter; blue warmth, then back to the other again; a change, two stars, one blue, one red, dancing together… My mind concentrated. On a destination. A particular destination in mind. Only that. Only there.

"It's beautiful," Zhang murmurs, her arms tightening around me. Reflected in her eyes: a growing arc of blue and white and green.

A sun golden yellow, hot. I turn to feel the warmth of its radiance, even through the failing shield of our shared v-suit. This sky is not black or star-filled. It's blue.

There's no reason the Discontinuity need open only onto cold dark vacuum.

The tug of gravity, of a world entire, pulls us towards the gap, to our inevitable destination.

A horizon. Beyond the blue shimmer. Rushing towards us.

There is someone there, a silhouette figure. Strange yet familiar. Running. Waving. In welcome or farewell.

The gap opens as I close my eyes.

And say my final crossing prayer.

Doomed Youth

Fiona Moore

"Is it just me, or are there more ants than usual this year?" Joanie asked. She was throwing stones at the bungalow roof to try and chase away a three-foot-long drone which had landed there by mistake, and was attempting to inseminate our chimney.

"It's nothing to worry about," I said. "CNN says rising and falling ant populations are normal; this is just an unusually bad spring." Down the street two other drones were having a standoff with the man next door's poodle over a scrap of rancid beef from a garbage can, and another was poised on the roof of a car, denting the metal with its weight; the rest of the flock were circling, vulture-like, on the air currents above the town, sniffing for the queen.

"Seems like we've been having a lot of those lately," Joanie said. She'd finally managed to peg the drone on its shiny bronze rump with an egg-sized rock, which connected with a satisfying *doink* and left a mark on the big insect's thick chitin. It shook its head distractedly, then, with a *what was I thinking* air, flew off into the cloudless sky to re-join the others.

"It's probably the climate change –" I started to say, but we were both interrupted by a contralto screech rising behind us.

"THEM! THEM! *THEM!*"

"Oh God," Joanie said with an eyeroll. "It's the Ant Lady."

"The what?" I was turning to face the source of the screaming. It was a thin old lady, stringy grey hair about her face, clutching a filthy ancient doll with a plastic head and hands and a ragged pink cloth body, standing in front of the house next door. I could see blinds going up and startled faces crowding the front windows.

"The Ant Lady," Joanie repeated. She grabbed my hand and pulled me into the house, the screen door banging tinnily behind us.

Q, the third housemate, had woken up, either due to the

screaming or the noise of the drone, and was wandering into the hall in his undershorts and Aperture Science T-shirt, scratching. The nickname was a university affectation that he'd nagged all his friends into adopting, and, once he'd finally realised how stupid it sounded, he couldn't manage to get rid of it. "What's going on?" His black puff of hair radiated out in all directions, uncombed; his eyes were bleary, his chin unshaved. He suddenly focused, looked out the living-room window. "Oh, her again. Ant-THEM! for Doomed Youth."

"Groan," Joanie said, rolling her eyes ostentatiously.

"Should we call the police or something?" I asked.

"Nah, she'll be done in a minute," Joanie said, and indeed the noise was already fading. I looked out the window myself, through the cheap sheers the landlord had stuck us with, and saw the old lady, quiet now, wandering purposefully towards one of the two-story houses further down the street.

"So what's the story?" I asked, as Q wandered into the kitchen and switched on the kettle sleepily.

"The Ant Lady?" Joanie settled down on the sofa. "Q, if you're making coffee, do me a cup, okay?" Q grunted. "Yeah, it's sort of sad. She was one of the victims of the original ant infestation."

"Really?"

"Yeah, it was actually not too far from here, just a few miles up the road. She was only a kid at the time, but she lost both her parents to the ants, and the shock sent her crazy. She couldn't say anything but "Them!" for months, apparently. They put her in rehab and then a foster home, but she never really totally recovered. Anyway, she was in and out of institutions most of her life, but managed to get married and have at least one kid somewhere along the way. When they cut the budget and closed the mental hospital she was in, they sent her to live with her daughter. She's harmless, mostly. She's even okay with the ants most of the time. Don't know what set her off today, I guess it's the mating season, with all those drones everywhere."

"Great, we'll be hearing that scream for weeks," Q handed Joanie a coffee, draped himself hairily over the armchair and dug about for the remote control.

"Should have put that in the ad," Joanie smiled apologetically at me. "Housemate wanted, female preferred, non-smoker, quiet neighbourhood except for the crazy ant lady."

"It's okay," I said. The house was an easy commute to the university, where I was a less-than-enthusiastic graduate student and tutorial assistant in epidemiology. Joanie and Q were coders at a local software company, which accounted for the furniture-lite, tech-heavy state of the living room. The neighbourhood had once been a post-war suburb, but urban sprawl and demographic changes had made it something less easily definable, a mix of original residents hanging on to properties bought in the Fifties, Sixties and Seventies, students and expatriates renting cheap and reliable properties, and, in the wake of a few rumours that the area was about to gentrify, property speculators buying up old bungalows to demolish and turn into McMansions for millionaires. Our neighbour to the west was a quiet man in his eighties with an overly aggressive black poodle, our neighbours to the east were a small, cheerfully noisy, knot of twentysomethings from somewhere in the Ukraine, war refugees on a two-year contract to the abovementioned software company. "So, the original breakout was around here? Wow."

"Yeah, you can still visit the site," Joanie said. "Not much to see, though, just a hole in the ground. Not even an interpretive centre or a gift shop."

"Wonder what caused it?" I asked.

"Communists, they said at the time," Joanie raised a sarcastic eyebrow. "Caused a standoff with Khrushchev or somebody. Later on, they blamed the aboveground nuclear tests."

Q pointedly turned up the volume on the TV, drowning us out with a news report on the civil wars in Romania and Poland.

"Seems like Russia's determined to rebuild the damn Soviet Union," Joanie remarked.

"It can do what it likes," Q said, as the report switched to one on the ongoing slow collapse of the European Union. "None of *our* business."

"Even if the UN..."

"There's no way the President's going to be stupid enough to commit troops anywhere," Q said. "Public wouldn't stand for it. America stands alone, all that shit. Anyway, who'd fuck with Russia these days?"

I left them to it and went back to my room to work on my thesis. By the time I'd emerged from the stacks of demographic data on leprosy outbreaks since the Industrial Revolution, the dispute had been resolved and the participants were nowhere to be found.

The next day was Monday, and I went in to the university as usual. Instead of going straight to the computer lab, though, I went to the library, to look up the original ant infestation.

There it was, in newspaper and video. It's become so easy to take the ants for granted: some places are more populated than others, but they've spread pretty much everywhere in the world since the fifties. I remember feeding one in St Peter's Square on an undergraduate trip to Italy, amused by the way it would hold the tiny bread pieces in its huge mandibles. But here were the reporters, incredulous and almost hysterical about these giant insects. Pictures of attack survivors, including several of a pigtailed little girl, eyes starry with trauma – the Ant Lady as she was, I realised. Finally relief, as it was discovered they were vulnerable to flames, more relief when people learned that they wouldn't attack unless directly provoked, reports of trials of various poisons and sprays. People learning to live with a new threat. Occasional retrospective, ten-year-anniversary stories, twenty, then thirty years; others when some local bully went too far teasing one with a stick and got a near-fatal bite. I realised I'd been reading and watching all morning, and it was nearly one.

Going down to the sandwich shop, I checked my phone and read my messages, then the headlines. It was the usual low-level stuff, a few good news items about animal conservation in Africa and the President outlining a strategy to make America number one through the 3-D printing industry, balanced by others about the ongoing civil wars in Central and Eastern Europe, a retrospective piece about the Russian annexation of the Ukraine a while back (reminding me momentarily of the neighbours), and a subtextually-xenophobic piece about the number of refugees – political, economic, sexual, or just plain bombed-out – from the Middle East, Pakistan, Europe, North Korea, fill in the blank, and whether we could afford to support them. An item on some kid – born in the USA, with Afghani parents – who'd been arrested with a knapsack full of homemade explosive at a rock concert in upstate New York. A political analysis arguing that the President had benefited in the polls from the domestic rise in economic growth, but needed to be careful to keep the electorate on side once people got comfortable again. Articles on climate change, on the increase in reported drone and worker numbers this year, with a warning to motorists that, however satisfying the squish, it wasn't exactly good for the car to drive directly into an ant.

When I got home again I noticed a line of workers stretching from across the street and running through our yard, busily carrying scraps of some kind back to the nest. Q was sitting on the front porch, tablet on his lap, fast-food cartons at his feet, a home flamethrower close to hand.

"Couple of the little bastards tried to force the kitchen window earlier," he explained. "They're riled up over something."

"I was reading about them today instead of working," I sat down on the steps, accepted a French fry. "Never really thought about them much before now, but it's interesting. Nobody seems totally sure what caused them, or why."

"Nuclear testing, I'm telling you," Q said. "Nevada. Area 51. It all makes sense. So what's *your* angle?"

"Dunno," I said. "Maybe…" I considered my thesis. "I was thinking I might run the numbers, try and plot increases and decreases in ant populations, see what I can come up with."

"You got the time for that?"

"Sort of," I said. "I've still got teaching, but I'm waiting to get access to some data from the University of Edinburgh, so I can afford a side project for the next week or so."

The insect line gradually broke up and the participants pattered away in different directions. We watched people coming home, parking their cars, going in for dinner. A couple of the Ukrainians came back laden with bags of strange-looking ingredients and, not long afterwards, a pleasant odour of starchy comfort food wafted across to the porch. Down the block, I thought I saw the tottering figure of the Ant Lady, but I couldn't be sure.

Now that I'd become aware of her presence, I kept noticing the Ant Lady everywhere. I'd probably seen her a dozen times before; I'd moved in to the house in September, but I kept weird hours, so it wasn't too easy to get to know people in the neighbourhood. But now I kept seeing her; walking to the dinky little corner store, being helped into the passenger side of a car by a stout fortysomething who was presumably the daughter, wandering up and down the street on some unknown errand.

One day, though, when I was at the store buying milk, spaghetti and cheese, I felt someone behind me, turned, and there she was, just a little too close.

"We may be witnessing a Biblical prophecy come true," she said, matter of factly.

I was too surprised to be polite. "Uh, what?"

"And there shall be destruction and darkness come upon creation, and the beasts shall reign over the Earth," she said, nodding. It sounded like a quote, but I didn't know from what. The Bible, I guessed. "Even the smallest of them have an instinct for industry, organisation, and savagery that makes us look feeble by comparison."

I took my basket of groceries resolutely to the cash register, where the fat man who ran the store smiled a bit and shook his head knowingly. "That everything?" he asked. Then, quietly, "don't worry, she's a regular here, I'll make sure she gets home okay."

"Thanks," I said.

"Used to be a good neighbourhood," the fat man shook his curls as he ran my purchases through the ancient scanner. "Everyone looking out for each other. Still is, mostly. Problem is, those damn immigrants –" he suddenly stopped, realising he might have said something very stupid.

"It's okay," I reassured him. "I'm from Seattle." I hated myself for condoning his racism, however implicitly, *She's Asian but she's from Seattle, she's One of Us.* Wanted to mess with him; tell him, casually, about how my parents, refugees, spent their new American lives in a frustrating Catch-22 system of paranoia, called *communists* by their neighbours, *bourgeois traitors* by their families, having to run the gamut of mysteriously declined job applications, office-temping jobs well below their degree level, patronising bosses too polite to say what the stoners downtown would, *slope, chink, commie*. To this day, my mother is still convinced that she's under surveillance from both the FBI and the Chinese Communist Party. But I'd had a long and tiring day and didn't really want to become one white guy's object lesson in multiculturalism.

"Yeah," he said with relief. "People like those Polacks at number seventeen."

My smile got a little bit tighter. "I think they're basically harmless," I said, handing over my credit card. I was also certain they were Ukrainians, but didn't think pedantry would help.

"Oh, I'm sure *they* are," he said. "But it's, well, we've got *all* these Polacks, and ragheads, and Koreans, and what have you, coming over and taking jobs Americans could have had. You know. Working for that software company, too," he shook his head. "We're teaching them to hack us, is what we're doing."

"I don't think it works like that," I said, thinking of Joanie and Q, but he still wasn't listening to me anyway.

"And who knows who they're talking to? Sending an e-mail home to mom, and she sends it on to the Taliban, next thing you know…." He shrugged expressively. "Oughta arrest them all. Don't send them back. Lock them up for good so they can't blow anything up. Anyway, have a good night." I took my bag, nodded to him, and, feeling there could have been some way I might have handled that better, left.

"So, you still working on your ant project?" Joanie asked. Outside the living room, the rain hit the windows hard. A distant backbeat and some high guttural lyrics were faintly audible from a stereo system to the East.

"Kind of," I said. "I've got a few rough correlations. The first breakout was in the 1950s, yeah. There were pretty regular large infestations across the country until the early seventies, then they seem to settle down. A couple rises in the eighties, then pretty much nothing until 2001."

"Why 2001?"

"Not sure," I said.

"I remember the surge in 2001," Joanie said. "Mainly because it was my fifth birthday, and my dad arranged an outdoor picnic, which we obviously couldn't have." She smiled. "Wound up having a picnic on the dining room floor. Lotta fun for a kid."

"But the numbers drop again round about 2007ish," I went on, "then, well, it turns out you're right, there's been a steady rise for the last few years."

"Like I said, climate change?"

"I've been trying that," I said. "Working with air pollution stats, radiation levels, global temperature rises. Not much correlation with air pollution or temperature; some with the radiation levels, but it's not really consistent. It's just crazy enough that I'm going to start trying economic growth and syphilis infection rates next."

"How about Internet penetration?" Q looked up from something he was doing to a Raspberry Pi.

Joanie snorted.

"No, really," he said. "It's as good as anything else. And it was round about the turn of the millennium that the general public really got hold of it. Eternal September, all that."

"Eternal September was in 1993," Joanie pointed out in a *you-dumbass* voice.

"Anyway, there was a dip in ant numbers in the 1980s, right when home computers were taking off," I said. "Seems to me the Internet's just been gaining in participants since it started, not rising and falling. Besides, how the hell would Internet use affect ants?"

"I don't know, maybe they feed off the Wi-Fi or something," Q said. "Whatever."

I fell into the local habit of avoiding the Ant Lady. If I saw her at all, I just smiled a greeting and hurried away, like everyone else.

About a month after the incident at the grocery store, I made a final effort to communicate with her. I was sitting out on the lawn doing some marking, when she strolled past, her usual peculiar little smile on her face, carrying a newspaper blaring the usual warning about the Balkans.

"Hey," I said, impulsively.

She looked up at me, wide eyes startled. I could see a bit of the little girl from the 1950s, there in the suntanned and wrinkled face.

"How you doing?" I went on, already regretting the effort to make conversation. "Lotta sunny weather for the time of year," I ploughed on. "Good for the lawn I suppose."

The lady quirked her smile and shrugged.

"So what's your name?" I asked her.

The Ant Lady leaned in, conspiratorial. "The enemy," she said.

"Uh..." I was a little spooked. "Your name is 'the enemy'?"

She shook her head. "We haven't seen the end of this. We've only had a view of the beginning of what may be the end." She smiled, then spoke as if quoting. "When we entered the atomic age, we opened the door to a new world. No one can predict what man may eventually find in that new world."

I took a chance, risked her screaming. "You mean the ants –"

"Mom!" The daughter was bearing down on us. "I'm glad I found you. She wasn't bothering you, was she?" she asked me in a pleasant tone which could equally imply that I had been bothering *her*.

"No," I said. "Name's Kara Chong, I'm new here. Moved in a few months back." I stuck out my hand, clumsily. "Just thought I'd be friendly, say hi."

The daughter smiled a tense, suspicious smile that made my radar go off. Suddenly remembered a playground chant some kids had made up in fourth grade, *Kara Chong you don't belong*. "I'm afraid my mother doesn't talk very much," the daughter said. "She's harmless, but modern life confuses her a bit." She shepherded the Ant Lady away; the lady glanced back once, eyes knowing pinpoints. I didn't think anything confused her at all.

I went away with the nasty, insulting little chant earworming in my head.

I carried on working on the ant correlations for a while. But then the data came through from the Edinburgh Medical School and it was back to correlating leprosy outbreaks. The talk around the faculty was mainly about upcoming exams, a predictable scandal in which one of the professors left his wife for a graduate student who left him for a tenure-track post in Queensland, and the disintegration of Europe, about which everyone had an opinion, none of them informed. Life returned to normal, Kara Chong once again belonged, and the ant correlations began to gather virtual dust in a corner of my cloud drive.

Then, one Sunday, I got up as usual – late, but earlier than Joanie and Q, who had stayed up till 3 AM with some shipping deadline.

Went out into the kitchen, opened the fridge. Light didn't come on. Checked the stove, the lights. Nothing working.

"Power outage," I said to no one in particular, switched on my phone. No signal.

"Great." I made myself some cereal, went into the living room. The Wi-Fi router was silent and dark. I cursed the fact that I hadn't charged up my tablet the night before; I had maybe four hours of work time at most. Although perhaps my laptop... I tried to remember how much data I'd backed up offline.

"What's going on?" Joanie joined me in the living room.

"Some kind of power outage," I said. "Landline's out too."

Then, in the distance, we heard them.

A series of booms, faint, like someone beating a tympani, an irregular rhythm. I put down my bowl, almost dropping it, ran out to the porch. A flash of light on the horizon.

Abruptly the power surged back on. The TV squawked into life, tuned to CNN as usual. A serious-faced man speaking urgently, urgently. I caught the words *cyber-attacks* and *enemy powers* and *foreign hackers* and *terrorism* and *public utilities*. I caught the words *Pearl Harbor* and *Nine-Eleven*, and *loss of American lives*. Commentators came on, hastily assembled with words like *refugee policy* and *enemy within* and *Eastern Europe*. Sudden cut to the President in front of a podium, looking earnestly and resolutely at the cameras and drawing breath to speak.

And then, they came.

Boiling from the ground, surging, a living flood of chitin rushing out of the earth and onto the streets, thousands upon thousands of ants, flowing over everything. Joanie let out an inadvertent cry, jumped back in the house and banged the door. I heard her rummaging for the flamethrower against an auditory backdrop of Presidential platitudes.

Looking to the side, I realised that Q had left the flamethrower on the porch. I grabbed it, then, with some half-formed idea in mind of what to do, I stumbled forward, down the steps, out onto the lawn, in my T-shirt and shorts and flip-flops, staring, staring at the return of the ants.

That was when I smelled the smoke.

I turned around, saw. The blaze had caught thoroughly, was licking at the gables and the awning. The tide of ants reared, parted around the conflagration. On the lawn, two of the Ukrainians were chattering round a third, who was lying on the ground, moving feebly, making irregular small moans; a fourth was trying, in confused and accented English, to call 911. I saw the old man to the West start forward, then stop, a complicated look on his face, *help them* warring with *what if they're terrorists*? His dog was barking urgently, unheeded.

I started forward myself, only to find my arm gripped painfully, like an ant bite. Looked. The old man to the West hanging on, his kind eyes suddenly burning, threatening, his thin frame not pitiable any more but tough as wire. "What do *you* think you're doing?" he asked, suspicious, hostile. *Kara Chong you don't belong. Kara Chong you don't belong.*

Footsteps, more hands grabbed me. Roughly pulled the flamethrower from my grip and twisted my arms back. I saw the lights on the police car before I was slammed up against it. Behind me, the old man was speaking to them, almost wheedling. "She did it! She started the fire! The chink girl! I saw her. Look, she had a flamethrower!"

I looked frantically back. Q and Joanie were standing there, open-mouthed. "Help," I gasped, but they just stood there. Did they believe the old man? Or were they afraid they'd be arrested too if they said something?

I looked the other way and saw the Ant Lady.

She wasn't screaming, she was smiling, that little knowing smile from before. She had an anti-ant flamethrower in her hands, and was gazing, not at the surging insects, but at the burning house, the shifting noise of falling beams, the terrified Ukrainians on the lawn.

Nobody, of course, was paying any attention to her.

"Them," she crooned. "Them."

F Sharp 4

Tim Pieraccini

I hold my breath as the guard walks to the door. His footsteps sound rapid and sharp in the white-walled recording studio.

We dare not look at one another. He stands in the doorway for an interminable moment before grunting softly and pulling the door shut as he steps out. We women are alone.

I have not been the only one afraid to breathe. For a few seconds, along the length of the white leather sofa, there is nothing but the sound of escaping breath, almost like soft laughter. And still, we five F Sharps hardly dare look up, hardly dare acknowledge this tiny interlude of freedom.

Elzira Barros is less afraid of expressing herself. She leans back in her chair. "Thank fuck; I thought he was going to insist on staying."

Sitting forward again, she pats the mini-cam on the low table between us. "Before I turn this on, let me say, very quickly: there are some who suspect the truth."

She does not elucidate, but scans our numerically-arranged line, looking at each of us. She activates the m-c, waits for a moment as one lens adjusts to capture all of us and the other angles itself to frame her face.

"*Record.*"

Seen up close, she is somehow both more beautiful and less glamorous than she appears on our screens. Less glamorous because reality reveals the faint lines around her mouth and eyes and on her neck; more beautiful because she is here, before us, eyes flashing and hair shining in the bright studio light. It is so long since I have seen anyone besides the guards and the other Notes. We have Intflix, of course, but the zettapixels seem only to add a layer of unreality; I know many of us believe the images are manipulated. A closer view of Elzira Barros' skin seems to confirm those suspicions. I feel tempted to reach out, to put my fingers against her cheek.

As if she has sensed my thoughts she looks at me. "You're…" she checks her pad, "F Sharp 4?" At my nod, she adds: "You're from the Theocratic Union?"

"Syria," I whisper, after a moment. I can sense the other F Sharps looking at me. No one ever speaks about our lives outside the Chorus.

She clearly sees my discomfort; she looks along the line. "I understand why they chose this group. It certainly shows off Sir Johannes' fine commitment to diversity. Indian, Korean…? Canadian, Zambian…?" She appears to recall something. "But, of course, you know nothing of each other. You mix only with others of the same Octave, is that right…?"

For a moment it seems no one will answer. I wonder if the others are doing as I am – keeping their eyes down.

"That's absolutely right."

F Sharp 3 is the one who has spoken. She has a beautiful speaking voice, this Zambian woman, and when I look up and catch her eye I remember this is not the only attractive thing about her. I look down at once, feeling the blood warming my face at the memory of the tiny smile she has just offered me.

"*Pause*," Elzira Barros commands the camera. "*Delete.*" She waits a moment. I don't dare look up, and I wonder if the others do. "I'm sorry, I know you're not supposed to talk about anything other than the work and the performance. We'll start again. Please lift your heads, so we can see your faces."

I look up and feel the others do the same – although perhaps F Sharp 3 never lowered her head. Elzira Barros gives us a practised smile.

"*Record.* This interview, itself historic, is given to mark the announcement of a greater event – the very first live performance of a new choral work, the Kassian Anthems, by Sir Johannes Brugmann. This performance, on the Enceladus Inter-system Station, will be the largest live concert for over thirty years; as many as four thousand people will attend, from all habitats of the Solar System. I'm speaking to five of the singers who will have the honour of interpreting Sir Johannes' new work. These are the F Sharps, 2 to 6.

"F Sharp 2," she says, addressing the Korean, "I believe you were one of the first operated on to allow Sir Johannes greater range in his vocal compositions?"

The woman's principal response is a nod, but the tiny sound she makes is unnaturally low.

"And," Barros turns to the Indian woman, "you, I believe, number 6, have only recently been passed fit following your own procedure? I'm sure you're excited to be able to take part in the Kassian Anthems."

"I am." She has abundant loose black hair and calm maturity in her eyes, but the voice is higher than a child's. Because of the strict segregation I've never encountered these engineered Notes before; my immediate response is a mixture of revulsion and pity.

"The performance is still eight Terran months away," says Barros. "Presumably you'll be spending that period rehearsing?"

"Not all of it," says F Sharp 3. "It's planned to record the Anthems, so they're ready for instant distribution when the performance is over."

The Canadian, 5, speaks for the first time. "The concert itself will also be recorded." She is tall and slender, also with extremely long hair but of a very soft gold which seems to invite touch. "But only Sir Johannes will hear that."

My own hair is longer than it has ever been; we are encouraged to let it grow. Having it cut is allowed, but exorbitantly expensive – and we are not permitted to attend to our own, or each other's.

"Sir Johannes," murmurs F Sharp 3, "would obviously not permit the public to have unrestricted access to any work over which he has not exercised complete control."

I have drifted into thinking about whether I'll cover my hair when I return home, so I don't immediately realise what 3 has gently implied. The others have been more attentive. No one speaks into the hush that follows.

Even Elzira Barros takes a moment to recover. "A reason, perhaps, why his work has not been performed live before…? *Pause*." She consults her pad. For several seconds there is silence. Barros looks up, flashes another false-looking smile, gets to her feet. "Wait…just a minute. I…have remembered something I needed to send. I'll be back very soon – then we can *resume*." She looks from one to another of us, backing towards the door. "Excuse me."

The door closes. We are completely alone.

We have never been unsupervised since we entered the Chorus.

"My name is Megai," says F Sharp 3.

Both the engineered Notes make noises of panic. The Canadian whispers: "Don't be a fucking idiot."

"My name is Megai," she says again. She looks at me. Her face looms close.

My throat feels tight and dry. I open my mouth, but can only gasp softly.

Megai puts her hand over mine. Her skin is so dark, and so warm. I look into her eyes again. I first saw her face less than thirty minutes ago, but she seems so familiar.

"F Sharp 4, you're very beautiful, and I don't want to leave this room until I know your name." Megai looks past me at 5 and 6, and then back at 2. "All of your names."

"They'll be in here any moment," says 5. "As soon as they realise..."

"Yes," says Megai. "So we must not waste time. She – Ms Barros – has done this deliberately, do you see? She arranged an interview, insisted that no guards be present, then left us. She's given us this precious moment to speak..."

"Are you sure?" rumbles F Sharp 2. 6 looks thoughtful, but seems afraid to speak.

"She was acting...kind of weird, at the end there," says 5. "But we can't –"

"Ousa," I say. "Ousa is my name." It feels almost as though I'm speaking the name of a fictional character. I have not said my name aloud for three years.

"Shut up!" 5 jumps to her feet, scans the walls and ceiling, looking for signs of surveillance. "You know what'll happen if..."

2 and 6 sit stiffly, as if disassociating themselves from anything that is happening. Megai lifts my hand, holding it in both of hers. "I will see you again. We will sing together. Then the whole System will hear our names."

"But how...?"

The door opens. Elzira hurries towards us. Behind her a guard steps in, closes the door, and leans against the wall.

Elzira takes a seat and bends over the mini-cam. "I'm so sorry we had to *stop*."

Megai frowns, then her lips curve slightly. She nods once at Elzira, who does not smile, this time, but sits back. "Now, where were we…?"

The restarted interview follows the pattern I expected. We are given opportunities to say how talented Sir Johannes is, how great an honour it will be to participate in the performance; we talk about the skill and training involved in the Discrete method, how it is not like playing an instrument or singing in the normal fashion, but interjecting a note at the precise instant it is required. And we talk some more about Sir Johannes, about the exquisite discernment required to choose voices that will work alongside each other, in harmony in the chords or tripping from note to note – voice to voice – in the melody without jarring the listener.

Finally we talk about how our unlimited credit after we leave the Chorus will transform our lives.

Elzira Barros does not ask about our lives now.

Back in the Number 4 Wing, alone for the night after having very carefully answered the questions of my Octave under the eyes of our Supervisors, I lie on top of my duvet and try to picture Megai's face. I wonder what she meant: 'the System will hear our names'? Is she planning something? If so, she can only act alone, as Chorus members are permitted no unsupervised communication. Our everyday lives are carefully ordered to eliminate any possibility of concerted action, except when we sing.

I remember, suddenly, that we must rehearse, all of us, for a live performance in which perfection will be the absolute minimum demanded. This will mean congregating, all of us together, every few days at the very least.

My heart beats so fast that it is a long time before I'm able to sleep.

I have lived as a Note for three years. It would be unfair to call it imprisonment – after all, we're paid very well while we're here and will want for nothing for the rest of our lives – but I think, if I'd known the extent to which my activities would be overseen and regulated, I would not have signed up. It's impossible to discuss these things with my fellows in the Octave, but I'm not alone in feeling this. So much can be conveyed with a look, a twist of the mouth, a tone of voice. D 4 is especially adept at layering her responses to the supervisors; they frown, and stare at her, but they can find nothing concrete to object to. D 4 is French, and although we're prohibited from speaking anything but English, she manages to inject occasional words of her native language into what she says, and I see some of the others smile, as if at a joke.

For a long time I thought I was in love with D 4. She's very beautiful, of course. We all are, something I never understood in a group of women whose importance would seem to rest in their vocal cords alone. But that was before Sir Johannes visited our wing, and after a few perfunctory pleasantries, invited B Flat to spend the evening with him.

Just prior to his arrival, we had been invited to reread the penultimate section of our contracts. From the shocked looks on the faces of the others, I was not the only one who felt certain that the wording had been changed since I'd signed. Daily, I thank the Prophet it was not me Sir Johannes chose, but at the same time I would have given myself for my sister, B Flat. There was such a quality of innocence in her face, and in her voice. She stills sings Sir Johannes' music beautifully, but something in her eyes is not the same.

Sir Johannes has sent the voices of women far, farther than any product of human civilisation. His recordings – our recordings – are automatic inclusions in the databank of any probe sent into deep space, or aimed at a distant planetary system. We are the soundtrack to advertising, to official news broadcasts, to movies and to games, transmitted to every station and colony across the Solar System, and beyond. Even the pirate channels use our work, despite Sir Johannes' persistent attempts to have them hunted down.

Sir Johannes is the foremost champion of women; he pays the Notes at the highest existing contractual rate. He employs only women at his business centre on Phobos. His household staff is all female. He can be seen on any number of archived broadcasts over the decades, extolling the qualities that make women superior to men. This man, this legend of the music world, has spread untold joy and inspiration, all through the medium of the female voice. If there are some who are driven to wonder, as my parents did, why a 66-year-old man employs only women between the ages of 18 and 27, their voices are not part of the public discourse. And even my parents could not deny how much good could be done with unlimited, lifelong credit.

There is sound reasoning behind Sir Johannes' employee choices in regard to the Notes, we are told. Only women in the peak of health – regular exercise is one of our main diversions here – and the full bloom of youth can produce the absolute perfection of pitch and tone Sir Johannes demands, we are told. Sir Johannes travels the System – his commitment to diversity and equal opportunity is as legendary as the man himself – seeking only the very highest quality candidates, and rejecting 90% of those he interviews. The process can sometimes be a lengthy one; Sir Johannes commitment to his art and to the public cannot be overestimated. We are told.

There is no denying Sir Johannes' genius. Some claim he has entirely revolutionised vocal music by the Discrete method, employing a different singer for each note, and by pioneering experiments to increase vocal range. His latest work takes inspiration from the early Byzantine composer Kassia – bringing a woman to the fore yet again – but what he has done with the primitive melodies is unprecedented. We are told.

The total number of singers in the five Octaves is 60, so we're surprised when we assemble in the rehearsal hall and find 300 young women. It is explained that the concert will reproduce the multi-tracking used in the recordings; Sir Johannes has spent most of the last two Terran years travelling – recruiting. It has been a draining experience – we are told – so that the initial rehearsals will be conducted by his amanuensis, Hugo LaSalle. Professor LaSalle is stocky, dark and short, a striking contrast to Sir Johannes' willowy paleness. This is the first time I've seen him, but I don't pay him too much attention, because I see, easing through the thronged Notes, Megai. F Sharp 3, as I must take care to call her.

During the preparation there is no attempt to organise the Notes, so that Megai and I can stand beside one another, pretending to pay attention while instructions are being issued, and trying not to look at one another. I am getting glances and frowns from the members of my Octave. Megai's fingers are brushing against the back of my hand. In a moment when she's sure our overseers are fully occupied, she leans her head close to mine. "Get the real names of your Octave today."

I forget myself and turn to stare at her, but she looks serenely ahead, apparently attending closely to Professor LaSalle as he begins to explain the counterpoint of the second Anthem.

D 4 is Garance; it was not what I expected her name to be.

I am filled with pride, excitement and terror. Seven of us have exchanged names. Five have held aloof, so far, but there will be many more rehearsals, many more chances. Already there is a new bond between the seven; shared glances, tiny smiles, a certain daring in conversation. This small exchange has unleashed things long held in check. The guards have noticed, but seem to have put it down to the excitement of the rehearsal.

Elzira Barros is present at the second rehearsal; Sir Johannes seems to have been pleased with her interview, despite the minor security scare when we were left alone. Professor LaSalle is fully occupied in choosing from among the new recruits for the drone in the third Anthem, so he allows Elzira to take aside her five interviewees. We huddle in a corner of the hall; Elzira asks us the obvious questions until the nearest guard loses interest. Then she beckons us to huddle close.

"You know, I think, that the camera was still on when I left the room – before?"

Megai nods. The others appear stunned. I realise that I knew, but have been avoiding thinking about it.

"We have the recording," continues Elzira, "ready to broadcast as the concert ends. It is not much, but it shows the climate of fear and repression that you endure." She pauses. "But we will not show it without your permission."

"What do you think'll happen if you show it?" asks the Canadian, F Sharp 5.

Elzira smiles. "I will probably be arrested."

"I mean to us – to our lives?"

Megai turns on 5. "Are you happy? Is this life what you thought it would be?" She takes a breath before making her voice so soft I can barely hear. "Has Sir Johannes visited your Octave?"

5 drops her eyes. Suddenly afraid that I know what has prompted this question, I seize Megai's hand. Megai understands; squeezing my fingers, she shakes her head.

I am so flooded with relief I can hardly stand. 2, the tiny Korean, holds me up.

One of the stewards is coming towards us. Megai releases my hand, whispers: "All of you – get the names of your Octaves. For next time."

The Canadian swears dismissively. I want to tell Megai that I have seven names, but there is no time. The steward is there, and we're herded back to join the throng.

We didn't answer Elzira's question, and she's not present at the next three rehearsals. But progress is made; F Sharp 2 is Ji Yeon, 6 is Urvashi. The Canadian avoids us; she looks over when we gather, and I do think I see a faint yearning in her face, but she is clearly frightened, and with good reason. Nothing like this has been attempted before.

Back in Number 4 Wing, the atmosphere is different. Only two of our Notes are still nameless, and Garance is working on them. We have to exercise extreme caution, of course, but we look out for each other in a way that we never did before. If the guards have noticed anything, it will be an increase in minor accidents at one end of the refectory when two or more of us are seated together – at the other end.

We have been given sheet music for all the Anthems now, actual paper copies to study and annotate. As another warm-up for the concert, we will be recording the Kassian Anthems in our usual fashion, and for this we'll be allowed to have the sheets before us.

The sheets are a tool we can turn to our own ends. Thinking about what Megai wants to do, I've devised a system of notation which should be undecipherable. Still, we can't share it with everyone; we live in fear of those still known only by their Note numbers.

Megai clearly restrains herself when I tell her my idea; she looks as though she wants to hug me. Things become more difficult with each rehearsal, as the details of organisation are finalised; we all have our places in the hall now, each with our own Octave. The new recruits give us our only respite, some of them proving unsuitable and needing to be replaced, with the further direction and training that requires. Thankfully Octaves 3 and 4 sing side by side, and Megai is on the left of her Octave and I am on the right of mine, only a metre from her. In the breaks we can exchange the briefest of messages, and sometimes even a tentative touch.

Occasionally one of the newcomers will break down at the rear of the hall, and we have as much as two minutes of confusion to shield us.

At every moment, in the hall and in the Wing, I expect a hand on my shoulder, hauling me away. Every member of our Octave except C Sharp has given her real name; all have been incorporated into the design.

For the last two Terran months of the rehearsals, Sir Johannes is there, pacing around the hall as we sing, standing and staring, saying nothing. I've noticed that some of the Notes are quietly weeping by the end; the music we make is certainly very beautiful, a unique combination of so many different voices blending in the same piece. Even Professor LaSalle appears moved, and Sir Johannes' silence is considered a promising sign.

Our sheets are taken away from us, and destroyed; our conductors are satisfied that we know our parts. In fact, we know two versions.

It is too late to change any part of the plan. With Sir Johannes prowling our ranks, communication is impossible. We must, on the day, trust our memories and each other.

I can feel Megai's presence but dare not even turn my head in her direction.

Elzira Barros is present at the penultimate rehearsal. We never answered her question about the release of the footage. Her eyes seek out each of us, the special five, but if she asks for another interview it's not granted to her, and she remains at the front of the hall, beside

Sir Johannes. He never looks at her. We sing, and the tears flow down her cheeks. I am crying, too. Sir Johannes is a genius.

For the final rehearsal we are in the venue itself; a vast space styled as a European cathedral of the gothic period. After completing the recordings ready for release, we have moved to Enceladus Inter-system Station. How strange it was, singing alone in the studio, after these months of mingling our voices in that hall. How strange it is, after the years at Wing 4, to wake up in a dormitory with a view of Saturn. Garance and I have taken adjacent beds, and we are able to exchange looks the cameras never detect – but no words. And C Sharp is not one of us, and now it's too late. I wonder how many have refused to join in the other Octaves. I wonder who is there, at night, to share a glance with Megai.

We are gathered to watch an inter-System bulletin on the morning of the performance, in the artists' area of the venue. All 300 of us are there, and Sir Johannes – who seems oddly tense. I can't see Megai, but there are so many of us in such a small space, all crowded around the wallscreen.

Elzira Barros appears on the screen – but this is not one of her reports. The story is about her. She has been arrested for conspiring to destroy Sir Johannes' reputation. The man whose face replaces her image goes on to talk about footage she took, which has not been located, but which is said to implicate some of Sir Johannes' employees.

Megai's face appears on the screen. It is like a fist to my stomach. I'm saved from falling only by arms around me; Garance on one side, and Ji Yeon on the other. I can't hear what the man on the screen is saying; I'm protesting, denying, calling her name. Garance smothers my cries with her hand; luckily, in the general commotion only a few nearby Notes have heard me.

The man on the screen is speaking about a notation system – my system – with numbers beneath certain notes, in a seemingly random pattern they have been unable to decipher. They speculate that secret messages were being passed.

"Listen!" Garance hisses close to my ear. "We have only two

hours to go. You must hold yourself together. Only two hours. After that, you may crumble."

"B-but Megai…"

"F Sharp 3," growls Ji Yeon in her unnerving voice, "gave herself to them, to shield us. I'm sure of it. They found her, and she took it all upon herself. Now…it's all upon us. Don't disgrace her. Remember your duty…F Sharp 4."

Ji Yeon has been pronouncing the note numbers loudly, perhaps to reassure those around us. In the distance I see the Canadian, F Sharp 5. Her eyes meet mine for the briefest of moments before she looks away.

A stranger stands in Megai's position; a promoted reserve, without Megai's beautiful posture or proud tilt of the head. Her presence, her slight shifting, is a reminder that I have no idea what is happening to Megai at this moment. I have no idea what will happen to any of us after today.

We are arranged along the aisle, with the audience on both sides and each Octave facing alternate directions. My face is caked with makeup to disguise puffiness and pallor; it would wreck the performance to replace too many of us, so they have done the best they can. Sir Johannes himself stood directly in front of me and scrutinised my face, giving a final curt nod.

The clock numbers roll over; two minutes. I do as Garance advised – try to breathe deeply, without thought, following the breath. The 5s will begin, so I have a further 30 seconds to compose myself. I look at the faces in the audience; have they seen those reports? A tremor of doubt shakes me; these are all billionaires, chiefs of industry, wealthy entertainers. Will any of them care, when they know? Will this be in vain?

A swooping drone reminds me of the cameras, which will show the System everything that happens.

My first note is seconds away. I think of Megai, straighten my back, and sing.

The first anthem is a triumph. The second, a wonder. The third provokes a standing ovation. Sir Johannes is a gift to humankind.

There are tears on many cheeks, rapture on all faces. The high arched ceiling echoes with the cries of approbation, the whispers of astonishment.

The fourth anthem begins with the 5s once again. I am so tense I can't stop myself shaking. We left two bars blank, a space for a name we were never given. After that, we begin. I am afraid my heart will shatter my ribcage before those bars have finished.

The first solo note is wordless, a soft build. The second is F Sharp. It is a word.

It is not the word the composer is expecting.

It is not the word we are expecting. She sings alone for three seconds, the tall, golden-haired Canadian – Ellen! – as we all register that she has joined us. She is not singing only her one note, her F Sharp, and the others in her Octave hold back to let her be heard. Sir Johannes' hands freeze in the air, his jaw goes slack. The audience emits the faintest murmur.

We recover; we support her. We sing beneath her and lift her words, up to the level of the previous anthems. In a few moments her time is past, and the voice of Garance is heard behind me. It seems that all the voices, all sixty of the original Octaves, are supporting her, but I can't be sure. The new recruits have been stunned into silence, but the old Octaves give voice to their passion and their spirit, and this fourth anthem may be the most moving of all. It is Sir Johannes music, but not his words.

My heart is still beating fast, but I feel stronger now. My own moment is coming, and I close my eyes, apologising to my family, who will no doubt be watching. I hope they will understand.

The next singer is F Sharp 6, Urvashi, with her impossible vocal cords. The high notes pierce like daggers, driving the ten words home.

The audience has been stunned into stillness again. A few have looked towards Sir Johannes, and they know something is wrong.

It is my moment. Sir Johannes is shouting now, screaming at the broadcasters, at the security people. Men are running towards me.

Enveloped in love and defiance, I fill my lungs and sing the line.

"Ousa is my name. A slave is what I am."

The signal goes out to all planets, all places, and cannot be recalled.

About the Authors

G.V. Anderson is a British writer whose professional debut, "Das Steingeschöpf", won the World Fantasy Award for Best Short Fiction in 2017. Her stories have appeared in *Strange Horizons, Fantasy & Science Fiction, Lightspeed, Nightmare,* and *Interzone.* She is currently working on her first novel.

Chris Barnham's work has appeared in *Intergalactic Medicine Show, Compelling SF, Interzone,* and last year's *Best of British SF.* He lives in London, with a wife and three children, all of them much nicer people than him. He used to work for the British government, but now just makes stuff up for himself. His most recent novel is *Fifty-One*, a time-travelling romance, featuring a cop from 2040, marooned in 1940s London and forced to choose between saving the future or the woman he loves (*Interzone* said: 'better plotted than Connie Willis'). Check out www.chrisbarnhambooks.com and on Twitter @barnham_chris

Dave Bradley was born in west London, studied medieval literature in Oxford, and became a magazine editor in Bath. His beat was home computing and video gaming until, in 2005, he took the helm of SFX, the leading newsstand science fiction and fantasy magazine. Today, Bradley lives in Wiltshire and works as a media consultant, occasionally penning book reviews, but mostly planning conferences for game developers, a business that takes him all over the world. His story "Salvation", composed for a local writing group, is dedicated to author David J Rodger, a friend who died in 2015 – the story first appeared in an anthology celebrating Rodger's work, *The Hotwells Horror.*

Esme Carpenter started writing science-fiction and fantasy aged 12 and found she couldn't stop. Inspired by fiction regarded much too old for her, she took interest in the mechanics of world-building and how the fantastical affects the most human of characters; her work is focused on human struggle against insurmountable odds. She made her way to the University of East Anglia to study Creative Writing, and onwards to teach English. Her first novel, a middle-grade fantasy called *Against the Elements,* was published in 2012. While originally from York, England, she moved to California, USA two years ago to be with her husband.

Matthew De Abaitua's debut science fiction novel *The Red Men* was shortlisted for the Arthur C Clarke Award and adapted into a short film 'Dr Easy' by Shynola, produced by Film4/Warp Films. His science fiction novels IF THEN (Angry Robot, September 2015) and *The Destructives* (Angry Robot, 2016) complete the loose trilogy begun with *The Red Men*. "Extraordinary visionary… the most intriguing and disturbing near-future speculations published for some years." Strange Horizons. His memoir *Self & I: A Memoir of Literary Ambition* (Eye Books, 2018) was shortlisted for the New Angle Prize for Literature. He is a senior lecturer in creative writing at the University of Essex and lives in Hackney.

Sunyi Dean is an autistic mixed-race writer who was born in America, grew up in East Asia, and now lives in England, where she has resided for the past thirteen years. She has published five stories in 2018 via *Flash Fiction Online, Sub-Q, Interzone, Aurealis,* and *Andromeda Spaceways*, and is currently on submission with her agent for a full-length novel.

Malcolm Devlin's stories have appeared in publications including *Interzone, Black Static, Nightscript* and *Shadows & Tall Trees*. His collection, *You Will Grow Into Them*, is published by Unsung Stories.

J.K Fulton is the son of a lightkeeper, and spent his childhood growing up at a succession of lighthouses all around the coast of Scotland, from Portree to Portmahomack; these remote and lonely locations instilled in him a life-long love of both books and the sea. He has lived in Leicester with his partner Sandra since 1993; while Leicester is about as far from the sea as you can get in the UK, their home is stuffed with books, which is the next-best thing. His short stories have appeared in *Exuberance, Shoreline of Infinity*, and the *Leicester Writes Short Story Prize Anthology*. Under the somewhat transparent pseudonym John K. Fulton he also writes Scottish historical fiction for children, including WWI spy thriller *The Wreck of the Argyll* and Pictish fantasy adventure *The Beast on the Broch*. You can see more about his work at www.johnkfulton.com or follow him on Twitter @johnkfulton

Colin Greenland became the first British author to win the Arthur C. Clarke Award in 1990, with *Take Back Plenty*, his fourth published novel and the first volume of the Tabitha Jute trilogy. He is still writing, fitfully, some of it even science fiction, though "Before They Left" was the first thing he's had published for ages. It's an extra chapter for *Childhood's End*, he says, which Arthur never got around to writing.

Dave Hutchinson was born in Sheffield in 1960 and spent much of his working career as a journalist. His Fractured Europe series of novels has variously been nominated for the Arthur C Clarke, BSFA, Kitschies and John W Campbell Memorial Awards. He lives in London.

Anna Ibbotson grew up in rural Aberdeenshire but moved to Edinburgh 10 years ago and has since refused to leave. She lives there with her patient husband and impatient cat. She is a library assistant of all trades but still doesn't understand the Dewey decimal system. You can catch her wasting her time on twitter at @AnnaIbbotson.

Tim Major's love of speculative fiction is the product of a childhood diet of classic Doctor Who episodes and an early encounter with Triffids. Tim's most recent books are SF thriller *Snakeskins* and a short story collection, *And the House Lights Dim* – others include *Machineries of Mercy*, *You Don't Belong Here* and a non-fiction book about the 1915 silent crime film, *Les Vampires*. His short stories have appeared in *Interzone* and *Shoreline of Infinity* and have been selected for *Best of British Science Fiction 2017* and *The Best Horror of the Year 10*. www.cosycatastrophes.com

Fiona Moore is a London-based writer whose first novel, "Driving Ambition", is now available from Bundoran Press and whose second, "Rabbit in the Moon", has recently been acquired by ChiZine Publications Her fiction and poetry has appeared in, among others, *On Spec*, *Asimov*, *Interzone*. She has written and cowritten a number of articles and guidebooks on cult television, and has also cowritten three stage plays and four audio plays. When not writing SF, she is a Professor of Business Anthropology at Royal Holloway, University of London. More details, and free content, can be found at www.fiona-moore.com.

Mike Morgan is an ex-pat based in Iowa. Hailing from Hounslow in west London, Mike tries to preserve the traditions of his homeland in the chilly American Midwest, but all he manages these days is pulling crackers at Christmas and celebrating Pancake Day. As the years go by, his family back in

Blighty remark how increasingly American he sounds, and his friends in the USA remark how British he still seems (and shouldn't he quit that nonsense). So far, he's sold about twenty short stories to various publishers. You can read about them on his website: perpetualstateofmildpanic.wordpress.com. He's also on Twitter, as @CultTVMike.

Finbarr O'Reilly is an Irish writer whose work has appeared in Clarkesworld, The Best Science Fiction of the Year (edited by Neil Clarke) and The Year's Best Science Fiction (edited by Gardner Dozois). In his day job, he has worked as a journalist on magazines and newspapers for 20 years, most of these as a sub-editor. Like many Irish writers, he lives in self-imposed exile. He currently resides with his wife and two children in a small town in Lincolnshire, far from the sound of gulls and the smell of saltwater. Visit him at finoreilly.com or follow him on Twitter @finoreilly.

Tim Pieraccini is a writer and videographer. He has made about a dozen short films, some music videos and one feature film, All Heart. He is chief videographer for performing arts school The Brighton Academy. Known in the distant past (well, the 80s) as an artist and writer in Blake's 7 fandom, his stories have been published by *Doctor Who Magazine*, *Flame Tree* and *Parsec Ink*. He lives on the south coast of England with no pets or children, the number of books he hoards effectively forbidding other luxuries.

Alastair Reynolds was born in Barry, South Wales. He went on to study space science, and eventually worked for the European Space Agency in the Netherlands. He started writing science fiction not long after that birthday but took a little longer to get into print. He is now the author of eighteen novels, several novellas, and more than seventy short stories. His most recent books are *Elysium Fire* (2018), *Shadow Captain* (2019) and *Shadow Captain* (2019). He returned to Wales in 2008.

Donna Scott has over a decade's experience of editing genre fiction, and is a Director of the British Science Fiction Association. Together with Jamie Spracklen, she co-edited *Visionary Tongue* magazine, set up by author Storm Constantine to encourage new writers. She is also a slam-champion performance poet and stand-up comedian, currently touring as part of Oh So

About the Authors

Funny with *The Extraordinary Time-Travelling Adventures of Baron Munchausen*, an improvised storytelling show for children.

Teika Marija Smits is the pen-name of Dr Teika Bellamy, a mother, writer, editor and ex-scientist. Her writing has appeared in various places including *Mslexia*, *Shoreline of Infinity*, *Brittle Star*, *Strix*, *LossLit*, *Literary Mama* and *Reckoning*. When she's not busy with her children, or writing, she's managing the Nottingham-based indie press, Mother's Milk Books. She is delighted by the fact that Teika means 'fairy tale' in Latvian, and in spare moments creates fantastical art. She can be found at: https://marijasmits.wordpress.com and on Twitter as @MarijaSmits

Henry Szabranski was born in Birmingham, UK, and studied Astronomy & Astrophysics at Newcastle upon Tyne University, graduating with a degree in Theoretical Physics. His fiction has appeared in *Clarkesworld*, *Beneath Ceaseless Skies*, *Diabolical Plots*, *Daily Science Fiction*, *Kaleidotrope* and *Fantasy For Good: A Charitable Anthology*, amongst other places. He lives in Buckinghamshire with his wife and two young sons.

David Tallerman is the author of upcoming thriller *A Savage Generation* and the crime drama *The Bad Neighbour*, ongoing YA fantasy series *The Black River Chronicles*, the *Tales of Easie Damasco* trilogy, and the novella *Patchwerk*. His comics work includes the absurdist steampunk graphic novel *Endangered Weapon B: Mechanimal Science*, with Bob Molesworth. David's short fiction has appeared in around eighty markets, including Clarkesworld, Nightmare, Lightspeed, and Beneath Ceaseless Skies. A number of his best dark fantasy stories were gathered together in his debut collection *The Sign in the Moonlight and Other Stories*. He can be found online at davidtallerman.co.uk.

Natalia Theodoridou is the winner of the 2018 World Fantasy Award for Short Fiction and a finalist for the Nebula Award for Game Writing, an editor of sub-Q interactive fiction magazine, and a Clarion West graduate (class of 2018). Natalia's stories have appeared in *Clarkesworld*, *Strange Horizons*, *Uncanny*, and *Beneath Ceaseless Skies*, among other venues, and have been translated in Italian, French, Greek, Spanish, Chinese, and Arabic. *Rent-a-Vice*, Natalia's first interactive novel, is out by Choice of Games. Originally from Greece, Natalia now lives in Devon, UK. For details, visit www.natalia-theodoridou.com or follow @natalia_theodor on Twitter.

Matt Thompson is a London-based experimental musician and writer of strange stories. His work appears at *Black Static*, *Nature: Futures* and *Aliterate*, among others. He can be found online at http://matt-thompson.com, and on Twitter at @24wordLoop.

Lavie Tidhar is the author of the Jerwood Fiction Uncovered Prize winning and Premio Roma nominee *A Man Lies Dreaming* (2014), the World Fantasy Award winning *Osama* (2011) and of the Campbell Award winning and Locus and Clarke Award nominated *Central Station* (2016). His latest novels are *Unholy Land* (2018) and first children's novel *Candy* (2018). He is the author of many other novels, novellas and short stories.

Hannah Tougher is a graduate of the Creative Writing MLitt at the University of Stirling and currently lives in Glasgow. She has a love for strange and weird fiction. Her work has previously been published in *The Ogilvie* and *Idle Ink*. She writes short stories but has recently developed an interest for reading and writing flash fiction. She can be found on twitter @hmtougher.

James Warner's short stories have appeared in Interzone, Lady Churchill's Rosebud Wristlet, Ellery Queen's Mystery Magazine, and elsewhere. On behalf of San Francisco's Litquake festival, he organises the San Francisco Lit Crawl, currently the world's largest annual literary pub crawl. He is from Hayling Island originally, but hasn't been back lately. He also has a story in Jared Shurin's *The Best of British Fantasy 2018* anthology.

Aliya Whiteley was born in Devon in 1974, and currently lives in West Sussex, UK. She writes novels, short stories and non-fiction and has been published in *The Guardian*, *Interzone*, *McSweeney's Internet Tendency*, *Black Static*, *Strange Horizons*, and anthologies such as Unsung Stories' *2084* and *This Dreaming Isle*, and Lonely Planet's *Better than Fiction I* and *II*. She has been shortlisted for a Shirley Jackson Award, British Fantasy and British Science Fiction awards, the John W Campbell Award, and a James Tiptree Jr Award. She also writes a regular non-fiction column for *Interzone*.

More New Titles from NewCon Press

Simon Morden – Bright Morning Star
A ground-breaking take on first contact from scientist and novelist Simon Morden. Sent to Earth to explore, survey, collect samples and report back to its makers, an alien probe arrives in the middle of a warzone. Witnessing both the best and worst of humanity, the AI probe faces situations that go far beyond the parameters of its programming, and is forced to improvise, making decisions that may well reshape the future of a world.

Once Upon a Parsec – Edited by David Gullen
Ever wondered what the fairy tales of alien cultures are like? For hundreds of years scholars and writers have collected and retold folk and fairy stories from around our world. They are not alone. On distant planets alien chroniclers have done the same. For just as our world is steeped in legends and half-remembered truths of the mystic and the magical, so are theirs. Now, for the first time, we can share some of these tales with you…

Best of British Fantasy 2018 – edited by Jared Shurin
Jared spread his net wide to catch the very best work published by British authors in 2018, whittling down nearly 200 stories under consideration to just 21 (22 in the hardback edition) and two poems. They range from traditional sword and sorcery to contemporary fantasy, by a mix of established authors, new voices, and writers not usually associated with genre fiction. The result is a wonderfully diverse anthology of high quality tales.

Maura McHugh – The Boughs Withered
Kim Newman provides the introduction for this, the debut collection from one of the most exciting writers around. Twenty tales, including several original to this book, which represent the best short stories from an award-winning writer of fiction, non-fiction, comic books, and plays. A series of contemporary visions and murky pasts that draw upon the author's Irish heritage and so much more.

www.newconpress.co.uk

IMMANION PRESS
Purveyors of Speculative Fiction

Strindberg's Ghost Sonata & Other Uncollected Tales by Tanith Lee

This book is the first of three anthologies to be published by Immanion Press that will showcase some of Tanith Lee's most sought-after tales. Spanning the genres of horror and fantasy, upon vivid and mysterious worlds, the book includes a story that has never been published before – 'Iron City' – as well as two tales set in the Flat Earth mythos; 'The Pain of Glass' and 'The Origin of Snow', the latter of which only ever appeared briefly on the author's web site. This collection presents a jewel casket of twenty stories, and even to the most avid fan of Tanith Lee will contain gems they've not read before.
ISBN 978-1-912815-00-5, £12.99, $18.99 pbk

A Raven Bound with Lilies by Storm Constantine

The Wraeththu have captivated readers for three decades. This anthology of 15 tales collects all the published Wraeththu short stories into one volume, and also includes extra material, including the author's first explorations of the androgynous race. The tales range from the 'creation story' *Paragenesis*, through the bloody, brutal rise of the earliest tribes, and on into a future, where strange mutations are starting to emerge from hidden corners of the earth.
ISBN: 978-1-907737-80-0 £11.99, $15.50 pbk

The Lord of the Looking Glass by Fiona McGavin

The author has an extraordinary talent for taking genre tropes and turning them around into something completely new, playing deftly with topsy-turvy relationships between supernatural creatures and people of the real world. 'Post Garden Centre Blues' reveals an unusual relationship between taker and taken in a twist of the changeling myth. 'A Tale from the End of the World' takes the reader into her developing mythos of a post-apocalyptic world, which is bizarre, Gothic and steampunk all at once. 'Magpie' features a girl scavenging from the dead on a battlefield, whose callous greed invokes a dire curse. Following in the tradition of exemplary short story writers like Tanith Lee and Liz Williams, Fiona has a vivid style of writing that brings intriguing new visions to fantasy, horror and science fiction. ISBN: 978-1-907737-99-2, £11.99, $17.50 pbk

www.immanion-press.com
info@immanion-press.com